CHIEF

DORSE DUBOIS
WITH ROYAL CONNELL

FOCSLE

Published by Focsle, LLP, Annapolis, Maryland
Copyright © 2020 by Dorse Dubois

The Catalog-in-Publishing Data is on file at the Library of Congress.

ISBN
Hardback: 978-0-9600391-6-6
Paperback: 978-0-9600391-7-3
eBook: 978-0-9600391-8-0

Cover design by Alan Connell
Cover images: USS Ellyson (DD-454) © Naval Institute Press; clouds by Lieutenant Elizabeth
Crapo, https://www.photolib.noaa.gov/Collections/Sanctuaries/Papa/emodule/839/
eitem/36847; Dorse Howard (Hod) Dubois courtesy of the author

ACKNOWLEDGMENTS

A project of this sort comes to fruition as the result of a team effort. My USNA Classmate, Submariner Pete Smith consulted on the intricacies, capabilities and limitations of diesel electric U-Boats operated by the Germans in WWII. Another Classmate, Don Coullahan read the entirety of *Chief* and peppered me with useful comments and questions. Ms. Dixie Savage was helpful in lending her experience as a Nurse and Ms. Carol White, daughter of one of the characters in the book made helpful suggestions about Hod's early family life. Retired Chief Petty Officer David Law did his best to keep me well anchored to the Goat Locker where he spent a career. Beth Klein Johnson provided first hand background detail of life in the P.I. and in Japanese prison camps from her Grandfather's letters as a POW of the time.

And there is a startling contribution that comes from cyberspace, social media to be exact. For it was in Facebook over a period of several years and some 330,000 "likes" that I honed my craft. There I learned how to connect at the heart and benefited from instant feedback thousands and thousands of times. There was the closed group of Parents of Naval Academy Midshipmen in particular that listened to my stories and encouraged me to write more.

"You oughta' write a book," they said.

Just Sayin'.

Dorse DuBois

For this and all my writing projects, I dedicate my effort to my father.

Royal Connell

PREFACE

This is a novel of service to the Country. *Chief* is the first of a trilogy that describes three generations of a family's service in the nation's wars. *Chief* brings accurate first hand descriptions of life aboard ship during the depression years and World War II, affording a view of naval operations from the deckplates of the engineering spaces and gun turrets up and reaching all the way to CinCPac's headquarters in Makalapa, Pearl Harbor and MacArthur in the Philippines, Australia and Japan. We follow a farm boy from Texas hill country through each ship in his career; and along the way the extraordinary contributions of the Navy bluejacket make the case for the Chief Petty Officer as the backbone of the Fleet.

This work would not exist without the writing, guidance and encouragement of my friend and writing partner, Royal Connell. Both of us served tours at the Naval Academy, both of us graduated from that institution. Royal was an Instructor there and his encyclopedic knowledge of events away from the famous battles has served to show how, for instance, incidents at Conferences could affect hundreds of fleet units and thousands of men and their families. Most of those affected knew not of the intricacies, knew only service and survival. Royal and I shook hands on the agreement to partner in this endeavor at a hotel in Tampa, Florida. Though my name appears on the cover, *Chief* would never have been produced without Royal's guidance, knowledge of naval history and sage advice. He told me more than once that this was my book. The truth is that it is ours.

Some of the characters in *Chief* are historical, some fictional and one was made of steel, guts and luck. USS Ellyson, a Gleaves class Destroyer, pictured on the cover is the ship that Hod Dantes rode through World War II. She was known as a lucky ship, losing only one of her crew in hostile action while serving in many theaters and battles, always with distinction. Ellyson was the namesake of the Navy's first Naval Aviator, Commander Theodore "Spuds" Ellyson. Her crew called her the Elly May. Aboard Elly May we visit the characters who inhabit Chief's Quarters, the Wardroom and her battle stations in places like Pointe du Hoc, Normandy, Okinawa and Tokyo Bay.

Finally this book is dedicated to my Father, Dorse Howard DuBois, the erstwhile Texas farm boy who grew to become one of the stalwart cadre that mans and leads the Fleet.

Dorse DuBois
August 18 2019
Umatilla, Florida

CHAPTER 1

OYSTER STEW

The three kids, hiding to either side of the bedroom door were waiting for their Father to come out and kill them all, as he had promised. John, the oldest and biggest, tackled him about the waist as hard as he could hit him, dragging him to the floor as he came into the kitchen. Loraine, the youngest, scrambled to hold onto his legs, screaming, "No, Daddy, No, no nooo!" Howard went immediately for the shotgun, saying nothing, silent as could be, concentrating as hard as he could on getting control of the weapon, grabbing his Dad's fingers and bending them back, pulling and jerking on the stock while keeping the muzzle pointed away from any of them, as best he could. Loraine was screaming and crying, getting whipped about and banged into the floor by her Father's thrashing legs, as he kicked and tried to scrape her off of him, so that he could get up. But together with John they were keeping him on the floor. John was now on top of his Father, trying to ride him like a cowboy on a bucking bronc and he kept hollering, "The gun, Howard, get the gun or we're all dead!"

Their Father, like Howard, was silent, concentrating all of his considerable strength on freeing himself from the three kids. A couple times he almost succeeded, but Howard would shift one hand away from the weapon and stick his fingers in his Dad's eyes, gouging and pressing until his Dad would have to deal with him, knocking his hand away desperately while he quit trying to get up. Finally the squirming frantic mess of arms, legs and sweaty bodies slowed down and they just lay there, panting and out of breath and Howard was able to jerk the weapon away. He scuttled crablike off the pile, one arm holding the weapon, pointing it away from everybody. Their Father panted, "Alright, I'll let you live. Howard, give me the gun." But Howard instead shucked the shells from the shotgun and put them in his jeans pocket. Then he took the gun and put it back in the bedroom. He was always careful with weapons that way, assuming they were all loaded until he had opened them and emptied them. It was what his Dad had taught him. He found the rest of the ammo for the gun and picked it up, took it with him. He and his Dad stood and stared at each other, neither of them blinking. That was the day that Howard started thinking for himself, on everything, a lifelong habit.

Horace Howard Dantes was born in Lockhart, Texas on February 27, 1913. We know that he was named after his father, Horace Cleveland Dantes, and we know that he hated his name, for he never used it. Question is, did he also hate his Father? He had a baby sister, Loraine Ada Dantes, who in that charming southern way of hardly literate babies naming siblings, dubbed him "Hod." It was her best try at saying Howard, which was the name he chose to use. Horace eventually got transmogrified into Hawss, which sounded like Hoss and Hod would answer to Hoss or Hod; call him anything else and you answered to him.

His Dad was the oldest of six brothers, one sister, and held in awe by all of them. He was a natural leader, physically courageous and when called upon extremely violent, though perhaps not for the times in which he lived. As a youngster, and when his Dad was still alive, Hod would go to the hall closet and find his Dad's jacket, the one he wore in his first gun fight, the one with the bullet hole in it, and run his finger through the hole and perhaps imagine what it must be like to face an armed enemy. Most likely he admired his Father, at least until the Saturday they had oyster stew.

Horace Cleveland Dantes had been married three times, losing his first wife, Ada, to an infected appendix operation, his second to divorce and his third ran off and left him. Despondent, he one day announced to the three kids: John, the oldest, Hod and their little sister Loraine Ada that he was going to kill them all on Saturday, and then kill himself. Oh, and by the way, what would they like for their last meal? The kids all looked at each other and said, "Oyster stew."

The kids knew to believe him, for their Dad had killed before, and besides, there was the constant reminder of the jacket with the hole in it, hanging in the closet. Horace Cleveland had worked as a barber as a young man, and had gotten into an argument with a customer in his chair when the customer grabbed the straight razor off the tray and slashed at Horace, cutting his belt in two. The man fled from the shop, coming by two days later to say he wanted to apologize and asked that Horace meet him after work to make up, so to speak. Horace Cleveland didn't trust the man nor did he fear him. He agreed to the meeting, but went to it armed with an 1851 Colt Revolving Navy Pistol, one of 272,000 made and used in several wars, including the U.S. Civil War. His had been bequeathed to him from his Uncle John. They met in the street about a block from the barber shop, when his assailant drew on him and fired, the bullet tugging on his jacket, but missing him. Horace returned fire, his shot taking the man, Stephen Kreuz, dead center in the chest. There were witnesses, depositions were taken by the sheriff, and Horace was acquitted at a quick trial, on witnessed self-defense.

Kreuz' brother took offense, however, and noised it about that he was out for revenge. He waited until Horace was on a trip out of town and took up in ambush behind some bushes at the railway station, waiting for Horace's return on the train. Horace Cleveland's friends, however, had gotten word of the ambush and gone up the line on horseback with a mount for him. They rode hard back to Lockhart, arriving before the train. Horace spotted the brother, Tom Kreuz, hiding behind the shrubbery, walked up behind him and said, "Here I am." Tom spun 'round, jerking his shotgun up and fired as Horace ducked and fired three shots in quick succession. A wag from a nearby saloon placed a card, the ace of spades, over the cluster of entry wounds centered on Kreuz' heart. It was a tight group. Marksmanship would prove to be a family attribute, one passed down to Hod. Horace Cleveland was again acquitted on self-defense and his reputation grew. He and his brothers were high spirited. The saying was that they rode high, wide, and handsome. They also on one occasion rode their horses into the main saloon on the Courthouse square in Lockhart, seat of Caldwell County. It is not recorded whether they asked for beer for their horses, but they did fire off several rounds at the clock in the Courthouse tower, on their way out. They were rather full of themselves for the time, actually for any time.

But, back to the oyster stew. Saturday arrived, Dad made the stew they'd requested and noted that they didn't eat much of it. Plainly they'd lost their appetite. With a grunt he got up from the table and went into the bedroom for his shotgun. The kids had plotted their move, deciding they weren't going down without a fight. They quietly got up from the table and stood to both sides of the bedroom door, ready to jump their Father as soon as he came out. Then ensued the fight for their lives already described.

In their early years, after their Mother died, the kids went to live with their Grandmother on their Dad's side. As a widow she had married Mr. Crowell and they all lived at their farm, together with Mr. Crowell's four sons, five miles from Luling, in McNeil, Texas. It was a large group and everybody worked, especially Grandma, cooking and baking for that crew. Hod, when he first started plowing, could barely reach the plow handles, but it worked because the mule, Joe, was smart and knew what to do and turned by himself at the ends of the rows. Hod gathered corn, hauled water for Grandma, picked cotton and grew strong and tough, working for everything he got. There were watermelons in the summer and Hod would break them open with the heel of his foot, eating just the hearts, hot from the sun. Sometimes they would take ol' Joe down to Plum Creek and swim, diving off of Joe's back, swimming under his belly. Joe tolerated it, never stepped on any of them. After Mr. Crowell's sons grew up and moved out, it settled down to a smaller family with the same amount of work, a place with no running water and a kerosene fired stove and lamps. It was a hard life but it was all they knew, and life was good.

Of the three kids, Hod was the quiet one, usually not speaking unless spoken to. He doted on his little Sis and she loved him dearly. John was the flamboyant one, known for his open and loud personality. The Family thought Hod to be slow in the head, because he spoke so seldom. Perhaps they failed to notice the intense curiosity in his eyes, the look that was somewhere between a twinkle and a glint. There were others who noticed, though. The girls in school noticed the deep blue eyes and the twinkle; the boys tended to get the glint and were wary of him, his silence and the way he moved, strong and confident. The girls liked his confidence, though, and found him to be extremely good looking. Hod would have success with the gentler sex and it was to be a lifelong passion, a break from an otherwise often bleak existence.

After Horace Cleveland died, he also the victim of an appendix operation, the kids were split up, John and Loraine going to relatives' places in Beaumont, and Hod staying at the farm, with Grandma. Indeed it was Grandma who raised Hod, and he would visit the farm, later in life, as he crossed the country, between ships, often spending a week or two, pitching in and regaling her and Mr. Crowell with his sea stories. Upon his arrival, each time, Grandma would have him pull off his shirt and prove that he had no tattoos. And he proved an unusual sailor, no tattoos, no bad language and his stories were always funny, sea stories that were usually at his expense, describing his foul ups and mishaps.

When he finished the tenth grade, the family decided that he needed a better school than the one in Luling, and he went to live with his Uncle Bill in Beaumont. He was woefully behind and failing until he started to catch on, soon rising to the honor roll. In the eleventh grade he got a job as an usher at the movie theater, where he commenced an education of another sort. He was an usher until the movie started, then went up into the projection booth to relieve the guy showing the movie. Late in the evening the girl selling the popcorn and candy would close down the refreshments stand and join him, in the projection booth. With only one chair there she got around to sitting in his lap. That led to other things, sweet delights and a very nice education from an "older woman." Meanwhile at home Hod put in a large garden that helped feed the family and with his $7.00 a week paid for all his school expenses and his clothes. He was used to pulling his own weight, always had. Later in the Navy, he would save his pay and send most of it to his sister Loraine, so she could pay her own way, too.

It was 1932, the depths of the Great Depression, jobs were hard to come by and it wasn't easy to keep food on the table, much less have money or time for the 'extras'. Hod had been living with various relatives most of his life and had a very strong desire to be independent; so after he graduated from High School he decided to join the Navy. It was not easy to get into the armed forces, but it took Hod only about a month, when most recruits were waiting for six months or more. He almost aced the entrance examination and he was in excellent physical condition. He went to San Diego for boot training. His first breakfast in Boot Camp was beans and cornbread. When he went back for seconds, the cook said, "Son, you will make a good sailor, you like beans!"

All recruits slept in hammocks and they learned how to roll their uniforms and pack them in a sea bag. Most of their time was spent learning to march, first in squads, then in platoons and companies. They learned the manual of arms: port arms, right shoulder arms, left shoulder arms, present arms and how to stand at attention and parade rest. They were taught how to salute and had classroom training in the chain of command, knot tying and seamanship. All of them learned the names of the various ratings, or occupational specialties, and how to recognize Officers but most of all, they gained an instant and overwhelming appreciation for what it meant to be a Chief Petty Officer.

CHAPTER 2

NAVY BOOT CAMP – SAN DIEGO

"Alright, get a move on you sons uh bitches, we ain't got all day." It was the First Class Petty Officer, hustling the barracks full of them into formation outside on the grinder at 0430. They formed up in three ranks, tallest to shortest, had been doing it for about three weeks, now, dressing down at arm's length, while looking right and lining up with the man next to them. Then they turned their faces to the front and made tiny shuffling movements with their feet to be completely hidden behind the man in the rank in front of them. If they could have, they'd have also been invisible.

Petty Officer Shockey then called the muster, "Able, Aaron, Costain, Dantes, Daughter…" continuing until he had called out all forty names, each man singing out with a "Here!" when his name was called. When he was finished, he did an about face and saluted the Chief Petty Officer in Charge of Baker Company, Chief Locker, "all present or accounted for, Chief". By chance, Dantes and Daughter were of a similar height as well as alphabetically sequential. Their friendship had started when they wound up next to each other in formation and had opportunities to swap a few words and looks as they were getting used to the new routines. They'd been here for going on three weeks and this formation was not scheduled.

"Very well, Petty Officer Shockey," and Shockey saluted again, a perfect salute, forearm at a 45 degree angle with the deck, did an about face and marched to the rear of the formation, squaring his corners with military precision and marching, not walking, to his assigned position. "Alrighty then, this morning there was shit, in the shitcan!" the Chief bellowed. A pause and then several bellies started to shake with muffled laughter, as they all wondered something along the lines of, *well, isn't that what shitcans are for*? Daughter was speaking out of the side of his mouth, "Well I guess that explains why we're out here in our skivvies." Dantes did crack a smile at that, a quick one, but not quite quick enough.

"Dantes! You think that's *funny*?" He said Dantes funny, like dainties, and Hod didn't like people messing with his name, never did.

Now Shockey spoke up, "Daughter thinks it's funny too, Chief," and he grabbed both Daughter and Dantes and frog marched them to the front of the formation, where they were ordered to assume the leaning rest position, which was the pushup position with arms straightened.

Chief Locker then asked in an overly polite and solicitous tone, exactly what it was, that was so funny. Dantes started to answer, but Daughter interrupted, as though it were he, being addressed, "Chief it just seemed like a funny place to take a dump, Chief."

And Dantes knew better, but he chimed in, "And I knew it was probably paper, but thought you meant it was shitpaper, Chief, and I didn't think any of us would have done that. Sir. I mean Chief." The two of them were buddies that way. If one caught crap the other found a way to share it. It spread it out, made it less severe than it would have been, for just one of them. Boot Camp was working, as they were starting to think as a team and finding ways to co-operate and absorb the harsh attention they were getting as a larger and larger group, as others became less scared and more competent. The Blue Jacket's Manual would have referred to it as morale, or esprit de corps, if there *was* a field manual for that, lord knows there was one for everything else.

The Chief, of course, knew all of this, had been looking for it and was quietly pleased that it was these two, because they were plenty strong enough to take what was coming, and he wanted to do a number on the rest of the Company. But before he could get started, another voice spoke up, then two more, then the clamoring bunch of the whole company, saying, "Me, too, Chief, I thought it was funny, too." And lots of bellies were jiggling and chests were pushing out.

So, the Chief and the PO1 spent the next hour administering Physical Training, wearing out the Company, and running them in for one minute trips to the rain locker and a change into dungarees to get ready for chow. It turned out to be the last deliberately chickenshit thing the pair did to the Company. Now started the more serious phase of rebuilding the men, whom they'd been tearing down for almost three weeks. It was almost to the half-way point of their training and they needed to be focused on what they were doing, on the pistol range, in the rifle pits, the swimming pool, for survival training, boxing and the jump into the water from the rafters of the natatorium. There had been some attrition, but the ones who were left had proven their toughness and training now became more inclusive, more like what they hoped the real Navy would be.

In the messhall, going through the chow line, they held out their trays, getting eggs or oatmeal plopped on it, some toast and orange juice, a mug of coffee and maybe an apple. "So, you do much with firearms out there on that farm, in Texas," Daughter asked, "'cause I haven't the first notion of how to go about it."

"Yeah, some, but don't worry, they've been doing this for years, know what they're about." Dantes replied. "I hear the instructors are Marines."

"Oh great, this ought to be fun." And they finished up their chow, and headed back to the barracks to get into their infantryman's dress, which was dungarees with trousers tucked into leggings and a web belt with a bayonet scabbard attached. Their white hats were dorky looking as they were not allowed to stretch them at the rim, to put a salty curl to it nor to wear it at a cocky angle. That would come later, when they were aboard ship.

"Yeah, well remember," Dantes said, "the most important things are to get the front sight centered in the rear circular sight, with the bull sitting right on top of the front sight blade take a breath and let half of it out then squeeze the trigger, and not to jerk it."

Daughter cocked an eye at him, "So, you've done this a time or two?"

"Yeah, a time or two." They dry snapped for five days, practicing the prone, sitting, kneeling and offhand positions, learning how to unfasten and open and twist the slings on their rifles so as to wind smoothly around their fore-arms, and how to control their breathing and squeeze the trigger. Meanwhile the chickenshit Marines were standing on their ankles, to flatten their feet, and knocking their rifles about and the boots slowly got their muscles to co-operate and their firing positions to become stable, with very little movement.

The second week they took turns firing and working in the pits, running targets up for firing and down for scoring, and firing their weapons, the M1903 Springfield .30-06, called the battlefield tack driver. There was slow fire, timed fire and rapid fire, in all four positions. The Marines also fired, expecting to show these swabbies how to do it. Firing was to last for the week, in order to get everybody qualified, either Marksman, Sharpshooter or Expert. Dantes was one of the first to shoot, was given a chance to sight his weapon in, and to gage the wind. The range was 250 yards. He smoothly qualified expert, with the high score on the range that day. It stood up for the rest of the week, topping all of the Marine instructors. They asked him, "Fired before?" He answered, "Some."

They tacked on Pistol firing after rifle and gave it short shrift, compared to the week of dry snapping with the Springfields. The result was the same though, Dantes had high score, beating the Marines as well.

In boxing training they taught them to keep their chin down, dauber up, elbows in and to throw a lot of jabs. They also learned the left hook, right cross and uppercut. They were shown how to slip a punch and how to clinch and tie an opponent up. Then they matched them with someone their approximate size and they would go for three, three minute rounds, wearing head gear and that was it. Dantes' reputation had preceded him and he was matched with another boxer his size. He also happened to be boxing the instructor, and the first one to go.

Daughter said, "This is a put up deal, that's the instructor they put you with."

Dantes answered, "I'm to be taught a lesson; I will probably learn a lot."

The bell rang and they both advanced to the center of the ring and touched gloves. Dantes noticed the way the instructor shuffled his feet and how he led with his left and kept his legs spread, and he immediately copied him. He was only quick enough to partially block the first shot, a left hook that came whistling in to his right cheek, stunning him. Instead of retreating, Dantes leaped forward and tied up his opponent, one glove under each of his own arms, working him backwards into the corner. His opponent pulled loose and started in with body shots to his kidneys, when Dantes threw a hard left jab, straight into the nose of the instructor. Blood started to pour and Dantes got another punch in, a combination really, two shots to the gut followed by an uppercut. There was now blood in lots of places as both fighters were scoring and whaling away at each other. Dantes got on his bicycle then and concentrated on dodging and slipping the punches coming his way, as the bell rang, ending the round.

Back in his corner, Daughter was his corner man, sponging him off. "I think you've got him pissed, and that's not good."

"Yeah, but he's breathing harder than I am, and I think he's dropping his left a little bit, might be set up for a right cross. I think that's my best chance, a right cross when he drops his left. When you see it drop, I want you to holler, NOW, and I'll put everything into one punch and take my chances."

Round two passed swiftly, most of the punching done by the instructor, Hod taking all of his shots on the arms, and in his sides, mostly backpedaling, slipping and weaving, trying to stay out of his way while the instructor expended energy. As the bell rang for the third and final round, Daughter pulled the stool from the ring and Hod reminded him, "When he drops his guard, you holler NOW."

They both advanced to the center of the ring and touched gloves, when the instructor immediately uncorked a right cross, dropping his left with the effort. As Dantes slipped the punch he heard, "NOW" and put everything into a counterpunch right cross of his own, scoring cleanly to the left temple of his opponent. The instructor went down and did not answer the count, to the cheers of Dantes' fellow boots. The match was over. And Dantes had learned not to ever let himself get into a ring with a ringer, again. He much preferred to keep the odds in his favor, the turf, his turf.

The next week they were marched over to the base natatorium, carrying a spare set of dungarees, rolled up in a towel. They'd already been swimming in the pool, working up to a full hour without hanging onto the sides. Today it was going to be an hour, but fully clothed, except for the shoes. "Okay, listen up and listen tight!" PO1 Sharkey growled. "The drill is to swim around the perimeter of the pool for an hour, without touching the sides. At the end of the hour and on my signal, you will remove your trousers, tie the ends of the legs in an overhand knot and swing your trou over your heads, catching air in the wetted cloth and using your inflated trou as a flotation device. Any questions?" looking around. "Does anybody want to demonstrate this?" Almost as one, they all turned toward Dantes.

"Well, how about it Dainties, are you up..." but Dantes had already entered the pool in a smooth dive, right over the sign that said, "no running, no diving," and had surfaced, twisting and facing the company, doing a powerful treading underwater using his legs as though doing a scissors kick and sweeping slowly with his arms outstretched at the surface. His head was practically motionless and he wasn't even breathing hard. He looked expectantly at Sharkey, waiting for his instructions. "Okay, now bend forward, unbutton your trou and pull them off, one leg at a time." Dantes drew his legs up, bent forward and did this. "Now tie a knot in the end of the legs of your trou, both legs." It was done, in less than a minute. "Spreading the waist, grab your trou with both hands and swing them over your head, inflating them. Dantes did this too and rested one arm over the crotch with the knotted legs standing in a vee, pointed at the roof. "Very well done, Dantes." Now collapse your buoy and reinflate it by lowering yourself beneath it and blowing air up into it. It took Dantes four dunks and blows to fill his trousers and he again rested across the crotch of his buoy. Daughter led the applause, clapping, whistling and shouting and the rest of the Company joined in, their cheers bouncing off the enclosed space and making a helluva a racket until Sharkey regained control.

The Chief, who had been watching all of this, spoke up. "Dantes, I know you can do the swim, I'm passing you now. I want you in the pool as a lifeguard, looking after your buddies; if you see anybody who needs help it's your job to go to him and render assistance. Got it?" "Aye, Chief." And you could see the confidence grow among Dante's company mates as Sharkey blew the whistle and they all jumped into the pool. And, when it was time for the Company to climb to the rafters and the platform placed there, all the way up a skinny, shaky ladder, naturally it was Dantes who went first stepping off the platform, arms crossed on his chest, legs crossed at the ankles and head turned to the side and tucked. And he was followed by his company mates, going on the confidence he gave them.

Dantes was selected to carry the Company Guidon at the Graduation Parade and he also graduated at the head of his class and received his promotion to Seaman First Class, whereas the others were all advanced to SN2 and would have to wait several months aboard their first ships to make Seaman First. It was a pattern that would follow him throughout his Naval Career, and he expected nothing less of himself.

It was after the parade, they were back in the barracks for the last time together, as a company. They were made to roll their hammocks and all of their uniforms and pack them into their seabags. Then it was one more formation outside on the grinder, where an award for best recruit was given to Dantes. Shockey handed out their orders, to all of the men. There was excitement as they saw the ships to which they were headed. One of them called out," which ship did you get, Dantes?" He looked up and said, "Detroit, I'm going to the Cruiser fleet." They all looked to see if they were going to be on the same ship. Only one was, it was Daughter. Dantes grabbed Daughters orders and read it for himself, in surprise and with a big grin on his face. "I'll be damned," and then he felt someone's gaze on him, looked up and saw the Chief, looking at him across the grinder. And he knew. He walked over to the Chief and stood before him, looking at him directly in the eye.

"I think I should thank you for this Chief."

"Why, whatever gave you that idea, Seaman First Class Dantes? And by the way, you are out of uniform;" and he handed him a brand spanking new set of three stripes. And a very small smile surfaced on the Chief's face, stayed there for a second or two, and he said, "You didn't know that this was my last Company, did you? Dantes responding with raised eyebrows. "I've got my orders, too." Then they both grinned, broadly, nodding together and saying at the same time, "Detroit."

CHAPTER 3

TIJUANA

It was a short jaunt from Boot Camp to the ship, and Dantes and Daughter had a weekend before having to report aboard. They had been advised to report straight to their duty stations, but were of a mind to see some of the sights first. Shockey actually told them uniforms were okay in town, but if they thought of heading to Mexico it would be better to go in civvies.

Dantes looked at Daughter, and the twinkle was there, "Well, I'm for getting a brew or two in Tijuana, how about you?"

"Shockey said we'd better wear civs, going into Mexico" Daughter replied. "Less likely to get thrown into a Mexican hoosegow."

"Yeah but we won't have any room for civilian clothes aboard ship; it either fits in our seabag or we don't take it with us. I say we find a room to put our stuff and go to a store and buy one shirt, each, and use our dungaree trou. That ought to be civilian enough."

They found a rooming house, run by a widow lady in National City. It was just a two mile walk to the border, so they stored their gear, put on the shirts they'd picked up at a clothing store and their dungaree trousers, locked their room and headed out on their first liberty. At the border they made as if to show their ID and the Mexican Border Policeman just waved them through. With their haircuts and dungarees he knew exactly where they were coming from.

The muchachos y muchachas also knew a sailor when they saw one and they were soon surrounded by eight or ten kids, teenagers and younger. "Hey, Yanqui! You wanna' good time?"

Dantes just kept walking, he was used to Mexicans in South Texas, knew a bit of their lingo, Spanglish style. "Vamonos, yo no tengo dinero," he said in an aside.

"You no want mujeres, Senor?" the most persistent street urchin said.

"Quiero cervaza, donde esta la cantina, muchacho?" Dantes replied

The one kid, the most persistent, got in front of them, "Me Jaunito, I take you cantina, for cerveza Senores. I know the way. Best Cantina, best Senoritas. I show you." He was pleading and laughing at the same time as he shouldered aside his competitors.

Daughter said, "Don't know about you, but I'm thirsty and a senorita or two would go down pretty well, too."

"Yeah, well it's probably only a block away, but let's let him take us." And they went with Jaunito and a rag tag crew in their wake, marching in an exaggerated military style march, making fun of the newly released boots on their first liberty. It was pretty dark inside. The door was open with light coming in through a couple windows and the door. It smelled of stale beer, sweat and maybe urine coming from the head in the corner. There was an eight foot bar with a mirror behind it, making the space look twice as big. The bar tender kicked a skinny, mangy dog out the back door, came back behind the bar, put both fists on the polished mahogany surface and with raised eyebrows said, "Cervezas Senores?"

"Tequila, Senor, but no ice. Just neat, in a glass," said Hod, "y una Cerveza, tambien." Jose, for it was Jose's place, as the sign said outside, turned to Daughter, asking with his expression, and you, Senor?" "The same for me, said Daughter."

"El mismo, Jose, y pronto, por favor!" Dantes said, trying out some of the Spanish he knew from a Texas upbringing. They got their shots of tequila, knocked them back and started to notice their surroundings as their eyes adjusted to the semi-gloom. It was a packed dirt floor and a corrugated tin roof. They were seated at a small table with four chairs and before long two ladies came into the place, most likely given the suggestion by Jaunito. They exchanged glances with Jose and he nodded slightly. Jose couldn't afford to keep regulars in his place; besides, it was too small, no additional rooms behind curtains. They didn't notice Jaunito, outside earlier, getting some small change from each of the senoritas, then taking up station against the wall, guarding his position, such as it was, fleeting but none the less important for him. His job now was to shoo others away and give the four inside time to make time, so to speak.

There were a few Mexican workers who came into the place, sat at the bar and drank their tequilas straight up, out of jelly glasses. They were workers, heading home after a hard day, taking their ease and observing the young yanquis in the mirror behind the bar. Observing, too, the two senoritas. The two lovelies were not girls, not by any means. They sized up these two striplings and adjusted downward the estimate of their monetary worth; indeed Anna wondered why her brother had come and gotten her for these

Boots. Still, the evening had not yet started and who knows, there might be a few dollars to be had, a bit of fun in the process.

The tarted up, somewhat provocatively dressed pair sashayed up to the table and asked, "Okay we sit down and join you?" Daughter replied, "Sure, have a seat."

Dantes got up and held a chair for the prettier one of the two, saying, "Just for conversation, ladies, just for conversation." Anna, the older of the two, recognized this as just the opening of negotiations; with a quick glance at Consuela she replied, "Well of course, we hardly know each other, yet. You wouldn't buy a drink for a total stranger, right, Senor?"

Dantes replied, "My name is Dantes, and this is mi amigo, Daughter, and you have very good English, much better than my Espanol."

"Thank you Dantes and my name is Anna, and this is Consuela." Turning to Daughter she asked, "What brings you to Tijauna, Senor? Where are you from, San Diego, LA?"

"Actually, we're just out of Recruit Training, in San Diego, Anna."

"Hmmm, so interesting, Marines or Navy?"

"Navy all the way," said Daughter.

Dantes had turned toward Consuela, who seemed a bit more shy than Anna. Maybe it was because her English wasn't so good. She said to him, "Nice day, today. You stay long, here, in Tijuana?" Dantes noticed she seemed a bit nervous and he asked, would you like a drink, Consuela?" Anna picked up on that and signaled Jose, who came to the table.

"Gentlemen, drinks for the ladies?" Jose asked. Daughter said, "Yes, and I'll have another tequila, in one of those jelly glasses you've got behind the bar." "Shall I bring the bottle to the table, Senores?" Dantes asked, "Cuantos?" Jose said, "Two dollars, American." Dantes nodded. He felt fairly flush, with almost two month's pay in his wallet. Anna caught Jose's eye and said, "Four jelly glasses, Jose." That meant she was taking it easy on these two boots, no high priced watered down drinks for the girls. There'd be opportunity, perhaps, later to pry a bit more dinero from their companions, and they wouldn't have to share it with Jose. Besides, that tequila was about eighty five cents American, and Jose was getting more than twice that.

The USS Detroit (CL-8) was commissioned as an Omaha Class Scout Cruiser in July 1923, when Hod Dantes was but ten years old. By the time he reported aboard with his best buddy from Boot Camp, she was labeled as a Light Cruiser, and had been home ported in San Diego for over a year. She had spent her first eight years as part of the Scouting Fleet, either in the Atlantic or Mediterranean. Her first duty was to assist in the first aerial circumnavigation of the world in 1924 and in 1927 she transported the United States Secretary of State Frank B. Kellogg, from Ireland to France for the negotiations that led to the signing of the Kellogg-Briand Pact.

Aboard USS Detroit, newly arrived Chief Locker, who had already report-ed in for duty and settled into his berth in Chief's Quarters, dropped by the Ship's Office, and looked in through the half opened Dutch door. A Yeoman third looked up from his typewriter, squinting through his cigarette smoke, "Yeah, Chief, What can I do for you?"

"I'd like to know if two sailors just out of Boot Camp have reported aboard."

"Names?"

"A Seaman First by the name of Dantes and a Seaman Second, Daughter."

Riffling through a stack of paperwork, including a few sets of orders, he looked up, "No, Chief, nobody by those names has checked in, yet. Why, you know them?"

"Yeah, they were two recruits in my Company in Boot Camp, just checking on them."

"Well, Chief, any sign of them I'll let you know, leave word up in Chiefs' Quarters."

"Appreciate it, thanks."

"Uh, Chief, here's the ship's copy of Daughter's orders, he has until Monday morning to report in, probably the same for, and did you say Dantes?"

"Yes, he would have the same reporting date."

"Well, it wouldn't surprise me if these young bucks went on down to T-Town, you know, first liberty out of Boot Camp, and all that." Chief Locker grunted in agreement and turned away, headed forward to the Goat Locker, which is what Chiefs' Quarters went by, in most of the Fleet.

He entered the general mess area of Chiefs' Quarters, with a dining table and a few aluminum chairs placed around it and against the bulkhead, and the ever present lagged, painted and stenciled pipes and lines running in cable trays in the overhead. The bulkheads painted an industrial light green, dark green felt table cloth, just like the wardroom and a tiled deck in a black and white checkerboard pattern, buffed to a high gloss. Removing his cover he noticed the Chief Master at Arms sitting by himself at the table, nursing a cup of coffee. Lifting the coffee pot from its heater in the coffee mess, he tilted it toward the Chief, his expression asking if he could use a topping off. The CMOA nodded so he poured one for him, returned the pot to the mess and sat down across from him. "Name's Locker."

"Glad to have you aboard, Chief, Matt Grundy."

"Glad to be aboard, Chief, and good to meet you."

"Saw your orders, bet it was *lots* of fun, pushing those boots."

"Had its ups and downs, like most duty stations. I was ready to get back to the Fleet, though."

"I can imagine. Got any family in Dago?"

"Nope, no wife, at least not yet. You?"

"Not anymore," and his sour expression didn't invite comment. "That coffee tastes like it was brewed yesterday; steward needs to make a fresh pot. Not too many takers with a weekend coming on. We got lots of married on board, the rest of them liberty hounds."

"Well, after a tour in Dago, I know they are out there and know where to find them."

"I'll bet you do," Grundy grinned. "By the way, I saw the orders on a couple of brand new sailors, due in on board. You know them?"

"Actually, I do. They were in my Company and one of them is the honor graduate for the Company, Seaman First name of Dantes. He and his buddy, Daughter. I just checked with the duty yeoman and they haven't shown up, yet."

Grundy smiled, "You wouldn't have anything to do with them coming here, would you?"

"Well, I might have put a bug in the personnel Chief's ear, about a month before graduation, once I knew I was coming to Detroit." Staring at his coffee, he continued, "I'm a little worried, guessing they probably went on down to Tijauana."

"I imagine you might know that place, too, Locker, stationed in Dago, and all."

"Yes, but mostly by reputation, didn't head down there too often. How about you, Chief?"

"Well, as you know, I get involved with all the non-judicial disciplinary cases, prepping them for the X.O. So, I have a pretty precise bead on the worst places, the really bad actors, have actually pulled a few sailors out of some pretty nasty situations."

Chief Locker perked up, looked at the CMOA with some intensity. "Matt, I have a really big favor to ask."

"You want to go down there tonight, or give it a night, go find them tomorrow?"

'Let's go tonight, I'm buying."

"Got yourself a deal, Locker. You didn't say your first name?"

"Wallace. And no jokes about wall lockers." They both laughed and decided to go south after an evening meal, on board.

Chiefs Locker and Grundy, departed the quarterdeck with the permission of the Officer of the Deck. They were third in a nest of four light cruisers, so it was a ritual they had to repeat two more times, just to get to the pier. The Chiefs, by custom, didn't have to show liberty chits, were treated more like Commissioned Officers in that regard. They went to a pay phone on the pier and called a taxi to meet them and it showed up at the pay phones in five minutes.

"Where to, Chiefs?" as they got into the back seat of the cab.

"Take us down to the border crossing." That got them a second look in the rear view mirror. The driver wasn't used to seeing too many Chiefs going into T-Town. He also didn't see, for what it was worth, that one of the Chiefs had, under his jacket, a Colt .45 1911, semi-automatic pistol, a favorite weapon of choice in the services for more than twenty years, now. Chief Grundy had access to the sidearm and Chief Locker was carrying it, as he had qualified regularly with it on the range in Boot Camp.

"Want to make a stop or two on the way, Chiefs? Better booze over here, trust me."

"Nah, we're gonna' wait for some of that good tequila. Thanks, anyway." Chief Grundy replied. They had talked it over on board ship at dinner and decided to take a firearm and also to stay sharp, no booze. The exact words were, "We're on a mission; doesn't mean we can't have some fun, just no booze." They weren't particularly worried about a hassle from the Federales, the CMOA had some contacts in law enforcement, should they need them.

They got out of the cab and said they might be looking for a ride back to the base, maybe around midnight and what time did the driver get off? "Gotcha' covered, gents, I get off at 2300 and will be down here by 2230."

"Oh, and it could be a little crowded, we'll be a likely party of four, coming back."

"No hay problema, Senores," with a wave out the window as he drove off.

So it was a little bit like pulling liberty in a foreign port. Place smelled different. It was a mixture of diesel exhaust, bad sewers and food being cooked and hawked on the streets. Place was dirty, garishly painted and bathed in ugly and occasional lighting from street lamps and signs in some of the windows. Most of the shops were open, it was a weekend, after all, but they were empty except for shopkeepers, mostly bored, some hopeful. And the ever-present kids. The seasoned Chiefs were toughened to most things, but regretted seeing the kids in the streets. In fact, that's what they thought of the two sailors they were there to find, they too were kids, their kids and they wanted to find them before they got into too much trouble.

There was a mariachi band, just three old guys, a fiddle, a trumpet and a guy who only played castanets. They all sang and actually sounded pretty good, decked out in the bell bottom pantalones with silver beads, short waisted jackets, frilly shirts and the decorated sombreros, though they didn't need them for protection from a sun that had long since turned in for the night. They played "La Cucaracha," which seemed appropriate, got two bits in return and moved on to find another gringo, sing another song.

First they went to the jail. Might as well start there and work their way into the bars and bordellos, shacks and back alleys. If they didn't find their kids it was still a good idea to let the locals know they were there, on semi-official business. Didn't hurt to give a couple bucks to el Jefe, while they were there, either. It was the way it seemed to work in all these liberty ports, world-wide.

Grundy turned to Locker, "If they're in one of the better restaurants, they are probably not in trouble, yet, so we have time to get to them later, if needs be. I say we go hit the dives and ask around, check there first."

"Sounds good to me, Chief." It was maybe strange, maybe not, but the kids gave them a wide berth, there was no clamoring, no crowding. These were serious looking men who carried themselves with a great deal of authority. They entered a bar on the first corner and described their sailors, asked. "We haven't seen them here today, Senores," they were told. Locker said, "Matt, let's try some of these alleys, I can just see them getting mobbed by a bunch of kids, right off the bat, and getting shanghaied into one of these dives, with lots of promises.

They went into a place, sort of dark, a few kids hanging around, sat at the bar and asked after two young sailors, probably dressed in some sort of civilian get up. "Not in here, Senores." And the bartender went to the door and waved some kids in. Then ensued some rapid Spanish punctuated by scowls and threats and the oldest kid turned and said, "Si, I help you find them."

Locker paid the barkeep a dollar and grabbed the kid by the shoulder, "Mas dinero por usted, pero solamente por mis dos amigos." The kid nodded and took off, the Chiefs following. They would wait in the dirt street while the boy went into the bars, asking. He would come out and head in a different direction. By the fourth bar, a place called Jose's, the kid was in there longer. He came to the door and waved them in.

Jose was wiping glasses, looked up at them. "Si, Senores, I think I have seen the two men you look for. It was just two of them?"

"That's right, probably two of them," Locker said. "Did you see a couple of brand new sailors in civilian clothes, today? Maybe four hours ago, or more?"

"Si."

"Can you describe them, please?"

"One of them, muy guapo, you understand guapo?"

"Yes, handsome, the senoritas would like him, muy mucho."

"I think they are the two who went with Anna and Consuelo. But of course I cannot guarantee.. maybe three or four hours ago." And he turned his back and busied himself at the rack of bottles.

The Chiefs exchanged a glance. "Jose, I have a proposition for you." It was Grundy speaking. "We are willing to pay for help in actually finding our shipmates. We are also very well acquainted with El Jefe Gonzales at the Station. If I were to tell him that we were mistreated by someone, I think that person would get a little visit from the Chief. He might even close this rat hole down, if we complained. It would cost you mucho dinero to get permission to open up again, I think."

Jose shrugged, "Antonio Gonzales is mi hermano, Senores. I think maybe he is not so quick to lock me up."

"Four dollars"

"Ahh, Senores, not less than ten."

"I also am very good friends with El Jefe's Boss, Jose, he your brother, too?" It was Grundy edging closer to the bar, scowling.

"Maybe just ocho dolares, entonces."

"Five and not a penny more," said Locker, and we will pay the kid, when we see our sailors, after he takes us to them." Another torrent of Spanish directed at the kid, and Jose nods, says, "Juanito will take you there.

CHAPTER 4

TIJUANA RESCUE

At Jose's Bar, earlier that evening, Dantes slammed his empty cerveza on the rough table, declared to the other three, "this has been muy Bueno, mi amigo y mis amigas but all good things come to an end." And he reached over to Daughter, nursing perhaps his fourth tequila, took the tequila from him, downed it and says, "Hasta la vista, senoritas, let's go, Daughter."

Anna had been watching closely, waiting for exactly this to arise and she turned to Consuela, nodding toward the head, "We're going to the powder room, be back muy pronto, senores." Daughter looked up, mumbled something and put his head down in his arms, on the table, started to snuffle.

As they primped in a bit of broken mirror, propped against the wall over the sink, "Consuela, we have some time invested in these two, I don't want to let them go, not just yet."

"I think they have had enough, Anna, so young and guapo, I think it's better we see them off, while the one you have can still walk."

"No. There's yet time to spend, and besides, it'll be fun with these yanqis."

"What do you have in mind, Anna? I think there are others out there, some who can afford to pay. Besides, these are just muchachos, not hombres."

"I think we will take them to my place, show them a good time and they will pay us."

"You think so? My senor is too smart for that, I think."

"We'd better get back out there before they go outside and get lost," Anna said, with a last second adjustment of her lipstick.

Dantes had gotten Daughter to his feet, had him by the arm and they were being obstructed by Jose, who was standing between them and the door, busily wiping down the table and thanking the senores, wishing them a good evening. As the senoritas came fluttering up he did the hand off, caught Juanito's eye at the door and ushered the four of them from his establishment with much bonhomie. "Adios, Jose, adios and it was a good time," say the pair as they were swept from the place, barely sidestepping the dog shit just outside the door, headed out to see what else the night might have in store.

Dantes looked around, saw Juanito, "M'hijo, walk with us to the border crossing."

Anna frowned, stared at Juanito and slyly pointed to her arm. Juanito caught on and said, "Jefe, you want tattoo? I know perfect place to get really good ones!"

Before Dantes can say no, gracias, Daughter straightened up and says, "Exactly what I want, my first tattoo." Anna chimed in, "You can have him do a pretty senorita, something to remember me by!"

"Not a good idea," said Dantes, "and it's time that we.." But Juanito had already grabbed Daughter and together he and Anna were steering him in the direction of what served as the seedier part of downtown. With a big frown Dantes and Consuela followed until they came to a place with a glass storefront, pictures of patterns taped to the inside. "This is the place, my Uncle, he runs it. He's a very good artist," said Juanito. They went inside and the uncle looked up, sized them up and said to Daughter, "You like tattoo?"

"Yeah, show me some pretty senoritas, maybe with not too much clothes on."

Dantes said, "senoritas with no clothes on, yes, tattoos, no."

"You telling me I can't get a tattoo?"

"Nope, I'm telling you, you gotta' pick. We don't have enough dinero for both."

With a leer at Anna, Daughter said, "Guess we are gonna' have to skip the tattoo." Anna replied with a come hither grin, pecked him on the cheek and laughed, "Well, then, I know just the place!" And off they headed for Anna's place.

It was a garishly painted cinder block and plywood roofed place, with a kitchen, small living room and one bedroom. Juanito had gone and they were left standing in the middle of the place. "I have little to offer, just juice and a little bit of rum." The three of them fell onto the one large couch while Anna went into the kitchen area and came back with some juice and a half filled bottle of rum. She poured two glasses of juice and adds a dollop of rum, offered them to Daughter and Dantes. They settled back into the couch and before long Anna started rubbing Daughter's leg, moving her hand up his thigh. He put his drink down and pulled her closer.

Dantes and Consuela were kissing and hardly noticed as the other two headed for the bedroom. In another ten minutes they came up for air and Dantes raised his voice and said, "What you up to, Daughter?"

"Two times," he replied, laughing.

Dantes laughed, "You always were a bull shitter. Drunk as you are, you couldn't get it up even once!" He got up and went into the bedroom, lighted only by a couple of candles. And there they were, naked and on top of the spread, Anna on top of him. Consuela came up and put her arms around Dantes from behind and started to undo his dungarees, button by button. She pulled his trousers down and he spun into the bed, pulling her with him and she landed on his front, and as his hands went up her skirt, her hands grasped him through his skivvies, then freed him from them. They both tear off their clothes and then it became very active and crowded as they tangled together while the other two watched.

An hour later they woke up in a tangled mess, the four of them, and Anna got up and went into the small privy, and relieved herself into a pot. Daughter heard a scratching, scuffling sound, "What's that?" Consuela said, "it's the rats, in the rafters." And she went in her turn to the privy, leaving the two ship-mates together alone.

"Well, Daughter, you about ready to head back to the room in National City?"

He looked over at Dantes, "What, you don't think we can stay here for the night?"

Dantes took a peek at his watch, "Well, it's plenty late, I suppose we could stay; I'm just not sure how many people have the key to this place. That and I'm not too keen on sharing it with a pack of rats." Just then the 'girls' came back in, having freshened up with some water from a pitcher in the privy and dabbed a bit of perfume on themselves. As though Anna had heard them, she went over to the door, turned the key in the lock, padded naked back to the bed and threw herself on Dantes, as Consuela lay next to Daughter.

"So, Senor Dantes, you ready for a real woman?" And four eyes got big and all doubt was removed as to where they would stay, for the night.

About three blocks away, in a cousin's house, one Jesus Garza was eating some arroz con pollo and knocking it back with a cerveza. He checked the time, thought he would soon head for home and relieve those two young gringos of their money. His girlfriend, his Corazon, was with him and they'd enjoyed an hour or so of lazy sex in the bedroom before she heated up a meal. Jesus acknowledged Anna as his wife, but didn't mind shopping her out; in fact it was his main way of making money, that and pushing marijuana. With a grunt he got up from the table, checked that his pistola, a .22 Cal semi-au-tomatic pop gun, was loaded with a full magazine and a round chambered, safety on. He didn't need heavy fire power and didn't need the noise that went with it. This was to be a quiet and brutal four or five minutes, perhaps without the necessity to actually shoot someone. He had shot un hombre, two months ago, and disposed of the body, then lay low. This time it would be two gringos.

He figured it would be safe to do it again, if necessary; and he liked the feeling he got when he jammed the pistol against an estupido gringo and fired several rounds into him. He'd been smoking some of his finest and was ready to go.

Leaving his cousin's place he walked casually toward his own place, arriving at the back, outside the bedroom. He waited awhile, listening closely at the bedroom wall, and could hear sounds of pleasure, sounded like those gringos were getting laid and laid good. Well, he hoped they were enjoying it, they would not think that he, Jesus, was so much fun. In fifteen minutes the noises stopped. He waited another ten minutes and then went around to the front, letting himself into the living room, moving slowly and silently. He decided to wait and stood in one spot, listening, stood there for a couple of minutes, getting ready.

Meanwhile the Chiefs were walking from Jose's Bar through the neighborhood, making their way to the place where Jaunito tells them the two sailors are. Juanito stopped them and asked for the cinco dolares. Chief Gundy says, "Uh-uh, not until we see our friends." Jaunito led a bit further on, pointed to the next house and said, "Aqui, here is where they are." He nervously again held out his hand. Chief Locker looked at him suspiciously, "Que esta la problema, muchacho?"

But Juanito has fled, looking over his shoulder, scared and not even waiting for his money, running away as fast as he can. The two Chiefs headed for the house, running.

Listening, also, was Dantes, who had heard the scratching of Jesus' key at the door and was now fully alert, trying to decide if it was rats scurrying that he'd heard, or maybe someone at the door. His eyes were fully opened and he was listening for any other noise. As his body tensed he felt Anna also tense and move as though sleeping, getting into position where she was ready to hold him down, into the bed. They lay like that for another full minute or two, but by now Dantes was convinced that someone else had entered the house and was in the next room. Dantes feigned a yawn, freeing both his arms and hollered out sharply, "Daughter, get up!"

At that point Jesus burst into the room and went straight to Daughter, who was still waking up and pistol whipped him. Consuela was screaming and crying in the corner as Dantes threw Anna to one side and cold cocked her with a vicious right cross.

The Chiefs outside heard the muffled shout, ran to the door and finding it still unlocked, pushed it open and crashed into the space just left by Jesus. "Dantes, where are you guys!" It was dark in the living space and Jesus knew his way in the dark, was now in the bedroom, going for Dantes.

Dantes heard the Chiefs and shouted out, "There's a guy with a gun." And he jumped off of the bed and the unconscious Anna, leaping for the pistol wielding Jesus. The two Chiefs burst into the dimly lit bedroom and Locker shouted, "*Dantes, get the gun!*"

All of a sudden it was Hod, four years earlier, those words ringing in his ears, "Howard, get the gun!" as he struggled for his life with his own father, tearing, punching and fighting for his life like a demon. With one hand on the pistol he was tearing into his assailant with the other, firing vicious jabs into his eyes, breaking his nose, a savage growl rising until he held the weapon with both hands, pointed down at the floor.

Chief Gundy now held his Colt .45 on Jesus as he kicked him in the ribs and the head, rendering him unconscious. Dantes got up from the floor and went to Daughter and made sure he was breathing as things quieted down, just the soft weeping of Consuela in the corner. Chief Gundy retrieved Jesus' pistol, while Locker went into the privy and got the water pitcher and a towel, wiped the blood off of Daughter and held a candle close to his face, assessing the damage. He was essentially okay so the Chief threw most of the pitcher of water in his face and he came up sputtering and disoriented.

Chief Gundy, said, "If you two have had enough fun for the night, I think we should be heading back to the ship." Dantes was already getting dressed, then picked up Daughters' clothes and helped him into them. Locker looked at Gundy, "Leave them all where they are, or take them down to the station?"

"Nah, we'll maybe give ol' what'sisname here another kick or two, make him stay night night for long enough to get us across the border. If we turn this bunch in we're going to have some explaining to do, ourselves."

Locker nodded, "What I thought, too, Chief." Neither Daughter, who was coming around rapidly, nor Dantes who was dressed and calm, said anything. They both knew well enough how lucky they were and also knew when to stay silent. They had screwed up and they knew it. They did NOT know what the Chiefs would do to them and were not in any hurry to find out.

Dantes went over to Consuela, who was looking scared and shamed, drawn up into a ball against the wall and quietly gave her a five dollar bill. He hid it from the others, and said nothing, but Locker knew what he was doing, and he actually approved, as silently as Dantes had done it. Some stuff you didn't talk about.

It was getting pretty close to midnight as the four of them got to the taxi stand on the other side of the border. The walk had been a quiet one, the two young lotharios chastened and not strutting at all. They were taking refuge behind the chasm of military seniority, maintaining silence unless spoken to and keeping their eyes in the boat, to themselves, not even talking to each other. Both of the Chiefs were armed, and the CMOA would lock up the Navy issue Colt .45 in the armory aboard ship and also dispose of the pistol they had taken from Jesus.

The taxi driver got out and opened the doors, sensed immediately that there had been an incident and he, too, stayed totally uninterested and asked, only, "where to, the ship?" Chief Locker looked at Dantes, who said, "No, we'll be stopping at our room in National City," and he gave the driver the address. They pulled up at the end of the pier where Detroit was berthed, the two Seamen having first changed into their uniforms. As they got out, Daughter pulled out his wallet and paid the cabbie. Locker let him. He figured it was part of the cost of a liberty in Tijauna. There would be other costs, as well, but the two of them had performed pretty well, for a couple of sailors on liberty. The Chiefs would probably laugh about it, when they got back to Chiefs Quarters, and were telling each other a couple of sea stories about when *they* were boots on their first liberty. But for now they just made their way across three quarterdecks, requesting and receiving permission to cross until they got to Detroit. Locker took Daughter below to the sickbay after first having the quarterdeck messenger roust the duty corpsman to unlock the place. Daughter had his wound, on the side of his head disinfected and bandaged.

Meanwhile, Chief Grundy took Dantes down to Chiefs Quarters, got the Chief Bos'n up and asked him to take his orders until tomorrow, for the Ship's Office, and to assign him a place to hang his hammock in the First Division berthing space. Dantes took both seabags below to sling his and Daughter's hammocks, but before he headed below, he turned quietly to Chief Grundy, about to say something. The Chief held up his hand. "Sailor, you screwed up and we both know it. But you also showed me something in the way you handled yourself in that fight for the gun. In my mind they cancel each other out. The only reason you are alive tonight is because your Chief Locker was not going to let you go down there alone and get into some serious trouble. It's enough to say that I fully understand why he thought you were worth it. Now, keep your nose clean and I wouldn't recommend any more trips to Mexico. Those folks down there have a long memory." With that he turned on his heel and headed for the Goat Locker.

Down below in the First Division berthing space, Dantes was trying to stay awake until Daughter gets there and turns in. Daughter came down the ladder, entered the compartment and groped in the soft semi-gloom, found his hammock, whispered to Dantes, "You awake?"

"Yeah, you okay?"

"I'll be better in the morning, but at least it's still the weekend, what's left of it. Reckon they'll let us sleep in?"

"Guess we'll find out." And Dantes relaxed in his hammock, felt a small movement, heard the noise in the hammock hooks, probably a tide shift or something, he thought, gave a twitch and was asleep.

In his dream, nightmare really, he is wrestling with his Dad on the kitchen floor, only the face is Jose's and it's not a shotgun it's Jose's pistol. They are wrestling silently, four hands on the pistol and someone shouts, "The gun, Howard, get the gun!" He yanks the gun away and Jose turns back into his Dad, with his hand out, "Gimme' the gun, Howard, gimme' the gun."

And the ship shifted again, just a bit, enough to cause the tear to drop and run quickly down his face as his eyes opened and he stared into the dark. When he fell asleep again he is lying to his Grandma about what he did in Tijauna, feeling the burn of shame crawling up the back of his neck. And Grandma seems to know and she is hugging him and he is only a kid, an orphan, and this farm is his home.

5 August 1932

Dear Loraine,

I hope you are doing okay, living with the folks. I miss you and think of you often. Whenever I can I'll include a draft for some spending money for you and so you can help pay the expenses of Aunt Leta and Uncle Bill. This letter includes $25. Please let me know if you don't find it. I worry about losing it in the mail.

I thought you might like to know a little about living conditions on the U.S.S. Detroit. For First Division, my Division, there is one small washroom, with a tile deck, and a rack all around the bulkheads with holes in it to hold a bucket. Everyone has his own bucket. There is a steam outlet where you can heat your bucket of water. We are allowed to use two buckets of water, that is when we are in port and more water is available. We have to bathe and wash our clothes in those two buckets, and everyone keeps clean. Living in close quarters means bathing every day. If someone fails to take a bath, he gets a couple of warnings, and that's it. A party of shipmates takes him into the washroom, strips off his clothes and gives him a good scrubbing with sand and canvas. We generally do it at night and call it a blanket party. It's usually enough.

Sleeping quarters are on the second deck, which is also the mess deck, no bunks. We sleep in canvas hammocks swung from the overhead. They are rigged fore and aft so that when the ship rolls, when underway, gravity keeps us in our hammock. The pitching motion as the ship's bow rises and falls is slower than a roll and generally less violent, unless you are all the way forward in the ship. After you get used to it, your hammock becomes quite comfortable. A few old hands have cots, which they set up on deck. When enough people get transferred, and I have enough seniority, I will rate a spot on deck for a cot. Everyone respects these rights and no one ever sets up his cot in the wrong spot. But there are always some pranksters. For instance you might come back to the ship some night after a binge ashore, and find your cot nailed together.

One sailor always hangs his socks over a steam pipe, over his cot, to dry. His socks were stolen a couple of times. So, he tied one end of a string to his big toe, and the other end to his socks. When he woke up the next morning, his foot was up about 3 feet above the cot. Someone had taken his socks, pulled his foot up, and tied the string to the steam pipe.

We don't have cafeteria type meals served. We have tables that seat ten men, five on each side. When not in use, the tables are swung on the overhead. One sailor is detailed as mess cook and brings the food down from the galley in tureens. Each mess cook serves two tables, 20 men. Things like meat and desserts are rationed. So, to get the best piece of meat, or an extra piece of pie, you tip the mess cook each payday. The mess cook, if he is smart, will buy a carton of cigarettes for the cooks in the galley. That way, he gets the best from the galley to feed his mess and get better tips.

Reveille is at 5:30 each morning, unless you had the mid-watch. Then you can sleep in 'til 7. The mess cooks have to get up at 5:00 and have coffee ready when the rest of the crew gets up. We turn-to on deck at 6:00 and work until 7:15, and have breakfast at 7:30. We quit work at 11:30 in order to get cleaned up for lunch which is at 12:00. We start work again at 1:00 and work 'til 4:00. In the evening, on free time, we play cards, cribbage, acey ducey, or go ashore when we rate liberty. Half the crew has to be aboard at all times to stand watches and be available for emergencies.

Mainly I compare the Navy to life at the farm. We worked harder on the farm, because there it was necessary to work to survive. With jobs so hard to come by, living on a farm at least meant getting enough to eat, and Grandma's chow was the best. Survival aboard ship mainly means not falling overboard in a bad storm, or having an accident when handling the gun mounts and ammunition. If we end up in a war, survival will depend upon our ability to fire our six inch guns rapidly and with great accuracy. I find I'm getting used to shipboard life and I'm looking forward to going to foreign ports, something you get to do when your home can steam across the horizon.

Say hi to the folks and tell them I'm doing fine and am looking forward to seeing them again some day, hopefully soon.

Love,

Hod

P.S. I just heard we're going to be in some big fleet exercise. The rumor is that it will be in the vicinity of Hawaii. Maybe I'll get to go ashore there! Some time in Pearl Harbor or Honolulu would be a really nice break from shipboard routine.

----

15 August 1932

Dear Howard,

You're so grown up! You sound so grown up! Is it okay if I still call you Hod? Is this really my brother? Thank

you for sending me some money, it's appreciated. I hope
that you're keeping some of it for yourself. It does
feels good to be able to contribute to my own keep. It's
difficult to come up with extra spending money and I hate
to ask Aunt Leta for it. She does give me a small allow-
ance when I help with the chores. I am so proud of my big
brother and I really miss you around here.

Hawaii! Wow, that seems like halfway around the world.
I'm going to go to the library and find a book about Hawaii; that way I'll know what you're talking about when
you write about those places. I can't wait until I'm
grown up, too; but you won't see me using a bucket for
water to bathe and do my laundry in. And aboard ship,
there's no privacy, is there? I can't imagine anybody
playing any tricks on you, because you usually play them
on others!

You haven't asked and but no, I don't have a boyfriend. But some of the boys have been looking, and are
being very nice. Uncle Bill says I can't have one until
I'm 16!

Hod, I have a question. I'm remembering the night we
were going to eat oyster stew and wondering if you ever
think of that. Do you worry that any of the three of us,
you, John and me, might be turn out the same way? Was he
crazy or a murderer and are we going to grow up to be
like him? I know this much, I never saw anybody so brave
as you, that day. And regardless of how we all turn out,
as a family, I am proud to be your sister.

Love you,
Loraine
PS Bo had puppies I'll tell you about them in my next
letter.

CHAPTER 6

In the years following the Great War, which we now refer to as World War I, the technology of war at sea, indeed the whole concept of world relationships, underwent a dramatic, if often confusing evolution. With the end of the war, President Wilson expended all his political capital trying in vain to establish a worldwide organization to prevent such a World War from ever happening again. His efforts at creating a League of Nations where governments could air their problems met with a stunning defeat by his own congress who failed to ratify the treaty. The League's charter was flawed in any case with no enforcement option to assert its will.

Additionally, in their rush to exact revenge for the Central Powers' wartime escalations, the Triple Entente of Britain, France and Russia sowed the seeds of a second world war by their reparations clauses in the Treaty of Versailles. The League of Nations was ill-prepared to deal with the growing unrest caused by the smothering effects on the economies of central Europe that were thus caused.

At the Washington Naval Disarmament Conference in 1921, the United States virtually dictated to the major navies of the world that they would all take a step back from the increasing arms race that brewed after the end of the war. The outcome was the famous ship building ratio of 5:5:3, whereby for every five tons of battleships the U.S. had, Britain could have five tons and Japan could have three. To the Japanese, this was a loss of face, since they considered themselves to be a first level sea-power. And most navies other than the U.S. responded to the treaty requirements by building really big cruisers to make up for the loss of battleship tonnage.

As a concession to the Japanese, language was inserted that prevented the U.S. and Britain from fortifying any of their possessions in the western Pacific, essentially giving the Japanese a free hand in the region.

In 1928, another flawed effort to prevent worldwide conflict surfaced in the Kellogg-Briand Pact, which essentially outlawed war as a means of resolving differences between nations again, without any means of enforcement. It was this series of negotiations for which the USS Detroit was a means of transport of the U.S. envoys.

By the early 1930s, when the Naval Arms Treaty was expiring, many of the world's major navies had abrogated or flatly ignored the treaty restrictions and were embarking on renewal of their sea-going forces. In the U.S., the New Deal brought about beginning the replacement of obsolete ships with newer, more capable versions as a means of putting people back to work during the great depression.

The slow-down in ship construction didn't mean that there was no innovation. WW I had taught some new lessons. The failure of the landings at Gallipoli caused the United States to consider amphibious warfare as a developmental doctrine. And under the brilliant minds of some U.S. Marine officers, notably LT COL Pete Ellis, the United States was able to formulate the means of executing the war in the Pacific after Pearl Harbor.

The Battle of Jutland also caught the eye of the Navy strategists. The former Queen of the Seas, Great Britain, proved that the large scale fleet battles of the past might not succeed in future naval conflicts. However, even coupled with General Billy Mitchell's proof that the airplane was a valid weapon against capitol ships, this was a lesson that was not easily incorporated into the mindset of the world's naval leaders. While aircraft at sea were acknowledged as useful in a scouting role, and there was an interest in building ships just to carry aircraft as their main battery, the naval world still concentrated on the Battleship as the primary weapon of sea-going conflict.

Technology brought leaps forward in naval warfighting capability. Increasing and changing means of lethality in turn called for changes in tactics. The United States often working with Great Britain, completed a series of tactical war games, some involving fighting refereed miniature tabletop exercises, others involving great numbers of fleet units at sea. The idea was to develop tactics that would bring battles to successful conclusions, to codify these lessons learned into tactical doctrine and disseminate the doctrine throughout the Officer Corps.

It was a case of technological leap frogging, improved battleship weapons could strike at greater ranges, using plunging fire that made ships more vulnerable at a distance. Plunging fire involved rounds hitting lightly armored decks instead of heavily armored sides which defended against flat trajectory close range fire. But at long range, small errors in aim point grew into misses at distance, requiring better accuracy. The vertical stable element of the Ford fire control computer enabled more accurate aiming, during rolls and pitches but lookouts in the mast tops were only so good at estimating misses and adjusting fire onto target. Due to the curvature of the earth, they simply weren't high enough to see the splashes of misses and therefore not able to correct fires onto the desired targets.

At that time, scouting aircraft were carried aboard Cruisers which catapulted them into flight and these seaplanes were able to observe fall of shot and bring salvoes onto targets. Now range was extended far out from the gun platforms and the probability of a hit was increased as well, an increase in lethality that begged new thinking, new tactics to push successful attacks or to repel them.

Thus in the thirties much effort was expended in conducting Fleet Problems, which were massive at sea exercises of fleet units of all types, refereed and scored and then modified for the next such exercise. It was Blue Forces against Black. Ernest King was the Captain of an Aircraft Carrier participating in these exercises. Isoroku Yamamoto, a hero of the Battle of Tsushima Straits had been a student at Harvard, then an attaché in Washington, then a respected Commander in the Imperial Japanese Navy and tactical thinker. He, too, was greatly interested in the Black on Blue Fleet Problems, sought the results and then bent them to the use of the Imperial Japanese Navy.

One such exercise was run by Admiral Yarnall, in 1932, who left his battlewagons at home, but brought his carriers to the fight. He conducted an attack on the US Fleet at Pearl Harbor by a fictitious Asian Island Nation at 0730 on a Sunday Morning. The attack coming in virtually undetected from the North West with the refereed result being the destruction of the defending battleships and annihilation of the fleet. And, yes indeed, the lessons learned in the employment of air power were duly noted by the future architect of Japan's attack on Pearl Harbor.

In 1932, SN1 Dantes' first cruise aboard Detroit, was to Hawaii to participate in Fleet Problem XIII. He was but a deckhand, albeit a smart and active one, and had been getting trained as a pointer on a 6" gun mount, in short range gunnery exercises. Eager to learn and help his mount get an "E" painted on it, as well as looking forward to the extra $5.00 per month prize money that went with it, his horizons didn't extend very far from his ship, though his very existence would be affected by lessons learned and decisions made in places very far away. Dantes and Daughter, his buddy from Boot Camp were both looking forward to a little liberty in Pearl Harbor and Honolulu.

On the starboard bridge wing, in the second dog watch for those who had eaten evening meal first, then come topside to relieve the watch so the others could eat. Dantes is the starboard lookout. His duties were to maintain a sharp watch from the bow, all the way aft, looking for any surface or air contacts. Since they were halfway to Pearl Harbor, some 1,300 miles distant from land and steaming with only a small escort of tin cans, they didn't expect many air contacts, except for the routine launches and recoveries, twice a day, of the scouting seaplanes. Dantes had stood many of these watches at sea in the local operating area, off San Diego. He enjoyed the activity and the responsibility. And, he was excited to be headed overseas, so to speak, for the first time.

"Commander Lodge is on the Bridge, Sir!" the Quartermaster of the Watch sang out. There were a couple salutes and greetings exchanged as Lieutenant Commander John Lodge USN stepped in and closed the pilothouse door. He wasn't, strictly speaking, ship's company, but was a member of the DesPac staff as Detroit was the Flagship for all of the Destroyers in The Pacific Fleet. The Commodore for the tin cans was a four striper, a naval Captain and Lodge was his XO. As the Skipper of Detroit wasn't on the Bridge, Lodge contented himself with stepping out to the starboard wing, encountering Dantes there.

Dantes saluted, "Good evening Commander." Got a return salute and a grin.

"What's your name, sailor?"

"Seaman First Class Dantes, Sir." Lodge looked him over, noted his clean uniform, confident posture and relative youth.

"You're pretty young to be a Seaman First, aren't you, Dantes?"

"Yessir, Commander."

"First cruise?" thinking this sailor could hardly be a year out of boot camp and he was used to sailors who took months to become full Seaman and stayed in the rank for the full four year term of their enlistment.

"Sir," and Dantes glanced momentarily at Lodge, then put his binoculars to his eyes and started another sweep of his sector.

"How'd you make First Class so fast, Dantes?"

"Actually made Seaman First in Boot Camp, Sir." And then Lodge understood that Dantes had to have been the honor Graduate of his Company. His interest quickened and he asked,

"What do you know about what the ship is actually doing, Dantes, besides heading for Pearl?"

"Scuttlebutt is that we're to take part in a Fleet Problem, number thirteen, Sir, I believe."

Lodge smiled, ever impressed by the speed and accuracy of below decks intelligence. With slight exaggeration it could be said that the men often knew the details before the Wardroom did. Of course, with twelve years in, himself, he knew the source of that information. The stewards kept the Chiefs informed and the Chiefs in turn were the source of lots of general information, for they were the ones who would translate orders into action, the work that would accomplish the ship's objectives.

"Dantes, we will be joining up with a total of 132 other vessels and mount a simulated attack against the Fleet units berthed in Pearl."

"Sir, by simulated I think you mean that we won't actually be firing our main batteries." Dantes was enjoying the attention and the chance to learn something. Lodge was enjoying himself, too, curious to gauge the awareness of the crew and already mightily impressed by this fellow, Dantes. "Right you are, Dantes, in fact all of the participating units will receive orders to be in positions to attack by certain times and referees will decide if they would have scored hits, if they had fired. Besides, we will be employing aircraft carriers against battleships in Pearl and the cruisers and destroyers will mainly be used as escorts to protect against submarines and other surface units."

"Figure we're testing this out as a precaution against the Japanese, Sir?" And he then held his breath to see if he was going to be mocked or censured for speaking out of turn.

Instead Lodge laughed out loud, delighted that this sharp sailor could see through instantly to the reason for these exercises. "Where are you *from*, Dantes?"

"Farm in McNeil, just a few miles from Lockhart, Texas, sir." And they both chuckled in the knowledge that this farm boy was something more, much more than a farm boy from Texas. Just then they heard the QM of the watch sing out, "Captain's on the Bridge, Sir!" and Commander Lodge, graduate of Harvard with a degree in International Relations and a decidedly up and coming member of the Officer Corps, took his leave of the young Texan turned seadog and stepped over the coaming of the water tight door to the pilothouse to greet the Commanding Officer.

Cruising easily at 10 knots, the Detroit pretended to be the carrier and exercised the destroyers as though they were screening the main body, a circle at 2,000 yards around the Detroit. They would run flag hoists up signaling the new course of the heavy, then when the hoist had been repeated on all of the other screening ships, the hoist would be two blocked, that is run all the way to the top and executed by dropping the hoist to the deck. This first signal was to start the screen to the positions they would occupy on the new course. Just as they got there, the Detroit would, herself, turn to the new course and the whole formation would be headed off in a new direction, all screening ships in their positions.

These maneuvers were also practiced with signals by flashing light and by radio commands. On all of the maneuvering screening ships the Junior Officers of the Deck would be working out the heading to their new stations on maneuvering boards at flank speed, usually 25 knots. During the boring Mid-watches, Dantes had gotten the Quartermaster of the watch and occasionally the JOOD to show him how the Mo-boards worked. It all reminded Dantes of a giant watch, with a rotating bezel, the screening positions the numbers on the edge of the watch face. He liked to try to work out the maneuvering board solutions in his head and then check to see how close he was to the command given to the helmsman. He'd noticed that the Officer of the Deck was also working the solution, either on the maneuvering board or in his head, too.

Too, Dantes had studied Morse code and became proficient at reading flashing light messages, as well as the signal flag hoists. Eventually he had been taught semaphore by the signalmen, a way of talking with your hands, with positions for each letter. It took some skill to read it and an entirely different skill to send it. The sailors who were really good at it could move smoothly from one letter to the next without pausing, doing the motions in miniature in front of their waists. It appeared to be a nautical dance and a fast way to send messages when within sight and close aboard. Sailors would chat by semaphore to other sailors on ships sailing alongside during underway refueling. For Dantes it was only a matter of pride, to be able to do more than what was strictly his own job. It was also, in his mind, a matter of preparing to "strike" for a rate. He was showing initiative and learning the craft of a Signal-man against the day when a position might open up and he could be selected to take the test and compete for a coveted Crow, or promotion to Third Class.

Two days out from making anchorage or picking up a mooring buoy at Pearl and the maneuvers had wound down, the task group was making a steady and lazy ten knots toward Oahu and the deck gang was titivating ship, preparing for the likelihood of senior visitors while awaiting the start of the Problem. It was a brilliantly clear light blue sky and a sparkling deep blue ocean with just a couple of knots of breeze and very little roll, almost no swell. The bow wave creamed aft in brilliant white and a large pod of dolphins played at the bow riding on the bow wave, flashing back and forth across the prow of the ship. The men were stripped to the waist, getting some sun and saving the work of washing their shirts. Dungarees, too, were rolled up into shorts and hats put aside as they worked with a will. One of the First Class Bos'ns had a ukulele and had permission to play it for the others. Every now and then a sailor would do a hula dance, swaying his hips and aping for his shipmates, with a skivvy shirt twisted in front to look like a bra. Of course his buddies whistled and hooted obscenities and everybody laughed and thought of those hula girls in Honolulu.

The nominal man in charge of this Divisional working party was another First Class, BM1 Hanky. He was, to say the least, not very smart. He always had a mug of black coffee in his hand and sported a knife on the end of an intricately knotted lanyard as well as a finely twisted necklace about his neck, at the end of which was his badge of office, a shiny silver Bos'n's pipe. Nobody called him Hanky, everybody called him Boats. He wore his jumper in cold weather or his dungaree shirt in warm, with the pipe tucked into the pocket on his left breast. His white hats all had stretched rims so that they flared, all the way around their circumference. He never wore it back on his head, it was worn down in front and was always blindingly white and perfectly clean. Boats never was seen to do any work, himself; he only told others what to do. And, he usually didn't do that until he saw the person already doing the task. He would see someone working and he would tell that worthy to do exactly what he was already doing.

The answer was always, "Yes, Boats." It didn't do any good to protest that you were already doing the task, because Boats would only look at you with a strange uncomprehending look in his eye and stomp off, muttering to himself. Nobody knew how many times he had failed the Chief's exam or how many times he had been busted. He had a gut hanging out in front of him and a truly amazing collection of tattoos, everywhere except above his collarbone. Yes, he had hinges at his joints with flat head screws tattooed to hold them in place and spider webs and there were stories that he had one on his penis. It was a normally sized and entomologically correct housefly, complete with legs and wings, right on the top of his dick. When he got really drunk on the beach his shipmates would tell the bar girls about Boats' tattoo. They liked to see it and he liked to show it to them, and how it got bigger. There were different ways to ship over and Boats always found a way to do it aboard Detroit, with the promise that he would continue aboard the ship that had been his home ever since she had been commissioned, back in '23. Boats seemed to sprout from the deck plates, was ever a presence, claimed he would die aboard her and most people thought he probably would.

Some wished he would go ahead and do it. The dying, that is. There are chasms in the Navy, some of them that measured the distance from Enlisted to Commissioned status, some might describe a knowledge gap, comparing the intelligence of one sailor or type of rating to another. Boats had his own chasm. A separation from perhaps the world, a world in which he was wedded only to the Detroit, and his coffee mug and apart from any and everything else. For Dantes it was inconceivable that a human being could be so stupid and still function. As he would say to Daughter, "We had a mule, Joe, and a blind horse, Prince, on the farm that were way smarter than Boats."

"I once watched Joe get over the fence and we had it fixed so's he wouldn't be able to do it. We put a harness on him and hung an iron bar from it that was supposed to tangle in the fence and stop him from jumping the fence. But ol' Joe was smarter than that. I watched him get next to the fence, parallel to it and two feet or so away from it. Then he would start swaying back and forth and swinging that makeshift anchor until he had it going with a pretty good arc and then he would lunge with his head sideways and launch that anchor over the top of the fence. Then he would jump the fence, with the iron bar already on the other side. Joe was smart enough to make the turns at the ends of the rows of cotton on his own, when I was barely big enough to reach the plow handles." They were swabbing down the deck as Dantes told his story and Boats came over to them and told them to swab the deck. The two just kept a straight face and said in chorus, "Yes, Boats."

CHAPTER 7

PEARL

Detroit at anchor in the roads off Pearl Harbor along with the other major units of the Battle Problem Strike Fleet. Admiral Yarnall had summoned his major combatant Commanders aboard his Flagship and they were gathered in Flag Country, eager to hear what the Admiral had to say. Though his staff had planned the Problem the information had been held closely. Some of today's attendees were reminded of an earlier time when Nelson would entertain his Captains, his Band of Brothers, and go over and over his plan and particularly his tactics, over dinner and with his best wine. The Admiral came into the compartment and the buzz of conversation died down as the Admiral said, "Take your seats, gentlemen." There was a scraping of chairs as they settled into groups around the tables.

"Gentlemen, as you know our series of Naval Problems conducted up to this time has produced a doctrine and the results have been used in training all Commanders and indeed the entire senior Officer Corps in how we are to operate in fleet engagements. If I might summarize, that doctrine emphasizes engaging first with heavy battleship fire from long range, using spotter aircraft to ensure accuracy. It is by attacking and hitting first that we anticipate being able to bring the enemy to battle quickly and with devastating effect." There was general agreement, shown by nodding heads, faces turned with interest toward the Admiral. "And, up to this time the primary use of aircraft has been our spotter aircraft as we depended on them to correct fires onto targets at extreme ranges of up to 35,000 yards, where the high trajectories required result in plunging fire down through exposed decks, putting the enemy's battleships and cruisers out of commission. Well, I'm here to tell you that I've left my battlewagons home." A murmur of surprise swept like a wave through the Commanders assembled. "And I intend to attack with all of the aircraft at my disposal, launching early on Sunday morning from northwest of Oahu, and use bombing attacks and torpedo runs to sink the battleships at their moorings. This is the way to seize the initiative and deny the enemy the initiative. We're about to break you into smaller groups with your counterparts on my staff. They will hand out your Operation Plans. Be ready to discuss our tactics in approach to the battle site, the attacks themselves, withdrawal and general rules for scoring and safety of maneuvering. One final thought, we are depending upon surprise so we will use the cover of weather when it is available to us and we will maintain strict radio silence. I will have the ass of any Commander who breaks discipline and gives our target any radio signal with which to triangulate and determine our position. By the way, this exercise is supposed to start, as you know, on Monday. Last I heard, the enemy operated seven days a week." The assembled Officers chuckled.

"Now before we break up, I'd like for Commodore Dick Cochrane to say a few words about our likely future enemies, the Japanese. Dick is a scholar among scholars when it comes to naval history. Dick?"

"Well Admiral, I don't know about the scholar part of that intro, but as most of you know, I've spent the better part of my Navy career here in the Pacific. I've watched the Japanese and their dealings with their Asian neighbors, and I can tell you they are a difficult people to understand, and a lot more difficult to defeat. In fact, no one whom they've taken on has been able to beat them.

"So let me start with a little of the Admiral's history lesson. Since joining the western world in battlefield technology in the latter part of the last century, they have developed a real trend. Back in 1895 without any warning they were going to take a hostile action, the Japanese fired on and sank the British ship Kow-shing owned by the Indochina Steam Navigation Company of London, thus starting the Sino-Japanese war. The ship was chartered by the Chinese government to ferry troops to Korea. It was on her way to reinforce Asan when it went to the bottom with 1,100 troops plus supplies and equipment.

"At the start of the Russo-Japanese war, the Japanese government perceived a Russian threat to its plans for expansion into Korea and Manchuria. After negotiations broke down in 1904, the Japanese Navy opened hostilities by a surprise attack on the Russian Fleet at Port Arthur, China. When the war was over, Japan was left occupying Manchuria but unable to sustain an occupational army against the Russian Bear who was very likely to go lick his wounds and then throw more men at the Japs than they could withstand. So the Japanese asked Teddy Roosevelt to mediate a peace treaty. Teddy dictated the terms of the Treaty of Portsmouth but forced Japan to withdraw from the mainland. He got the Nobel Peace Prize and the Japanese became more resentful of the U.S. for having "insulted" them.

"So, bottom line gentlemen, the Japanese are envious of potential sea power in the Pacific, they have a tendency to start wars against stronger opponents by conducting surprise attacks on their navies, they are merciless and unrelenting both during and after any battle, and they have already defeated all potential powers in the Pacific except the U.S. So keep those thoughts in mind while you are planning."

With the Commodore's warnings still ringing in their ears, the assembled officers quietly headed for their groups, to continue the brief in more detail.

LCDR Lodge, the junior man there, turned to his boss, the Commander of all Destroyers, Pacific with a keen look of excitement on his face. "Like the Admiral's notion of playing for all the marbles and no rules, do you, Lodge?"

"Yessir, I like it a lot."

"Well it's a cinch the battlewagon community isn't going to like it so much. They've been used to being the cock of the walk for a long time, now. If this attack is judged successful it'll be the writing on the wall for them. They'll be relegated to second class status. Personally I like the notion of turning over the apple cart, right off the bat.

"You know Lodge, I heard Col. Billy Mitchell speak back in 1924 when he was on an inspection tour of the Pacific. He was saying that Japanese air power shouldn't be counted out. They are good, he said, and if we were suddenly to be at war with them tomorrow, it would be at least two years before our air forces could catch up. He believed war with Japan was inevitable but our stick in the mud, overly cautious senior officer leadership can't see the handwriting on the walls of their own battleships. President Wilson tried to get the world to back away from large seagoing battles with the Washington Naval Arms treaty in 1922. But telling countries they couldn't build battleships caused them all to go out and start building really big cruisers instead. Now even we are starting to rebuild our battleship fleet. People may think that the high road to world peace leads through everyone being nice to one another, but the fact is that human beings are inherently distrustful of each other and war is the ultimate expression of that distrust. I don't know what it will take, but the Navy needs to shake itself into the world of the 20th Century and get to building aircraft carriers instead of continuing to waste our resources on preparing to fight the last war.

"Everybody knows this is to simulate a Japanese attack on our forces at Pearl. They are sneaky bastards. I'm fine with it so long as we use the lessons learned and start the move to engaging with naval air forces before it happens to us. This could make clear where our emphasis ought to be, and it isn't on those slow moving battlewagons. Sea battles will be conducted from well over the horizon, likely by opposing forces that never see each other, just carriers and their protective escort formations, turning into the wind and launching their aircraft out to the best available position, provided to us by our patrol aircraft. Those ships in Pearl ought to be sitting ducks."

After completing the detailed briefings and receiving their sealed orders the assembled Brass made their manners to the Admiral and departed in order of seniority over the side to their gigs and motor whaleboats. Signalmen on board the flagship notified each of the ships by flashing light that their Skippers were returning, so they wouldn't be surprised by their arrival, would have time to get the side boys at the quarterdeck. Getting aboard their ships, each of them repaired to his cabin, opened his orders, and then called his XO and Ops Officer in, to go over the plan and their part in it in detail. This was going to be a fight for sure, potentially none the less lethal for not using live ammo. Politics were involved and this was a deliberate challenge to the entrenched battleship navy and battleship mentality. Depending upon results, careers would be altered, some ended. It was a case of being willing to pose the most challenging of circumstances and then openly deal with the results, whatever they might be. The Naval Profession demanded nothing less.

Back aboard Detroit the word was passed to Ops that they would be observing strict radio silence, no exceptions, for the duration of the operation, starting now. They went over the Op Plan that night and disseminated it to the Department Heads and made ready for their coordinated departure that night, at 0200. When Pearl Harbor woke up the next morning, there would be nothing but an empty sea to greet them.

A similar set of meetings had taken place ashore, involving all of the units based at Pearl. They had gone over the CinC's plans to engage the Blue forces and defend Oahu and all of the facilities and bases on the island. They reviewed doctrine, formations and tactics for the three day exercise, starting on the following Monday. As the meeting broke up they left Headquarters Pacific Fleet and headed over to the Officers' Club, there to be joined by their ladies for something to eat, conversation and some dancing to live music. Life in the islands was good, when you got the time to enjoy it.

Bridge, USS Detroit, at sea in Fleet Problem XIII

"This is the Captain speaking," the sound of his voice coming over the speakers in every compartment throughout the ship. "As you know, we are engaged in a bit of practice warfare, the kind where we only pretend to fire our weapons and have referees stationed aboard the units of both sides to determine the relative success of attack and defense. Our Commander, Admiral Yarnall has decided to inject a bit of trickery into this exercise. Although our Fleet Problem is supposed to start on Monday, three days from now, we are preparing to actually launch our fleet attack as a surprise, on Sunday. After all, we don't expect any potential enemy to give us warning of his intentions, do we? It will be our carriers that play the key role, and their aircraft that conduct the actual attack. We've learned that the carriers normally moored in Pearl are at sea, so we must assume that they have been prepositioned to attack us, before we can get our aircraft launched. It is our job to protect our carriers and strike first. I expect all hands will do their duty to the best of their ability. That is all."

Dantes turned to Daughter at the mess table, passing him the tureen of fried chicken, "I kind of like the notion of surprising them. If it's to be a fight, then give them no chance, no chance at all."

"You heard the old man, Dantes, this is just practice, just a game. Why so serious?"

Dantes looked up from his mess kit, "Some things you don't just play at, making war or making love, for that matter. Seems to me they both deserve your best effort," he laughed. The rest of the table in their mess joined in and before long there were obscene comments about what their practice of the latter would be like, once they got back to Pearl. Still, Dantes mused about what the Skipper had told them, appreciated how seriously he must be taking this, taking the time to keep everybody informed. He wondered if he would see Commander Lodge again, and get the chance to hear what he thought.

Saturday passed in a rain storm, the ships maintaining strict and accurate defensive positions in their screen of the carriers, with Detroit even taking a turn at plane guard in the wake, 1200 yards aft of and slightly to the port side of the "bird farm" as they called her. Dantes had the watch at the helm and was concentrating on holding the ship's head within a degree or two of the ordered course.

"Dantes, do you enjoy being the helmsman?"

"Aye, Sir," he replied to the OOD, continuing to keep his eyes on the compass rose and making small adjustments to stay on the ordered course.

"Have you noticed that when we turn, I have to give you several commands, trying to maintain position on the quarter of the carrier?"

"Yessir, I have, Sir."

"Why do you suppose that is?" Dantes had been thinking about that very thing, thought it was an awkward way to go about following the carrier.

"Sir, the carrier's turns are wider than ours. They just set right standard rudder and follow their own turning radius. If we use standard rudder, our turn will be tighter than theirs, Sir."

The OOD grinned, he'd expected nothing less than a reasoned and articulate response from Dantes. "Despite the fact that the slipstick wizards in Washington have supposedly calculated that a "standard" rudder will make all ships to turn in the same radius, they really don't do they? So, can you see the wake of the carrier, Dantes?"

Danes looked up from the compass and forward, out the right hand window of the pilothouse, then immediately back to his compass. "Yessir, I can see the wake, just forward and to starboard. It is cutting right about midway back on the fo'c's'le, I'd say the fourth stanchion in the life line."

"Very well, Helmsman, the next time we do a turn in his wake I will just order you to follow in the carrier's wake. To do that you will use small amounts of rudder adjusting to keep a constant picture of that wake, cutting right at that stanchion. If the wake moves aft in a right turn you will increase rudder, if it moves forward you will ease rudder. Understand?"

Dantes grinned, just like a teenager given the keys to the car, for his first date. "Aye, aye, Sir." And they both knew that his answer meant I understand and will obey."

"We'll let you warm up, some, Dantes. Helmsman, follow in the carrier's wake."

"Follow in the carrier's wake, Aye, Sir." The Quartermaster noted it in his log and Dantes got envying looks from the other enlisted members of the watch. Not even the Bos'n's Mate third had gotten a chance to drive the ship, any ship, in this manner. With the resulting smoothness at the helm, the ship started to gain on the carrier, so the OOD took a few turns off and then after a while, added half of them back in. Of course Dantes had noticed them getting closer; but he wouldn't say anything; that would have been taken the wrong way. He laughed to himself; he was steering but didn't have control of the speed. It reminded him of the time his Dad had somewhere to go and told him to drive the car back home.

It was a model T Ford and his feet couldn't reach any of the pedals. His Dad got it started, told Howard to take it home, jumped out and slammed the door. Howard had gripped the wheel as tightly as he could, shoulders all bunched up, herding the car more or less in the right direction, but worried about how he was going to stop it, back at the house. He had steered it before, sitting in his Dad's lap, but this was different, way different! He kept it going without messing with any of the levers and without stalling and when he got to the yard he dropped down out of the seat and jammed on all three pedals: low gear, reverse and brake as the vehicle bucked and rattled and stalled to a stop, missing the garage. He was only nine at the time. But then his Dad had singled him out, he thought, always giving him stuff to do that he had no idea he could do. For instance, he never taught John how to shoot, but he taught Howard and they spent a lot of time and a lot of ammo, shooting out at the farm.

Sunday morning early, 0400-0800 watch aboard Detroit. The Fleet Problem attack force, positioned 100 miles to the northwest of Oahu had turned into the wind and was preparing to launch aircraft using the light afforded by nautical twilight. After joining up in formation for the run in to Oahu, the air group would have an ETA of 0730 at Pearl Harbor. The carriers would continue in formation to close Hawaii, shortening the return trip for her aircraft. The surprise was total, as the attacking aircraft made bombing and torpedo runs against the Fleet tied up in Pearl Harbor as well as the fuel farms and the airfield at Hickam, and the Marine Barracks and aircraft at Kaneohe. Upon completion of the attacks the attacking force broke radio silence, joined up in formation again and returned to the strike carriers. Late that afternoon all ships had returned to their anchorages, and Commanders and Staff were summoned to the Flagship for an initial debriefing with Admiral Yarnall.

"Gentlemen, initial reports from the referees are that the attack was a near perfect success. Comments from CincPacFleet are not so complimentary. The Battlewagon Skippers are growling about our not following the rules. I believe I will let those comments just go unanswered, as I expect they will not be able to identify any potential adversaries who will not also use surprise in any such attack." A general wave of chuckles swept the group. "But make no mistake; this Fleet Problem will have exposed the weakness of heavy surface combatants to air attack. It will now be our job to devise the means, tactics and doctrine with which to defeat such an attack, were it to be launched against the United States. Imperial Japan is still smarting from the restrictions that forced them into second class status as a naval power and they are very involved in projecting their might across the Pacific."

In the months following the completion of this Fleet Problem studies were conducted at the Naval War College and plans were refined for successive Fleet and table exercises that would build on the lessons learned. And in the War Ministry of Japan, a rising Naval Officer, Isoroku Yamamoto, who had gone to school at Harvard and served as Naval Attaché in Washington, would learn of these results and study them with great interest. He understood America, knew her strengths and weaknesses and now he had a blueprint for attacking her.

CHAPTER 8

THE DRIVE TO MAKALAPA

While the USS Detroit lightly pulled at her anchor in Pearl Harbor, the entire First Division, except for those on watch, was standing at attention in two ranks on the main deck. Morning Quarters was held in roughly the port quarterdeck area, one of the spaces that they regularly cleaned and maintained. Muster had been taken and all hands were present or accounted for. The Chief reported this to the Division Officer, who reported it to the Department Head. "Very well, have the men stand at ease."

The Division Officer said, "First Division, at ease," and the Department Head went forward to Officers' Call, where all Department Heads reported to the Executive Officer.

"Very well, Gentlemen, you have the Plan of the Day. In addition there will be liberty today for the Port Section. Liberty to commence at 1200, uniform will be whites. Liberty is to be for all hands who are performing up to snuff, and that ought to be most of them. Any sailor who is not performing well should be doing extra duty, more serious cases should be placed on report and the reports forwarded to me, for screening before taking them to the CO for non-judicial punishment or worse, court martial... Any questions? No? Then Attenhut! Dismissed! Oh, First Lieutenant, a word with you."

"Sir."

"You have a Seaman First, named Dantes, in First Division. He has been requested as a driver of the Commodore's staff car this afternoon, up in Makalapa. His service record says he has a driver's license. Have him ready to go ashore at 1200 as part of today's Shore Patrol. He will have the added duty as driver."

The First Lieutenant responded immediately, "Aye aye, Sir," but his raised eyebrow signaled a question. Makalapa was the fabled Senior Officers Quarters located at Pearl Harbor, a conclave of residences in a tight, small group on a quiet street of well-tended lawns and gardens where CincPac, CincPacFlt and several three stars lived with their wives and families.

"Don't ask. I have no idea how this came about, just that he was requested by name for this duty. Didn't say how long it might take so it might be a good idea to have him dressed in his best whites and packing a spare uniform in a small duffle." With that the XO turned on his heel and headed for the Wardroom.

Back at First Division the Division Officer reported that the Plan of the Day had been read to the men. "Very well, Mr. Smythe," then turning to the Department he raised his voice slightly so as to be heard, "There will be liberty today, commencing at 1200 for the Port Section. See the Chief for your liberty cards. Chief you may authorize liberty for all hands in good standing." Everybody knew he was reinforcing the Chief's authority; you didn't keep the Chief happy, you soon wished you had. "Dismissed." Holding Smythe back, he said, "What can you tell me about SN1 Dantes?"

"Good man, Sir. Hard worker and keeps his nose clean, smarter than most, always asking questions and learning all he can. I could use a dozen more like him."

"Look, he's been requested by name for duty as the driver of a staff car, going to be driving somebody up to Makalapa today. Handle this yourself. Have him in his best whites on the quarterdeck at 1200 and I suggest he take a spare uniform with him in a small handbag, don't know how long he'll be ashore." "Aye aye Sir."

Still standing where they had fallen in, Daughter turned to Dantes, "Our first liberty in Honolulu, buddy. Whattaya think about that?" And both men were smiling, if not smirking.

"Well, I have to admit I am looking forward to seeing some of that hula dancing they talk about," Dantes replied. Just then Ensign Smythe approached, and said, "Dantes? Dantes came to a semi-relaxed position of attention, "Sir?"

"You have Shore Patrol today."

"Ah, Sir, I'm in the port section."

I know that, Dantes. But you have been requested as driver of the staff car today. Come by Junior Officer Quarters at 1130 in your best set of whites and carry a toiletry kit and spare uniform in a handbag, word is that you will be duty driver or something like that and going into the Senior Officers area on the base in Pearl. Understood?"

And a thoughtful look flashed across Dantes' face before he answered, almost absentmindedly, "Aye, aye Sir."

And you will go as part of today's shore patrol party. Chief Gandy, the Master at Arms will muster the Shore Patrol on the Quarterdeck at 1200, you'll get your instructions from him.

Meanwhile, Daughter looked on with amusement mixed with a touch of envy. *Hasn't been the first time Dantes has stood out, won't be the last,* he thought. Smythe moved off, headed for his quarters and the two deckhands went below to their berthing compartment, Daughter teasing Dantes about what he would be missing in Chinatown, in Honolulu, all the while knowing he'd like to be along for the ride in that car. Knowing Dantes' luck, it would probably be the better liberty.

Below in the compartment men were unrolling their hammocks and stringing them up to hooks in the overhead. Others had lowered a mess table, grouped around it and broken out an acey deucey board. The seabags were all stowed against the bulkhead, out of the way of traffic, for there were no lockers and no bunks. Each seabag was stenciled with a man's last name and most were locked with a padlock that passed through four grommets. Every sailor learned how to fold his clothes and pack them into his seabag. The saying was that they were ready to go anywhere on 30 minutes' notice, and a full seabag. Just now Dantes had rigged his hammock and broken out his dress whites and best shoes, polished to a gleaming shine. They had learned how to spit shine their shoes. Everyone had a pair that they saved for inspection, and one for everyday working wear. Because of the way they were smoothed and tightly rolled, their uniforms had no wrinkles. Too, they had been washed by their owners in the head with one of two buckets of water they were allowed daily, when and if the water was available.

Though his shoes were perfect, Dantes gave them a miniscule coating of black polish, breathing on them to provide a bit of moisture. He used a well-worn handkerchief and wrapped it around two fingers. When he was through he'd spend a minute or two with some soap, getting the polish stain off his fingers. His white hat had been well broken in, with the rim stretched so that it formed a uniform halo like rim. He would wear it without a cant to either side, slightly lower in front than in the back. It was a sharp, aggressive look and on Dantes it looked outstanding. Moving to the head, he still had a bucket of water yet to draw for the day and he did so, hitting it with a burst from the steam hose there to warm it up. Then he stood naked and gave himself a Marine bath, wetting down, then soaping then rinsing, with the water running through a drain in the center of the sloped deck. He dried off quickly and pulled on his skivvies, boxers and a pull over tee shirt. All this time he was thinking about how he had gotten this assignment. It had to be connected to Commander Lodge, he knew that. He was looking forward to the day and the time they'd spend together. You see, Dantes had talked to no one about his conversations with Lodge. Dantes assumed that Lodge had shown the same forbearance. After all, Dantes was but a Seaman First, and he and Lodge worked in very different worlds, even if on the same ship. Still they seemed to have something in common, though Dantes could not have imagined what that would be.

Back at his hammock, Daughter brought him his own neckerchief, holding it out, "Here, I got mine pressed by one of the snipes in the engine room. They have a steam line rigged to a polished bit of steel that the shipfitters fashioned. It's hollow inside and there are little holes to let the steam out. A guy there presses neckerchiefs with it."

"I heard some scuttlebutt to that effect, what did it cost you?"

"Ahh, forget it, we can't have the Admiral thinking we're not sharp, on the Detroit. And here, you can use this handbag for the stuff you're going to carry with you."

Dantes smiled his thanks and started packing his toiletries and spare uniform articles.

Commodore Dick Cochrane, ComDesPac's quarters, aboard Detroit, the evening before.

"Ahh, Lodge, thanks for coming."

'Yessir," delivered with an easy smile.

"Look, I got this message from CincPac's Aide, asking if you would be available to call on the Admiral at his quarters, in Makalapa. Something about a tennis match. Not my business and of course I already replied that you'd be honored, all that. Tell me, do you actually *know* the Admiral?" And he looked up from his seat at Lodge with an inquiring look.

"In a way, Sir. My Dad and he were classmates and shipmates. Our families know each other."

"And the tennis, you any good at the game?"

"Been awhile, probably pretty rusty, but yessir, I've played," he laughed.

"Next I suppose you'll be telling me you beat Big Bill Tilden."

Lodge laughed, "Not exactly, I played him in the Philadelphia Championships, before he was 'Big' Bill Tilden, and as I recall it wasn't even close. He played for a Business School, and was really good."

"Where'd you play your tennis?" with an appraising look, sizing him up.

"Ahh I played for Harvard, made the Varsity my last three years there, Sir."

That got an admiring look from the Commodore, "Well, look, you can have my staff car, it'll be at the landing and I don't plan on going ashore tomorrow. Anything else we can do for you?"

Lodge paused and with a thought a bit of delight showed on his face. "Sir, I wonder if I might have someone as my driver, someone from the crew."

"Well, I can ask. I'm sure the Captain would be pleased, just whom did you have in mind?"

"It's a Seaman First, name of Dantes, Sir."

"Your families know each other too, Dantes, huh? Maybe his family owns the Chateau d'If!" the Commodore looked up, grinning. "I'll mention it to the Skipper and I'm sure it'll be okay. The Aide said you'd be expected at 1300 for an informal luncheon and some tennis. And, why don't you make a good liberty out of it while you're over there... I won't expect you back for a couple days." And with that and a respectful thanks, Lodge departed, leaving the Commodore sitting bemused and sort of proud of his staffie.

Junior Officers Quarters.

The crew referred to this area as Boy's Town. It sat in the deckhouse next to a paint locker on main deck. There were chained framed bits of canvas, stacked four high as makeshift bunks. There was a couch in the middle of the space and a pipe that ran athwartships with about a foot or two for each officer who bunked there. Uniforms and civilian clothes were hanging on the pipe and there was a head with two stalls and a urinal connected with a door that closed. It was 1130 and Smythe sat on the couch, waiting. There was no actual door to Boys Town, just a curtain across the narrow opening into the space.

Dantes knocked twice on the bulkhead next to the curtain, sounded off, "Seaman First Dantes, Sir!"

"Come," said Smythe and Dantes pushed the curtain aside and took a step into the center of the space, facing Smythe. He put his handbag down at his side, and stood at attention with his cover in his left hand, facing Ensign Smythe and staring at the bulkhead over Smythe's head. "At ease, Dantes." And Dantes relaxed, but still held an informal position of attention, and dropped his gaze to that of his Division Officer's. Smythe stood and looked Dantes over.

"You're looking sharp, Dantes. In addition to being the staff car driver, you'll be on Shore Patrol. Chief Gundy has your instructions. This is your first Shore Patrol duty, is it not?"

"Yes sir."

"I don't know if you'll be getting a sidearm or just a nightstick, but your service record says you're an expert pistol shot, that right?"

"Yes sir."

"Any questions about your duty? If not just be at the Quarterdeck at 1200."

"Aye, Sir."

"Dismissed."

1150 Quarterdeck, liberty party and Shore Patrol gathered and ready to go ashore.

Dantes spotted Chief Gundy and Chief "Wall" Locker standing together about the time they saw him. Chief Gundy raised his chin, with a pleasant look on his face and Dantes took that as an invitation to approach. "Chief Gundy, Chief, good to see you. I'm reporting for Shore Patrol Duty, Chief," looking directly at the Master at Arms.

Gundy smiled broadly, "I'm counting on Honolulu being a bit tamer than Tijauna, Dantes."

Dantes smiled back, "Don't know what would have happened if y'all hadn't been there that night, Chief." It was actually difficult not to call the Chiefs 'sir', such was the respect and in this case genuine affection and awe that Dantes had for the two of them.

Chief Locker spoke up, "You're looking sharp, Dantes, looks like you've put on some weight, all of it muscle. I'm hearing some good things about you from First Division."

Dantes blushed and before he could answer, Chief Gundy added, "That's not all we're hearing. Scuttlebutt is that you've been invited up to CincPac's place for barbeque and maybe a swim."

Dantes face looked horrified, "No Sir! I mean you know not to trust that messdecks skinny, uh Chief."

"This didn't come from the messdecks, Dantes; it's evident that you've made one hell of a good impression on SOMEone. Now I suppose you're going to tell me you're just the driver for this afternoon's soiree." And Dantes relaxed and finally realized his leg was being pulled. He grinned and allowed that was so, asked if the Chief had any Shore Patrol instructions for him. "Nah, other than if and when LCDR Lodge turns you loose, you should head over to the Royal Hawaiian. We'll have a command post set up over there and we will be able to use you and the vehicle. We'll issue you your sidearm then and team you up with a Petty Officer, send you out on patrol.

"Aye, Chief. Does Chief have any advice for me, before I head up to Makalapa? Looking directly at Chief Locker.

'Wall' Locker looked at him a little squinty eyed, said "As long as you don't have Daughter leading you astray you ought to be okay. While on Shore Patrol it'll be no problem as you'll be mainly pulling other sailors out of fixes. But I would steer clear of Chinatown. That is a place where anyone can get messed up. You know the saying, "Stewed, screwed and tattooed?" That's where that expression originated and all they care about there is your money. Now that I think of it, not so different from Tijauna. Just use your common sense, Son."

Dantes looked his Chief in the eye, "I won't let you down, Chief." Just then the Chiefs noticed Commander Lodge, who appeared to be looking for Dantes. Locker nodded in his direction and Dantes made his way over to him, saluted and said, "Sir, I have the keys to the staff car, patting his handbag"

"Very well, Dantes. I have directions up to Makalapa, so it ought to be no problem finding the place where we're headed. They actually have the names and titles of the occupants on little signs, out front." The OOD, a Lt (jg) with the long glass under his arm came up and said, "Sir, the Commodore's barge is alongside, if you're ready."

They went to the ladder that was rigged over the side and there was a motor whaleboat idling, attached to the side by a boat hook. First Dantes then Lodge saluted the OOD and the colors and requested permission to leave the ship. It was granted and Dantes took his seat well forward, reserving the stern sheets for the Commander. When he was seated Lodge told the Coxswain to make for the Fleet Landing and they settled in for a short ten minute ride to the beach. Those aboard Detroit waited their turn for the motor launch circling just off the ladder. It would probably take two or three runs to get them all ashore. They waited with excited patience. The old hands who had pulled liberty in Pearl before were regaling the boots with stories about Chinatown and the sights to be seen on the beach. It's safe to say nobody envied Dantes his "duty."

Leaping to the landing, Lodge told the Coxswain not to stand by, that he would just catch a regularly scheduled motor launch back to the ship. Then they both walked to the car, a '28 Dodge four door painted haze gray. Dantes unlocked the doors and they both got in up front as Dantes familiarized himself with the layout and controls.

"Dantes, if you haven't driven one of these, I have. I can drive us to Makalapa."

Dantes flushed and said, "It'll be just a minute, Sir, I think I can get a handle on it."

"And I'm convinced you are correct. Carry on, Dantes." Dantes briefly thought about telling the Commander about his first time driving a T-Model Ford, at the age of nine, thought better of it, put it in neutral, pushed the clutch in and stepped on the starter. The car coughed and roared into life as Dantes had the gas pedal pushed too far. He flushed again, brought it back to idle, put it into low gear and slowly pulled away from the curb. "Turn right at the next corner, Dantes." And off they went, with Dantes (and Lodge) getting more relaxed by the minute.

Within ten minutes they had turned into the Makalapa quarters area, and were very slowly, in low gear, proceeding past the three star name plates until they came to the most imposing structure of all. Dantes pulled to a stop, verified the name and shut down the car, neatly parked by the curb. "Thanks, Dantes, and very well done. I didn't want to distract you with conversation on the way over here."

"That probably helped, Sir."

"Well then, let's take a couple minutes before going in, chat a bit. Frankly I've missed our occasional talks on the bridge. Do you have any thoughts or questions about the Fleet Problem we just completed?"

"Yessir, I'm thinking that the Admiral you are visiting might not be so happy that we violated the rules by starting essentially a day early. At least that's the scuttlebutt, Sir."

"And what do *you* think about jumping the gun that way, Dantes."

"Sir, it made perfect sense to me and I think that the defending forces should have anticipated it. It added realism to the whole exercise and must have caused a lot of consternation, when the results were known. And Sir, I do have a question, will our enemies also have access to the results of our Fleet Problem?"

"Whom do you think that enemy might be, Dantes?"

"Well, Sir, it's Japan, of course, and possibly Germany. But here in the Pacific it would definitely be Japan."

"In answer to your observation about the Admiral, I expect that he's secretly pleased that we went ahead and pulled a surprise strike. He's the guy in charge out here and he wants to understand the real threats and be ready with sound tactics when an attack of this nature is launched. Regarding the results getting to the Japanese, yes, it will happen. My concern is that they will actually learn more from our exercise than we will. Now, why do you suppose I wanted to have this conversation?"

"Sir I appreciate that you have allowed the conversations we've had. I haven't been in the Navy very long, but long enough to know that this is probably very unusual."

"Dantes, I've been in the Navy for twelve years and I find *you* to be very unusual. I like your inquisitive nature and the way you think and carry yourself. I wanted this talk just now so that you would have had a chance to know what you think and why. That's all. Oh, and the Admiral is known for his earnest desire to know what his sailors think. It would surprise me if he doesn't actually ask you for your opinion. I just thought you deserved the chance to be ready. When he asks, just speak up and tell him what you think, not what you think he wants to hear. By the way, I agree with everything you just said. Now let's go in and meet the Admiral and his wife. I'll bet they set a really fine table." And the two of them got out of the car and headed to the front porch where a white jacketed steward had opened the door and was standing there with a big welcoming smile.

CHAPTER 9

LYDIA

As the two of them entered CincPac's personal residence, at 37 Makalapa Drive, Commander Lodge handed two of his cards with the upper left corners dog-eared to indicate that he called in person, to the steward, who thanked him and admitted them to the foyer taking their covers and putting them on a mahogany table. "Please come with me, gentlemen."

They proceeded into the drawing room, nicely furnished and immaculate, several photos on the walls, Dantes gawked as he looked around, Lodge took account and anticipated what would come next. "John! So nice of you to come. Welcome to Makalapa," a trim and tanned lady beamed," and do introduce me to this handsome sailor with you!" And she turned a gorgeous smile on Dantes, who was completely taken aback and tongue tied.

"Auntie Jane, this is an outstanding sailor from USS Detroit, Dantes, who just happens to be the honor graduate of his training command Company."

"Thank you for coming, Dantes, and what shall I call you? Last names seem so formal." There it was again, having to deal with his execrable first name.

Completely mesmerized he choked out "Why, Hod, Ma'am, it's what my sister calls me, its short for Howard."

"How charming! So Hod it'll be." She turned to Lodge, "and how are your parents, and family, John?"

"Doing very well, Auntie Jane and they would like for me to extend their well wishes. They speak of you often in their letters, hope to perhaps visit again, soon."

'We look forward to it, John, both Uncle Fitz and I. We are expecting some more guests this afternoon, they will be here shortly. In the meantime may I offer you some refreshment on the lanai?" And the three of them headed to the back of the house where a table for eight was set and a pitcher of pineapple juice sat on a white cloth napkin sweating into a pool of its own making.

"There's a changing room over there, by the tennis court, with some aloha shirts in it and shorts, lots of sizes. Please do change into clothes of your choosing and get comfortable; until the breeze picks up it can be a little warm. Oh, and do serve yourselves something to drink and there are also some appetizers there." And with that she left them to go off into another part of the house.

"Are you sure she meant for me, too, Sir?" Dantes asked.

"Absolutely, Dantes. I expect one of the seats at that table is for you, and you are a guest here, today. Same as me. Let's shift our uniforms into something less formal." They proceeded into the thatched coconut palm changing room and picked out colorful and comfortable shirts, put them on, along with some shorts, hung up their uniforms, and returned to the table on the lanai. The steward poured them some juice and they nibbled a bit from the goodies on a silver tray.

Just then a distinguished gentleman, well-tanned and casually dressed in shorts and a Hawaiian shirt, face beaming in a broad smile, entered the lanai, "John, so glad to see you! It's been too long!" "Uncle Fitz, yes it has, Sir! Allow me to introduce a shipmate of mine, Seaman First Class Dantes." The Admiral turns to Dantes with interest, "Dantes, my wife was telling me just now that you were honor graduate out of boot camp, that so?"

Dantes, blushing down to his heels, stood smartly to attention, "Yes, Admiral, but it was just for my Company, Sir."

"Good lad! You know, at one time I commanded the training center in San Diego, so I know how tough it can be and can appreciate the honor you no doubt earned." He turned to the appetizers, "Have you gents tried the pork? It's regular luau fare, wild pig, roasted in the ground in ti leaves on hot lava rocks." And he speared a piece and popped it into his mouth. "John, I want you to stuff yourself, maybe it'll slow you down, on the court," he laughed. "So, how's your old man, John, still as ornery as ever?"

"He's doing well, Sir, and is looking forward to you and Aunt Jane visiting in Boston, next time you find yourselves in the neighborhood."

The Admiral beamed in response, "That will be great, we'll look forward to it." Just then the steward brought three Naval Officers onto the lanai. They were all dressed in shorts and aloha shirts, and the steward had their handbags with racquets, towels and such, and he proceeded to the court, to place them there. The Admiral made the introductions and it was a funny scene, well-tanned legs sticking out of shorts except for the two seagoing members of the group, with their pale legs and arms. They had exchanged small talk for ten or so minutes when Mrs. Fitzgerald entered with the last guest to arrive, a smashing looking young woman whom she held by the arm.

All present turned to them in a respectful silence. The woman standing next to Auntie Jane was a stunner. About five feet five inches, dishwater blonde hair, long but just now pinned up behind her neck, a small waist flaring to a heart shaped bottom and perfect breasts and a face that when she smiled could break your heart. Every man there took it in with a quiet deep breath and tried to look like he wasn't looking. "Gentlemen, this is a dear friend of mine, Lieutenant Lydia Eliot Crowninshield. She's stationed at the Naval Hospital in Pearl where I got to know her through my volunteering there. I expect you'll all introduce yourselves later, meanwhile let's sit down to lunch", she smiled, "You'll find place cards at the table."

Lodge noted with pleasure that his 'Aunt' had placed him next to the Lieutenant, and not the male one. He held her seat for her and the Admiral held his wife's and then the Admiral sat as did the others, shortly after. At the head of the table was Jane Fitzgerald, with the Admiral at the other end, with Dantes seated next to him. There was a sleepy buzz of conversation as two stewards quickly offered the meal, ladies first, then the others, with the Admiral last. "Dig in, Gents, I'll take all the advantage I can get, for later on the court." And sure enough he ate very sparingly, mind already on the matches to come. You see, the Admiral hated to lose.

Jane leaned toward Lydia, "I want you to meet LCDR John Lodge, Lydia. Our families are very close. And John, this is my very best friend on the Island, Lydia Crowninshield."

"That's Lieutenant to you, Commander," she smiled at him, mischievously."

Lodge almost fell into her eyes, recovered quickly and laughed, 'Well, I'll drop my handle if you will," and they both laughed and shook on it. The other Officers present got the message, Miss Lydia was off limits, at least for now. Dantes had watched the whole performance entranced, and with a very small smile tugging at the corners of his mouth. This might be very foreign territory for him, but the byplay he'd just witnessed he'd seen already in many places in his young life. Attraction and interest between the sexes was shown in an international language; everyone knew it, on sight. He sat back and relaxed, for the first time.

The Admiral touched Dantes on the shoulder, "Say, Dantes, do you suppose you could give me a hand, this afternoon?"

"Sir? Of course, any way I might be of use..."

"Well, you see I'm such a poor player that sometimes my shots go over the fencing and there are lots of balls we don't take the time to retrieve, while playing a match. Ever see a match, or play?"

"No sir, can't say as I have."

"Well look, when we start warming up I'll show you a bit about the job I have in mind for you. It'll make all the difference between just batting it around and actually playing matches." Dantes answered with an Aye, Sir and relaxed even more with the thought that at least he was going to earn his way at this shindig. And the Admiral saw the reaction he was looking for and knew the kid would be okay. There were two more who noticed this bit of byplay, Jane and Lodge; they both had the same instincts; one was the hostess, the other the one who had put Dantes into this situation. Both felt some protective responsibility.

As the stewards cleaned up after dessert the Admiral suggested that they give Lodge some time to practice, perhaps knock off some rust, Lodge replied, "Ha, I suspect it's *all* rust, Sir." He looked up expectantly at the strange faces down the table. The youngest, the Lieutenant, spoke up, "Sir, I've been nominated to serve as a warmup partner and asked to discover any weaknesses and report." Lodge looked at the Admiral accusingly. "Not me," Uncle Fitz said, probably one of those ringers I play with, seems every week." They all laughed and protested their innocence, but the Captain spoke up. "Well there is an advance report that you used to pull your own weight, on the courts." "Don't know what you've been told, Sir, I just hope not to embarrass myself." Knowing nods among the players and, "Yeah, that's what they ALL say, sounds like a ringer to me." You could tell that the competitive juices were rising and they were eager to get started. They didn't know whether they would have to go easy on this guy or whether it might turn into a real match. Chairs scraping and being excused from the table, there followed a general migration to the courts.

Uncle Fitz gave Lodge his choice of racquets and he banged them against the heel of his hand, testing the tension, the gut giving off a satisfying ping as the racquets bounced. He quickly picked the most tightly strung one of the batch and took a couple of balls to the backboard installed at one end and started banging forehands and then backhands into the board. He moved in close for some volleys, then back for some high bouncers and a chance for some overhead smashes. Finally, knowing he was being watched, he pulled a trick he used to play in college, he totally switched hands and repeated most of his warmup routine left handed. Shaking his head as though he was mortified, he pulled a face and said, "Might as well get this over with. I hope I can give you a game." Then the Lieutenant, the male one, took one end of the court, the one that had the sun in *his* eyes, and signaled new balls and continued Lodge's warm up for another five minutes. Lodge said okay and he returned the favor. When he had had enough warmup Lodge approached the net, "By the way, name's John Lodge." "Glad to meet you, Sir, I'm Rod Kinney." They spun a racquet for serve, Kinney won and they went to their ends of the court to serve. Kinney meanwhile was trying to place the name, wondering if he had heard of this guy before, and the stewards had moved several chairs out to courtside for the spectators. Both players went to a water pitcher and took a sip from paper cups there and then took their positions.

Kinney wound up and sent a straight shot into the body, screaming across the net. It was long and it was expertly deflected to the side by Lodge. Dantes, who had been instructed briefly by the Admiral, ran after the ball and held it. Nobody was acting as referee or linesman, the players were doing those tasks for themselves. Kinney nodded as if to agree that his serve was long, then arched his back and delivered a curving spinner as his standard second serve, this one going off the top string of the net. Lodge called "let," as it fell almost into play. Kinney looked at him, "Sir, I think that was out." "If you don't mind, Rod, I need a few more, to get used to the speed." So Kinney wound up and delivered his very best shot, scorching the chalk line. Lodge ran around his backhand and creamed it just over the net for a winner, looking rather relaxed as he did so. They played two sets, Lodge winning a close one and then Kinney taking over the second. It was obvious that Kinney was in the better shape and he gallantly said he'd had enough, thanked the Commander and they both headed to the sidelines.

You have some amazing shots, Sir, I can't believe you don't play regularly." Can't match your conditioning, Rod, and you have an excellent game. Maybe with a LOT of practice.' and he laughed. There were two courts and both were busy, with Dantes and whomever else wasn't playing fetching balls, to keep the action going. Lydia had changed into a tennis costume and was hitting against the backboard. He watched her with interest as 'Uncle' Fitz came up to him. "If you'll take it easy on an old man, I'd like some mixed doubles, you and Jane against me and Lydia." "Of course, Sir, I'd be delighted. Don't know about who's going to have to take it easy, though," he said with a chuckle. "Just a friendly, social game or two, John, I've been looking forward to it." Lodge nodded, his eyes on Lydia, and he wasn't checking out her game. Auntie Jane peeked from the kitchen window, her eyes twinkling and a soft, happy smile on her face.

The mixed doubles match was the last one of the afternoon and it was a friendly one. Lodge mainly concentrated on keeping the rallies going, in general not going for any kill shots, content to let the others go for those. Fitz knew what was going on, so after the first game, which he and Lydia won, he suggested changing partners. The Admiral brought some more intensity and Lodge just kept hitting them back, letting Lydia take the shots from Jane, while he mostly took the ones from Fitz. On that basis John elevated his game some, too. He took some points from the Admiral while Lydia did the same with Jane. When it worked out the other way, the Fitzes did pretty well, otherwise it was the younger players who gracefully and quietly sewed up the second game. The Admiral was ready for a rubber match, but Lydia protested tiredness, said she thought she'd had enough. Thus came to an end a very pleasant afternoon of social competition.

The invited Officers made their manners and departed, Captain first, then the rest, Jane saw them to the door with many thanks and "let's do this again, real soon."

"John, I had the stewards move your uniforms to the guest bath, in the house. Why don't you go and take advantage of the shower in there? I took the liberty of having them spiffy up your uniforms. Lydia, dear, please make yourself at home in the master bedroom." With alacrity and thanks, they both took advantage of the facilities and then repaired once again to the lanai, where it had cooled nicely. The Admiral took Dantes off, to show him his study and Jane busied herself in the kitchen. Fitz had mentioned that he had a bottle of homemade wine, the only legal booze in Prohibition, and it was sitting on a smaller table with two glasses.

As the cicadas came out and the sun was going down, Lydia and John took seats at the small table, and John poured a bit of the hooch into a glass for each of them. Meanwhile the Admiral had Dantes sitting in an overstuffed chair, examining some of his mementoes from the China Fleet duty and his time in the Philippines. The Admiral said to Dantes, "Dantes, tell me, what you thought of the Fleet Exercise." Dantes made as if to get up, and Admiral Fitz shushed him back. "I am too uninformed of what my sailors in the Fleet think, Dantes, and I value your input, your observations. You'd do me a favor if you'd just give me your impressions. Really. Thankful for the warm up he'd been given by Commander Lodge, Dantes leveled the Admiral with his twin steely blues and repeated, word for word what he'd told Lodge. "Worried about the Japanese, are you?" "Yessir, I think that what we may have done is confirm for them how to proceed against us in the Pacific, if it comes to that." "Well, Dantes, it IS going to come to that, just between two sailors, and it will be our job to be ready to beat the hell out of them. I thank you for your confidence and willingness to confide in me. There are many who would be afraid to do so. Likewise, I have shown confidence in you; I expect that you will not be sharing our conversation, back aboard ship." "Of course not, Sir." This time when he rose, the Admiral didn't stop him and they meandered back into the kitchen where Mrs. Fitzsimmons had some hot chocolate and cookies ready. Dantes thanked her profusely and ate several.

Out on the Lanai, the dying rays of the sun bathed Lydia in a golden glow, showed Lodge to something less than full advantage as he had a bit of a bright red sunburn. It was not noticed by Lydia, at least she was in no mood to break what was becoming a delightful spell. She'd asked him where he played his tennis, giving him the chance to puff his chest a bit and he deflected it, talked instead of how much fun it had been and how out of shape he was. He knew by her string of names of famous Brahmins of Boston that she must be of the elite, as was he, when you got down to it. She in her turn made light of the chance proffered, admitting only to being from the Boston area. There was the joke about the Lowells speaking only to the Cabots and the Cabots speaking only to God, with the Lodges never getting a look in. Of course the point was, if you *were* a Brahmin you didn't talk about it, at all.

When the other three came out onto the lanai, both looked at their watches and were surprised at how late it had gotten. Jane said, "Shall I call a cab for you, Lydia? For she had arrived by taxi, earlier in the day. Surprising even himself, Dantes piped up, "'We already have the staff car and I'm driving, no need to call a taxi, Ma'am!" Everybody smiled at that, it was agreed in an instant and the party slowly made their way to the front door, with Dantes carrying everything but Lydia's purse and handbag. All gave profuse thanks all around and all of a sudden there they were in the car with Lydia offering to give directions back to her housing on the base. Inside the house, Fitz said to Jane, "Well you certainly pulled *that* off well." And Jane got a faraway look in her eye and put her arm around her Fitz and leaned into him, really tightly. The stewards had repaired to their quarters and now with a kiss the Fitzgeralds did, too.

But it seemed the night was not yet over in the car, as Lodge suggested dinner before calling it a night. Lydia hesitated, wary and thinking this might be about to turn into a pattern with which she was too familiar. She was a little more suspicious when John further suggested a nice restaurant at one of the large and famous hotels. John, noticed her reaction and quickly added "I am not familiar with any of the best places, only assumed they were at a resort of some sort, and that you would probably know the best places. Dantes can drive us there and we will drive you to your quarters, as well." He smiled in his most charming manner, no leer, and she smiled back and said she'd be delighted. Turning to Dantes she said, "Driver we'll go to the Royal Hawaiian. If we get there before seven we can have a nice dinner and catch the hula show after." With that settled she gave Dantes the directions and he started up and, noticing that his driving was improving, headed out on Kamehameha Highway for Waikiki.

As they pulled up to the portico, Dantes mentioned that the Shore Patrol was headquartered here for the night, and he would take his leave and check in with them later. He mentioned that he was sure they could find him and he might just take in the hula show, would catch chow with the Shore Patrol. With Lodge thinking Dantes was a genius, the two of them alighted and headed into the hotel as Dantes pulled the car around to the parking lot.

At dinner he learned, with gentle prodding, that Lydia had gotten her degree and then been trained as a surgical nurse. She found out that he had played his tennis at Harvard and speculated that he must have been pretty good. It was indeed an enchanted evening as John bought plumeria leis for each of them from a flower girl and they ordered steak and potatoes, finishing with a pineapple and papaya fruit salad. There was an orchestra and they got in a couple of dances before it was time for the show. The music was exotic and enchanting and they both felt they fit together perfectly. It was quickly becoming hard to let go of each other when each song stopped and the band paused for their next number. Outside there were tiki torches lighting the way to lounge chairs next to a grassy area where the performances would take place. They walked hand in hand, were shown seats up front and settled in for the show.

There was the soft, rhythmic hiss and crash of the surf at Waikiki as a backdrop as the hula troupe came out in a line, hips twitching to the beat of insistent primitive drumming. They turned to face the audience and produced bamboo canes and gourds and a chant in Hawaiian started up. Down on their knees they performed in unison a series of postures with both instruments, banging them on the ground, on others' instruments and on their own bodies. The leader called out the cadence from time to time and directed them to the next part of the performance without stopping. It was a large Hawaiian woman in a brightly colored muumuu and she had a deep, melodious voice. With a crescendo it all came to a noisy stop and in the silence three maidens in real grass skirts and bodices came swaying out to perform, their dances emphasizing the hands and the story they told, in Hawaiian sign language. Again the woman in the muumuu called out the phases and did the chanting. This too came to a halt and finally the stars of the show, a gorgeous couple, the man dressed in a breechcloth, the woman more scantily clothed than the other hula dancers, took to the front, the drums started again and they performed together. Hips were gyrating wildly by the end and the man was sweating profusely at the final crash of the drums. To the applause of the audience, the slack key guitar took over, playing some old Hawaiian favorites as a quartet sang the songs, gently swaying. John and Lydia both turned toward one another and it was obvious that it had been a stimulating and exciting night. John held his hand out and Lydia placed her's in it. And they just sat there for awhile, listening to the surf, when Lydia cast off her shoes and said, "a walk on the beach?" John said sure, shucked his shoes and got up slowly, hoping not to show the extent of his excitement. They walked slowly to the water then along the beach, feeling it in their toes, arms about each other's waists. She waited for his kiss and he held her and told himself not to do it. They hugged lightly with smiles and then headed back to the hotel.

As they were putting on their shoes, Dantes walked up, Lodge asked him, "Get some chow, Dantes?" "Sir, and I saw the show, too. I have the car waiting in the portico, if you are ready, Sir." "Excellent, Dantes, thanks!" And they all went to the car, the couple again getting in back, Dantes started the car while Lydia gave him directions to her quarters on Base. Lydia had moved closer to John, for the ride home, Dantes was brilliantly not in a big rush, he suggested that they might finish off with a quick trip through Chinatown. The Shore Patrol had told him how to get to it, said it was a pretty interesting place. Lydia had heard of Chinatown, too, and she spoke up and suggested perhaps not tonight. Instead they drove along the boulevard fronting Waikiki for a mile or two, then turned at last and headed to the Base. The plumeria scent was intoxicating, she was beautiful and they were snuggling, his arm loosely around her shoulders, her arm resting on his thigh. John turned his glance away from the surf and looked at her and kept looking. She turned her face up for a kiss and her wrist just accidently brushed against him. Starting with tennis the evening had been building in excitement and now they were both aroused. She glanced up. Dantes was keeping his eyes on the road, but the thought that he could watch had started a tingle. *"You're sick, girl,"* she thought to herself but that didn't stop the tingle. Soon the kisses grew more heated. John put his hand in her lap and she crossed her legs and withdrew from their kiss. Dantes moved the mirror down. "I think Dantes was watching," she said, which to John meant Dantes was no longer watching. He moved to kiss her again but she looked straight at the front seat and then back at him. *I could've sworn she wanted more, for sure I did! Maybe if Dantes hadn't been along we'd have…* And he imagined them parked like two teenagers on Lover's Lane watching the submarine races…

Whew! That was close! Her eyes closed as the car swayed and rocked in a turn and she imagined what he would have done, if she'd let him, what she wanted to do with him. Her eyes again open and her consciousness back in the confines of the car, she smiled to herself. *Opportunities like this are a dime a dozen. I'm asked out all the time. But not with someone like John; he could be a keeper. Mmm, there is tomorrow maybe…*

They straightened their clothing and took notice of where they were. In another five minutes or so they'd be back on Base.

"So, Dantes, did you have a good time tonight?" Lodge asked. Dantes put the mirror back up and told them it was the best time he'd ever had. John and Lydia looked at each other and their looks said the same thing, best time they'd ever had.

At the Nurses quarters Dantes pulled to a stop and Lodge got the door for Lydia. They both stumbled over each other, saying what a grand time they'd had. She said her number was in the base directory, at the general number for the hospital, and that in the evenings there was a phone in the lobby of the quarters, though there was not always someone there to answer it. John said, "I have tomorrow off, too. If you like we might go on a picnic. I have the staff car for a couple of days of liberty." She said "Will Dantes come with us?" with that same mischievous look she gave him at Makalapa when they had just been introduced. Lodge, snapped his fingers, "Just remembered, he has Shore Patrol, so I guess it'll just be us." With that she gave him a real kiss, leaning into him and said "Goodnight, John. It was a wonderful time." John replied, tomorrow at Ten?" She said, "Ten it is," and went into the barracks that served as nurses quarters.

CHAPTER 10

CHINATOWN

After a seemingly forever moment, Lodge re-entered the staff car. He was obviously entranced by the turn of events. Hod waited for him to come out of it, but finally interrupted the pleasant thoughts. "Sir, if you don't mind, I need to check back in with the Shore Patrol."

"That'll work out fine, Dantes, you know the way, so drive us there. I think I'll get a room there, myself, at least for tonight." Arriving at the Royal Hawaiian Dantes parked the car and handed the keys to Lodge. "Good Job, Dantes, I enjoyed it and hope you did as well."

"I appreciate your including me, Sir," he nodded. As they parted, Lodge turned and asked, "The Admiral, did he ask your opinion, as I thought?"

"Yes sir, he did. And I told him pretty much what I told you."

"And what did he think of what you said?"

Dantes paused, remembering his promise to the Admiral, "Sir, he thanked me, said he needed to know what his sailors were thinking." Lodge paused, too, just a half second, realizing that Dantes was not really answering his question.

Lodge smiled, "He's an inspiring person, don't you think, Dantes?"

"I do, Sir," Dantes smiled back, both aware that a very neat observance of a propriety had occurred, and Lodge was reassured of Dantes' discretion. "One more thing, Dantes." Dantes looked up, "Miss Lydia has invited, and actually we both invite you to join us on a picnic today, if you're available."

"I thank the Commander and ask that you will convey my thanks to her as well, but I am planning to be trying out for the ship's pistol Team, tomorrow, Sir."

"That sounds like a lot of fun, Dantes and I bet you'll be good at it."

With that Dantes headed to the ballroom off the lobby where the Shore Patrol contingent was seated at tables. "Ah, there you are, Dantes," boomed

Marine Gunnery Sergeant Clancy, of the Detroit Marine Detachment, a sea-going Marine and noted marksman.

Dantes replied, "Reporting for duty, Gunny."

"You look none the worse for wear. Ready to go on patrol?" Dantes looked at the Gunny and nodded his assent. "Okay then, let's get you outfitted," and he was issued a web belt, a Colt .45 Cal. semiautomatic 1911 pistol and holster and an armband in dark navy background with gold SP embroidered on it. He adjusted his belt, hooked the holster to it and put it on. Then he depressed the magazine release button on the side of the grip and popped the magazine out of the pistol, noted rounds in it, pulled the receiver back and locked it in the open position. Looking from the breech end he looked through the barrel, holding it to the light and ascertained there was no round in the bore. He then flipped the catch down with his right thumb, letting the receiver slam home and snapped the trigger, letting the hammer fall on the empty chamber. Finally he put the magazine back in the grip housing and holstered the pistol, slipping the safety on. The Gunny noted with satisfaction that at no time had Dantes pointed the weapon at anyone or anything.

"Every weapon's loaded, right, Dantes?"

Dantes looked up and said, "That's what my Dad taught me in Texas, Gunny."

"That where you learned to shoot?"

Dantes nodded, "There and Boot Camp, of course, Gunny."

"What I hear, you beat all of your instructors in Boot Camp."

"Well, paper targets are easier than squirrels and such, Dantes replied."

Clancy smiled and gestured toward the door. "I'm going to take you out with me, tonight, and I'm looking forward to tryouts for the pistol team, tomorrow.

Chinatown, Honolulu, Hotel District.

They got a ride in the SP wagon to downtown, Honolulu, about fourteen miles from the Royal Hawaiian. Alighting a couple blocks away, they started walking in, Dantes in step with the Gunny and to his left, about a half pace behind. It was a fairly leisurely pace and both of them kept looking in an arc that went from aft of their waist to the front, crossing over slightly into the other person's arc. At corners and street crossings they looked behind them and cleared the area visually. They made way for the few civilians and the sailors generally made way for them.

It was noisy, with lots of shouting and laughter, but the first thing Dantes noticed was the smell. It was food, actually, and smelled pretty good. Clancy glanced at him, "First time ashore, in Honolulu, isn't it?" Dantes' eyes gleamed with excitement, trying to take it all in, all at once. "Hawaii is a bit like one of their favorite meals, poi. It's a great big mixture of Chinese, Portagees, Japanese and Hawaiians. And it's hard to describe. That smell of chow, that's from the street vendors and it's Japanese food they're selling, called yakitori. It's the Nip version of barbeque, chunks of chicken on bamboo splints and cooked over a bit of charcoal. Sometimes they will add some onion or even pineapple, but that's mainly the Hawaiians. And they all seem to use soya sauce to add to the taste. And, you can find beef or pork, even fish sometimes, instead of chicken. In the P.I. they call it monkey meat on a stick."

Dantes looked up at that, "Monkey meat, huh?" He knew that P.I. stood for the Philippines and that the .45 pistol had been instrumental in putting down the attacks by the Hukbalapap, there. He figured that monkey meat was slang for chicken just as S.O.S. was short for shit on a shingle, a sailor's name for chipped beef on toast.

"Hell that's nothing, they eat dogs over there in the areas visited by the China Fleet. And you are better off taking it slow, eating anything you find in those bars and streets." Dantes made a mental note to get some yakitori tonight before they turned in.

As they reached the hotel district it became much more crowded and they both placed their right hands on their weapons. Now the sidewalks were crowded with sailors lined up at the doors of the hotels and rooming houses and winding around whole city blocks, blocking off the interspersed places of business: eating places, shops and stalls, and making it difficult for anyone to get into the establishments. The houses of ill repute were mostly three story structures. As they pulled to a stop in front of one of them, Clancy took Dantes by the arm and out of the flow of traffic, and explained.

"You see, Dantes, these are almost legal in that they are protected by the Honolulu Police. Everybody knows they are here and what they are for. The Mamasans run a tightly controlled business and that includes getting the girls weekly medical inspections by doctors, and providing clean spaces, called bullpens, in the larger hotels. The girls are restricted to their rooms for the most part and may not be accompanied by anyone when out of doors." Dantes sniffed and inhaled a whiff of disinfectant, nodded. "Come on, we'll go into one."

"Here, on the first floor, the bouncer sits and he rejects any trouble makers. The other person is the cashier. She takes your money, three dollars if you're military, two if you're a local civilian. That's about a day's pay for a piece of ass. She gives you a chip that shows that you've paid. You are now cleared to go upstairs where the madam will have you pull your crank out and give you a short arm inspection and wash you, nice and clean. Finally you get to go up to the top floor where all of the beds are. In a bullpen it's a room divided into four compartments and it's like an assembly line for getting laid. In the first quad you get undressed and wait until called into the second quad. In the second quad the girl services you. In the third quad you get cleaned again and in the fourth you get dressed. A girl on a busy night will have to service about twelve customers an hour. She could do fifty in a four hour workday. The locals generally use a back entrance, the military the front door. That's because lots of sailors don't like to think that colored people are fucking the same women. But they are. And, if you ejaculate prematurely or fail to come, they will give you a rain check."

Dantes looked at the Gunny with big eyes, and the Gunny said, "Wondering how I know so much about how these places run?" Dantes nodded slowly, anticipating the answer. "Because I've been coming down here for years, have my favorite place and favorite girl. Mamasan knows me and she keeps a clean place. Local authorities like it because the rate of infection is low and the cops permit it because they are getting paid off and they also permit the movement and sale of booze, make money from both."

Dantes gave a wry look and said, "Henry Ford would be proud."

"Yes he would," the Gunny replied, "Love, mass produced on an assembly line. Since we're on duty we'll abstain, tonight."

And Dantes tried not to look relieved as he said, "Dang, just my luck." And he knew why the Lieutenant had turned down a ride through Chinatown. He had caught more than a glimpse or two in his rearview mirror of the two of them back there before turning the mirror down. He had felt the excitement fill the car, stimulate him, too. There were none of those feeling here, this evening. He thought back to the movie house in Beaumont, up in the projection booth, remembering how Joan had squirmed around in his lap, and they kissed and after a few times doing this they had gone further, much further, after he had installed a hook on the inside of the door so they couldn't be surprised. There the scent was not of industrial cleansers and disinfectants, it was chewing gum and maybe some popcorn, and a bit of a dab of cologne down the front of Joanie's chest, where she liked to be kissed. Other smells too, and he knew that he much preferred the backseat of a car or a little projection booth to places like this.

Gunny was looking at him, broke into his reverie, "Probably time to move on, we can probably hit one of these places tomorrow, maybe on the way back from Diamond Head."

As they proceeded down the row of houses, Dantes heard some shouting between two of the rooming houses. He thought one of the voices was familiar. He grabbed the Gunny by the arm, "I want to go back there and see what's going on." Gunny took in Dantes' excitement and concern and said, "Let's go." Running down a darkened alley they ran into a slow motion scuffle. Three sailors were taking wild swings at each other in no particular order. One of them was Daughter, on his feet, one was on the ground and the other was backed against the wall of one of the houses. They all reeked of alcohol and to stop them would be doing them all a favor. They didn't look particularly pissed or dangerous and probably didn't even know why they were fighting.

The Gunny stood back and waited to see how Dante would handle it. First he went to the one on the ground and checked him to see if he had swallowed his tongue and was breathing okay. That done he approached the one against the wall and asked him to sit down, right where he was. The sailor did as he was asked. Then he turned to his shipmate, and asked, "What's going on, Daughter?"

"What, you got the dooody, Dantes?" "Yeah I got the duty and if you keep your yap shut we may get you out of here and back aboard ship without busting your chops. You got that, Daughter?" "Yeah, I got that."

Turning to the Gunny, "This one's ours, my messmate, actually, and the other two are from other ships. If possible I'd like to keep my shipmate off the report sheet. And if these other two continue to behave, I think the same for them as long as we get them down to fleet landing." And he looked up at Gunny who was nodding, "Sounds good to me, Dantes, always do these things with the least fuss possible. These guys are just a little past their limit is all. We can get them back to the landing and let the SP there handle them until they get back aboard. You go get the SP wagon and have them bring it here, I'll watch them."

Slamming the doors to the wagon the Gunny and his sidekick headed back to the main drag and stopped for some monkey meat on a corner. It smelled delicious and Dantes was still just a growing boy; he was hungry! Gunny gave him a sidewise glance, "You know, I could hold the fort while you went across the street and went in for an inspection. Tell the Mamasan there, her name is Su Ling that I sent you for a numbah one good time. She'll take care of you and unless I miss my guess it'll be a freebie."

Dantes colored then and looked up at the Gunny, "Think I'll pass, Gunny. Why she may never come back to you if I did that." Gunny laughed, blowing his yakitori onto the street, "Good man, Dantes, good man. Look, let's get this load back to fleet landing and head back to the hotel and get some shuteye. We have a pretty full day ahead of us on the range at Diamond Head."

The next day at Diamond Head.

There were five of them, various rates and ratings plus the Gunny who was in charge as team Captain. Dantes was the only new hand, all the rest had fired in various matches in the past year. Dantes was getting a tryout because they had an opening and because he came recommended, from Boot Camp. They were down in the crater and had their pistol cases at stands along the firing line, facing a row of targets at twenty five yards, with the butts another fifty yards further and against the rising crater wall. Each case had pistols and cleaning gear and ammo. Plus there was a single carbide lamp that they shared and used to blacken the sights of their pistols.

The pistols had all been modified and had special front sights that were filed to a shine and a sharp edge, then blackened. The sears had also been filed in order to ease the pressure needed to get the hammer to fall. Under the Gunny's command all weapons were safed and laid upon their wooden platforms and then they all went down to the target frames and put up their targets. The frames were all hooked together and set up so that they could rotate ninety degrees using a lever at the far right hand end of the target line. With all targets up the Gunny rotated them to face the firing line and they went back to their firing positions.

"Lock and load five rounds." And five magazines slammed into their receivers and the slides were released, stripping a round off the top and into the breech of each of the pistols. "This will be slow fire, five rounds. Safe your weapons when through. All ready on the right, all ready on the left, all ready on the firing line. Commence fire." And a desultory staccato rippled through the enclosure as the shooters took their time in getting off their five shots. When Gunny saw five safed pistols he called out, "Cease fire." And the line of them went down to the targets with small rolls of white and black glued patches. Gunny followed Dantes and checked his target with him. "Not bad, Dantes, four in the black and one in the eight ring. Two of those in the black are bulls. Well done for a first time. Go ahead and patch your target." Of the other four shooters all had all of their shots in the black except for one, who had two in the white. They fired several more times, going from slow fire to timed fire to rapid fire, with less time each time to get their rounds off. Performance fell off with the speed up in firing rate, that is except for Dantes. He was getting the hang of it and taking less time meant less shaking for him. He imagined the targets were squirrels and wasted no time, getting his shots off as soon as he had a good sight picture, Poppopoppoppop until the slide stayed open.

They all crowded around Dantes' target, a couple of them whistled. "Ain't seen nothing like *that* Gunny." All of Dantes' shots were in the black, in a tight group, just off center to the left. Gunny looked at Dantes, "Can you explain why your group is off to the left?" He asked. Of course he was joking. Dantes took him seriously, "Gunny, I believe if we take just a little bit off the sear it won't do that. I must have pulled instead of squeezing, but at least I did it consistently." He looked up wondering what he'd said as the rest of them laughed. For awhile after that they called him Mister Consistent. Dantes was just happy they didn't call him jerk off and that he had made the team.

CHAPTER 11

AT THE BEACH

As he sat parked outside Nurses' Quarters, at Pearl Harbor, he looked at his watch for the third time, having gotten there ten minutes early. Now it was ten, just, and she came bouncing, skipping down the short porch, smiling and squinting in the brilliant morning sun. She had a handbag and a picnic hamper with her. Lodge jumped out of the car, grinning from ear to ear, "My you look fine, this morning!" She grabbed him by the arms, gave a squeeze and turned to the back of the car. Opening the door she put the hamper in and turned back, "There's not much in this hamper. I borrowed it from one of the girls, I thought we could stop at one of those little grocery stores in Pearl City and get bread and cold cuts, maybe a few other things for sandwiches." And turning back toward him, "You don't look so bad, yourself, Commander."

"Hey, I thought we agreed to drop the handles," feeling a bit deflated at the way things seemed to be starting off. Lydia smiled, "Of course I can call you John," she paused and got that mischievous look on her face, "or maybe even Darling!" And with that she got in the car in the front and scooched over to be closer to him. He started the car and his smile brightened as they headed toward Pearl City. They chatted as he drove keeping his eyes mainly on the road while she took advantage and gave him a long looking over. She saw a very handsome and fit man in his early thirties, a serious person whose eyes and smile marks said he liked to have a good time. He, too, was dressed in civilian clothes, informally in shorts and a short sleeved shirt, loafers and sun glasses in his shirt pocket. Things had gone so well and so quickly last night that she wondered how much of her feelings were based on fantasy, how much on reality. From where she sat, the reality was comforting, yet disturbing at the same time. This morning the picture was in sharp focus not at all like the dimly lit backseat of a car. Daylight and a night's sleep had way of doing that for a girl.

They pulled up to a mom and pop store, went in and got some soft drinks and an opener, a loaf of bread, jar of mustard and some spiced ham. She looked around until she found a wooden ice cream spoon, a shaped stick, showed it to the proprietress, she nodded and put it all into their hamper, he paid and off they went. "I was thinking we might try Waimanalo; there's a nice beach there and it's situated on a military reservation." She was impressed, surprised actually, to see that the Commander had done some research since last night. "And we can stop in at Hanauma Bay, maybe Koko Blow Hole along the way." She leaned back in the seat, relaxed for the first time, in his presence. Every once in a while it was nice to let someone else be in charge, do the driving so to speak.

"Ohhh, that'll be so nice, John; I've been to neither place but I've heard about Hanauma Bay. I've brought my Brownie camera and we can take some snapshots!" John nodded and turned to look at her for a moment. "I've brought my swimsuit." "Oh I have, too." And they rode along companionably for the next twenty minutes or so. John slowed and pulled over to the side, where there was a small shopping center, one of the stores with colorful clothing outside, flapping in the breeze. He shut the car down, "I want to get a small gift for my Auntie Jane; maybe you could help me with size, selection, that sort of thing." She smiled her assent, "I *love* to shop! And they went into the store.

"Do you have any pakemuus?" she asked the shop owner. Seeing john's quizzical look she said, "It's an elegant Japanese version of the muumuu, high collar, fitted waist and slit up the side, almost to the waist. I happen to know she wants one, as a surprise for her husband." The shop keeper asked about size and Lydia said, "Just about my size." She brought several to the front and laid them out, all the same size, some plain some patterned and most out of a soft clinging silk. "Which one do you like?" Lydia asked, looking from the dresses to John.

"Hmmm, I like two of them, the soft pink one and the deep purple one with the choke collar and embroidered frogs."

"Shall I try the pink one on for you?" And he nodded and smiled gratefully. She disappeared into a changing stall behind a curtain and soon popped out again, posing with one hip thrust toward him and pulling her hair back into a tight mass behind her, with an exaggerated sultry look. John's eyes betrayed him, she was gorgeous, lovely. John turned to the shop lady and said, "I'll take them both, please." And he could have meant the model and the dress, but the lady took it as the sale of two dresses. They took the time to have them giftwrapped and then hopped back in the car, next stop Hanauma Bay.

They stopped at the top, pulling off the highway, got out of the car and just stood there, overcome by the beauty. The bay was made from an ancient volcano crater at the shore, with roughly a third of the wall crumbled into the sea. The remaining bowl contained sparkling white sand and every shade from light green to the darkest blue. They moved together, not saying anything and naturally put arms around each other's waists. Just then a car passed behind them, beeping and hollering, disappearing in a cloud of laughter. It broke the spell and they made their way back from the edge, got in the car and headed out toward Waimanalo.

They stopped at Koko Blow Hole, got a little wet from the spray, pointed out Rabbit Island and finally got to the gate of the reservation, where their staff car was waved through. Driving into the last of the offshore breeze they headed down to the shoreline, found a place to park and got out of the car. She had a blanket and they took it all with them to the high tide line, spread out and sat down to lunch. They had the place almost to themselves, just a couple families several yards down the beach. Lydia put on her large brimmed sun hat and John his sunglasses. She made the sandwiches, assumed lots of mustard, while he opened a couple of soft drinks, now only slightly chilled, but sweet and bubbly, just the same.

With a bite of sandwich poking his cheek out he turned to her, "Say, this tastes mighty good, right now." "Mmmm," she answered, swallowing a huge bite of her ham sandwich. They were washing it down with soda when she turned to him, "So, John, tell me about yourself." He looked at her, thought for a bit, "Actually, I'd be surprised if our family trees didn't get tangled up a bit, a few generations ago. Almost surprised I didn't know you, or of you, growing up." She laughed, "You mean the Brahmin thing. Of course there has to have been some contact over the years; it's a small state, an ingrown sort of region, New England. I'm curious to know about the connection between you and the Fitzes."

"It's a family thing. My Dad and the Admiral were Classmates at the Academy and shipmates on their first ships after Graduation." My Dad was probably expected to go to Harvard and went Navy instead. I was expected to go to the Academy and went to Harvard instead. That illustrates a family trait, don't know whether to call it independence or stubbornness," he grinned. "And of course my Mom and Auntie Jane were bosom buddies, growing up together as young Navy wives.

Lydia thought a bit, "I do think we almost came close to knowing of each other, except for it being maybe a five or six year age difference. I was trying to think of my tennis years and I think I do remember something about you and your tennis. We probably had the same group of tennis coaches in Boston youth tennis, but you were always a step or several ahead of me. You *did* play Bob Tilden, didn't you?"

He laughed, "Yeah, not that I gave him too much of a match. We played a few times and I was good enough to make the squad at Harvard, but that's about it." He paused, remembering those days, "And your family, what did they think about you, going into nursing?" accompanied with an interested look, because this was getting a little bit personal. "I mean, my grandparents were scandalized that my Dad would go into the military; they had other plans for him."

She laughed in delight, "This seems so familiar. Of course you know or you wouldn't have known to ask. The Cabots and the Lodges and the rest of that lot don't think that nursing is a vocation befitting a young lady. Too, too messy, don't you know. Besides, I didn't *need* to work, we had money and why in the world would I choose something so, well, *earthy*? He looked up at her appraisingly, "And does that describe you, Miss Lydia? Earthy?" She smiled again, caught up perhaps in delicious memories, maybe pleased to see some New England stuffiness melting away. "I suppose that's just something for you to find out, Commander. And they were both enjoying a bit of light flirting.

"Mmmm, I do have a personal question for you, John, along these lines. You are handsome, *extremely* well connected, eligible doesn't begin to describe your seeming bachelorhood, yet here you are, unmarried still. You must have left a trail of broken hearts all the way from Boston to, well, to Honolulu. Oh, I've dated around, but in my case it was never the right one and I knew it. What can I say? I'm picky."

And with that he jumped up, "I'm changing into my swim shorts." And he headed back to the car, stood on the other side of it and quickly stripped and donned his trunks. As he returned to the blanket, Lydia passed him, got her suit from the car and did the same. John cheated, he looked. He didn't know it, but Lydia had looked, too. They returned to the blanket, lying on their sides and picked up their conversation

"You didn't press me on the earthy bit, John but I'd like to answer, even if only indirectly. Here on the Island, for sex the enlisted go down to the Hotel District and are serviced. That's not available to Officers, so they often turn to, you guessed it, Nurses. The assumption is that that's what we're here for, and without hesitation they assume that they will be serviced, too. But in private." Her color had heightened and her discomfort was showing. John took his sunglasses off and moving closer, gently put them on Lydia.

"Lyd, I noticed your reticence at Makalapa. And I probably figured most of that out, for myself. It is the reason I didn't kiss you the first time I had the chance, and the reason I didn't press for even more, in the car on the ride back." "Too much, too fast," they both said and nodded at the same time, then laughed together nervously.

"And then, there's the question, how long will you even *be* in the islands?" And she held her hands out, palms up, thankful for the glasses.

"Interesting question. My Boss the Commodore tells me that the Detroit, his Flagship, is being detached from the Task Group and we will be here likely for several months." And, I am going to be up for a change of duty station within the next six to nine months. There were mild hints at Uncle Fitz' that he knew that, makes me think I can probably have the billet I want, and I'm due for a spot of shore duty. No guarantees, but those are the likelihoods. You know the Navy." And John just stopped talking and was comfortable in the silence. He took her hands in his and held them, just looking at her, then the water, then back at her.

She was in a modest one piece suit, but as she lay there, cleavage was showing, they both knew it and both liked it. He moved closer, leaned in for a kiss and put one hand on her hip. She bent closer, made the kiss a good one and her breasts rose to the top of her suit. John raised an eyebrow, "Ready to go in?" and he stood up, pulling her with him. At that point she took a deep breath, dug her heels in just a bit, hesitating, "John it is hard to even define "too much" of a good thing, but it's very easy to go "too fast." They both nodded and then they ran down to the water, warm and inviting, and it was time to take a break from their conversation.

They stood at the very edge of the water, letting the receding wavelets pull the sand from beneath their feet, gradually sinking into footprint sized holes and growing more and more unbalanced. There were crooked lines of foam, bubbles popping silently in the breeze and the hiss of broken shell fragments clicking together by the thousands and terns darting, gulls circling. The crashing waves were thrusting onto the virgin beach and leaving their gobs of white foam, then withdrawing to do it again endlessly. Getting dizzy watching the water pull the sand in one direction and then change direction to flow in again, and about to topple in their tracks, they finally went deeper into the waves, pulling their naked feet from the sucking sand and wading out to the first sand bar. They crossed it and waded back into the water on the seaward slope of it and stopped in water up almost to John's shoulders. It was too deep for Lydia to stand so John took her waist and swept her legs up and cradled her lightly in his arms, the displaced water bearing most of her weight. The sun was perfect, warming them, as if they needed that. The waves and the undertow pulling them this way and that and they stayed that way for a while, kissing until the kissing got heated and his hands started to move.

She swung her feet down to the hard sandy bottom and came up reaching for him and wrapped her legs around his waist. She was leaning into him, her breasts flattened against his chest. The push and sway as the swells passed was delighting them both, lifting John just off the ocean floor then depositing them again with a bump in the troughs between swells. Each time they bumped she bounced lightly off of John. He wasn't backing away from the contact, was rather moving with and against the waves and enjoying it. He squeezed her tight and her breasts were pushed up even higher. There was color in her face and neck and the blood suffused her chest as she reciprocated the hip motion and in a tight voice she said "John, I'm not a tease, I just want more time. Is that okay with you?"

"I mmmf and his kiss smothered what else she was to say. And they rocked together in the sea feeling the incredible closeness. She reached up and started to kiss him and he looked at her, in mock seriousness, "That enough time?" he asked. She thought about saying yes, thought just a little longer and kissed him again instead. "Here is where we use will power, John. Just petting for now?" she asked. Her expression was hard to read. . Finally the sounds faded away, not even the surf was heard, just soft sighs and ahhs and little smiles and constant kisses in the swirling water..

After a while they turned to go in. They waded and kept turning to each other and kissing. It was taking a long time to get back to the beach. They noticed that it was deserted, only their car. They went as far as the dry sand bar, still a hundred yards offshore. There they sank to their knees and just looked at each other. "Thank you, John," she said.

They walked all the way to their blanket and spent another two hours wrapped in each other and in the blanket, giggling and talking.

"I want you to know that I feel a little bit weird about all this. I want more but also want to go slowly enough to enjoy it and to allow a friendship to grow," Lydia said.

At that he propped himself up on one elbow and she found out exactly what he *did* think. "It is always the woman who has the most to lose, who risks the most, not least of which is pregnancy. I think I am ready to pick one and settle down. I know I want a woman who is passionate and who has an enormous capacity for love. The way we met, at Auntie Jane's place, that wasn't by accident. She and I are very close and our families have always been close. It was a set up to introduce us. Aunt Jane knows us both and she approves of you. What she did told me the families would approve wholeheartedly. These past two days have been the most exciting for sure. I have worried about what you might think, had to remind myself that it is best that you see me as I am, that I have to be myself whether that appeals to you or not.

He continued, "You don't have to say anything back, in fact I'd rather you slept on it for a while."

"I want to say just one thing, John. Well, maybe two. Thank you for being just the way you are and explaining. A girl wonders."

Back at the Naval Hospital, ten days later.

"Mrs. Fitz, how nice to see you!" The Admiral's wife was on the premises, reporting for her volunteer duty. Knowing she enjoyed Lt. Crowninshield, the word was passed for her.

"Lydia, I've thought about you a lot, this week," Mrs. Fitzgerald said

"Oh, how nice of you to say," Lydia smiled, looking distracted.

"Perhaps I've come at a bad time?" The Admiral's wife was looking at her closely. Lydia appeared to have missed some sleep, maybe some of the glow Jane was used to seeing.

"Not at all, Mrs. Fitz, I.."

"Oh please just call me Jane, Lydia. By now I feel almost like your Mom."

"Do kids ever call their parents by their first names?" she asked, some of the mischievousness and sparkle back. They both laughed, moving to a couch in a corner of the lobby. Jane took another look, seemed to decide something, then asked.

"And what did you think of John Lodge, Dear? Perhaps it's none of my business but I hold the two of you in my highest regard, love, even. I will admit to deliberately throwing you together, perhaps I made a mistake?" A line appeared between Lydia's brows and grew. "To the contrary, Auntie Jane, perhaps you succeeded too well." Jane just sat patiently, waiting confidently, looking at this young woman for whom she had such feeling. "He's been gone for maybe a week, and I'm sure it's because the Detroit is at sea and I miss him terribly."

Jane smiled a soft smile. "That's what happens with our Sailors, Lydia, they go to sea, and honestly it's part of the mystique, maybe what makes them different from all other men. Those of us who love them simply have to share them with a mistress called the Sea, and trust that we are flesh and blood mistress enough for them. We have to be just as strong as they are."

They were holding hands together, facing each other just the way a mother and daughter would do. Lydia let her hands loose, turned aside and brought out a package. It was wrapped as a gift and Lydia handed it to Auntie Jane, "This is from John. We shopped for it the day after we played tennis at your place in Makalapa. He wanted you to know how much he loves you and means this as a gift to both you and the Admiral."

"Oh, Lydia! How nice! You see, this is just exactly like John and like a Sailor. They appreciate women more than the kind of man who's around every day. Why it's like Christmas every time they come home from being gone at sea. Christmas and a honeymoon, all over again." And she beamed, perhaps a little self-consciously, remembering her last such honeymoon. "May I?" she asked, looking up from the box.

"Of course, Auntie Jane." And then they both took in a bit of a breath, looking at the silken oriental muumuu. Jane was delighted and Lydia seemed to have brightened, too. "Ohh, this is perfect, I *love* this shade of purple; and John picked it out, you say?"

"Yes, it's his choice, though I *did* model a pakemuu for him, for you." "Well thank you *both*!" Jane said, still looking at the gown and feeling its silkiness.

"So tell your Auntie what is bothering you. Only what you care to share and if you like, I will tell you about John."

She took a deep breath. "I have had to put him off and in spite of it, I am falling for him. We have to wait until we at least know each other and it is almost too hard. Anything else is just crazy. But we have talked and we agree on so much, and do have a lot in common.

"But Lydia, Dear, you are both such attractive people, and healthy adults and are the type of person who doesn't beat around the bush, so to speak." And both gave a small smirk, not even pretending not to notice the double entendre. These men are sometimes impossible to be with and absolutely miserable to be without! I can't speak for John, of course, but I've known him since he was a baby and I know he is an honest man with intelligence and character.

Lydia looked up from her lap, grasped Jane by the hands tightly, and said, "Thank you, if I may call you, Auntie Jane."

"We must get together, perhaps for lunch one day. Maybe I'll wear this," and Jane held up her pakemuu to her front and pulled the split open and went ooh la la with an appropriately sexy stare and they both collapsed in laughter. The rest of the staff within hearing heard the shrieks and smiled in their turn. Crazy old bat!

CHAPTER 12

WHALEBOATS PREPS

The First Division was again formed at Quarters. "Alright, listen up to the Plan of the Day. All nonrated working party this morning to bring ammo aboard and strike it below. A reminder that today we'll also be holystoning and the appearance of the quarterdeck is not up to standards. It *will* meet standards. Any Questions?" As the Division Officer prepared to dismiss them a voice from the rear rank piped up, "Sir, any word about the whaleboats, about whaleboat racing?" Ensign Smythe looked at his POD and the Chief coughed, the Division Officer looked at him, nodded and the Chief spoke up saying, "That information was put out last week and I have a copy of the notice in the paint locker. There's always that ten percent that doesn't get the word, so I will repeat it, the ship is forming a team of volunteers. It will be limited to only nonrated personnel. Come up on the fo'c'sle after dismiss and we can sign you up." Then he turned to Ensign Smythe, "Thank you, Sir."

"Fall out!" and Dantes turned to Daughter, "Did *you* hear anything about whaleboats?" "Nah, and I would have remembered. Probably one of them forgot to pass the word. I bet there's a stack of flyers sitting there in the paint locker. Why, you interested?" "Sure, aren't you? Sounds like fun." "Dantes, you crazy or what, that's gonna be nothing but more work." And he laughed and sauntered off to fall in for the working party.

The ammo was brought aboard from the barge alongside in cargo nets and lowered by boom and electric winch through hatches directly over the magazines, several decks below. There a working party formed a line and in bucket brigade fashion they passed the projectiles from man to man until they were ensconced in their racks and ready for fuse insertion and distribution by hoist to the turrets and mounts above. The projectiles weighed 105 pounds each so the men in the line were either large and strong or they were relieved often. A couple extras were there to do the reliefs as needed and the work went fast.

The powder was separate and in stitched silk bags that weighed 34 or 34.5 lbs. The smaller men could handle the powder easily.

Right after noon meal Dantes took Daughter with him up to the paint locker. "Don't give me that bull about too much work. This is going to be fun. Besides it'll be a break from other stuff. Like holystoning." Daughter looked at him in mock amazement, "Don't give me that, you enjoy holystoning, too!" They picked up a flyer from the stack and read it. "Hmm, says only nonrated need apply. We'll race against the other cruisers and the battle wagons will do the same. Looks like ten men to a boat, not counting the Cox'n. And it says whaleboats, no motors, no sails, and no rules. What do you suppose they mean by no rules?" Daughter shrugged. "Well I think they mean you can cheat if you're not too obvious", Dantes said. "C'mon and let's take a look at our whaleboat."

They went up on the boat deck and found the whaleboat in its cradle with a tarpaulin lashed over it and with the davits for lowering it twisted away and secured at the side of the ship. Dantes looked for the oars, didn't see them and loosened the corner of the tarp and peeled it back to reveal twelve oars, ten plus two spares. Eyes sparkling he pulled an oar out and hefted it. It was fairly crude and about eight feet long with a round grip and flared blade to catch the water. Looking further he saw a bag of brass oarlocks, pintles and gudgeons, hardware for shipping the oars and the rudder. As he put it all back and secured the tarp, Daughter could see that he was thinking.

After 'Knock off all ship's work' they called away the whaleboat racing crew and some twenty nonrated sailors showed up on the boat deck. As it turned out they had had to make an announcement about the whaleboat practice, as no one had gotten the word or seen any flyers. And although the Deck Department had the most nonrated, there were some in other departments who were striking for a rate but were still Seamen. They were eligible too. Boats was there with a muster list and he called off the names. As he got no answer he scratched that name off the list. Finally he looked up and said, "Tryouts this week and then next week we'll start training." He looked up, "Who has ever rowed in one of these?" Nobody held up their hand. Boats said, "Really?" They sort of chuckled a bit, and one worthy said, "How hard can it be, Boats? We just get in the seat, put the oar in the water and row"

"Well there is putting the oarlocks in as well as shipping the rudder. Look, you two take off the tarp and we'll get our boat ready to put over the side. Dantes, you take half of these men over to the port side and start rigging that boat, too. I'll come and check on you." Several of the Seamen moved to Dantes' side with eager looks and grins on their faces, all of them go getters. When Boats came over to check on their progress they had their boat already rigged and hooked up to its davits and were ready to board and lower away. Dantes looked at Boats and said, shouldn't we the call away the small boat detail?

Boats said, "Dantes, get them to call away the small boat detail. Dantes turned to Daughter, "Go get Hicks, if he gives you any guff, tell him Boats said, and have them call away." "Yeah, Boats, I know, call away the small boat detail."

When they all showed up the BM3 swiftly took charge and with the smoothness born of practice the detail hoisted the boat from its cradle and pushed it outboard, over the side of the ship. Then they took the block and tackle bitter ends and threw some round turns on cleats on deck to hold the line taut. The crew got in the boat and Hicks being the smallest man in First Division, why, Dantes just naturally made him the Coxswain. It turned out that several in the boat *had* rowed in whaleboats, they just didn't raise their hands when asked to volunteer. The detail started paying out line and the boat moved jerkily down toward the surface, some twenty feet below. They had shipped their oars with ease and thrust them out to the side as all of them got used to the feel of the oar in their hands. As they got in the water Dantes gave himself the aft-most position on the port side and he sat Daughter on the thwart next to him, as the crew sat in pairs, five rows, ten oarsmen to a boat. Plus Hicks the Cox'n. Once in the water Dantes turned to his crew and said, watch my oar, I will be the stroke oar and everyone else will match what I do with my oar with yours. Got it? There were nods and answers. He turned to Hicks and said, "Mainly just stay seated and don't fall overboard. When there's anything to say, I'll tell you." Hicks grinned in answer because he was getting a free ride. "And use the rudder as little as possible but keep us from hitting anything."

There was a five knot breeze rippling the water, that's all, no swells. The sun was fairly low in the sky so Dantes put it behind them, picked out a course clear of shipping, told Hicks to pick out a point on shore to aim at and said, "Ready all!" He leaned forward with his blade perpendicular to the water then dipped it in and pulled. Most of the others did the same and Dantes just kept repeating the motion: lean forward roll your wrist and drop the blade in, pull as far as your body would let you, using your back and arms and when you got to the end of the stroke, drop your wrists and let the blade come out of the water. They went along that way for about a minute and Dantes told Hicks, "Let her run." He got up and stood in the middle of the boat, directly on the keel. "Okay, now. No kidding has anybody done very much of this?" Two of them said yeah. Dantes said, "I will demonstrate what I'm doing and I want you two to correct my method if it's wrong." One of the men, Sykes, said "Nah let me just show them."

He unshipped his oar and held it before them resting on the gunwale. "See? My wrists are up," and he demonstrated. "This is the catch, where the oar goes into the water. At this point you are leaning forward as far as you can reach. When the stroke oar goes in the water, your wrists are up and you tilt the oar down into the water by raising your arms and pull together. At the end of the stroke when you are leaning all the way back, to get your oar out of the water you simply drop your wrists. That will angle the blade so that our motion through the water will pop it right to the surface again." Dantes said, "Everyone try that out, with your oars out of the water. Practice it a few times. Okay, now do it slowly but with your oar in the water. "Sykes, you correct any hand positions you see that are not quite right. We'll just sit here and dry snap for a while until it feels more natural." Okay let's try again and I will set a slow cadence to give us a chance to get used to the feel of this."

They ran their drill with oars in the water and the improvement was significant. The crew was smiling and chattering happily as they glided with some power, nearly getting space between their puddles. "Let her run." Hicks repeated his command loudly and all of the oars matched Dantes' in a horizontal position straight out from the gunwale. Dantes turned on the thwart and said, "Next we're going to learn how to stop. We'll get some way on the boat and then we'll practice putting the brakes on. So they did that, getting up to speed and then dropping their blades into the water and holding the handle of the oar away and steady as they rapidly slowed to a stop. Then they practiced turning on a dime, using the oars with one side pulling and the other side pushing. Dantes turned again, "That's enough for our first time. We'll take her home." They returned to the ship to find that the other boat had already been hoisted out of the water. They were feeling pretty good about themselves and looking forward to the next practice.

A week later Dantes ran into Chief Locker. "Afternoon, Chief." "Afternoon Dantes, care to join me on the fantail?" "Yessir." "Thought you learned better than that in Dago, Dantes. The 'Sirs' are saved for the Commissioned Officers." "Chief, it was the way I was raised, is all. On the farm in Texas we were taught to say Sir to those we respected." "Yeah, well there are few enough privileges to pass around in this man's Navy and that one is reserved for the Officers. Regardless of what you may think of the occasional one who doesn't come across right, they've all earned their title. Just as you have; Seaman First is no mean title, Dantes." "Aye, Chief and it's you who gave it to me." "No again Son, it's you who earned it." They strolled aft along main deck between deckhouse and lifeline, an occasional gull wheeling close to look for garbage as the smells of a ship generally wafted downwind with the breeze when anchored. Too, the ship would stream with the winds and tides, and the fantail was often enough the first part of the ship that the gulls encountered, flying into the wind and looking for a handout. The space was wide enough for the two of them, maybe four abreast, and occasional men greeted the Chief. He'd been aboard like Dantes, just less than a year but was greatly respected throughout the ship. He and the Chief Master at Arms were instant buddies and few if any knew why or had heard the story of what took place down in Tijauna. There were a few others back aft since the smoking lamp was lighted throughout the ship so most were smoking. When through they just tossed the butts overboard then headed back to work or about their business.

Dantes looked inquiringly at his 'Sea Daddy'. "So, the Commodore has shifted his broad pennant ashore." and he returned Dantes' look. "Took that sharp Commander with him." Still no comment from Dantes. "There was comment about you, getting the assignment as his driver." Dantes nodded, "It's a bit surprising to me that an almost brand new deckhand would get mentioned." 'Wall' Locker laughed, "Old women have nothing on sailors when it comes to scuttlebutt." Dantes grinned too, but didn't offer anything. Locker grinned in turn, "I see you have kept the common sense I saw in Dago." Dantes said, "Chief it was a great time. I was included almost as one of the family, at CincPac's Quarters in Makalapa. I have never seen anything at all like the life lived by the top brass. But when all is said, they turn out to be people, just like everyone else." "I have just an idea of what you're describing, Dantes, but everyone has their imaginations. I imagine that there has been talk about you and the Commander, the Admiral, who knows maybe even their wives and girlfriends." At that Dantes gave a really sharp look. "Yeah, it seems there were some from Detroit that saw a certain staff car cruising along Waikiki. You are smart not to comment about anything that went on, very, very smart. Another thing and I imagine you have anticipated this. Some of the talkers are jealous, might try to cause you a little trouble." Dantes nodded. "Do like my Momma taught me, don't start a fight but if you find yourself in one be damn sure you finish it." As Locker turned to leave, Dantes said, "Chief?"

He turned back, curious to hear what Dantes might say. "Chief I wonder if there might be a way to get some time off for my whaleboat crew, for training. We don't need much, just a half hour before knock off so there will be a small boat detail readily available to put us over the side. Also it would be good if we could leave our boats in the water and avoid the work of putting the boat in the water and picking it back up each time." Chief squinted at him, wondering what made Seaman Dantes think of going to a Chief, not even in his own Department, to get something like this done. Dantes of course read the look, "We nonrated get our scuttlebutt too, Chief. Word is that you and Chief Gundy have special pull up the line, that if you want to get something done out of the ordinary, go to a Chief. In particular go to one of you." He continued, "With the extra time we will be able to get in longer workouts and stand a chance at winning some races." Before Locker could answer, "And I have some ideas for modifications to the rig on the boats. Nothing big or that couldn't be removed after the racing season, but I think it'll result in a faster boat." Chief showed interest, asked about Dantes' modifications, nodding that he understood, gave Dantes an admiring look, cocked his head in a grin, "What'll you think of *next*, Dantes?" and he headed back up to Chief's Quarters, having made no promises.

Two days later, bringing his boat in for hoisting the JOOD hollered down from the Quarterdeck, "Tie up aft by the Jacob's ladder. You have permission to leave your boats secured there." "Aye, aye Sir," Dantes hailed back. The next morning at quarters the Division Officer, Mr. Smythe announced that the whaleboat crews had permission to knock off at 1530 to shift into athletic gear and go to whaleboat practice every day. The next day he was summoned to the shipfitters spaces where he talked with an SF1 about the modifications he had in mind for the oars and the oarlocks. They worked up a sketch of the modification to the oarlocks. The SF1 showed some skepticism about extending the oarlocks out away from the side of the boat, thought they could fail in a race. "What do you think of extending the oars," Dantes asked. The Petty Officer smiled and brought out a sketch he had already done showing a metal sleeve pushed onto the oar handle and kept in place with screws. "And finally we will need a collar on the oar that we can adjust as well until we find the ideal pivot point," Dantes said. The collar will serve to butt up against the oarlock and set the distance of each blade out from the side of the boat." "Got it," the SF1 replied. "Thanks and please do these modifications only to the port whaleboat oars. We'll need to run tests against the other boat to see how much difference they make." Before leaving, as though he'd just remembered, Dantes handed over a carton of cigarettes which was gratefully received. A mock salute in return and Dantes was happily headed down to the berthing compartment for noon meal. *"Those cigarettes didn't cost too much,"* he thought, *"especially since the crew chipped into the pot to get them and two more cartons from ship's stores. Never can tell when you might need a bit of cumshaw."*

The modifications were made within a day, tests and adjustments made in another afternoon and Dantes and his crew were ready to test their new oar set out against some competition. The coxswains from Detroit's two boats agreed on a rendezvous and met for some racing. Ready, set Go! Hicks shouted and both boats surged forward. Dantes' boat was setting a stroke of fifty strokes per minute. The other boat was at sixty. Dantes' boat smoothly pulled away from the other boat by several lengths and then picked up the pace to 60 strokes per minute, leaving their competition floundering in their wake thirty yards behind when Dantes finally gave the order to let her run. Dantes looked up to Hicks, "I have one more idea of a small change that might help us get just a bit more speed." And they talked about it and Hicks nodded that he'd be willing to try it and thought it might work.

The decision was made to single up to one boat, Dantes' boat, for the rest of the racing season and the four best oarsmen from the Starboard whaleboat were kept as spares for boat number one. The starboard whaleboat was hoisted aboard because it was no longer competing and the oars on Dantes' boat were wrapped in a tarp and lashed securely in the boat to keep her modifications under wraps until the big race, which was scheduled to take place in another month. What Dantes had done was extend the oar blades by about fourteen inches with the collars placed at the ideal point on the oar to ensure that each oarsman had enough leverage to pull that blade through its arc. It made for a much more powerful thrust for the boat, as long as the crew could provide the muscle power. He went and looked up the race course distance and found it was two miles. With the Quartermaster's help he set out two buoys that were two miles apart and that became Detroit's practice course. Then he set a man killing practice routine of rowing for two hours each day with the modified oars and using the practice course for sprint practice. The longer rows built their endurance and the sprints gave them coordination for the race at high stroke rate. At the end of three weeks they were sprinting for the whole two miles. Regatta day was in three days.

For his final preparation he and his crew turned their boat over on the boat deck and scraped off all marine growth on the bottom that they could find, then applied a liberal coat of wax and hand rubbed the bottom to a high gloss, absolutely smooth. The ship was taking notice and excitement was running pretty high. Two days before the regatta the cruisers and battlewagons were aligned down the course and starting and finish lines were marked with buoys.

They were ready to go.

CHAPTER 13

NUUANU VALLEY

LCDR Lodge knocked on the bulkhead next to Commodore Cochrane's Cabin door and entered when bidden. "Lodge, pull up a chair." John sat, made himself comfortable and gave his attention to his boss. "I got word today from CincPac Staff that I am to debark and shift ashore, join the Admiral at CincPac Headquarters. Naturally you'll come with me."

"Sir."

"I'm aware that you are also soon to be receiving orders for your first shore tour. That being so, I think that the timing in this case will work in your favor. You should know that I have recommended you for early promotion to Commander and told the assignment officer at BuPers to hold off on any new assignment for you until we know the results of the Board, which is meeting now, as a matter of fact. If it all works out you will already be ashore on my Staff and then if promoted will likely get a more senior position with CincPac or one of his subordinate Commanders."

Lodge looked at his boss, and gulped, "Sir, I don't know quite what to say. My deepest gratitude, of course, but I will be sorry to leave my position with you, Sir."

Cochrane considered that and the fact that his staffer knew *exactly* what to say. Furthermore he knew his man and expected that he said exactly what he thought. He stood, indicating that their chat was at an end, held out his hand to Lodge, "Ohh, I think we will find ourselves together quite a bit over the next several months and years, John, and I look forward to it."

"Sir, thank you for your confidence in me. I won't let you down." And with that he went to his much smaller stateroom, his mind racing with the possibilities: going ashore, possible promotion, shore duty and maybe, just maybe some time to sharpen his tennis game and to conduct a proper courtship of one Lydia Eliot Crowninshield!

They moved ashore two days later, a small group, and took up working space at CincPac Headquarters, with one noticeable change, Admiral Fitzsimmons had his own ideas of an initial billet for Lodge. He had endorsed Cochrane's Fitness Report on Lodge, strongly recommending him for immediate promotion. Anticipating the result he simply made some room for him on his own immediate staff, figuring the promotion for Lodge would follow shortly.

Shortly after that, the next day in fact, Lodge made a visit to the Naval Hospital where they passed the word for Lieutenant Crowninshield.

"Thought I'd take a chance that you might be available for lunch," Lodge opened, looking at her semi-seriously, "I apologize for the lack of notice.." and his voice trailed off as just her presence was making the words a little harder to find.

"Oh John, I appreciate that and of course I am glad to see you. Give me five minutes and I'll meet you in the canteen?" He nodded and watched as she walked away, then with a bit of an elevated pulse and a fantastic outlook headed to the lunchroom.

They picked up some navy bean soup and baloney sandwiches from the line and were seated at a table for two. They were getting glances because it was unusual to see the Lieutenant with a man, any man. At lunch or any other time. She actually had a reputation as a bit of an ice queen, distant to the male population in general and turning down invitations regularly. They dug into their soup while it was still hot, Lydia eating greedily, a bad habit she had picked up as a nurse from having to grab meals on the run. Lodge wondered how she kept her figure. As for him, he had suddenly lost his appetite. He laughed to himself, *I wonder if I'm breaking out in pimples. This feels like teenage years: no appetite, tongue tied, can't concentrate, and on a permanent high.*

He sipped a spoon or two of his soup and she said, "don't like it? I'll eat it." He swapped bowls with her and dabbled at his sandwich while she drained his bowl as well. The attraction between them was totally mutual but the effects were opposite. She had a ravenous appetite. And now it wasn't just for food. Finished with her meal, (she was going to save the sandwich for later) she looked up at John.. Her heart was beating like Gene Krupa, that new jazz drummer she had heard just before moving to Hawaii, but she waited for him to say what was on his mind.

"ComDesPac has shifted his pennant ashore and CincPac has poached on the Commodore's staff and taken me aboard in a temporary assignment to CincPac Staff. There have been broad hints that I can expect shore duty for my next assignment and that it will be here, in Pearl. So I don't know exactly what I will be doing, but I will be likely doing it here for some time to come." Her face lit up with one of her devastating smiles that made all the colors brighter, "Oh John that's fabulous news, and if we weren't in public.. Well it's just the best possible news I could have heard." And she did reach her hand across the table to be held for just a second or two. John flushed with pleasure and just sat there, the two of them just sat there. Funny how at times like this the sounds fade away and time seems to pause while you take it all in. Her elbow slipped from the table and it was as though she awoke with a start and they both laughed, breaking the spell.

"When can I see you again?"

"Well, let me check my dance card."

"Getting lots of invitations, are you?" She looked at him incredulously, "Well, yes, from time to time." "Anyone I know?" "Hmm yes actually Rod Kinney has asked if I'd like to play Tennis." Lodge colored a bit more, and she giggled, "I was too busy to take lessons with Rod, had someone else on my mind." "Tonight okay?" he asked. "John Darling, yes tonight would be okay and I'd like for it not to be public. With *you* I don't worry about appearances, but as the local ice queen I have certain, ahh sensitivities to observe."

"I feel the same way, don't want to set tongues wagging. I have an appointment this afternoon with a real estate person. Going to see what's available on the island for rent, also going to pick up a used car. What say we leave it that I will pick you up around 1700 and we'll do nothing special, keep it private and maybe spend some time getting to know each other." She looked at him steadily. "Anytime with you is special, Commander and it will be good to slow down and do what you said." They both smiled, he got her chair and stood as she headed back to work. *"Rod Kinney, huh? I'm not at all surprised."*

He called the real estate guy that Auntie Jane had recommended and he said he'd pick The Commander up.

Downtown Honolulu. The door lettering said "J. Akuhead Pupule Real Estate." It was a local nickname, as Kavika Kalaniola had many friends who knew him as Aku. He was a skinny intense middle aged native Hawaiian with a little Portagee thrown in. He had almost no walk-ins, lived by referrals and his telephone. He was extremely well connected. "Welcome to my office, such as it is." Lodge grinned, looking around at the various mounted fish on the walls, and pictures of local big wigs, he assumed. "You come recommended highly by a very fine lady, Mrs. Jane Fitzsimmons." "Yes, that's my Auntie Jane. We're very close." "What can I do for you, my name Kavika means David by the way, you can call me Dave, if you wish, Commander." "I'm John, and I'd like to call you Aku," he replied. "You know Hawaiian?" "I know only that your sign means crazy fish head, Aku, and I like crazy people. A lot." They both laughed, "Maybe I'll teach you some Hawaiian, John, we'll see."

"So you want a rental place?" "Yes, at least to start, nothing too fancy, but it would be nice if it was out in the country a little bit. Furnished would be good too, but not a deal breaker if I have to supply enough for housekeeping. And I need to pick up a used vehicle that runs, I hope you can recommend me to a friend of yours who can fix me up. And one more thing, it would be super if you could do all of this in the next two or three hours." Lodge sat back and enjoyed how Aku's face fairly lit up the room.

Aku held up a finger, got on the phone and placed five calls in succession. He was talking what sounded like pidgin English, regular English and some Portugee thrown in and he was talking rapidly. He slammed down the phone and rocked forward. "You got an account locally?" "Not yet. I can make out a draft on my family's bank in Boston, however, if that will suffice." Another smile spread across Aku's skinny face, "That's going to work out just fine, John. First let's go get your car. You have your choice of three. You'll pick one and we'll use it for the rest of our stops. That way you can get used to driving around the island."

In a whirlwind tour they found themselves up in Nuuanu Valley, the route that Kamehameha had taken with his warriors when consolidating his power in the islands. The place was owned by the Bishops, an old family in the islands. It hadn't been for rent, but for Aku and anyone close to Miz Jane, why it was suddenly available and at a fair price. Furnished of course. It was the first and only place they went. There was even a garage for the used Chrysler sedan. John looked at Aku with genuine amazement and total affection. "Aku, you are simply the very very best at what you do." Another smile and Aku handed him the keys. "Any time, John, anything I can do."

John grabbed him by the shoulders, "I will have one more request but I'll need a bit of time to get used to Hawaii and then I will come to see you. Thank you so much!" And then John drove them back to Aku's office, he left several checks drawn on the Boston bank, checked his watch and saw he had more than enough time to head in to Pearl and pick Lyd up for their evening alone.

Parked outside Nurses' Quarters, Pearl Harbor.

Lydia with her hair brushed back into a ponytail, eyes sparkling walked up to the car and took a turn around it as though she was judging a bit of horse flesh. She looked at Lodge, "I had you figured for something a bit sportier," she kidded and jumped in front as did Lodge. "How in the world did you get such nice and sensible wheels in so little time? I would have shopped for days, weeks before I could narrow it down to just *three* choices, much less actually buy one." He looked askance at her and said, "I know this guy... he's a hell of a salesman." Lydia was dressed in knee length pedal pushers and a colorful striped polo shirt that just fit with no extra room. In front the stripes were stretched, emphasizing her breasts. That's why she had the dang shirt, anyway. She looked really good and she knew it. She did it for John and hoped he knew *that*.

John got his eyes back on the road and headed out Kamehameha toward Nuuanu Pali. They would stop before going that far, but Lodge didn't say where they were going. "So, mystery man, got a private place where we can, uh, talk?" only solicited an "Ummhmmm." So she just decided to let him have his surprise and settled back with the window rolled down and her left hand placed innocently in John's lap. After a while they pulled off the road before getting too high up in the valley. It was a dirt road, a drive really and it gently wound through small turns in a couple hundred yards up to this very nice looking cottage with all kinds of plants and flowers and a magnificent view of cloud shrouded cliffs and peaks. She had never seen so much green in her life.

"How did you find this place," she said, running up to the door. He unlocked it and swept her up and carried her across the threshold and set her down with a kiss. "Uh, I know this guy," he said. "Oh and it's furnished! Did you borrow it from somebody just for us to use?" "Nope, this is my new home. I've rented it. Welcome." She looked at him, one finger to her lips, "and this guy, I really have to meet him." "Ahh, nope again, not sharing you any more than I have to. We can stay here and talk about whatever we want for as long as we want and no one will bother us, Dear." And her eyes shone at the sound of the little endearment. She'd been calling him Darling for some time now.

They checked the fridge and found some pineapple, pineapple juice and beer. There was rum on the shelf in the pantry. Lydia found two plates, got some pineapple and served it to the kitchen table along with two beers. Then they just sat and opened the beers and downed about half before eyeing the pineapple. Then he was eyeing her. She noticed and reached into her pants pocket and pulled out a folded piece of yellow legal sized paper. He leaned in to try to get a look. He could tell it was a list, but before he could make out any of the items she held it away holding her hand out in the stop sign. John eased back and knew when to let the lady be in charge. In reality she had always been in charge but he wasn't complaining so far.

"John, please forgive me for ambushing you with this list. I knew that if you started giving me that look of yours I was going to be lucky to remember my own name, much less what I wanted to talk about." "I know the feeling," he replied. "John, what can I call you besides John?" He looked non-plussed. "Well, what does your Mom call your Dad?" she asked. "It depends upon a lot of things, it…" "Enough. My Mother calls my Dad lots of things, but he likes it when she calls him Honey," Lyd said. "I've heard Auntie Jane call her Fitz Honey. She calls him Honey Fitz sometimes too." John replied. "Well okay but just so you know, I'm looking to call you something else. Now we'll start with the list if that's okay with you, Hon."

"What are you thinking right now, Honey?" she asked.

"Hard to think. I'm glad we're doing this but I think it's a bit formal. You asked at the beach if I thought it was weird that we could do heavy petting and leave it at that. I understood the reasons for it, at least I did at the time. I told you that the woman has the greater risk. Right now I'm glad we did what we did and did not do what else we wanted to do."

"When you do get married will you want kids?"

"I'm not opposed to them. I was raised in a Navy family until my Dad got out and I don't remember much about it. I think it takes real skill and devotion not to mess it up. And that was with my Mother at home, not in the Navy herself."

"Hon, why the Navy for you? And why Harvard instead of the Academy? And what do you want out of your Navy career? And do you think there are sexual things that are taboo between man and wife?" and she went on and on to the bottom of her list and then said, "I only wanted the list to get over my actual shyness at asking such questions and because I really want the answers. But I don't want them right now, all at once. I wanted you to know that I can talk about anything and everything and I realize not all women are that way. I chose to let you see some more of me. And we can take time to get the answers from each other. I'm not going anywhere any time soon and I will not see anyone else."

She looked around the kitchen, "Hmm, what does the rest of the house look like?"

And he took her by the hand and they walked into the bedroom.

Of course neither talked to anyone else about how they spent their time. Jane had shown interest during her visits to the hospital, had given Lydia ample opportunity to volunteer information, but there was not a hint. Still, Jane knew that Lydia was happy. She was self-assured, had always been that, but there was something else and Jane knew not to ask. She also knew this; on Lydia the confidence looked good and she hoped she had guessed the reason. The weeks rolled by and on weekends John didn't shave. Lydia went without makeup at 'home' the whole time. Thank God neither of them snored. They got frisky every night.

Finally John's duty took him to Hong Kong and four other ports with Commodore Cochrane. He was gone for almost three months. After the first night, she stayed in her quarters for the entire time, couldn't handle their bed anymore without him in it. And that's when the ache started, the physical longing that told her all she really needed to know. She now belonged to John and she knew it.

John was incredibly busy while he was gone; but he made up a list of his own, or at least he tried. He thought it would be easy but he kept trashing it.

He realized that he knew all the answers. He knew her when she was horny and when she wasn't interested. He knew her attitudes about many things, knew her better than he knew anybody else, knew things from her childhood. He realized how much he missed her and that this must be what being in love felt like.

CHAPTER 14

WHALEBOAT RACE

The last three weeks had gone by quickly and the ship had pitched in with some special preparations. First Division had requisitioned some dark blue paint and some of a bright gold color and unbeknownst to the Brass had painted the whaleboat a shiny blue with gold trim along the gunwales. They had lettered "Detroit" in gold lettering on the port bow and "Lahaina Moku" on the starboard bow. The sickbay had chipped in when his crew came down with blisters and then when the calluses on their hands built up and cracked and tore and bled. They stung when salt water soaked into the cuts. They got regular treatments in which the blisters were bandaged and then the calluses that replaced them were carefully trimmed and treated with surgical spirits which hardened the surface layer of skin on their hands. The mess cooks put aside good cuts of meat as well as extra rations for the race crew and for the last three days the crew was put on light duty so that they would be relatively rested and ready to go. Finally the equivalent of the old sailmaker made racing shirts out of very light canvas, sanded until it was soft and stenciled "DETROIT" on the fronts and "CREW" on the backs. Everyone was proud of their ship and they had turned out a fine looking crew and boat.

On a trip to Diamond Head with Gunny Clancy, Dantes had approached the management at the Royal Hawaiian Hotel and asked if they could provide a local contact who was involved in Hawaiian canoe racing. After a short discussion they left with the name of a Hawaiian who made canoes and raced them. His yard was at a small beach in a farming area, and it was an operation run by Holokai and his brother Kaikane Kekoa.

"Good to meet you, Dantes, Gunny. What can we do for you," Holokai asked. Dantes explained that he had gotten their names at the Royal Hawaiian, and that he was preparing for a boat race, not a canoe race but a whaleboat race to be held at Pearl Harbor within the month. The brothers smiled,

"That sounds like a lot of fun, guys, whaleboat, you say?" "Yes, we carry them aboard ship as a multipurpose boat. They were originally used by whaling ships to approach the whale and stab it with a harpoon." "The brothers responded with keen interest, "You know we have had a long whaling tradition in Hawaii, and Lahaina, Maui has been a whaling center for many decades." Dantes explained that he was looking for a paddle for his whaleboat. He wanted it to have a blade on each end, it possible, for use by the coxswain, or steersman.

A small smile crossed Kaikane's face, "I think I know why you want this paddle, Dantes. Your boat comes with a rudder, no?" Dantes nodded. "But each time your steersman uses the rudder to correct course it slows the boat down." And he grabbed Dantes by the shoulders, laughing, "You want to add a little bit of speed each time you correct course instead of subtracting it!" Dantes laughed with him, "Yes! And it might just be enough to make the difference in a two mile race between winning and losing." The brothers talked quickly in a smattering of Pidgin English and Hawaiian and then turned to Dantes. "We don't have such a paddle but we can make one. It will take us less than a week, maybe three days at the most. We will carve it out of koa wood, medium sized blades maybe eight feet long total." "That sounds perfect," and Dantes' expression asked, "How much." "My friend'" Holokai said, "We will make this paddle for you for free because you go to sea, just like Hawaiians. Our names mean seafaring person and master of the seas. We come from a long line of seafarers here in the Islands."

They shook on it and Hod told him about *his* first name," Hod" and that he had been given his name by his sister. "Sounds almost Hawaiian, Hod," Holokai said and of course Hod invited them to come to the races. They said they would like to do so and would give them their answer when they came to pick up their paddle.

Race Day at the finish line.

There was to be one race for the Cruisers and then one for the Battleships. The Battlewagons had their ship's Bands on main deck and paraded on their foc's'les and had set up tarpaulins for shade at the quarterdeck with seating for spectators and dignitaries. They were playing John Phillips Souza's, "Stars and Stripes Forever," and "Anchors Aweigh" as well as other martial airs. It was a festive atmosphere with perfect weather and no swells, just a bit of a breeze blowing across the course and at roughly right angles to it. A tug had been provided for all boats to get them to the finish line. When the race was called away each boat would row to the starting line, two miles away, as a warm up.

Dantes looked up at Hicks and his gaily painted war canoe paddle. It had shallow carving on the shaft but a smooth grooved area where Hicks would hold it when paddling. The carving depicted a whaleboat and a Hawaiian canoe joined by a square knot of friendship. The rudder and its hardware had been removed and a seat put in high in the stern to allow Hicks room to see and to paddle. He had gotten good at steering with it. Dantes thought that with a side wind blowing all boats would have to be using their rudders for the whole race. Likewise Hicks would be paddling for the whole race, just to keep them on course. They both looked over at the Kekoa brothers in their canoe. Permission had been granted for them to be at the finish line for the races. They had several burly Hawaiian paddlers and two guests of honor aboard their boat. They had brought food and drink and were ready to make a day of it. Waves and good wishes and thank yous shouted across the water and then Dantes took his boat to the starting line at an easy pace.

Word of the race had gotten around in Honolulu and the papers had picked it up. There was a nice little story about the Kekoas and their contribution to the race. The Mayor of Honolulu, George F. Wright called CincPac Head-quarters and invited the Admiral and his Staff down to Iolani Palace for a luncheon. It was a fine time and a friendly Hawaiian way of getting invited to the races and of course Admiral Fitz responded appropriately. As the Cruiser boats headed toward the starting line the Mayor, who was seated next to the Admiral and had been tipped in advance, looked through his binoculars and exclaimed, "There it is, the boat with the Hawaiian war canoe paddle!" The Admiral had already noted the one boat that was painted blue and gold and he took another, closer look. "That's Detroit's boat, I believe, Mayor, one of our Cruisers." Lodge, seated just behind the Admiral with his date, Lieutenant Crowninshield laughed in delight as he too looked through some binocs with a bright white sleeve over the leather strap. "I'll be damned and that's Dantes in the boat as the stroke oar. He had mentioned that he would be trying out for the whaleboat crew." Now Lydia and Auntie Jane were smiling and looking fondly at 'their' Dantes. Just then the steward brought some iced juice on a tray and another passed along the rows of seats with canapes and when they looked up, Detroit's boat, the Lahaina Moku had already pulled into the distance, easing rhythmically and lazily along toward the starting line.

All the boats got lined up and stern to the starting line which was marked by a buoyed line from one end to the other. Cox'ns were instructed to take hold of the line as a means of holding the boats in place until the start. There was an ebb tide which meant they would be rowing against a current; adding perhaps a minute or two to their elapsed time. Hicks repeated Dantes' softly spoken order to the crew, "Ready all!" And then a pause and a shot was fired from the starter's pistol in his motor launch and they all dropped their blades in and pulled. Further down the course, the Cruisers and Battlewagons sounded long blasts on their ship's horns and spectators rushed prematurely to the lifelines at the sides of their ships, straining and squinting for a look.

Dantes set an average pace of fifty strokes per minute, figuring to see where they stood in relation to the other boats. They slowly fell back to third place out of six boats, almost holding their own. Dantes said to Hicks, "Power ten." The order was repeated and they started to gain on the other boats. "Going up." "Going up!" and Dantes increased his stroke to 65 beats per minute. It was the stroke they had used in their sprint sessions and his crew was used to it and ready for it. Now they were moving on all of the other boats it seemed a half a seat at a stroke. The pace was too fast to get spacing between their puddle sets but they were advancing a boat length on each stroke and dipping into undisturbed water with each stroke and they pulled immediately ahead.

The other boats were noticing their advance and some of the crews broke discipline and called to up the stroke. When they did so they started falling behind a little bit faster. Meanwhile Hicks with the war canoe paddle was chipping in on nearly every stroke as the wind across their beam would have otherwise blown them off course. The motor launch had sped out to leeward and maintained speed with the pack and was there to keep an eye on things and make sure they didn't drift too far off course. Dantes had jockeyed for the upwind position at the start, figuring which way things would be likely to move and not wanting to have to dodge any boat being blown into them. As it happened, most boats stayed in their lanes or close to it and they all fell behind Lahaina Moku. "Dropping five." "Dropping five!" as Dantes eased his stroke just a bit and settled out exactly on 60 strokes per minute. The other boats also settled but as they did they fell further and further behind. Dantes could see that they had three lengths on the closest pursuer and were still gaining. He called for a silent ten. Hicks held up ten fingers and the crew put all they had into each stroke for ten strokes. Dantes asked for a silent twenty and the twenty power strokes were added to the previous ten. Dantes asked, "How far?" Hicks answered "500 yards." "Tell the crew five hundred to go and that we will do a power set for the last 100 yards."

And that's exactly what they did, finishing in a powerful display and at Hicks' call "let her run" they remained poised in the forward position, then again on his command they shipped oars and stood them up vertically with their dripping blades shining brightly in the sun. 'Boats' had done a great job as their blades were painted blue and gold divided diagonally across each blade. It was a handsome sight as the crew sat at attention holding their oars like so many knights with their staves, a salute to the viewing party!

Aboard CincPac's Flagship Admiral Fitz stood with a beaming smile, the guests with him as he rendered a salute to Lahaina Moku. The winning boat responded with three cheers for CincPac! Hip, hip HOORAY! Hip, hip HOO-RAY! Hip, hip HOORAAYYYYY!! As the other boats crossed the line they too were applauded.

The motor launch was motioned to the Flagship and the starter was given a request. He nodded and saluted and then took the launch over to Lahaina Moku, idling within speaking distance of the Coxswain. "Dantes?" getting a nod in return, "the Admiral requests you come aboard with your crew. You can tie up at the Jacob's Ladder." Dantes looked back at his crew and gave a fist pump; there were smiles all around. He asked the Starter, "Sir would it be possible to add two additional guests?" *Who does this swab think he is?* And as he hesitated, "I'm pretty sure he won't mind, Sir." *Yeah, like this halfwit actually knows the Admiral.* "I would like to go over to the Hawaiian canoe just over there and pick up two additional passengers." Not wanting to appear indecisive and thinking *what the hell* he said "Permission Granted," and started marshalling his Battlewagon boats for their run up to the starting line.

Lahaina Moku pulled alongside the Kekoa's canoe and excited laughter and words flowed. "Holokai, Kaikane we're invited aboard the Flagship at the Admiral's invitation! Come get in my boat and we'll take you there." And with great glee and much pride the brothers nimbly stepped aboard and they were quickly transported to the Flagship and tied up and went aboard, the crew first, followed by the two brothers followed by Dantes. When Dantes got aboard they were already formed up in a single rank and he just stood at the end of the line, next to the brothers. Admiral Fitz, along with CDR Lodge and Auntie Jane and the Lieutenant were moving slowly along something like a receiving line, stopping at each man and asking his name and saying well done, shaking hands and making compliments, the sailors awkward and wide eyed in their replies. As the reviewing party got to Dantes and the Kekoas a steward came and got the nine oarsmen and Hicks and took them below to the mess decks for a meal.

The Admiral shook Dantes' hand, "Well done, Dantes, extremely well done." Lydia and Jane felt comfortable with Hod and they smiled admiringly up at him, congratulating him. Just then the Mayor sidled up and stood next to the Kekoas with Lodge and the ladies looking on with interest. "So, Dantes, are you ready to race against the Battleships' boats?" "Of course, if that is what the Admiral wishes, Sir," but he looked a bit discomfited and cast a glance at Lodge. Lodge spoke up, "Just tell the Admiral what you think, Dantes." And Dantes' confidence leaped with his memory of the last time he had been told that, and how well it had worked out that time.

"Sir, I think it's apples and oranges. The Battlewagons race their equals as do the Cruisers. Besides, if this wind holds up there's a pretty good chance we'd beat the Battlewagon boat. And that might be very hard for the Battleship that lost to Detroit. It's supposedly all in fun, just like a tennis game, but we all want to win, Sir." Seeing that the Admiral was taking this in he continued, "If I might, Sir, I'd like to introduce my friends, Holokai and Kaikane Kekoa.

They provided the paddle that we used for the race." Admiral Fitz chatted with them for a bit and then turned to Dantes, "Why the paddle, was that your idea?" And Kaikane spoke up, "Sir, Hod Dantes is one very smart sailor. He knew that in order to steer with a rudder you slow the boat down every time you use it, just a bit. He wanted to be able to add to the boat's speed every time a course correction was needed. That's what he described to us at our yard, Sir." Admiral Fitz, with understanding dawning on his face exclaimed, "Then that explains your comment about the wind. As long as the wind was blowing all boats off course they would be subtracting speed to correct while you would be doing the opposite, adding speed." "Exactly, Sir." Lodge spoke up, "Was that it, Dantes, or were you not yet finished?" He knew that look when Dantes had something he was just busting to say.

"Thank you, Sir. Yes Sir I wanted to suggest that perhaps we could have a race between the Kekoa canoe and our boat." Admiral Fitz said, "And that's not apples and oranges?" "Sir, it is until we swap boats and that evens everything out. Their craft is much faster and more stable than our boat, and they will certainly beat us on one leg of the race. But on the other way back it might be a different story, Sir, it would be for fun and no worry about winners and losers." Just then the Mayor of Honolulu spoke up, "Well I think it's an excellent idea! Think of the boost in relations between my community and yours Admiral!" The two leaders, one military the other civilian, were now eagerly discussing the possibilities of a race from Waikiki to Diamond Head and back and Dantes and Lodge were looking at each other, both of them grinning.

CHAPTER 15

MORE LETTERS HOME

Dear Loraine, I really enjoy getting your letters, please keep them coming.

Let me start by answering your question about Dad and whether or not we are going to be like him. I find that as time passes I forget the tough times and remember mostly the good. I think it is usual to tend to remember the best and gloss over the bad; it's a natural thing. I remember him as a rough sort of man who made his way in the world and pretty much did everything he wanted to do. As for whether or not we might end up being like him, I suppose there are worse fates. For instance we know he was a crack shot with firearms and I'm finding that I share that talent with him. I got the best scores in rifle and pistol shooting in Boot Camp. While I don't know how or if that will be useful to me in my time in the Navy, I think it is a good thing to be able to hit what you're aiming at, in the Navy, or anywhere for that matter.

I admire his courage in facing down the two brothers who tried to kill him and I think that his courage is passed down to all three of us as we demonstrated that night he came through the bedroom door with his shotgun. We did what we had to do in order to survive, just like he did when he was a young man. I think that we should

just be proud that we are a family of Texans who can take
care of ourselves, no matter what. I'm sure he didn't
hate us, but maybe he hated his life at that time as he
was not very happy in his marriage after our Mom died. I
know that I missed her and if it weren't for Grandma I
don't know what I would've done.

It makes sense to me not to talk about that night with
others, not even the folks in Beaumont. It's our business
and nobody else's. If any bad comes from this it might
be that it will be hard to fully trust others. I leave
it to you whether that is a bad thing, but I will try to
be ready for whatever comes my way. I want you to know
that you were a very brave fighter and we could not have
won the fight and survived it without all of us pulling
together. Keeping something as shocking as that bottled
up inside might be like pus building up in an infected
cut; resulting in a sore or a memory that never heals.
So you should feel free to talk about it with me anytime
you need to or want to and I will do the same with you.
I know that if someone ever hurt you deliberately they
would have to answer to me and it is likely that violence
would be involved. In that regard I expect I am like our
Father.

I do have some memories of him and some stories that
you might not have heard or remembered. He had an air
about him that attracted both men and women and was a
jack of all trades and hard to pin down. He was strong,
ambidextrous and liked to drink and gamble. I never saw
him get mean drunk but when he had a few drinks he would
tell of some of the things that he had done. He had a
temper but was never mean to us. I was riding with him
one day in a model "T" Ford. The road was just a pair
of ruts and there was a man in a buggy ahead of us. He
would not move over and let us pass. Dad was mad and
when we finally came to a spot with enough room to pass,
we started around the buggy. As we got abreast of the
horse, Dad reached out and punched the horse on the side

of the head and knocked him to his knees. Dad could also be gentle and kind. He would come to the farm to visit us as often as possible and would always bring something for us. I remember one Christmas especially when he carried a big trunk into the house. We opened it and it was full of oranges and apples. That was something we never had to eat; they didn't grow in our orchard. This is the way I'll remember Dad, as a strong and kind man who often showed his love for his family. The Dantes' lived in Mississippi and the Indian Territory in Oklahoma and all their travels were made in a covered wagon. So if you consider the customs and the wildness of those days, the code of "an eye for an eye and a tooth for a tooth" you may understand why someone would kill another person in cold blood. I certainly don't think of myself as a killer but who knows what a person might do when in a fight for his life? Or in a war, for that matter. I expect that you do as you are trained to do and you do it without question.

A lot has happened since I joined up, all of it good. As you know I joined the Navy in order to make a living and escape the depression, like most young men my age. But the Navy has a way of changing you, I think, and it can be for the better. Totally by chance I had the opportunity to be in an Admiral's Quarters and it was magnificent. I suppose I will never again see anything quite so fancy. My Chief from Boot Camp is on the Detroit and he has looked after me and my buddy Daughter, and he has helped us stay out of trouble. I've had the opportunity to row whaleboats on the ship's team and to try out for the pistol team and make it, as well. As it happened an Officer, a Commander took an interest in me and has spent time talking with me about the Navy and the world situation, especially here in the Pacific. I've come to believe, as he does, that we are sooner or later going to be fighting a war here and the likely enemy is Japan. I actually hope that I am as ready to fight and win as our

Dad was. He did what he had to do in killing those two
brothers. In what's coming against us it will be much
bigger guns and much bigger fights. My reason for being
in the Navy now is much more than having a job; it has
become my job to train to be the best sailor I can be in
order to defend our country. I'd like to tell you about
some of that training and what it's like to fire the 6"
gun mounts.

The Detroit is armed with six 6"/53 caliber broadside
guns and two twin 6"/53 caliber turrets. The caliber (6
inches) is the diameter of the bore. The length of the
bore is 53 calibers (53 x 6"). This does not include the
length of the powder chamber.

I'll never forget the first time I heard these 6" guns
fire. Shortly after I came aboard we started training
for short-range battle practice, the most important gun
firing exercise of the year. If a gun crew gets all four
hits in the allotted time we get an "E" painted on the
gun shield and each member of the gun crew gets $15.00
prize money. In addition, the pointer and trainer get
$5.00 extra pay each month for a year, or until the next
short range firing practice.

The "pointer" sits on the left side of the gun, sights
through a telescope and moves the gun up and down, vertically, to keep the horizontal wire of his telescope on
target. The trainer sits on the right side of the gun and
moves it right and left, horizontally, to keep the vertical wire of the telescope on target. When the gun is
loaded, and the pointer sees the cross wires of his telescope on target, he closes the firing key.

I tried out for trainer and was good at it, and got
the job. I'll never forget that first short-range firing practice. I was sitting in the trainer's seat, keeping right on target. Then the gun fired - WOW. I bounced
about 6 inches above the seat, my hat flew off, I felt
the gun being loaded again, and then another blast. I
don't remember if I ever got back on target. When the fi-

nal round was fired, and I crawled out from under the gun
shield, I felt terrible. I thought I had let the gun crew
down. But, the entire gun crew were smiling. We had fired
all four rounds in the allotted time and the observers on
the bridge said that all four rounds were hits. We got an
"E" painted on the gun shield and I started drawing an
extra $5.00 per month.

It takes training and team work on the part of the
entire gun crew in order to get an "E". The gun captain
wears headphones and gets directions from "control" as
to when to commence firing and when to cease firing. The
man who operates the breech plug has to stand close to
the right hand side of the gun. He pulls a handle which
rotates the breech plug (unscrews it) in one motion. He
then puts a primer (like a blank cartridge) in the firing
lock. While he is doing this, and as soon as the breech
is open, the first loader shoves a projectile (wt. 106
lbs.) through the breech. The rammer man, with a long
wooden pole, then rams the projectile forward until it
seats against the rifling in the bore. The powder man
then puts the bag of smokeless powder in behind the projectile. The powder bag is made of raw silk (because it
will burn up without leaving smoldering residue in the
chamber). A grain of smokeless powder, for a 6" gun, is
about 1 1/2 inches long and about 1/2 inch in diameter,
with 7 longitudinal holes through it, so it burns from
the inside out as well as on the outside of the grain.
These grains are stacked in the powder bag and it is
laced up the side. A patch of black powder is sewed on
one end of the bag.

After the powder is in place, the plugman closes the
breech, and the gun captain yells, "fire one". If the
pointer and trainer are on target, the pointer closes the
electric firing key. Instantly, the primer fires, shooting flame through a hole in the breech plug, ignites the
black powder, it explodes and ignites the smokeless powder. The smokeless powder burns rapidly (almost instant-

ly). It generates tremendous gas pressure as it burns, which pushes the projectile down the bore.

The rifling (spiral grooves) in the bore cut into the soft rotating band around the end of the projectile and start the projectile rotating. It spins as it travels through the air. This rotation keeps the projectile from tumbling, thus making its trajectory stable, accurate, and predictable. When the projectile clears the muzzle, the gun recoils about 2 feet, and then slides back to its original position and the whole process starts over for the second round. Everything has to come together in order. If anyone slips up, wastes time (a second or two), or if the pointer and trainer are off target, you run out of time and no "E".

So I hope you enjoyed this little taste of Navy life. There's a lot to learn and we practice endlessly on load-er machines and in live firing exercises to get good at what we do. It's serious business and I am finding that it suits me well. I like the feeling that I am preparing to defend our Country and I'm proud of my ship and the Navy.

I'm proud of you too.

Write when you have time and give my love to all the folks.

Love,
Hod

————————————————

Dear Hod,

How exciting your life is now, in the Navy! Hawaii and San Diego and firing big guns and racing in boats and going to visit the Admiral. Did he ask you about life on the farm, in Lockhart? Just being funny, I can't imagine how Admirals and such would be interested at all in Texas goings on or what people from hereabouts think about anything. If he were really smart he might want your opinion about the Navy, though. You are the smartest one I know, in so many ways. It won't take you any time at all to figure out your way to the top and to become the very best at what you do.

I liked the way you explained Dad to me. I like being able to be proud of the menfolk in our family and you have sort of restored that for me in our Dad and of course it has always been that way for me with you. I'm thinking the gal that finally gets you will be someone very special!

We don't hear too much about war, in Beaumont. In school it amounts to learning about The Great War and how that started and ended. It seems it was mainly a great land battle with little involvement by navies. I know that the people in Europe are fearful of Germany starting up again. I hope that you will not have to be involved in any of that fearsome fighting at sea. And we don't hear too much about the Japanese.

On another subject, I want you to know that I do read parts of your letters to Aunt Leta and Uncle Bill. They love you and act just like a mother and dad to me. They love hearing about your exploits and adventures. I am saving all of your letters and read them from time to time. You and John are all the real family I have left and you both mean so much to me. Down at the movie theater where you worked they still ask after you. Do you remember the girl who used to work at the counter selling candy and popcorn? She sure remembered YOU! I only saw her a couple of times but she always asked about you. Well, she found a beau and married him and they've moved somewhere, Cuero, I think. The folks at the movie say they have had a baby boy. I think she named it Howard…

Just teasing again. I hope you are happy and think of us here in Texas often. You are too generous with me, sending what must be all your pay to me. It really helps out and helps me hold my head high with pride for our family.

All my love,
Loraine

CHAPTER 16

WESTPAC

Admiral Fitz and Commodore Dick Cochrane met in Fitz' study after knock off on a Friday. Jane brought them a pot of coffee and two charged cups, was thanked and quietly went outside where they could see her, tending some flowers.

"Goddam prohibition, anyway," Fitz muttered. Cochrane replied, "I saved a case of Johnny Walker and actually brought a bottle over with me, if the Admiral would rather try something harder,". Fitz grunts, "Why didn't you tell me in the first place," he laughed and went into the kitchen with the coffee pot and Dick followed with the cups of coffee. They poured it all down the sink, cleaned up and filled a bucket with ice and took a couple whisky glasses down from the cupboard and headed back into Fitz' study.

"You know I sat here with a Seaman First named Dantes one afternoon and heard straighter skinny out of him than I'll get from any three four stripers you could name. Present company excepted," he quickly added, "though you no longer count as a four striper, Dick, since your name got approved for Rear Admiral." They both leaned forward and clinked their glasses and took a long satisfying pull on their Johnny Walker Blacks. They sat there companionably, the Admiral now just the Fitz that Dick knew twenty years earlier, Dick just a shipmate and they finally both eased into comfortable postures in their chairs, sipping the fine scotch and letting the knots loosen and the memories burgeon, crowding out the present with hard lessons and good times from the past. Dick waited for Fitz to speak first and enjoyed the wait, letting the scotch waft into his face. Fitz broke out a mahogany cigar box and offered it to Dick. He lit up and Fitz soon followed. Outside the door the lady who loved one of them more than he could imagine smiled and went into her sewing room and stretched out on a little bed there. This had all the earmarks of an all-nighter and she was happy for them both. It had been too long…

"These youngsters don't know what's coming," Fitz said. "Don't I know it and it's because they don't know their history," Dick replied. "Hell, history is one thing but relatively recent history is another," Fitz said, "I know you spent a lot of time in the China Fleet, must have gotten to know the Chinese and the Japanese as well."

"Well, the Japanese are like a bunch of foreign talking Marines, Fitz, they come with lots of traditions and their own warrior code, Bushido. They will take death before dishonor and feel a deep kinship with and responsibility to their ancestors. And like the Marines, they fight all out to win; there is no alternative to victory. Their heroes are like something out of mythology, fantastic stories of superhuman talents and skills and the ability to deceive their enemies is highly prized, duplicity is to be admired if it gets the desired result. What we would call sneaky they find to be sagacious and completely legitimate. How they draw the line between falsity in their international relations and in business competition and their personal lives, I don't know. Their caste system is ironclad and an enormous amount of energy goes into appearances. Their women are strongly subordinated and there is practically no upward mobility. When I think of the concept of freedom my mind turns to countries like ours and the Brits. Japan is too tightly controlled to be thought of as free."

"Ought to make for a ready-made system for warfare, scalable if they have the population and the resources, and at least initially overpowering, whomever they pick as a target," Fitz said. "Exactly, and they are quick to learn and to adopt successful tactics and technological advances."

"They have contempt for all Gaijin and though the Chinese are not exactly foreign, more like distant relations, they have contempt for them too. Japan got the jump on all of the other nations in Asia as a direct result of Perry opening them up to foreign influence and industrialization. Japan was a different breed of cat, never sinking to the powerlessness of China and instead swiftly reforming and modernizing their military and particularly their Navy. There were the Sino Japanese wars that Japan tried to downplay as a series of incidents in order to escape sanctions and meanwhile many countries set up business in their cantonments in China and had their way with her. This was not lost on Japan and they contested with the Russian Fleet for local dominance and won. They went about gathering resources including appropriating Manchukuo from China. In summary the Japanese are feeling their oats and now have a military and a strong warrior caste that wants to use it. They need resources, especially oil, and they know where to get it. As it sits it's ourselves, the Dutch, the Aussies and the Brits that stand in their way."

"Tell me, Dick, what do you know about Yamamoto?" "He's more a contemporary of yours, Fitz, a hot runner who is smart, connected and politically experienced. He is their Navy's best strategic thinker and has often been at odds with the aggressive Imperial Japanese Army. His name, Isoroku means the number 56, the age of his father when he was born. His family was of a middle Samurai rank and he probably had few prospects until he was adopted by the Yamamoto family, of much higher Samurai rank but without any sons. It was a mutually beneficial arrangement that opened doors for him while conferring the rewards of a sparkling career on his new family. He studied English at Harvard and the word is that while there he hitchhiked to Texas and spent a lot of time in the Texas oilfields. He's a Japanese Naval Academy Graduate, fought in the Russo Japanese War where he lost a couple fingers at the Battle of Tsushima Straits, Commanded a Cruiser as his first command, shifted over to aviation and commanded the carrier Akagi. His areas of greatest tactical experience are gunnery and aviation. He did two tours as the Naval Attaché in Washington, speaks English like a native and once visited our Naval War College as a Captain. I'd say that if any Japanese knows and understands the United States it is Yamamoto."

"And you say he opposed the Imperial Army." "Yes, he was against the invasion of Manchuria and supports gun boat diplomacy rather than invasion. It is my guess that if he survives he will be the head of the Imperial Fleet." With upraised eyebrows, "Survives?" "Yes, well the Imperial Japanese Army is aggressive and its senior Officers have great influence with the Emperor. To oppose the General Staff is generally not conducive to a long life." Cochrane grimaced, "We are all students of Sun Tzu, certainly all Asian military leaders are steeped in his teachings. Sun Tzu says 'if you know your enemy and know yourself, your victory will not stand in doubt.' It seems plain to me that the Japanese see us as a potential enemy and they have sent Isoroku Yamamoto to America to learn about us." With that the Admiral Selectee sat back and let his friend top off his whiskey glass. When he'd done the same with his own glass, Fitz looked at his friend over the rim of his Johnny Walker Black and said, "And now it's our turn. I'm not sending you to Tokyo but I do want you to go on an information gathering expedition. We'll frock you first and you can take Lodge with you and I want you to pulse our friends the Dutch, the Staff in the Philippines, the Brits. You will go to Hong Kong, the P.I., the Dutch East Indies and Australia and I want you to find out whatever you can about what the Japs are up to and what our capability is if we are called upon to oppose them. We'll want to put on a good show while we're at it, so you can have a cruiser as your transportation. Lay plans for at least two months, maybe more. We can lay on refueling and resupply if and as required."

Two weeks later the Detroit embarked Rear Admiral Cochrane with LCDR Lodge as his accompanying Staff Officer, broke out his broad pennant and got underway. They'd managed to coordinate their port visits with liberty port visits by deployed units and were expecting to complete their cruise in two months.

Several weeks later on the Detroit's Starboard bridge wing, somewhere in the South China Sea, it was after the Second Dog Watch and Admiral Cochrane had just come from the Flag spaces to get some fresh air. The Chow Line had been secured and the ship's company had knocked off all work. Only the watchstanders were evident by their presence. The normal daily noises of the ship had calmed and an air of peaceful watchfulness had settled over the entire ship. The noise of the ship's fairwater slicing through the slightly rolling swell sounded a gentle shush to any topside sailor who might venture to raise his voice above a muted conversational tone. The ship was too far from land to attract the noisy gulls and the dolphin and flying fish playing in the ship's bow wave made no sounds in their frolic. The sun's orange orb was approaching the horizon and the ship's Navigator was on the flying bridge with the Quartermaster Chief to observe sunset and, as nautical twilight set in, to shoot some early stars for a decent positon fix. The smoking lamp was already out on all topside spaces since the glow of even a cigarette could be seen for miles over a dark ocean surface and the more diligent among the sailors were already rigging light traps in anticipation of Darken Ship being set. It was the time of evening that being at sea was made for, where the immensity of God's creation was overwhelming proof of His omnipotence to even the most doubting of Thomas'.

Lodge quietly exited the Bridge and slipped one of the dogs down to secure the Water-Tight Door from swinging. He approached, clearing his throat to gently intrude on Cochrane's consciousness. Mostly as an excuse to get to talk with his mentor, he carried with him a routine note from the Flag Watch Officer.

"Excuse me, Sir. The Watch would like to inform you that they have received a message from CinCPac. It's routine stuff but before you turn in you might want to see it." "Roger that Commander, I'll make sure to stop by there on my way below." Cochrane paused, not taking his eyes from the surface of the sea. "Isn't this the most peaceful time of a ship's day, Lodge? I was just sitting here and thinking that if it weren't for the fact that we're the human part of one of the most technically advanced weapons of war the world has ever known, this would be a perfect depiction of God's Peace on Earth. Of course the irony is that despite this peaceful feeling, I am discomforted by the knowledge that it will all evaporate sometime in the very near future into something the rest of the world can scarcely comprehend."

"Sir?" Lodge softly replied.

"Lodge, I've spent most of my professional life here in the Western Pacific, and most of that time I've been watching the Japanese slowly and patiently taking over whatever territory they can to consolidate their hegemony over this corner of the world. Ever since Perry opened their eyes to the technology and imperial reach of the West, the Japanese have made maximum effort to assimilate the lessons they can for their own purposes while molding them into their warrior code.

The Japanese mind, particularly their military mind, is very like a sponge in that it soaks up every little detail, just as we do, but the similarity stops there. They filter everything differently than the rest of the world. For centuries they have kept all foreign influence out of the islands. They dislike and distrust all foreigners. They beheaded any Gaijin who dared venture upon their soil even by mistake or in times of extremis. They were totally isolated from the rest of the world by choice. That created some unique situations. First, ethnically they are a virtually pure people. Second, they developed their codes of war, of honor, indeed of life in a separate, parallel path to the rest of the world. They don't play well with others at all. They view all other peoples as you might view a mongrel, junk yard dog, for exactly the same reasons. They have particular distain for the other Asian races. Westerners can be understood because to them we are savages. But, the Chinese, Koreans, Mongols and so forth, in their eyes, should have known better. Since those people have been trading and interacting with the West since Marco Polo, they have become tainted and not worthy of Japanese respect.

They have a surplus of population on a series of islands which are almost devoid of natural resources and cannot support their basic needs. Since they have the attitude they have about others, and they view them as dogs to be subjugated, it is only natural that they feel it their right to take what they need from their neighbors. At the end of the last century, they saw Europe and even the U.S. take claim to what they view as Japan's rightful hunting grounds. While the West was defined by its growing Nationalism, Japan started as a nationalistic state and became even more so. They viewed the Dutch in the East Indies, the Germans and Spanish taking over the islands of the South Pacific, the French in Indo-China and the Brits in India, Hong Kong, Singapore and even Australia as a direct threat to their way of life. Then when America fought the Spanish and took their holdings they were even more worried. They understand the axiom of logistical superiority. Europe can only barely hold on to their possessions in the East by having exceptionally strong Navies, but America sits on the other bank of what they view as their very own lake, and is their primary threat for control. They've read and understand Mahan's *Influence of Sea Power*. They know strong Navies can be maintained only by establishing a world-wide network of coaling stations.

"That's why they came in late to the party at the end of the War in 1918. They declared war on Germany too late to do any fighting, but not too late to have a seat at the table when the spoils of war were divided. They grabbed all the formerly German islands in the Marshalls, the Carolines, and the Marianas and made them their own. Then when we tried to relegate their Navy to second class status at the Washington Naval Arms Talks, they elicited promises from us and the Brits to stay out of their backyard by not fortifying any of our bases in the region. All of that just to keep their lines of supply from the Dutch East Indies and French Indo-China intact and free from Western interference. They need the rice, the rubber, the oil, in order to support their industrial growth. Economics drives politics every time. And they need the industrial growth. In order to match and surpass the West to re-take their 'rightful' place of superiority, they must have the resources.

"That's also why they invaded China, Korea and Manchuria and fought the Sino-Japanese and Russo-Japanese wars. They believe it their right to do so. We ignore their nature at our peril. Their people believe their very lives are meant to honor the Emperor. To them he is divine, he is a God. And in fact, their highest honor is death as a sacrifice for him. That makes them a very dangerous enemy. In a fight, they will gladly die rather than surrender, and we underestimate that as a motivation for their national greed. And as troops in the enemy lines, it's not enough for us to achieve military superiority on the battlefield. Victory requires us to become their executioner in order to beat them."

After several moments to take it in and try to make something of all of it, Lodge quietly replied. "Sounds as if you think that war with them is not only inevitable, but almost scarier than the Great War in Europe was just 15 years ago."

"You're absolutely right! Many brave Americans will be sacrificed in a bloody war over national pride and greed. And the horrible thing is that it's not out of the question that if it comes to war, we'll end up fighting Germany in Europe at the same time. With the Treaty of Versailles, we've set them up for failure, and failure brings out the crazies in the form of irrational leaders," Cochrane responded.

And with that, both men stood silently taking in the dying rays of the Sun as its top crescent hung briefly above the horizon, before suddenly popping out of sight with a brilliant green flash.

In the First Division Berthing Compartment, Dantes was shining his shoes as they passed the word for mail call. The non-rated with the duty got up and went to the post office to get whatever there was for First Division. He came back and started passing it out on the mess table and calling out names when he didn't see somebody sitting there. Dantes! Yo! "You got two." Daughter sidled up to him and grabbed the letters and sniffed them. Dantes looked up with amusement, "Not going to find any perfume on those," he said. "What? No lady friends writing to you Dantes?" "Gimme those, I've been waiting to hear from my Sis." Daughter paraded around the table, bouncing and holding the letters in his cupped hands as though they were hot! "You mean to tell me you got no women panting after you, Dantes?" And he laughed and dropped the two letters in front of Dantes, managing to miss the open lid of Kiwi polish with water in it. Dantes picked them up and stuck them in his pocket. He'd read them later, when he had a bit of privacy and more time. Right now he was getting ready to go topside for the 2000-2400 watch and he wanted to look sharp. Not everyone polished their shoes but Dantes always did and he had a sparkling clean set of dungarees and white hat to go with his shoes. He had a deal with the Machinist Mate in Main Control to let him use their steam iron, the one that the shipfitters had cobbled together and hooked up to a low pressure steam line. He checked the time, still plenty of time. He made it his policy to be on station to relieve early, at least ten minutes early. That way he often got to relieve on the helm instead of just lookout. Early bird got the worm and he liked steering the ship. He also figured there was a chance he'd run into Commander Lodge on this watch. It was three days out of Pearl and he hadn't seen him yet. The scuttlebutt was that they were going to several ports and he knew that the first one would be the P.I. Perhaps the Commander would tell him what the purpose of these visits was. Then he might or he might not have something to write about to Loraine. She enjoyed hearing about the ship, he just had to be careful that he didn't breach any security rules.

Finished with a turn at the helm and lee helm, Dantes had rotated out to the port wing of the bridge and donned his binoculars and was scanning his sector from just across the bow to dead aft when he heard the soft clang of the starboard pilothouse door being opened and closed. He heard someone greet the Commander. *Yep, they all seem to like the starboard wing*, he thought. He even thought he knew why. It was like driving a car, the vessel on the right or starboard side had the right of way and a Conning Officer or Commanding Officer could often be found there, just checking things out for himself. A little disappointed at missing Lodge he just bore down and concentrated on sweeping his sector, when he heard the door again and then the one on his side, the port side.

"Evening, Dantes." A slow smile crept out on Dantes' face, "Commander, good evening to you, Sir." "Been awhile, Dantes, you staying out of trouble?" Dantes' quick mind pictured Lieutenant Crowninshield and a swift rejoinder to his superior about trouble was swallowed. "Yessir, doing my best, Sir." But the "Sirs" were not overly formal; they were more conversational. This was a conversation between two sailors who respected each other, and their relationship was an easy one in spite of the yawning gulf between them of their stations in life, one a former Texas farm boy, the other a Boston Brahmin. They hadn't been so far apart when Lodge was in the backseat of the staff car with the Lieutenant and he had been driving and had turned the rearview mirror down. Of course the Commander knew first hand that Dantes kept a closed mouth with private business and with privileged communications and he very much enjoyed his chats with Dantes.

"What do you know about what we're doing, Dantes?" "Not nearly as much as I'd like, Sir, scuttlebutt…" "Nah, anybody can start scuttlebutt, I want to know what you *think*, Dantes, not what you've heard. Just then the OOD came out on the port wing, asked Dantes if he had any contacts, looked Dantes up and down, greeted the Commander and went back inside the pilothouse. With a little extra time to think, Dantes said, "Sir I believe we will be tussling with the Japanese in the next big war and I think that both nations are getting ready for it. My guess is that we are going on an investigation of some sort, seeing what we can find out about their preparations and their intentions and perhaps as well make a judgment about our own readiness to defend ourselves or to attack them." With that he stole a glance at Lodge to see his reaction. "Right on, Dantes. The Japanese have been sniffing around, sending their intelligence gatherers to places like Washington, D.C., and Boston and they have a large contingent in Hawaii on a permanent basis, monitoring our Fleet units and gathering whatever information they can get. We can't very well go to Japan and get our intelligence from the Japanese, there is no freedom of movement there as there is in our country. So we go to our friends in the region and keep an eye on their movements and what they buy and where they concentrate their strength."

"By the way, Lieutenant Crowninshield sends you her good wishes and asked to be remembered to you." "Thank you and please say the same to her for me whenever you get the chance." Dantes could see that Lodge wanted to say something more, and he waited. They both spoke at once, "That was a very fine evening." And then they both laughed. Dantes saluted the Commander who returned it and saying goodnight exited the bridge. Back in the compartment after watch he found that Daughter had rigged his hammock for him. He stripped down to his skivvies, put away his watch standing uniform and rolled into his hammock with his letters and a flashlight. He barely had time to get the flashlight off (it had a red lens cover) before he fell asleep, the letters unread.

CHAPTER 17

MANILA

Hod was standing the helm watch on the special sea and anchor detail as the Detroit entered Manila Bay. The Island of Corregidor had just slipped by to Port and he could see the twin volcanoes of the Bataan Peninsula beyond it. Off to Starboard they had just passed Fort Franco and Fort Drum. Fort Drum was interesting; it looked like a battleship built on a rock with cannon everywhere. He was concentrating on the helm orders and his gyro compass repeater but so far they were steering a fairly straight course, allowing his mind to wander. Manila! Just the name made you think of things foreign, like bamboo and thatch, manila line, street vendors with exotic food that the sailors called monkey meat on a stick. And the women were reputed to be good looking and friendly. Very friendly. "Mind your helm there, Helmsman!" And Dantes blushed under his pressed whites, down to his toes. He cursed to himself for his inattention. It was the first correction he had received on the helm.

Lots of the crew had been to the P.I., especially the old hands and they'd been telling Hod all about the beautiful women, the glorious sunsets, the palm tree lined avenues, the busy streets, shopping districts, especially the Escolta and of course of the bars and bordellos with their warm red lights welcoming the sailor in from the sea. One mentioned often was a place called La Playa. It was a restaurant and bar operated by a bunch of American ex-pats from Shanghai who had a love for gambling and making money off the many Americans and Filipinos with their Las-Vegas style casino, craps, roulette and black-jack tables. It was bright, colorful, noisy and always busy. They kept pretty women moving in the crowd and offered cheap drinks to keep you at the tables and the roulette. Sometimes the drinks were free, anything to loosen you up and get you to spend. Rum was cheap in Manila.

Cruising at 15 knots the trip from Pearl had taken three weeks and Hod was looking forward to getting off the ship. This was nothing like the San Antonio, Texas area where the water was confined to swimming holes, rivers and creeks. It was hard to imagine that there was this much water in the whole world. Seeing it from sea level was a lot different from the globe in his old school room back home. He had missed home but that was all forgotten this morning as he anticipated going ashore. He wondered what it would smell like. Tijauna smelled like beer, booze and bad whiskey. Honolulu had the sweetest smelling orchids and flower leis. He'd heard that Hong King smelled like diesel exhaust, others said it smelled like money! He finally wanted to get some monkey meat on a stick that the Gunny had been telling him about, the real thing. Letters from Loraine had kept him grounded, but he hadn't seen mail from her since the mail call they'd had a couple days out of Pearl. He wondered if and how the miracle of the mail system would catch up to them when they arrived in port.

Every sailor on board had those same desires. Strangely enough, it usually didn't take most of them very long in port before they wanted to get back to sea. For one thing they always ran out of money; for another they needed to get back aboard to get a decent night's sleep in their own hammock. True, the hours aboard a Navy ship could be and usually were chaotic, but the routines were set up to ensure that every hand was given enough rest to be able to function. Liberties and port visits were designed for recreation, something different. It was a great system and it had worked for centuries for everybody but the Brits. In the old days they had pressed their crews into service and had they let them ashore the crews would have deserted. In order to keep them happy aboard ship they kept them semi-drunk with Navy issue grog, a mixture of rum and water. When they got drunk they got in trouble and were lashed with the cat o' nine tails. The US Navy had started out with grog and lashings but soon did away with both.

Lodge found that he missed Lydia, missed her a lot. She had been staying in the house up Nuuanu Valley ever since he had moved ashore with the Commodore and had gotten a new assignment on Admiral Fitz' Staff. Certainly they both had enjoyed and gotten used to the pleasures of married life, without all the responsibilities that marriage would entail. But now he found he was fretting just as though he had those responsibilities, felt deep inside that he was responsible for her, furthermore he started thinking less of himself for claiming Lydia without doing the right thing by her. He had never missed anyone like he was missing her now, and it drove him to his desk to write her letter after letter, even though he didn't know when those letters would ever leave the ship. He laughed to himself, *I will probably see her before these letters do.* Yet still he wrote them almost every night and in them he said something he had never actually told her. "I love you, my Dearest." Going to sea was an adventure for many reasons, not least of which being the chance to encounter attractive women in foreign ports. But now there was a bittersweet aspect that tugged him in two competing directions. The adventure was still there, but the desire to be home and back in her embrace was a very lonely feeling that had never been there before. Now when the thought of finding a woman ashore crossed his mind it also occurred to him that Lydia could be having the same sorts of thoughts about, for instance, *Rod Kinney*! He didn't *know* if she was writing letters in the night and missing him as he was missing her. Certainly it was her right to consider other men, after all she said that there were invitations, lots of them. He had thought that they were just playing it cool, enjoying the time together, with no commitments, but now he wondered and thought perhaps it was just a bit of Brahmin self-respect, that Lydia of course was not going to speak first. She was waiting for him! At least he now hoped that was the case. And so he tortured himself with these thoughts each night as he tried to fall asleep. No more the self-contained Naval Officer, but instead a very smitten and lonely guy who needed to see his woman and hold her and believe the evidence with his own eyes. For the first time he really understood the line in Robert Louis Stevenson's poem *Requiem*: "Home is the sailor, home from the sea…" Home now was more than just a place, it was a tangible state of being which included another person. Furthermore he discovered that it would not be the same place without her. She had made a home out of a mere house, claimed it without a word just as she was now claiming him. He was a goner and he knew it. And it wore on him not to be able to tell her these things, except to a scrap of paper in his small, lonely stateroom.

After many long discussions with ADM Cochrane on the transit, Lodge was anxious to fill in some of the gaps in his knowledge of the atmosphere of the Far East, particularly what the folks in the region actually thought as opposed to what the bigwigs in Headquarters said they thought. ADM Cochrane had made it clear that much of the prevailing thought, the commonly accepted wisdom of the people who made the strategic decisions, was colored by professional bias and filtered by ignorance of the actual situation.

They already had appointments set for calling on the commander of the U.S. naval forces in the Philippines as well as a tentative meeting with a man named Manuel Quezon who seemed to be the most influential leader in the islands. As they approached the anchorage, Lodge along with every man on the weather decks, strained his eyes to gather in the view. Each of them was looking for his own sights to see and for the chance to experience all that there was to do in an exotic foreign land.

The overall city was a surprise. There were lots of tall buildings and a very cultured look of Spanish influence was everywhere. Lodge had already spied the Manila Hotel sitting near the base of Pier Seven, the longest pier in the eastern pacific and maybe the whole world. The hotel stood five stories tall and fairly dripped of exotic opulence. The roof was covered with a jungle of plants and flowers which gave an air of sophistication unlike anything Lodge had ever seen. They had already made reservations to stay there while the ship was in port. It would be their base of operations while conducting their meetings for the next few days. Truth be told, his overnight bag had been mostly packed for days now. He had thrown in his razor and shaving kit this morning and had it ready on his bunk awaiting the word that the barge was ready to take them ashore.

It was different coming into port as a part of the admiral's staff instead of as a watch stander driving the ship. For the first time he got to actually watch the whole evolution without being responsible for the outcome. He could pick out the nuance of minor course and speed orders to the helm and lee helm. He was able to watch the leadsman in the chains casting his line and calling out the depth of the water as they approached the anchorage and the Boatswains on the fo'c'sle as they prepared to drop the hook. This was a dance that had changed little in well over three hundred years of sail to the age of steel ships. There were still a few of those oldsters around that considered themselves a part of the last of the era of wooden ships and iron men. The materials of construction and the technology had changed but the dance was constant.

The Navigator had long ago looked up on ship's drawings the distance in feet from the hawsepipe to the pilothouse. His job was to put the hawsepipe directly over the assigned anchorage while getting fixes on the position of the pilothouse, for the pilothouse is where the Navigator plotted his lines of bearing from known objects on shore. The LOB from three such objects gotten at the same time on the Navigator's mark when plotted would tell the Navigator where the pilothouse was at the time the bearings were shot. The devices used to measure the angle to the landmarks were peloruses, gyro repeaters of the ship's gyro compass. Of course by the time that position was plotted the ship had already moved some distance, so you ended up knowing where you had been but not where you were at any instant in time. As a consequence the Navigator laid out in advance three bearings that converged on his chart to the spot where the pilothouse should be when the hawsepipe would be directly over the anchorage. In the final approach he received constant bearings on his sound powered phones and with a little lead time he recommended to the OOD to "let go the anchor." By the time the order was relayed and the anchor was let go the hawsepipe and anchor should be directly over the anchorage. At the time the anchor started its downward plunge a final set of bearings was taken to determine how close they had gotten to the target. Immediately upon letting go the Conning Officer would back down slow in order to pay out chain in a line and not a pile. This way as the chain paid out it would tend away from the stem of the ship and not grind against the side. The ship's reputation around the fleet was made or broken with such detail, and the Detroit was proud of her ability to properly perform those acts of seamanship that counted to other true sailors.

The "let go the anchor" order was relayed to the First Lieutenant who was in charge on the fo'c'sle. Within seconds everyone came to life as a sailor used the sledge hammer he was holding to knock the bale off the Pelican Hook which held the chain from moving. As it snapped open, the chain leaped from its state of rest and charged across the deck like a freight train at full speed running off the end of a destroyed railroad trestle. All hands knew to stay well clear of the area to avoid being caught by the angry chain and strained through the hawse pipe as the huge anchor ran free. A little known fact was that although the anchor flukes did grab a piece of the sea bottom, it was the weight of the chain that did most of the work of holding the ship in place when at anchor. The entire length of chain was put together with a series of shots, the length of each shot was 15 fathoms and the end of each shot was marked by a painted code of red, white or blue paint so that the crew would know how much chain was out. The second to last shot was painted entirely yellow and the last shot entirely red; to warn the crew that it was nearing the bitter end. Everyone knew that if they ever saw yellow running free that it was too late to do anything but try to save themselves as the bitter end was about to pull out a good portion of the bow as it went over the side.

This day as the chain paid out it slowed as well until the proper length was over the side, at which time the capstan brake was applied and the Pelican Hook was re-applied to take the strain off the capstan. The bale was then tied off so that it wouldn't accidentally slip and have the chain pay out unattended. Finally the First Lieutenant sent his report to the bridge. The anchor was set with 50 fathoms of chain on deck, tending 010 degrees relative, under light strain. The length of chain on deck was determined by the painted code marking the shots, and it was laying off the starboard bow at about 10 degrees. One of the sailors had put his foot on a link of the chain to feel if there was any bounce or chatter indicating unusual movement of the chain. By experience he could tell that the ship was pulling against the chain only slightly therefore being under light strain.

While this was going on the Boatswain's Mate of the Watch gave a whistle on his pipe signifying that the ship was no longer underway and announced the ship was anchored, and to shift colors. Immediately the National Ensign on the jack staff was lowered and the Ensign on the stern and the Jack on the bow were broken. Day shapes were hoisted from the signal bridge to warn nearby ships that the Detroit was anchored and unable to maneuver. The boat crews were busy swinging out the Barge and the whale boat to respond to any requirements for boating. It was as if all shipboard evolutions were waiting with bated breath for the anchor before leaping into action. Within minutes all was quiet and the ship had transitioned from an underway routine to being in port at anchor and ready to react to an entirely new set of events. And on the bridge an anchor watch was set with Quartermasters taking bearings and entering them into a log, and plotting them as well. As the tide and winds shifted the ship would move some; the watch was set to be able to determine that she did not move too much. A set of two Danger Bearings was drawn on the chart and the chart crosshatched in magenta where the ground was dangerous or too close to shoals or another vessel. The magenta color was used because it would still show up in a red light whereas the normal color for danger, red, would not. The price of good navigation, even when trying to stay in the same spot, was constant vigilance.

Flag spaces, where Admiral Cochrane was going over some last minute staff matters with Lodge. "We all set with a vehicle?" "Yessir, is should be at the landing when we get there." Cochrane smiled, "You know, the evening when CincPac informally gave me this tasking he said something that I'll not soon forget." Lodge returned Cochrane's look with interest, waiting. "I think you'll find this interesting as well. Admiral Fitz actually brought up the name of a Seaman First with whom he'd had a sit down conversation in that same study where we were knocking back our scotch. Said he spoke more sense, more intelligently about the coming conflict in the pacific than any three or four Captains he could name." Lodge beamed at that news, "Sir, of course he was talking about Seaman Dantes, the man who was my driver in Pearl." "What on earth do you think he was saying?", Cochrane asked. Now it was Lodge's turn to remember and respect a confidence. "Sir, I confess that Dantes and I have had several conversations on the bridge when Dantes and I happened to be there at the same time. He asks extremely good questions and thinks faster than most. In all likelihood Dantes shot straight with the Admiral and I would guess that the Admiral expected him to keep their conversation to himself and he has done so. My guess, if you want it, Sir, is that he sounded very much like a Commodore I know, and offered a succinct evaluation of the situation in the Pacific, albeit without the Intel we expect to get on this cruise." Cochrane chuckled, "Lodge, I want that man with us as our driver and unofficial assistant aide for the rest of this trip. He may be driving us, and hauling our cases from time to time but I would also value his eyeballs on the scene as well." "Aye, aye Sir. Might I suggest that we do this in combination with a shore duty assignment so that we can arm him in an inconspicuous manner? He is a crack shot, and member of the Detroit's pistol team. I've been reading classified accounts of insurgent activity, some of it pretty close to Manila, Sir." Cochrane immediately agreed and Lodge then suggested that they might also include in their shore party Chief Radioman Locker, who would be useful in securing their communications. A nod from the Admiral and a "very well" and Lodge was off to visit the XO, to get it nice and legal.

The Messenger of the Quarterdeck watch came into First Division compartment and called out, "Dantes?" Dantes and several of his shipmates looked up with interest. Dantes, who was getting ready for liberty, pulling on a fresh set of whites, paused and answered, "Here." The Messenger went up to Dantes, "OOD said to inform you that you are going over on the beach as Shore Patrol, assigned to Admiral Cochrane's party and you will also serve as his driver. Here are the keys to the staff car. You will be staying with his party for as long as he needs you; OOD says you can put in for any reimbursement when you get back and keep your receipts." "Tell the OOD, Aye, aye and when do I have to report." "Right now or as soon as you can drop by the armory and draw a weapon and brassard." Daughter, who had the duty, said he'd go get the weapon and sign for it, to save Dantes some time. "Don't want to keep the Admiral waiting, Dantes. How many does this make for you, now, Two?" And at that the rest of his mates laughed and kidded him, some of it envious and all of it good natured.

On the quarterdeck a ladder was over the side to the waiting barge, already hooked on and standing by. Hand gear and a couple of boxes had been swung into the craft and all were waiting for Dantes to get in the barge, as junior man, followed by the Chief and then Lodge and finally the Admiral, who was piped over the side as his flag was hauled down. When he was settled in the stern sheets the crew in the bow cast off and they were headed to Fleet Landing. Chief, who was seated next to Dantes, gave him a barely noticeable jab in the ribs and said under his breath, "What you got me into now, Dantes?" Dantes, with some familiarity and also under his breath replied, "I'm not believing that you don't already know and frankly I was going to ask the Chief the same question." They both smiled and remained silent for the rest of the trip to the landing.

CHAPTER 18

THE TAYAGS

Admiral Cochrane approached Manuel Quezon in the Army Navy Club in Manila. "Thank you for agreeing to meet with me here, informally, Sir." "The honor is mine, Admiral; tell me, what brings you to Manila?" Cochrane smiled, "I am sure your intelligence operatives know well what brings me here and have briefed you extensively." Quezon smiled in his turn, appreciating the compliment, left-handed though it was. With the initial polite fencing out of the way, Cochrane wanted to know of Quezon's concerns, "I *have* of course tried to keep up with your movements in the Philippines, for to know what you are up to is to know where we and the P.I. are headed." And Quezon replied, "And I truly hope that the United States and we make that trip together. As you are no doubt very well aware, we are moving inevitably to an independent Philippine Government. At some point after Colonial, Insular and Commonwealth types of government we will take our bow on the international stage as a fully independent Nation." Cochrane nodded, took a sip of his tea and with his silence encouraged Quezon to continue. As Quezon took a sip as well, perhaps to gather his thoughts, the Admiral said, "I expect that when that happens that you will be President."

"Sir, who is President is not as important as that we move forward together. I am very concerned about the Japanese. They collaborated just two years ago with a semi-religious sect or movement, the Tayag Insurrection that was also pushing for independence but with Japanese aid. We know that the Japanese would not be a benevolent ruler or partner like the US has been ever since Dewey defeated the Spanish in the Battle of Manila Bay. The Japanese are showing their true colors even now in China and Korea. They have no resources of their own and are moving forcefully to take them from other countries. With our position here in Manila Bay, some would say the Paris of Asia, we sit astride Japan's trade routes and lifelines. They covet our resources and strategic position and absolutely mean us no good. Yes, there is a transition coming and it will be critical to do it in such a way that when you leave you also leave us with the means with which to defend ourselves."

Cochrane leaned forward, reached out across the table to Quezon, "Sir, I am Dick Cochrane and believe you to be totally correct." Quezon took his hand, shook it as he stood at the table and stepped closer, "And I am Manual Quezon, your friend for as long as you are a friend to my Country and my people." Cochrane had reserved a small room for this meeting and he now asked Manual if it would be alright if he invited his Aide, Commander Lodge, to join them. Quezon nodded, once, with a smile and remained standing while Cochrane went to the door to fetch him. Lodge entered with a briefcase and introductions were made and the three of them sat down as Lodge got another chair and opened his briefcase. Quezon noted that it had a hand cuff attaching it to Lodge's left hand. "I wanted to be able to record our remarks and understandings as we go forward," Cochrane said, I will sign a copy and you may as well, if you wish. It won't be a formal agreement between our two countries but it will be an accurate record of our discussion. These remarks will be classified SECRET and we will take precautions to handle them as such, as I hope you will also do." Quezon nodded again and listened closely as Cochrane brought Lodge up to speed on their conversation to this point, with Lodge taking notes. Lodge looked up, "Sir, I took the liberty of ordering a small lunch, if…" And both Cochrane and Quezon smiled their agreement and Lodge went to the door to signal a waiter.

Over sandwiches and tea the two leaders discussed how the US had behaved in the P.I. in the past. At one point Cochrane brought up BG Arthur MacArthur, USA who had been the Military Governor General in the Philippines. He mentioned that he did not get along too well with the US civilian Governor Howard Taft. As a consequence he was reassigned and promoted, shifting his flag to a new assignment, while Taft went on to become US President. Manuel looked up with interest, "You know we are well aware of his son, Douglas, who became the youngest Chief of Staff of the Army. He also served here in the Philippines in various engineering assignments. Of course we would welcome him back with open arms and there would be no problems with our President, here, were he to join us. I think we are going to need a lot of help building our armed forces into an effective fighting unit." Cochrane replied with a wry look, "Manuel, I actually played against MacArthur on the baseball field, when the Naval Academy team played the West Point team. He played right field in the 1902 game and ran down a deep shot of mine to the wall, threw to the left fielder serving as relay and a strike thrown to home plate snuffed out my inside the park home run!"

As they all chuckled appreciatively, Lodge spoke up. "Sir, not to change the subject, but I am interested in any possible immediate threats. You mentioned the Tayag insurrection, which was put down only a year ago and that it also had ties to the Japanese." "Yes, well the leader of that group, which numbered some 40,000 at its height is thoroughly discredited." "And the Japanese, have they continued their subversive activities?" At that Quezon looked uncomfortable for the first time that afternoon. "I am not fully briefed or up to date on Japanese involvement. Sorry I can't be more informative. Our soldiers, though ill equipped, are brave and fierce. We will not be found wanting as an ally if and when it comes to that," Quezon said. And rather than make excuses for how busy he was in these uncertain times he just looked at his watch. It was clear that the meeting was over. After he had been ushered to the door and his waiting Jeepney, Lodge turned to his Boss in some embarrassment, "Sorry for the way I handled that," he said. Cochrane smiled, "It needed to be said and it was better that you were the one who did it." Cochrane looked at his watch, "About time we headed for our meeting with the Navy folks. We're set up in the Manila Hotel?" "Yessir and I also have Chief Locker and Dantes in a room right next to ours. It was good of CinCNav in the P.I to come over from Subic, saves us a lot of time."

In the Manila Hotel they were met in the lobby as they came in from their staff car, with Dantes trailing and the Chief not far behind. After a minute or two of catching up, for many on both staffs knew each other, they repaired to Cochrane's Suite where a large table had been set up. The Chief sat off to one side with the chained briefcase and Dantes took up position on a chair out in the passageway. CinCNavPI proffered a small stack of documents to the others around the table. They listed all seagoing assets for which he was responsible as well as their manning and commanding Officers. The second sheet showed The Ship Repair Facility, Subic's capabilities and assets and listed their manning in terms of skills, both Navy and civilian. A short paragraph described the work orders they had fulfilled over the past year. Then there was a reckoning of his annual expenses and the projected shortfall for the coming fiscal year. After reviewing the stack and asking for clarification a few times Cochrane pushed back in his chair and said, "Al, what can you tell me about the Nips?" Captain Al Jordan USN also pushed back and took a pull on his coffee. "Sir, they are way too active for my comfort. They pull in here on one pretext or another, saying they need repairs and it's all bullshit. Their fleet units are topnotch, well maintained and those arrogant S.O.B.s want us to know it. When they go on liberty they pick fights and belittle practically anyone with whom they come into contact. We get regular reports of bargirls and Mamasans getting beat up or worse. They are arrogant and full of hatred for the Flips and especially for Americans." Cochrane wrinkled his brow, looking up from his coffee, "Any contact with their Senior Officers?" "No Sir, not much. And they've had invitations. It's as though they go out of their way to put us in our place. I'd say they are taking our measure and figure that we're just a bunch of uncivilized dogs waiting to get our asses kicked. If that's all they do." "Word out of China and Korea is that they take heads and kill at the drop of a hat. And I'm talking prisoners of war as well as non-combatants," Cochrane replied. "Yessir, to them all foreigners or *gaijin* are beneath their contempt. It's as though they are justified in taking anything they want and they usually do it in the most brutal fashion." It was a grim party that pushed back from the table and shook hands all around to the tune of thanks for hosting us, thanks for the skinny and what are you guys doing tonight? Cochrane said, "There's a shindig here at the hotel tonight, Uniform I'm informed is Barong Tagalog and there will be real booze and real women and dancing. No Japanese though. You gentlemen are welcome, I'm sure." And with that they all shuffled out the door checking their watches, some of them going down to the lobby to get rooms, others looking into getting back to Subic tonight.

Back in their somewhat smaller two bedroom suite the Chief and Dantes sat for a bit, with iced San Miguels in a bucket. "Dantes, I'll take the watch tonight, cover the party and the dance. I'll keep control of all the classified stuff we have and handle anything that the Commander might have for me communications wise. Why don't you go on liberty and see the sights, try to have a good time without getting into a gun fight with a drug running pistol waving husband, for a change." At that Dantes gave a small grin, "I reckon I'll take off my Shore Patrol brassard, then, and leave the pistol with you." Sounds good, son, and have a good time but stay out of trouble, if you will."

Dantes went into his room, called down to the front desk and inquired about a Barong, size medium, which the front desk was happy to provide for him. He showered and sent his uniform down for laundering and put on his spare trousers and the barong when it came, looked in on the Chief who whistled at him and said, "Look out for the women." Then he sortied out to the front and hailed a Jeepney. They were lined up down a tree lined road, coming instantly on the signal of the lobby guy from the hotel. Dantes didn't know how much to give him so he just thanked him and got a very nice smile in return. He also caught some glances from two ladies standing on the corner, figured that they were in business but no business of his. He told the driver he wanted to go to the bars and dancehalls where the girls were. The driver smiled and said, "We got girls in *all* the bars, and Mamasans too." "Okay but I don't particularly want to go where the Americans usually go. I want to go where the locals go." "Dat's where the black man go and the people from out in the bush and just everyday Filipinos and Filipinas go to have fun," the driver replied. "Sounds good to me. Take me where you might go, later on tonight." With that the driver put his gaily decorated and garishly painted Jeepney into motion, honking and tooting the many horns mounted on it, driving like he was being chased and had a death wish. They pulled up in front of a one story place, nicely painted with the door open and inside there was a wooden floor, not packed earth as he had seen in Mexico. He paid the driver who said, "Maybe see you later on tonight. Be a little careful, they're not too used to Americans in this place." And he was gone in a cloud of dust and gas fumes.

Inside it was not too busy. Dusk was just setting in and the girls were still arriving, as well as the early bird regulars, on their way home looking for a beer and a dance, maybe more. It was cool and not too bright, with lighting at the bar and a semi-gloom at the tables. It smelled like beer and a bit of flowery perfume. Maybe the working men smelled like sweat, he didn't know. He noticed that all the girls looked him over but none of them came over to him. Finally a guy from behind the bar stood by his table, "You lost?" he asked. "Nah but I am a bit thirsty," Dantes replied. The bar tender didn't ask he just went to the bar and came back with a San Miguel. Dantes looked at it, said, "You got Kirin?" There was a bit of respect when the bar tender came back with the beer with the Dragon on the Label. Dantes didn't necessarily care for Japanese attitudes but the word down in the compartment was that their beer was superior. More expensive, too. At last a girl, very pretty and nicely dressed came over and asked if she could sit down. Dantes got up from his chair and seated her, just like he used to do for Grandma. At that *all* the girls took a second look. "I'm Rosa," she said holding out her hand to be shaken. "Dantes," he replied with a grunt and a bit of a smile. "First time in the P.I.?" she asked. "How could you tell?" he replied. "Not too many white men come in here," she answered. "You must be pretty brave," she ventured, or *pretty dumb*, she thought. "I'm not looking for trouble, I just want to dance." "Do you know how to dance like a black man," she asked. "No, but I might like to learn." Well the way it works in here and in all these places is you buy me a drink and then we dance." "Rosa, then I guess all we will do is talk 'cuz I ain't buying any drinks just to dance." With that she smiled, thanked him nicely and got back up from the table and went over to the place where several tables were pushed together and the girls sat like vultures, looking over the men that came in.

With the ice broken and the place filling up the rest of the ladies started making the rounds, always asking could they sit down, sometimes getting a watered down 'drink' sometimes not. The music started, records not live music, and soon most of the tables had drinks and girls and earnest conversation with some dancing. The Mamasan nodded in his direction with a bit of a frown and suddenly he was besieged with a parade of women, all asking buy me drink we go home, or buy me drink we dance, maybe *then* go home. Always Dantes just politely said no thanks. Then finally Rosa came back to his table and just sat down. She asked him where he was from. "Texas", he said. What was he, in the Navy, she asked. What did he want to do, here in Manila?

And did he have any brothers and sisters and where did he get those big blue eyes.

So they talked for awhile and he asked her if she would show him some of the moves the black guys made. She looked quickly over at the Mamasan and said, "Okay, but not for long." Five minutes later they both sat down and she started to get up when he motioned the barkeep and said a drink for the lady, please. Rosa sat down and nursed the drink and was glad the Mamasan didn't get after her to hit the tables again. They talked for quite awhile and she really seemed interested in him. Rosa pointed out a few of her friends, saying, "That one was once a mere maid and now she is making better money right here," or "Maria over there has been doing this for years, is in love with a Naval Officer and hopes he will come back soon." Dantes was learning quickly. "So, the real money is made when you take a man home for the night?" "Yes, and there are expenses, too. Usually they need a ride back to work or to a ship in the morning. We have regular boyfriends who have scooters and they give them a ride."

Just then a rough looking customer came in the door and looked around. Rosa nudged him and said, "That one, he's Tayag." "What's that," Dantes asked. "He is with a group of fighters that consider themselves insurgents. Their group were defeated and lost power about a year ago but he comes in here and spends money and when one of the girls takes him home he talks very angry about the United States. I think you should watch yourself around him. These men, they carry machetes. You know machete?" "Yes, I'm aware that they are used to cut sugar cane in the States." "Well here in the P.I. we still have head hunters. They're used for that, too." She looked at him appraisingly, "You want to go home with me?" "Not tonight, Rosa, not tonight. But thank you. Perhaps I will see you tomorrow night." He looked over at his driver, the one who had brought him here. The driver excused himself and came over to his table. "You ready to go back to the hotel?" "Yes, and I'd appreciate a ride." He didn't notice the Tayag listening in on their conversation, but Rosa did. She came out to the Jeepney with him and warned him again. "That Tayag was giving you a lot of attention. He knows you're American, everybody in the bar knows that. He's already turned down going home with his favorite girl tonight. You be extra careful, Dantes with the blue eyes."

Back in the Manila Hotel Dantes checked in and went up to his room. "All in one piece?" Chief asked. Then he said, "The Admiral and the Commander are dancing and whatnot in the Ballroom. Put on your uniform and take up a station where you can monitor goings and comings. You're back on Shore Patrol duty until they are turned in, assuming that they do that in their own beds." Dantes did as he was asked and returned to the Chief for the .45 Pistol. Chief got it out of the room safe and Dantes checked the chamber, checked the magazine, racked a round into the chamber and flipped the safety on. He holstered it and quietly left the room and strolled up to the ballroom. The dance tonight was being held on the roof, amidst all of the greenery and lush foliage planted up there. It was a beautiful view and a soft, pleasant night. Lodge saw him and made his way over. They stood at the parapet and looked out toward the Bay. "Beautiful night," said Lodge. "Yessir. I think I like Manila." What he was going to say next Hod would never know because just then there was a commotion at the entrance to the Ballroom.

He ran over to the noise with his hand on the holster and was amazed to see three men in fairly shabby clothing, one of them the Tayag pointed out to him by Rosa. Two had knives across the throats of women in ball gowns and the other, the Tayag whom Dantes had seen at the bar, had a machete and was striding purposefully toward the Admiral. In an instant Dantes quickly shot both of the men with the knives and then turned toward the Admiral, shouting, "Stop!" The Tayag hesitated just briefly and that's when Dantes went Pop-poppoppapop, the pistol bucking only slightly and under precise control by Dantes. The Tayag slid to a stop, having fallen forward on his face, with blood starting to pool under his chest and spreading. In a delayed reaction several women screamed and then were calmed by their dance companions. Dantes had already run back to the entrance and stood in the door, checking to see if there were any more coming. Manual Quezon and the Admiral examined the machete wielding attacker and with an embarrassed and apologetic look on his face Quezon turned to Cochrane and said, "A Tayag, one of the band that Commander Lodge was asking about this afternoon." Lodge meanwhile had joined Dantes, "That was some shooting and you made your mind up so quickly!" "Sir, it was Tayags, and they're known for their hatred of Americans." And Lodge looked even more closely at Dantes, wondering where he had come up with that knowledge. The Admiral came up as did the hotel people. They were apologizing that they hadn't stopped the men sooner and greatly relieved that an armed sailor was on hand. "You just never know when these insurgents might show up. I thought the Tayags were shut down," said the hotel Manager. And now Lodge was truly impressed. Dantes had identified them in an instant. *How could that be?*

The party was over for sure, the police had come and were interviewing everybody and hotel workers had to be stopped from cleaning up until the crime scene had been processed. Within an hour all was calm and a bedraggled bunch of party goers were allowed to go home. Manual Quezon talked to the Chief of Police who was now also on the scene and Dantes was given back his weapon and thanked profusely by the police and Quezon himself. The Admiral just stared hard at his driver and beckoned him over. "That was some shooting, sailor. Thank you and well done." Dantes was thinking of his Father's gunfights and also thinking that he was glad he had inherited some of his Dad's traits. Almost absent mindedly he replied, "Sir" to the Admiral, who looked with concern at Lodge and asked him to see Dantes back to his room. The police set guards in several places and the hotel Manager hoped that they could keep this out of the newspapers. Chief was concerned about shock, and kept an eye on his sailor until he had gone to sleep.

Dantes did so almost immediately and slept like a baby.

The morning after the Dance, the Chief and Dantes walked into the hotel's dining room. Lodge motioned to the two of them to join them at their table. They did, took seats and the waiter approached and took their orders quickly and efficiently. The two Officers made as if to wait until their food arrived and the Chief insisted they eat before it got cold. Meanwhile the Admiral poured a coffee for each of them, lingering over Dantes' cup before he handed it across the table, fixing Dantes with a piercing and a bit of an emotional look. "Dantes, it is no exaggeration to say that you most likely saved my life last night." Dantes didn't know what to say and so he just sat silent and waited for the Admiral to finish. Cochrane continued, "And due to political considerations and the wish not to embarrass a fledgling Philippine Government we will make no fuss about it, whatsoever." Dantes looked respectful, stayed silent but nodded his understanding. "I will mention to your Commanding Officer something extremely complimentary about your duty performance, of course, but I would prefer to keep this one close to the vest, not to talk about it." There it was again, an Admiral talking to him, a mere Seaman First, and asking him *not to talk about it*. "I understand, Sir, Aye, aye Sir." And a strange look passed over Lodge's face as no doubt he and Dantes were thinking almost the same thing. Lodge spoke up, "Sir, I am personally acquainted with Seaman Dantes' reliability and integrity." "And now we're all acquainted with his marksmanship as well as his extreme effectiveness in an unexpected emergency," the Admiral added.

As the wait staff were clearing away the breakfast dishes and scrubbing imaginary crumbs into their waiting palms with rolled cloth napkins, Lodge shook his head, "no, thanks" to another pot of coffee and they all hunched forward over the table for the business part of an impromptu meeting. Cochrane looked at Lodge who then asked, quietly, "Dantes, tell us, how did you know that those assailants were Tayag and that they were most likely going to attack? I mean, your recognition of the situation was seemingly instant and there was no hesitation in your action." Cochrane added, "We had only learned a bit about the Tayags yesterday afternoon from Manual Quezon and even he didn't have the most up to date information."

Chief Locker had heard some of Dantes' story in their room and he had joked with him, "*happens every time, the bargirls and the Mamasans always get the skinny first!*" In any event he waited in some amusement to see how Dantes would handle the inquisition he was about to receive. To his surprise and delight, Dantes came off sounding like the salt he wasn't, quite yet, "Sir, you know scuttlebutt; some of the best comes from the Mamasans and girls in the bars." A bit of a smile played at the corners of the Admiral's mouth but the Chief just sat there and beamed like a proud Sea Daddy.

Dantes described the salient points of last night's liberty: the Jeepney driver, going to a place at Dantes' request where the Americans almost never went, getting a free dance lesson in how a black man danced, being befriended by Rosa, a bargirl who noticed the Tayag who "happened" to come into their place and her mentioning to him the Tayag hatred of Americans. "Sir, it was she who noticed him listening to my conversation with the driver, she who told me he had refused to go home with his favorite girl that night, she who warned me, twice, to be wary of the Tayag and mentioned their use of machetes. I just figured that I'd better get back before any trouble got started. If it hadn't been for Rosa I wouldn't have been informed at all, wouldn't have had a warning. Maybe some in that quarter don't like Americans, but she certainly does. Of course I had no idea that he would come to the hotel and bring two more with him. And it was Chief who also warned me to stay out of trouble, Sir. So as you can see, Sir, I was just lucky."

Cochrane smiled at that and asked, "Do you think you could find her again? "Yes, Sir I think so." Lodge then picked up the conversation, "Dantes, we need more information about the Tayag and more specifically, the Japanese with whom they have been collaborating. We think that the Japanese are funding the Tayag and building an organization that would be useful to them, sometime in the future." Dantes knew exactly what they were talking about, as he already believed that they were going to be at war with them before too very long. "Sir, if I might offer a suggestion?" "By all means," the Admiral said. "I think that the Mamasan might be the one who knows the most about the Tayags who come there, into her place and I couldn't say for sure whether she sides with the US or with our likely enemies. So, if I do find Rosa, say tonight, it would be a good idea to get her out of the bar, someplace where she could talk freely, without being overheard. If I go, I would find out from her about Mamasan, perhaps without making the Mamasan suspicious."

Cochrane looked up at the Chief, "How does this all strike you, Chief?" "Sir, it will take someone with experience to talk to the Mamasan, if we think she might be cooperative. Dantes has a good idea about checking the situation out first with Rosa, though. Depending upon what Dantes finds out from Rosa we can make plans that might include the Mamasan. Also, getting him in and out of the bar quickly would reduce the chances of another run in with Tayag people, in case they frequent the place in numbers. Not everyone will know about the ruckus on the roof last night, but it's a sure bet that the Tayag will be missing that guy with the machete and it's only a matter of time before they will be asking questions." "How much to buy her out of the bar for the night, Chief," Cochrane asked. "It's been so long that I wouldn't know, anymore." Without missing a beat, Chief answered, "$20 US in Manila for all night with an early start, less in Po City."

Turning to Lodge, Cochrane asked, "How much and when do we tell the locals?" "Sir, after we have something that confirms Japanese involvement I say we go to Quezon and partner with him, let them take it from there with any assistance they might request." "Make it so, and let's give Dantes a little extra for Rosa; she's taking a pretty big chance and has already helped save our bacon. We can afford fifty US… and Dantes piped up, "Could we afford a hundred?" They all laughed nervously and Cochrane nodded at Lodge, to make it so. Lodge paid the tab and they all made their way back to their rooms.

By midafternoon Dantes had his money and a set of inconspicuous clothes and Chief had the Staff car for backup. They each had a .45 and they had also requisitioned Gunny from aboard ship, with a third. All three were outfitted with civilian clothes, all three had extra cash and they had talked some about how to run the operation. Lodge came down the hallway for a briefing, approved the plan and Dantes turned in for a nap until the sun went down while Chief and Gunny drank a few San Miguels in the living area of the suite, going over contingencies.

At 1700 they piled out into the portico and Chief said, "Remember the danger signal? The one where you are saying you need help?" Dantes answered, "Sure, Chief, it's the Coast Guard salute," and he hunched his shoulders and held his arms out to his sides, palms up, as if asking for help or expressing bewilderment. Chief and Gunny smiled, "You got it. Now go out there and have some fun. We'll be in the background and we'll leave you alone. If you get her to her place, all you'll have to do is come out and give the signal and we'll find a way to get you out of there. It'll be totally your judgment as to how much you will trust her; just don't tell her anything about the Admiral's involvement." "Aye, aye, Chief."

This time Dantes started out walking down the tree lined street until he came to the Jeepnies. There were maybe twenty of them, all different and all garishly painted and gussied up. As he walked past the first car without getting in he got a dirty look. He knew he was supposed to get in and take them in order. But he wanted his driver from the night before and thought he'd at least give it a try. As he got toward the end of the line he saw it, at least he thought it was his ride from last night. He rapped on the window and startled the driver who was asleep. He recognized Dantes and rolled the window down, looked him up and down, "You supposed to take the first car in line." "Yeah, but I want you," and he pulled out twice the fare for the trip and stuck it in the window. The driver said get in, took the money and peeled around, headed away from the hotel. "Where to?" Oh, I don't know, take me on a sightseeing trip and also I'd like to drive through that neighborhood where you took me last night. Remember?" "Yeah I remember." Nobody noticed the grey navy sedan that was following about a block back.

After a tour of churches, downtown and statues and Government buildings they went into the bar district where he was expected to go. It was brightly lighted with music blaring out the open doors and lots of girls on the sidewalks. They parked and actually went into a place and had a Kirin, turned down five offers and then headed out again. "Take me to the place where Americans don't usually go," Dantes said. I want another dance lesson. The driver looked at him as though he was crazy and headed for that part of town. Before he got there but by the time Dantes knew where he was he told the driver to stop, paid him a nice tip, got out and told him good night.

At about 1830 he showed up at the bar, went inside and sat down at an empty table. It was pretty busy and Rosa wasn't in sight. About the time he started to be concerned he felt arms around his neck from behind, and Rosa's voice, "Hello, Dantes with the big blue eyes, you come to see me?" And she sat in a chair next to him and put her hand in his lap, her other elbow on the table and said, "Well, you going to make me dance with you first, or you just going to buy me a drink?" Dantes called immediately with sign language to the barkeep, for a drink for Rosa. The Mamasan looked up from her notebook and smiled, this was more like it. She never forgot a customer. Dantes smiled at Mamasan and when the music started he and Rosa got up to dance. "You seem very different tonight," she said. "Ahh but you seem the same, Rosa, just like I remembered you." She smiled and rubbed up against him on the dance floor. As they sat down, Rosa was thinking about how she could drag this drink out and maybe spend more time with him before she had to go to another table. She was surprised when Dantes said," I would like to go home with you tonight, Rosa." A look something like momentary disappointment flashed across her face. *Maybe he is just like all the rest.* But she looked at him with a bit of merriment, "That usually takes place at closing time, Dantes. I can't leave early, not unless you pay a lot more." Chief had told him to expect this and to offer $15 and ask Rosa to do the talking. She came back and said, "She says no, you must pay more. Why not stay here for a few hours and then we go?" Dantes said, "wait," and he went over to the Mamasan. She looked up and said, "Too early. Buy some drinks and then you can go, maybe for $20." I think maybe now and maybe for $25." "I understand you got the hots for Rosa, she's a very pretty girl. But she hasn't done her work for the night. You want to go now, you got to pay, pfff $35 US." And she looked at him like she knew it would be turned down. Dantes put two twenties on the bar, said five for Mamasan and went back to get Rosa.

On the street they hailed a Jeepny and Rosa gave him instructions. On the way Dantes had him stop at a liquor store and he went in and got a bottle of rum and some Coca Colas. Then they continued down smaller and smaller streets to dirt paths and tiny houses and finally to a little place on the end of the street. They got out, he paid the driver and they went inside. As she went into the privy he found two glasses and mixed some rum and Coke, no ice and took a sip. Rosa came out, sat down at the table and looked at him, really looked at him. He gave her a drink and sat with her. She finally broke the silence, "Dantes, you surprise me. You seem very different from the sailor last night who wanted to get a free dancing lesson." " What do you mean, different," he asked. "Ohh last night no money, tonight lots of it, free spending. Last night not knowing what to do, tonight full of confidence. Which Dantes is the real one?"

Dantes had already decided to trust her. He put down his drink and said, "The Tayag you warned me about?" She nodded, a frown crossing her face. "He's dead, along with two others." Her face showed total shock and surprise, so he knew that the word hadn't gotten out yet. "But, how do you know that," she asked. "I actually saw it. It was an attack on some Americans but it was broken up and someone had a gun and shot the three of them." "You *saw this*" she said, with disbelief in her voice. "And you are still alive to tell of it?" "Yes, well it had lots of people upset, I'm surprised there was nothing in the papers about it," he said. Rosa continued to stare at him. "And just what, exactly, are you doing here, Dantes?" He turned toward her and said, "I'm here to thank you, I believe that the Tayag was out to perhaps do me some harm and your warning helped me to stay out of trouble." At that she relaxed a bit, but still had a questioning look in her eyes. "Thank me? How," she asked. "I have some money, and I thought it would be the best way to say thank you." Rosa took a large swallow of her drink, "This is the real stuff," she coughed, "not like the watered down champagne they sell you for us." "What do I have to do for this money," she asked; "I've done nothing for you yet." He gave a large sigh, "I want some more information on the Tayag," he said. "It's not too healthy to be talking about them. I took a chance when I warned you last night." Dantes took fifty dollars out of his pocket and put it on the table. Her eyes got big when she saw it. Dantes asked, "Mamasan, she knows everything that goes on in her place. Is she friendly to Americans or more sympathetic to the Tayag?"

"Mamasan is friendly to everybody. Everybody is her customer." "Yes, but do you think she is loyal to the Tayag or does she appreciate what the Americans are doing to give the P.I. their freedom?" "These are political questions, Dantes, are you really a politician?"

Dantes laughed, poured another drink and said, "I think she is perhaps afraid, if anything, about the Tayag and sympathetic toward the Americans." "And I think that you are right," Rosa said, with a toss of her hair as she held her glass out to be refilled. Dantes looked at her, "Don't be afraid, I am going to go outside and tell a couple of men from my ship something and that they can go." Rosa looked again at him, nonplussed. He got up, went outside and gave the signal, adding the come here sign. Both Gunny and Chief were there in less than a minute. "Go ahead and speak to the Mamasan. I figured you might as well do it now, before the word gets out about three dead Tayags." "Okay, you staying here?" "If I don't get thrown out, yes. See you tomorrow back at the hotel."

With that he went back into the small home and this time went into the tiny living area and sprawled out on a threadbare couch. He had noticed that the money was no longer on the table." Rosa came into the living room dressed in her nighty. "There is a toilet but you have to pour the water," she said. "Also, don't mind the skittering sounds in the ceiling, it's the rats. They make noise all night. You get used to it." Then she went back in to her bedroom, turned back the sheets and got in bed. Dantes went into the head, washed himself and went to the bed and looked down at her. She smiled up at him and patted the bed next to her. "I don't understand exactly what you're up to, Dantes, but I like you, the real one. Come show me the real Dantes."

Across town the Chief and the Gunny knew the bar from their earlier surveillance. They parked a couple of blocks away and went in. Gunny took a table where he could watch the door and bought a drink for the first girl who approached, while Chief went straight to the Mamasan. In Tagalog he bid her good evening and asked her how was business. She replied in admiring English that business was fine but she was always looking for opportunities. Chief suggested they might have more privacy in her office whereupon they repaired to a small locked space behind the bar and next to the head. She was all business as was he. They sat down she offered him a cigar and they both lit up. "How may I be of assistance," she squinted through the sharp fumes from the cigar. "We need some information on the Tayag and especially their Japanese friends, the ones whom we think are funding them." The Chief replied. She leaned across the desk and stuck her hand out, "You may call me Mamasan but my name is Rosario Gabangabang." Chief said, "Locker, Wallace Locker." For just a second he thought she was about to crack wise about Wall Locker, but she didn't. Instead they talked about her sources and their connections and the reliability of her information, all without mentioning names. At the end of a half hour's discussion they had an agreement and a price. They agreed to meet at the hotel in the morning to conclude their business at breakfast. As he was about to leave, she said, "There's been no report yet but I am hearing that there was a shooting last night and that three Tayags were shot and killed. You know anything about that?" "As an official response I must say no, Rosario." She smiled at him and said, cryptically, "That Dantes of yours, he is really something, isn't he!" Chief kept the surprise off his face, nothing surprised him anymore when it came to these Mamasans. He just smiled and let himself out of her office, picked up the Gunny on the way out and then they headed back to the hotel, figuring that Dantes could probably handle what he had in his lap for the night.

In the night, with the rats skittering in the rafters and their bright eyes peering over the edge, looking down at the bed, a young sailor but not still a kid, a Texas farm boy no more but an international lover in the making was all tangled up with a real woman. One who liked him and was soft toward him and who took him into her arms and gave him what he had wanted, it seemed, all of his life. He could not get enough.

CHAPTER 20

HONG KONG

Pulling out of Manila occurred without incident, the ship coming to short stay with the anchor chain retrieved and hosed down and stored back the space that held the giant links, all of them except the last shot which held the anchor itself. The OOD gave permission to bring the anchor aboard and there was one long blast on the ship's whistle to indicate change of status from anchored to underway as the anchor broke ground and started its final travel straight up, followed by three shorts, indicating backing down. Using the starboard engine ahead one third and the port engine back one third the OOD pivoted nearly in place, spinning to his initial heading for departure. As the anchor was hawsed and snubbed and operations ceased on the fo'c'sle the special sea and anchor detail was secured except for the watchstanders in the pilothouse and Main Control, in the forward engine room.

Relations on a Flagship tend to follow a pattern of Senior Officer staying out of ship's business and ship's Officers, especially the CO, painfully aware that the ship was under constant scrutiny for everything from the appearance of his ship and crew to the way she performed, under all conditions. Cochrane gave a satisfied grunt and left the Flag Bridge with Lodge in tow. Before heading to Hong Kong, their next port of call, they would pay a short visit to the US Naval Ship Repair Facility in Subic Bay, just a short steam away and on the other side of the peninsula down which they presently cruised, with Corregidor coming up on the starboard side. Pier space was available in Subic so the ship anticipated a couple of nights of liberty in Olongapo, referred to by China Fleet sailors as the "Pearl of the Orient." Olongapo, or "Po City" as the town was also known, was just across the Olongapo River from the base. It lacked any of the refinements of Manila but had all of the hustle and twice the filth. Po City was one long string of bars, clubs and shacks serviced by a fleet of Jeepnies and bar girls. It was known that if you wanted to know anything about the movements and schedule of US Fleet units all you had to do was ask in the clubs and bars.

In Admiral Cochrane's cabin in the Flag Spaces, he was saying, "Lodge, I won't be needing either the Chief or young Dantes during our stay in Subic. We'll take them with us in Hong Kong, however. Please let Chief Locker know that and ask that he keep a close eye on Dantes; I think it is reasonable to assume that there will be some sort of reaction for a sailor so young, having been placed in the situation he faced so well. Lodge nodded his agreement. "Also I'd like the Chief to pulse his network of Mamasans in Olongapo to see what they know about the movement of US Fleet units and also those of the Imperial Japanese Navy. Anything they may have heard about port visits, ships in company, Senior Officers. I expect that they hear from merchant skippers and the fishing fleet and we'd like all the Intel we can get. Lodge gave an Aye, aye and his look said, anything else Boss? "One more thing. It may be tough on Dantes not to talk about those shootings but I want a clamp down on any and all of our activities ashore. Have Locker see to it." Lodge passed the word on to the Chief and the Chief caught Dantes, coming down from his stint at the wheel after they tied up alongside in Subic.

"Dantes, Gunny and I are going over on the beach tonight and we thought you might like to join us. Commander Lodge and the Admiral won't be needing us while we're here and told us to get ashore and let our hair down," he chuckled. Dantes looked a bit surprised, agreed to meet on the Quarterdeck at 1830, after chow. As they approached the bridge into town the smell of the floating sewage on the Po River assailed their nostrils, contesting with the smell of monkey meat on a stick for dominance. Looking over the side Dantes spied kids swimming in it, hollering for the sailors to throw coins to them. Several sailors did so and the kids dove quickly to retrieve the money and then returned to the surface to repeat the exercise. There was a ruckus as a young Officer in civvies collided with a woman who had grabbed his hands and pulled them to her breasts, screaming as though she were being assaulted. Her confederate was out of luck, though, jamming his hands into the Officer's back pockets for his wallet. The Ensign had been warned to expect this sort of dodge in a crowd and especially on the bridge. And he had put his wallet in his front pocket with a twist. The woman quickly disappeared and the crush of liberty hounds pressed on into the streets of Po City.

Over San Miguels and a Kirin for Dantes, seated at a table in the cool "Willows Bar" the Chief mentioned to one of the bar girls that he would like to talk to the Mamasan. She looked at her watch and at the Chief, shrugged her shoulders and passed the word to the lady who ran things at the Willows. Locker turned to Dantes, "It's not strictly a carefree liberty; we also are tasked with finding out what we can about IJN Fleet unit movements. Oh, and by the way, I probably don't need to tell you that the Admiral expects that nothing will be said about any aspect of our time in Manila, especially the killing of those three Tayags." While Locker talked Gunny closely watched Dantes' reactions. Gunny *had* been fired upon in anger and had taken lives as required with whatever weapon was at hand. He knew that killing, no matter the surface reaction, took a toll. They needed to know how Dantes was affected, that's all. Gunny spoke up. "You feeling okay, Dantes?" "Sure, Gunny, why wouldn't I?" "Ohh, I don't know, I thought that this was probably the first time you've had to fire at someone in anger, first time to actually kill someone." Dantes shrugged his shoulders, "I've been around killing some, before. You get that on a farm. Hogs, chickens..." "The occasional Mexican?" Gunny interjected. Dantes looked at him closely, wondering if he had heard about the liberty he had pulled in Tijauna. Chief laughed, reading his mind, "No, Dantes, he doesn't know about your exploits in Tijauna. Look, it can be tough not being able to talk about something like this, that's all. This is your chance." Dantes took a long pull on his beer with the dragon on the label, "I'm fine, y'all, just fine." And he maneuvered the bottle precisely into the circle of condensation it had left on the cracked mahogany table, eyes to himself. *These guys mean well, but there's no chance I'm gonna' talk about this, not with them and certainly not with strangers. Yeah I been around killing and almost killing and I ain't talked about that, neither!* Locker broke into his introspection, "In about a week there will be scuttlebutt that'll make its way over the peninsula from Manila to Olongapo and it'll describe a young sailor killing, oh by then maybe ten, twelve P.I. natives, probably with a .45, a machete and knives. Some will mention your name but probably mispronounce it," and he laughed, again looking to see the effect it had on Dantes. Dantes looked up, a little pissed and letting it show, "Wouldn't be the first time somebody messed up my name," and he shrugged. Both of his companions snickered and just then the Mamasan came up to the table, was invited to join them, drinks were ordered and Chief and she had a relaxed and easy conversation about the movement of fleet units and arrivals in ports of call as well as those scheduled which had yet to occur. Dantes wasn't sure but he thought he saw more than a flat report about shipping pass between them. As the Mamasan got up and walked away, Dantes let a smile spread. Chief looked at him. "Don't you go getting any ideas, Dantes." "Oh, I don't know but that in a week or so we'll be hearing scuttlebutt about a certain Chief when he was but a mere Second Class or maybe a First Class, and how all the Mamasans who were only butterfly girls and not yet Mamasans used to take a sailor home. They'll probably get his name wrong, though, calling him Wall Locker or sumpin' like that." At that Gunny laughed so hard he blew his beer through his nose, sputtering and coughing red in the face. Chief was laughing too, *yep, I saw it in boot camp. His name is Dantes but he's gonna' be known as a tiger.*

At the Ship Repair Facility, Subic Bay, P.I., Admiral Cochrane and Lodge sat in the office of CDR Jock O'Malley, Commanding Officer of SRF Subic. "Thanks for a very fine report on the capabilities you have here at the Facility, Commander." O'Malley nodded. "I also got a complete listing of all Fleet assets from CinCNavPI as well as Commanding Officers, current deployments, etcetera. What I don't know is the actual physical state of our ships, whether they can be expected to fight effectively and for how long if called upon to do so. You, Sir, are the man whom I expect could answer those questions. You've been here, what, three years? In that time you have performed work on most of these China Fleet units. What I need from you is a detailed breakdown, and I don't mean a five minute briefing, of what's been fixed and what likely hasn't and any sort of insight you can give me as to what is needed to right our ships, if you get my meaning."

"Sir, how long will you be in port?" "You have another day, two maximum, to put together your best estimate. Of course you may also copy your reporting senior and you should know that I will be sharing your findings with CincPac in my report to him at the end of this cruise. Give me first cut before I go and follow up with any additional results by CLASSIFIED SECRET traffic to me aboard Detroit within three weeks. "Aye, aye Sir. Sir might I suggest we repair to the dining facility for a lunch…" "Make it a working lunch and invite any presenters whom you think necessary for detail." With that Lodge and the Admiral got up and headed for the dining facility.

Five days later, Detroit approached Hong Kong, made anchorage in the naval anchorage area, and received Custom Inspectors and permission to go ashore. Lodge had already arranged a call on the Governor of the Royal Crown Colony as well as the Senior Officer Present Ashore. Several invitations for drinking lunch aboard various Brit vessels had arrived by flashing light and Lodge and the CO were going through them when Chief Radioman Locker came into Lodge's stateroom with a clipboard full of even more. Lodge mentioned tasking for the shore party that would be accompanying the Admiral. "Chief, we will be taking both you and Seaman Dantes ashore with us in the party. We want to make the theme of this port visit connections with our Brit Allies. I expect that you will make contact with senior enlisted Brits and hook Dantes up, as well, with some Able Seamen. Our thought is to reduce and eliminate any barriers that have a nasty habit of cropping up in the absence of Joint exercises." Chief replied with a cheery Aye, aye.

Meanwhile Cochrane was with Phil Ryan, the CO of Detroit, going over a list of activities he wanted Detroit to sponsor and in which he expected maximum participation. "We can get the Athletics Officer to set up basketball games and baseball. Enquire if they can outfit us with cricket gear and challenge them to a match. I'll ask the Governor if we can hold some of this at the race track. Get the cooks all fired up, I want a good old Texas Barbeque ready for a party of maybe 300. I'll get the people invited. We'll do a feed at the race track and a smaller one aboard.

Government House, British Crown Colony, Hong Kong. "So good of you to come, Admiral." "Thank you for hosting us, Sir John." "I hear from my Secretary that you have a full schedule in mind for your visit with us, even a cricket match! Jolly good show, Admiral." "Sir John, thank you also for making the race course available for the athletic contests and picnic." "You are most welcome indeed. But you must let me pay for that feed you are putting on. Let's use your cooks and we'll provide the necessaries as well as the security." They shook on it and the Governor led the way into his secure spaces where the Senior Officer Present Ashore, Vice Admiral Tom Hardy (RN) was waiting with a briefing of Japanese moves in China as well as throughout the Pacific. Lodge was admitted and allowed to take notes. In addition he was shown several intelligence assessments. They were typed up and classified top secret and it was a stack of them. Most of them had been prepared by a Dame Sandra Tweedie something or other, with a whole string of alphabet letters after her name designating her decorations. Cochrane made a mental note to look them up; he was very impressed with the quality of the information and the conclusions and recommendations that were included. Looking up from his reading he mentioned his thoughts about the information and its author. The Staff and the Admiral all laughed or smiled. "Admiral, you have correctly identified our most outstanding senior intelligence operative. She is one of a kind, that one." And there were knowing looks around the room, though Cochrane declined the opportunity to comment further. Tea and coffee were served for "our American Cousins" and the briefing went on for some two hours. It was a sobered Cochrane who thanked his hosts for the information and expressed his admiration for the breadth and scope of their intelligence operation. Hardy responded, "Well, old chap, we are still the world's largest Navy. There are expectations that come with that." Cochrane smiled and left it at that and he and Lodge were seen to the door and their waiting car to take them wherever they wanted to go. At the car the Chief took charge of Lodge's notes and locked them to his wrist and Dantes busied himself at the doors, moving briskly and sharply under the gaze of the British hosts. "Fleet Landing, driver," said Lodge and soon enough they were back aboard Detroit.

Lodge had meetings with ship's Officers to check progress on the many details that enabled a whirlwind visit like this one to be successful. Chief hooked up with Gunny, headed ashore to places both of them knew from years earlier. Before going, Locker told Dantes to head for the Wanchai Pier and catch the Star Ferry to Kowloon. Once there he said to catch a rickshaw and tell the guy pulling it he wanted a good time. Same deal coming back, go to the Kowloon Star Ferry pier and catch a ride to the Wanchai side, then a quick stroll to Fleet Landing. And, have a good time!

Kowloon, across Hong Kong harbor from Hong Kong Island. The sweating rickshaw man held his hand out to be paid and took the twenty five cents American he was handed with a large smile. Dantes ambled into a likely looking place that had music and laughter blasting out the open batwing doors on the front of the establishment. The sign said "Good Time Bar." Inside there was a crowded bar with mostly Brit sailors drinking stout. Against the wall to the side were three cork dartboards set up and a crowd of Brits and Aussies around them, following the progress of the games with great interest. The accuracy of these players was incredible, as they took aim for tiny segments of wire bound space, the outer rings of numbered pie shaped slices. There were no scoring errors possible as the divisions between portions of the target were made of wire. You started with zero and added your score as you went, having to end on a triple and on the exact number, in this case 300, to close the game. Competitors took turns and usually threw three darts at a turn before surrendering the mark to the other player. Dantes noticed that most of the players had their own darts.

As he was watching, an Aussie by his uniform and accent sidled up to him and asked, "Whatcha drinkin' Yank?" "Kirin and I'm not a Yankee." The Aussie laughed, "Where you from, Mate?" And he handed over an ice cold Kirin. "Texas. That's a …" "Yeah, I know, that's where the cowboys come from. We got sheep where I come from," he said. He held his hand out, "Jake Fryar." "Glad to meet you, Hod Dantes." Well, Hod, you ever played darts before?" "Can't say as I have," Hod answered. "Wanna learn?" "You bet!" Jake and Hod went over to an unused board and Jake took his darts in a soft case out of his pocket. And handed one to Hod. "Let me see you throw it." Hod did an abbreviated wind up and tossed a looping trajectory that wound up putting the dart precisely in the center of the board. Jake laughed, "You could not do that twice in a row." Dantes said, "Probably not" and he took a second shot and again hit the center of the board. Jake waved him on to throw again and Dantes missed the center but still hit the board. "Not bad at all and I can see you have a good eye, it's your delivery that's all wrong." And he proceeded to put three darts in the center in a row, pulled his darts and did it again, started to do it a third time and Dantes said, "Whoa. I'm convinced. Show me a better way to throw." Two hours and several beers later Jake had Hod leaning forward toward the target, standing sideways to it, arm with the dart pointing straight at the intended target. With his upper arm held parallel to the deck only the forearm moved, in a rapid snakelike strike. Everything else stayed still. Also, they had gone over tactics and how to get to the number they wanted with the fewest number of darts, and how to hit the triples in the outer ring. Hod had the position down pat and was used to the notion of making small corrections. As to sight picture, why that was natural. Before the night was over Hod was throwing rapid fire triples, almost without aiming, it seemed. Jake didn't know if it was because he was such a great teacher or Hod was just a natural. He decided Hod was a natural but he was not able to keep up with Jake in the beer department. It looked like the place was getting ready to close down. Both were headed back to their ships. At the fleet landing they made plans to meet tomorrow at the fleet landing and laughingly shook on it and boarded the water taxi they'd hired to take them out to the anchorages.

The games were successful and Hod and Jake spent a lot of their Hong Kong liberty together. In addition to the race track and gardens they made it to the Peninsula Hotel with its magnificent Dragon Bar and view of Victoria Harbor and several bars in the Wanchai District. The day before Detroit was to leave Jake gave Dantes some addresses in Sydney, that of his parents and also the one for his Sheila and said he hoped he'd find the time to look them up and he was sure that his girl would have a friend in mind who might show him around town.

CHAPTER 21

QUEZON'S SURPRISE

One day out of Hong Kong, enroute to Soerbaja, in the Dutch East Indies, Lodge knocked softly at Admiral Cochrane's stateroom door and was invited in. The Admiral looked up, "Sir mail call was held and there was a letter for you." "That's unusual," and he held out his hand and took it from Lodge. He turned to go, as Cochrane had opened the envelope and was reading its contents. Cochrane held up his hand to stay him while he finished reading. A bemused smile broke out on Cochrane's face, "Well I'll be damned. This is most unusual. It is two messages, a formal one and a note. The note is from Manual Quezon and it talks about the other document which appears to be a land title. Quezon thanks us for our help in identifying the Japanese who were financing the Tayag insurrectionists and says that with this victory in hand it is no longer necessary to keep quiet about the events that took place on the roof of the Manila Hotel when we were there. Ah, and there's another inscription at the bottom of this land title. This land is given in perpetuity to Horace Howard Dantes in grateful recognition of his bravery in saving the life of Mrs. Luz Ramos Calderone and ensuring the safety of Manual Quezon. There's a PS that the legislature has passed a law exempting this land from any taxes and that the Calderones also look forward to receiving him at their Estancia at his earliest convenience."

He handed the letters over to Lodge. "These look authentic and binding to me," Lodge said. "I wonder how much land he actually got." A low whistle and Lodge said, "It looks like he owns some five thousand acres, give or take. The boundaries appear to be natural ones. Why do you suppose Quezon got involved?" Cochrane took the letter back and examined the deed more closely. Hmm, it also lists a Catholic organization as a previous owner. My guess is that this is also an opening shot against the Catholic Church and Quezon is just taking care of Dantes at little expense to either the Calderones or his Government. Land reforms are coming and until they are settled law, there's no telling how much this deed is worth," Cochrane replied. And with that they both sat down and reminisced about that night and Dantes' terrific and deadly accuracy in saving two women and certainly the Admiral and who knew how many others. "It was not lost on me that he fired first on the two that were holding the women and only when they were dispatched did he turn his fire on the one coming for me." Evidently it was also not lost on the Calderones," Lodge replied. "Shall I get him up here?"

"I think we will just routinely thank the CO for his support and mention Dantes and the Chief. As to his supposed gift of property, that will remain Dantes' business, plain and simple. We might suggest to him that he engage a lawyer to look out for his interests in the P.I. and help him if he asks, but I still prefer that we keep quiet aboard ship about our operations ashore," Cochrane replied. "Rather than draw even more attention to him amongst his ship-mates, I think it would be preferable that you let him know about his good fortune the next time you can manage to see him." Lodge nodded an Aye, aye, collected the deed and secured it in his folder and went back to his stateroom with a wry smile on his face. *This is getting interesting. What's Dantes going to get into next?*

Lodge's next move was to call Chief Locker and invite him to Flag Spaces for a sit down meeting. Chief showed up, was greeted and ushered into a small conference space where Lodge closed the door behind them, offered the Chief a mug of coffee and they both took seats, the Chief just after the Com-mander. The Chief waited for Lodge to begin but he thought he already knew or had guessed the subject of the meeting. "I'm aware of the special relation-ship between you and Dantes, Chief. I understand you were his Chief in Boot Camp." Locker nodded and smiled, and replied, "Sir I'm not the only one who knows and cares about our sailor," and he smiled a small smile. "Not too many Seamen Firsts get to go up to Makalapa and sit down with CinCPac." "Absolutely right and not too many Seamen Firsts who are called upon to take charge in a crisis and kill three men in the space of less than ten seconds. I'd guess that you're concerned about the possible effect on Dantes, Chief, especially as we've kept the whole thing quiet and he has not been free to talk to anyone about it." Chief nodded, waiting. "How do you think he is taking it," Lodge asked. "Well, he dropped off to sleep pretty quickly right after the police left, slept like a baby and hasn't mentioned it to me since. Sir, I wouldn't worry about him. I had planned to talk to him about it, was just waiting for the right time. Sometimes these things have to be his idea, Sir. He's the one toughest kid I know and yet it hasn't hardened him." Lodge let out his breath in relief, "Chief I think that if you and he can talk about this it will help him. If he actually needs any help." As Locker took his cue and was about to get up and leave Lodge said, "I still have to talk to him but it's about another matter, a private one that involves only Dantes. Do you think you could get him aside and mention that he is also wanted in Flag Spaces, something about a debrief to go over the time in Manila?" "Sir, absolutely. Would now be a good time? I believe he is not due on watch until the 2000 to 2400." Lodge nodded his thanks.

Dantes entered Flag Country, found Lodge's compartment and knocked. "Come," Lodge called out and Dantes, in his sharpest uniform, shoes gleaming stepped into the small room, was invited to sit and did so, "Thank you, Sir." Lodge gave him the papers received by the Admiral, explaining how he had gotten them and asked him to read them. After a time Dantes looked up, "This looks to be a title in my name for some land in the P.I., Sir." "Exactly so, Dantes, though I wouldn't be trying to cash in, just yet. The political situation in the Archipelago is volatile and who knows what the next set of leaders might do with things like land reform and civil rights?" "Sir, what might you recommend?" "I am sure that the Admiral would be willing to arrange for a lawyer to represent your best interests, with Manual Quezon's help, quite possibly Quezon's own lawyer. He could communicate with you through the mails and take steps to see that your deed is properly filed and that your property is looked after as well as your rights, so long as you have them." Dantes smiled and mused for a bit at his seeming good fortune. Then he looked up at the Commander, "Sir, thank you for all your help and all that you've done for me." Lodge replied that he was owed no thanks and thanked Dantes for his resolute action in saving lives at the hotel in Manila. "Shall I hold these documents for you, Dantes?" "Sir, thank you and would you please remember me to the Lieutenant when next you see her, Sir." Lodge chuckled; it seemed Dantes never ceased to amaze him with his presence of mind, as Dantes made his way back to First Division compartment.

In First Division they had also had a mail call and there was a letter from Loraine for him, sitting in the stack of mail on the mess table. It was the usual recitation of her girlish activities until he got to the end where once again she raised her continuing concern that she and Hod might somehow be dangerous to others or even themselves. Hod was about to scoff when it hit him like a ton of bricks. He began to shake as he thought about drawing down on those two with the knives and the horribly frightened women. He looked at his hands and with a bit of will he stopped their shaking, looked around to see if anyone was looking at him and was relieved to see that they were all reading their mail, too. Then the memory of his rapid fire shots into the back of the third Tayag who was going for the Admiral started his thinking and his shaking, all over again. *But I was fine, right after. I even had no trouble going to sleep. It was only a little different from firing at the range in Diamond*

Head. Fire as soon as you have a sight picture and don't let up until you're out of ammo. Those men needed killing.

The thoughts of that night had hit him, he imagined, in a delayed reaction. He wished that Loraine were where he could talk to her. *But you don't talk to your sister about something like THIS!* He checked the time, might as well leave his good whites on, he was due up on the bridge in less than a half hour. On his way up the ladder, past Chief's Quarters he ran into Chief Locker, just coming out into the passageway. Chief looked at him and cocked his head just a bit. Dantes hesitated with his foot on the ladder tread and it slipped, and he fell into the ladder, banging up his elbow in the process. He got up stifling his urge to cuss and Locker steadied him, continuing to look at him with concern. They both spoke at once, "You think we could get together…?" And Chief said, "After watch. It'll be quiet here in the Goat Locker. I'll wait up for you." While Dantes was on watch, Locker approached Gundy and told him he could use some private time with Dantes and Gundy offered him the use of the CMOA Office and gave him the key. Locker used some of the time to check in with the Ship's Chaplain and talk over the situation in general terms. The Chaplain told him that sometimes it took awhile for things to catch up with a sailor, no matter the age or experience. It could be an encounter with a first woman for a young sailor or just the accumulation of time away from home for the first time. The main thing, he said, was to be reassuring and not to be critical.

Locker was waiting at the door to Chief's Quarters when Dantes came sliding down the ladder, only his palms in contact with the rails at the sides, lightly landing on the deck at the bottom. Chief led the way to the CMOA's Office, they went in and took seats while Locker turned on just a small light in the desk cubbyhole. "I thought it was time, past time really, to talk a bit about what happened in Manila," Locker said. With a look of interest he asked, "Go okay with that girl from the bar, what was her name?" "Rosa, Chief, Rosa Vasconcellos." And his look at the Chief was a little bold, as if daring him to ask about their time together at her place. "It was helpful to know that the Mamasan was sympathetic. She in fact provided all we needed to know in order to root out the Japanese who were funding the Tayag. I'm told that Quezon was very happy to run them down and eliminate that threat. My guess is that he would have been ecstatic about what you did that night at the party. Once he got over the realization that he almost lost his life that night." *This is what he wants to talk about? How happy a politician was and how did it go with my "friend"?*

"Chief, are you worried about me, having to shoot those three? Worried about whether or not I can handle it? Because I am finding that it didn't bother me at all to do that," and his jaw jutted out just a bit. "I agree, Dantes, you certainly seemed to be in complete control as you shot those Tayags and slept like a baby afterward. But *some*thing *is* bothering you and before we go ashore on another of these intel gathering liberties I want to know what it is." Dantes just dropped his head, had no response. Chief pulled out a folder, "Says here that both your parents are deceased. I know something about that was an orphan, myself." Dantes looked up, "My folks are great, lots of Uncles and Aunts. We look after each other, plus my sister and I are close." Chief tossed the folder on the desk, "Tell me about your Dad." "He was a super Father, we knew…" "You were going to say that you knew he loved you, right?" Dantes just looked at the Chief. "Remember, you're talking to someone who knows what that's like, losing your old man and Mother. As time goes by you tend to forget the bad stuff and remember mostly the good. I know that's true for me." And his look just kept boring in on Dantes. "Tell me about him, he must have been very proud of you." "He was always a happy and strong man, doing stuff for us like the Christmas he came out to the farm and brought a big trunk of Oranges. We didn't have oranges on the farm, everything else but not them." Tell me more, son. Was he like you, are you like him?"

Hod was taking deeper breaths and gripping his knees, wouldn't look up. "Why are you doing this, Chief?" His voice had thickened and his face was getting flushed and he was getting worked up and extremely uncomfortable. Chief said, "My old man was a boozer, couldn't stay away from the bottle, liked to slap us around when he got boozed up. It was a long time before I trusted myself to drink. Tell me about your Father, Dantes, You have his name, right?" "Almost, except for the middle name. Whoever names their kid Horace," and he snorted an angry snort, "my sister did me a favor and changed my name for me and so I could use a nickname. I hate it when people make fun of my name! I've had a lot of fights over my name, people messing with it, saying it wrong." "So tell me more about your Father, Hod." Chief gave him no break. "You must have admired him. All boys need someone to look up to and it's usually their Dad. What did you admire about him? Was he handsome like you? Good in a fight like you?"

Hod looked up and Chief saw the boy, a chin starting to quiver, eyes to well and a defiant Hod almost shouted, "He was a crack shot, *OKAY? And he killed two men in fair fights, they were brothers and there* was a hole through his jacket where I could go and poke my finger through it in the smoke house at Grandma's…" And Chief jumped on that, "Nothing wrong with being good with a pistol, Dantes, you used one to very good effect at the hotel in Manila." "Chief you just don't *understand*." And Chief stood, "*Make* me understand, Hod, tell me." Tears streaming down his face Hod stood with his face burning with shame, "Chief, he tried to kill us all. My Dad went and got the shotgun and tried to kill us all." And he sobbed, great waves of emotion pouring out in gasps and a long crying keening sound, the total desolation of it all finally hitting him as he told someone, shared his deepest darkest secret. And the two men hugged and Hod dropped his head on his Chief's shoulder and he couldn't see Chief's face nor the tears that flowed down his cheeks or the smile as he kept saying, "Get it out, son, get it out. Get it all out."

Three days out of Hong Kong, Lodge's stateroom with Dantes. "Take a look at this draft, if you will, Dantes," proffering a handwritten letter from Admiral Cochrane to Manual Quezon.

```
Dear Manual, allow me to pass along Seaman Dantes' heart-
felt thanks for the generosity you and the Calderones
have shown him. He also has asked me to help him seek
legal representation in Manila in order that he may be
properly advised regarding Philippine law and custom and
have assistance in evaluating his new property and man-
aging it. He would appreciate your recommendation of an
attorney whom you know who would be able and willing to
handle Mr. Dantes' affairs there. Please feel free to
continue to address your correspondence on this matter to
me, at least until a lawyer is selected and arrangements
put in place between Dantes and his Attorney.
Very respectfully,
Dick Cochrane
```

Dantes looked up from the note, "Thank you, Sir and thanks also to the Admiral. I agree that this may eventually not amount to very much, but I should take steps to try to protect it." Lodge nodded, then asked, "Good liberty in Hong Kong?" "It was the best, Sir. Made a new friend while in Kowloon and have some people to look up in Sydney, when we get there." "I suspect you make friends everywhere you go, Dantes. We'll get this typed up for the Admiral's signature and off the ship with the next port visit.

Soerbaja, Java, a Dutch East Indies possession and site of their largest Naval Base in the Pacific. Advance exchanges of messages had resulted in scheduling a working lunch in Base Headquarters to be followed up by a tour of facilities, as it was to be a one day visit. Accordingly both Admiral Dick Cochrane and Admiral Dyck Tromp were in their short sleeve khakis, with Tromp additionally in Bermuda length uniform shorts. It was a hot and steamy day in Java. "As you know, Admiral, I am conducting a survey for CincPac and this is my fourth stop, with Sydney yet to come before returning to Pearl Harbor. I imagine that if anyone is informed and alert as to the possible moves of the Japanese, it would be you, Sir."

Tromp packed his pipe, lit it and sat back in his chair, "Dick, by the way I pronounce my name just about the way you do yours, I appreciate the compliment, though I suspect that you Americans would call it a left handed one. Yes, we have to be fully informed and as prepared as possible for a Japanese resurgence. With their rapid building program they are obviously putting in place a vast armada, one that will require millions of barrels of oil, of which they have none. We, on the other hand have vast resources in the ground and the refining and storage facilities of Royal Dutch Shell, but no fleet of a size that could begin to rival theirs. Nor will that change anytime soon. It's true that our Navy is developing plans for Battle Cruisers, we are calling it our Design 1047. We're doing it in collaboration with the Germans but it's not likely that anything will come of it, at least by the time we might have use for it. You see our Naval Staff have come up with the scenario that the Japs and the US will initiate hostilities with the likely outcome that battleships will have demonstrated their limited usefulness, leaving mainly carriers, cruisers and submarines. With our somewhat modest means as a military we have to be satisfied with a smaller fleet of smaller vessels, our hope for defense based on the attrition of the Japanese Fleet by your Navy, with we Dutch having enough left to possibly save our position here in the Pacific. Our Government has been cancelling program after program, refusing to fund naval construction, even the latest proposal for some destroyers." And he shook his head and emptied his pipe, which had gone out during his presentation.

"You know, The Brits seem proud of their size, think of themselves, and rightly so, as the world's largest Navy," Cochrane replied. Tromp cocked an eye, gave a bit of a smile, "Yes, but have you been aboard any of their ships lately?" He shook his head, "We get the occasional Limey vessel in here for port visits, and we always look each other over. They may be the largest, yes, but I think that they have some real competition in being the greatest. Both the IJN and your Navy will have a lot to say about that. By the way, we have indications that the Japs are preparing to construct a new class of battleships. Secret plans and drawings have been seen that call for eighteen inch guns. Funny, isn't it? They excel in carrier aviation yet still intend building these enormous battlewagons. It seems to me that the future of battle at sea will be decided in the air and under the sea."

"What about distribution of your seagoing assets?" Cochrane asked. "As you've surmised we have most of what we've got in the North Atlantic. Yes, Japan is a likely enemy but so also are the Germans. For the time being we are thin in the Pacific, preferring to defend the homeland and hoping that when the big boys finish their fight out here we will still be around, that there will still be a Dutch East Indies…" Cochrane said, "Dyck, I've come from the Philippines, met with Manual Quezon there. I honestly think that the age of colonialism is coming to an end. I saw a hunger for independence in the P.I., for full nationhood. I think that holding on to possessions will become increasingly hard, Japanese or no."

The tour covered the piers, shops submarine berthing, repair and storage facilities. It was not a very large facility but it seemed well run. The Dutch had a proud tradition in submarines, having invented and sold to the Germans their snorkeling systems for their diesel powered submarines. Back in Tromp's office, "I apologize for the shortness of our visit, we must be getting underway for Sydney, our next stop." Tromp fixed him with an enigmatic look. "Perfectly understandable, Dick, a natural itinerary. I imagine that the Nips have something similar in mind."

There was plenty of room in Sydney Harbor for Detroit to tie up to the pier, relieving them of the necessity of keeping boats in the water and also allowing them to hook up to shore power and secure their boilers and generator sets. It was also an opportunity to take fresh water on board as well as fuel and the ship continued to be busy, getting all of the water and fuel on board and into balanced storage tanks port and starboard as well as topping off the service tanks which were located over the keel so that the changing level as fuel or water was consumed did not change the trim of the ship. She would continue lighter in the water but heeling neither to port or starboard as levels dropped or were refilled from storage. The handling of these responsibilities fell upon the Engineering Department and they were done on a daily basis with reports written up and forwarded to the Chief Engineer for approval. In actuality it was two enlisted men, usually second class machinists or boiler tenders who did the actual work of storage, inventory and balance. Called the Oil King and the Water King, they were the first place the Chief Snipe or the CO looked when the ship was taking unusually large rolls in heavy seas. In order not to bob on the surface like a toy boat, the oil king had to take on saltwater ballast to replace the fuel that was burned. It was necessary to keep a low center of gravity at sea to avoid being rolled over in the storms often encountered. Similarly the oil king needed to judiciously pump water out when safe to do so and the weather allowed. No one wanted to see oil spills from ballast pumping operations in port. It was just another example of Petty Officers doing their jobs, vital jobs which were accomplished in obscurity, until something went wrong.

Lodge had told the Chief that this visit they would not be required as part of staff ashore, that the Commander would carry the briefcase and why didn't he and Dantes go ashore and enjoy themselves. Cochrane and Lodge met with the Admiral's opposite number, in a Government Headquarters building in Sydney.

"Welcome, Admiral, to our humble offices. As you can see there is not a lot of money to go around these days." "A common condition for Navies the world over, except for perhaps, Japan," Cochrane replied. "Yes, well the Crown sent Admiral Jellicoe out here after The Great War on a mission to assess naval needs and formulate a plan for an Australian Commonwealth Navy. He did a good job and made many fine recommendations. But the Washington Treaty intervened and largely as a result of disarmament after the war we find ourselves in quite a pickle. Jellicoe's recommendations fell on deaf ears and now we have formerly great powers with great deficits, facing a resurgent and active Imperial Japanese Navy." Admiral James Coons pushed the pitcher of iced tea across the table and Cochrane poured himself a glass. Settling back in his chair, "I paid a visit to the Dutch in East Java on my last stop." "Call on Dyck Tromp, did you? He's a good man, thoroughgoing professional." "Yes, and he is worried that he is number one on the Nippon hit list, has some very strong ideas about where to deploy any allied forces in order to prevent the Japanese taking over the Dutch East Indies oilfields." "Can't say as I blame him but I fear that the result in Java and Borneo is already a foregone conclusion. The Dutch have few resources too and those that they have they are keeping close to the homeland. They seem to have the idea that there will soon be a couple bullies on the block." Cochrane just sat there and took another sip of tea, waiting for the rest of it. "Their strategy, if that's what you want to call it, is to let the Nips and the Yanks duke it out, eliminating most large capital ships and hoping that their few heavy cruisers, which they don't even have yet, will prevail over what's left." *And how does that strategy differ from yours, Jim?* But Cochrane stayed quiet and took another sip of tea. A little red in the face, Coons continued, "Of course we also are dependent upon the US Fleet and that of the Royal Navy if we are to have any chance at all. The very fact that we *don't* have oil in the ground and that the Dutch do means that we will likely be number two on their list. And make no mistake, to feed their navy they will need that Dutch oil. Everybody knows it." And for the rest of their visit they discussed Australian readiness and capability to participate in some joint naval exercises that Cochrane had in mind. When he left he had a clear picture of Australian assets and their decided interest in participating in exercises with the US fleet.

Dantes went over with Daughter and wound up in the pub of the Lord Nelson Hotel. It was in a basement with sandstone walls and had its own brewery as well as a few dartboards. There was a Royal Navy Destroyer in port and they had run into some Limey sailors who had told them about the place. It was cool and smelled of the yeasty brewery and they had a pitcher of draft beer and some pretzels and were making inroads on both when an Able seaman stood next to them and asked if they were interested in playing darts for beers. Daughter said, "Nah, you guys almost do that for a living." And he laughed and downed the rest of his beer. The sailor turned toward Dantes, "You Yank, got any balls? Willing to try your hand?" Dantes kept the smile off his face, "Why, you offering any odds? I mean darts are practically your national pastime, except for Cricket. Or are you just looking to victimize unsuspecting sailors?" The sailor held out his hand, name's John Shands, and I think we might give you odds for the first go 'round, after all yiz might be fast learners." Introductions completed, Dantes said he'd be the one to throw for them and why not give it a go, with two for one odds to start?" He let the Limey explain the rules and then said he didn't have any darts. "That's okay Hod, we'll loan you some." "You want to go first," Dantes asked. "Nah, Yank, show us what you got." At that he smiled, for the first time, "Well, I tried to give you guys a chance. A practice throw, just to get used to the weight?" he said, reaching for the three darts in John's hand. "Sure, Yank, practice all you want."

Hod's first shot was dead center in the bull and the next two were in the trips ring at twelve O'clock and the one segment. He turned with a deadpan face and said, these may be a little bit light but I think they'll do. Starting at 301?" The Limies were shocked into silence, jaws dropping as Dantes efficiently fired his three shots for score: he hit two twenty point trips for 120 and added a single point with a shot to the dead center of the 1 segment. That gave him a score of 121. He figured three trip sixties to finish the game out on his next turn. He turned to hand the darts to John. John turned to his mates and said, "My fault, guys, he's a ringer." He threw his three and scored two inner bulls and a one, giving him 101 and left him needing 200 for the game. If you went over or didn't close out with a double or a bull you went back to the starting number. Hod fired three straight trip 20's to end the game. For style he did it in about two seconds, then sat down and asked for another pitcher, all this dart throwing had him thirsty! Daughter said out of the corner of his mouth, "You didn't learn darts in Lockhart Texas." "Nah, an Aussie 'mate I met taught me in Kowloon." Shands sat down at their table and they spent the afternoon swapping sea stories, drinking beer and in general getting to know one another. He finally asked the inevitable question, "Where'd you learn to play?" "Hong Kong, one night from an Aussie in Kowloon." "*One night!* That's pretty incredible. Besides those Aussies don't really know how to play the game." "What can I say, he was a great teacher." And they all laughed and Dantes excused himself. "What's up, Dantes, got a date?" "Maybe, I do have a number to call and an address. Never can tell. Those Aussies may not throw darts worth a damn but they do have sisters." He left them laughing with a promise to meet again the next day, same place.

She picked up on the third ring, just having gotten in from work. "Hullo?" "Hi. If this is Janie, this call is from a sailor who met Jake Fryar in Hong Kong. Jake taught me how to play darts in Kowloon and we spent quite a bit of time together. My name is Hod Dantes. We just got in port with the USS Detroit. Jake gave me your number and address, said you were his Sister or maybe his Sheila, but knew you'd welcome a call." She laughed a hearty trill somewhere between a giggle and an astonished guffaw and said, "Why of course Jake is exactly right, we simply *adore* Yanks here. And for the record, Jake is actually my stepbrother and a very protective one at that. Tell you what, give me some time to make a call or two and call me back. If you're free for this evening I'm thinking of calling a girlfriend. I'll see if she's available and maybe we three can get together for some fun on the town." "Sounds fun, Janie! Actually my best friend is also with me, here at the Lord Nelson. We'll both look forward to meeting y'all. And he hung up with a smile.

Janie picked up her friend, Mavis and they drove into town. Both girls were excited; it was a Friday with the weekend ahead of them and the Yanks were in town! They pulled up to the hotel, did a quick primp in the small rearview mirror and walked into the pub. Every head turned and one of the sailors gave a low wolf whistle. Janie glanced around the room until she saw the two Yanks. They made eye contact and Hod went quickly to their side, smiling a welcome and inviting them to their table. Daughter jumped up out of his chair, there were introductions all around and then Hod seated Janie while Daughter did the same for Mavis. "What are you girls drinking," Hod asked. Janie said maybe some white wine and Mavis said the same. Conversation in the room started back up again, the wine came in a carafe, house white, and Dantes poured two glasses for the ladies. "We really appreciate your taking the call and that you were both free. It's great to get to know someone in a strange port. We've been at sea for almost two months with short port visits in the Philippines and Hong Kong. *Very* nice to meet two ladies such as yourselves." Mavis looked up at Daughter and asked, "Where are you boys from?" And as the ladies sipped their wine the conversation eased and the smiles increased and the ladies heard a bit about life aboard a man of war and told them about their home town and what there was to do in Sydney. Dantes suggested dinner and did they know a nice place. The girls huddled and came up with a place, they said it was very nice. Janie had been there but not Mavis and she said it had a nice view of the Harbor. Janie drove with Hod in the front seat and the other two in the back, a happy buzz of conversation back and forth over the seat while Janie tried to concentrate on the driving.

It was a nice restaurant, white cloth napkins and someone to guide them to their table. The menu was fairly extensive and after a bit Janie opted for an inexpensive bowl of soup and a salad. The other three followed her lead and as the waiter went back to the kitchen, Dantes glanced around the room and saw a table with four Naval Officers seated together. They were in civvies and one of them was their Division Officer, Mr. Smythe. He returned the look, tipped his glass in salute, just a small gesture, nothing flamboyant. Shortly thereafter the waiter came to the table with a bottle of champagne and a bucket of ice. "It's from the Gentleman at the table and he looked toward the four Officers. Dantes thanked the waiter who performed the pouring ritual with a loud POP of the cork into his cloth napkin and poured, first for Dantes to taste and then the ladies and then the two shipmates. Dantes proposed a toast. "Here's to good shipmates, new friends and good times." The ladies said "Hear, hear" and they all took a sip. Dantes held his flute in the direction of Mr. Smythe and tipped it with a smile in thanks.

After dinner they moved into the adjoining room where a quartet had set up and were playing. As they walked into the room the musicians struck up a lively and nicely played version of the Star Spangled Banner. Everyone stood and the two sailors put their hands over their hearts. After they were seated the waiter came and took their drink orders and Dantes slipped him some bills, looking toward the band. The money was deposited in a hat onstage and Dantes received beaming smiles from the musicians. It was an exclamation mark to what was becoming a fantastic evening. The four Division Officers, when they came in, not being in uniform, received no such notice.

The four took their turns on the dance floor and Dantes turned out to be a fairly good dancer. His Grandma had taught him a few steps and told him that the steps weren't as important as enjoying the music and enjoying your partner. And he was enjoying his partner, very much. So much so that he was surprised to be tapped on the shoulder, not by Mr. Smythe, but one of the others, who asked if he could have this dance. Dantes smiled his assent, took his seat and watched them finish the dance. Smythe looked at Dantes from his table and gave a small shrug of his shoulders and Dantes thought about that, realized that Smythe meant nothing untoward, just a nice evening on the town. When Janie came back to the table she was thanked for the dance, however she didn't sit down but suggested to the other three that they might go to another place, a less formal beach bar that only the natives knew. Both men put money on the table and they left, getting friendly comments from some of the Australian patrons on their way out.

Janie took them along a beach road until they came to a place with a thatched roof and inside it smelled like a beer. There was no music, just beer on tap and peanuts and pretzels. There were couples in booths, all involved in each other and nobody paid them any mind. They took a booth, the couples together and across from each other. After half a beer Janie whispered in Hod's ear and they got up and went out on the beach for a stroll. The drinks and the champagne and the lateness of the hour had mellowed them and the moonlight and crash of the waves were fanning a spark that soon turned into a roaring blaze as they turned together and kissed. Daughter and Mavis had come out to the beach also but turned in the other direction, giving and taking a bit of privacy and soon taking liberties with each other. Janie excused herself and went back to the car and got a blanket out of the trunk. As she spread it in the lee of a dune, giving them some privacy, the other two went back to the car and got in the back seat. "Welcome to Australia, Hod," Janie said as she laid down next to him.

Two hours later they were back at the pier, the ladies dropping them off and plans had been made for the rest of the weekend, if the two sailors could get their liberty chits approved. It was to be an early start and the girls would be down at the pier at nine the next morning.

Hod knocked on the partition next to the curtain in 'boy's town' the next morning after they had been released from Quarters. Mr. Smythe came to the doorway. "Dantes, look, I had nothing to do with Mr. Lemon trying to hustle your date." "Sir, I appreciate that and thank you for the champagne. Sir I have a couple of liberty chits for the weekend, Daughter's and mine and the Chief has chopped them." Smythe smiled and approved them. "Well done, Dantes. Have a good time and be sure to be back on board by 0800 on Monday."

The girls showed up at five 'til nine, the two shipmates were on the pier waiting and they all piled into Janie's car. "Look guys, you're great in those uniforms but wouldn't you be a bit more comfortable in civilian clothes?" They went to Janie's place and changed into shorts and short sleeved shirts borrowed from Mavis's brothers. Janie had a picnic basket fixed and they stopped for some beers at a grocery store to add to it. Ready to get back in the car, Janie said "We want to take you to a place we call Royal Park. It's actually a National park with cliffs, water, beaches and forest trails." "Does it have Kookaburras," Daughter asked. "Yes and you know they're called that, the birds, because that's what their call sounds like," Mavis replied. Whereupon she gave her best imitation of the call and they all laughed. Dantes said, "I've heard about this place, and the native animals that you can find there, something called the wild Sheila…" Janie swatted him on the butt in fake anger and they all piled into the car for an afternoon in the park.

Before sundown and after they had about hiked themselves out, the girls thought it might be a good time for some rest. Janie drove them to Mavis' place and Hod was about to get out when Janie stopped him with her hand on his. The other two waved to them from the front door and went inside. "If it's okay with you, I thought we could spend the rest of the weekend together, just we two." Janie took both of his hands and kissed them in the palm. "You have such nice hands," she said.

Back in her kitchen with a couple of beers Dantes feeling a bit awkward, stuttered out, "I never understood exactly what Jake meant when he called you his Sheila and his sister. Either way…" and he looked up with wrinkled brow. Janie sat across from him. He actually is my step brother but he wanted to make it into something else. We moved in together as a family when I was only six and as the years rolled on he became my protector, actually he ran all my boy friends off, called me his Sheila. But we grew up and here I am, still single and on my own for ahh three years, now." Dantes nodded. "You would not know this but Jake's attitude toward me and to women is very like that of most Australian men. They are very close to their male friends, their "Mates," and they seem to take a bit of perverse pride in ignoring if not actually mistreating their women. That's one reason we girls in the Land Down Under find you Yanks so attractive, you know how to treat a woman."

Dantes took a pull on his beer and she continued. "Hod, I am not a loose woman. If you were going to be here I imagine our relationship could turn into something real. You are real but this time together is not, it's almost like a fairytale. You will be gone forever and I'll never see you again and all we have is two more nights." Dantes pulled her out of her chair and into his lap. As he ran his hands up under her blouse he said, "Then let's make the most of them, my Sheila."

At five minutes to eight on Monday morning it was a bedraggled Dantes and Daughter who were deposited pierside to make their way up the gangway to salute their way on board, and two tearful Sheilas who watched them go and then drove away.

After returning to Pearl Harbor, the Radioman approached Lodge's desk in CincPac Headquarters, "Sir, congratulations! We just got the Promotion List for Commander." as he handed it to Lodge. "Oh, and we also got this telegram addressed to you, Sir." He handed over a sealed yellow envelope. "It was delivered by the base mail courier." Lodge leaned back in his seat, signed for the UNCLAS promotion list, thanked the RM and checked the list for his name. *Hmmm, my name is at the top of the list. Why they jumped me some eighty or a hundred numbers!* He broke out in a smile as others looked in; some coming forward to give their congratulations, *word spreads fast!* The hubbub died down with hurried plans for a turn at the Club that night for an informal wetting down, albeit early. And then he remembered his telegram.

He flipped it over, only his name showing through the cellophane covered window in the envelope. *Who would be sending me a telegram?* A frown crossed his face, suddenly all thoughts of partying dismissed and he quickly opened the envelope, and read the message.

```
TO: LCDR JOHN LODGE
FROM: NANCY LODGE
    FATHER HAS HAD A STROKE IN VERY BAD CONDITION STOP
DOCTORS ADVISE RECOVERY NOT LIKELY STOP WE WILL BE FINE
BUT REQUEST COME HOME SOON IF AT ALL POSSIBLE STOP LOVE
MOM STOP
```

Lodge quickly strode to the Head Shed, asked in the outer office if he could have a minute with the Boss. The Secretary checked the Admiral's schedule, "He's clear for five minutes, you can go in now." And she looked up with some curiosity as she was about to congratulate him but he had already gone into the Admiral's office, and without the usual smile and bit of small talk.

The Admiral stood, beaming, "Congratulations, Commander! And they shook hands vigorously, but quickly taking in Lodge's pale expression he asked "What is it, John?" Lodge handed over the telegram, "It's my Dad, Sir..." and his voice trailed off as the Admiral read the news. The Admiral, now Uncle Fitz dropped the telegram on his desk. Both struggled to control their emotions and they didn't quite hug. But John dropped his head to hide his expression and Uncle Fritz gave him the time as he struggled as well. The Secretary quietly closed the door and canceled all appointments for the rest of the afternoon.

Admiral Fitz reached to his mahogany paneled bitch box, and depressed the lever," Get Air Ops at Hickam on the growler, ask when the next PBY is headed CONUS and if it's not today and by noon, get the Base Commander and make my personal request for a flight leaving ASAP. There will be a PRIORITY passenger, Commander Lodge and they have permission to embark others for a full flight, not however to delay departure for them or cargo. Cut Orders for three weeks leave for the Commander as well as travel authorization. Get Pay on the line and have him come in here with a month's pay for the Commander and I want it *toute suite!*."

Uncle Fitz turned to Lodge, "Give them our love and take good care of them and come back when you're goddam good and ready, hear me?" "Uncle Fitz, thanks." And with that he headed back to his desk and tried to call Lydia. No answer so he quickly found his vehicle in the parking behind Headquarters and headed over to the Sick Bay.

The desk called for her and she came into the lobby. One look and, "What's wrong, John?"

He took her hands in his, "My Dad has had a stroke and is not expected to live. I am packing and should be headed out on the next PBY for CONUS, in a couple three hours I suspect. Look, this is a tough time and a family time and I need to be there. If it were possible I'd want you there with me..."

Concern on Lydia's face melted into overflowing tears. "John, thank you for that, I feel the same way. I'll get you a box lunch from the canteen.."

"That's alright, they'll have something on the aircraft."

She stomped her foot, "John, I *need to do this*, don't you understand? It'll be at the plane and so will I, to see you off, SIR! And off she went, like the good wife she wanted to be.

Three hours later at the ramp, the PBY was turning up. "Here are your lunches, some for the Crew, too." He didn't say anything, so she added, "It's fried chicken and potato salad; eat the salad before it spoils."

He gave a small smile, "Yes, Mom." The prop wash was blasting them, blowing her hair in her face and they had to almost shout in order to be heard. He kept looking at her. With that look. The one from Waimanalo. "I've been back for three days from Hong Kong," he said. "I know. I missed you horribly." "Lyd I missed you too, more than I thought possible."

"*Oh God, don't cry now. He doesn't need that.*" The wind was blowing him too, but he stood rocking but steady on his feet, with his cover in his hand, all his gear was on the aircraft. *The way he's LOOKING at me!* She moved closer to him, aware that the cockpit had the window open and there were two Pilots staring at them and another crew standing in the side door, waiting for John to board. John was the best looking man she'd ever laid eyes on and just now she saw a small boy with a broken heart. She'd always been a sucker for small boys. He took a step toward her, put his arm around her, and pulled her into him so hard it took her breath away. With looks that would melt concrete they both shouted, "I love you." over the noise of the engines. And the kiss that followed was cheered from the aircraft. You'd have sworn maybe the concrete did melt down.

She stood there as the plane waddled like a duck into the water, got into takeoff position, turned into the wind and in a blast of spray took off. Then the tears came. Proud happy ones - and sad.

Many hours later at the Lodge home, in Boston, "Oh thank heaven you're here, John," she cried at the doorstep. She had seen the cab pull up and this handsome Naval Officer, her son, climb out with a Valpack in hand, stand tall and straighten himself and come to the door. They kissed and hugged and went on into the house while Nancy dabbed at her tears. To John's inquiring look she said, "He's home from the hospital. He's been sleeping. Let's see if he's awake."

"Hell yes I'm wake, tink anybonny couse sleep through all at bubbring! Get in here, Son." "Hey, Pop. You certainly went to extremes to get me to come home. What's it been, four years or five?"

"Hell don't know, all I know been too long. Pardon if I dawn gen up." Nancy brought a chair close to the bed for John, "I'll go get tea, or coffee if you want it, John" "Coffee would be fine, Mom."

Listening sharply and anticipating his Dad's slurred words, Lodge leaned close and framed his conversation so that simple answers, yesses and noes would suffice. "Uncle Fitz and Auntie Jane send all their love."

Upraised eyebrows and, "doin'? "They're as ornery as ever, Pop. I see them more often now that I'm on his Staff. They talk often of you and Mom. Say they can't wait to get together again."

'Cab', short for Cabot his middle name, smiled and drooled out of the side of his mouth. John took a napkin and wiped him dry. "No way live. Won't have to, much longer. Tell me ya nooos."

And Cab dropped into slumber while John talked about Hawaii, and a beautiful girl and his promotion and how much he loved his Dad. Nancy listened, sitting next to him with her head on his shoulder. And then Nancy talked about a small boy growing up, an only child who left and went to see the world, and how much his Daddy loved him and to watch him play tennis and Mommy too. And as he started to shake and rattle, they took his hands and held and kissed them. And when he had stopped, she got on her knees at the bedside and kissed her husband for the last time. Held him for the last time.

It was a large funeral held in a famous church and lots of famous people attended because John 'Cab' Lodge was well known and well liked. And in the crowded sanctuary were a couple who attended at the request of their daughter, a Nurse in Hawaii. By telegram she had asked them to go for her and to also send flowers. As the service proceeded his friends and politicians and titans of industry stood and spoke and offered their eulogies and memories of their friend, Cab.

Finally it was John's turn to speak, to say goodbye or whatever he wanted to say. Dressed in his Blues, tall and serious he took to the pulpit and looked out over the crowd. "Dad would be genuinely surprised to see how many are here. And I thank you for him. He would want you to all have a good time, so I'll say that for him. He knew how to have a good time and to honor him I ask that you do, too". And he broke out into a broad smile and gave two thumbs up with arms embracing them all and the whole crowd smiled and the laughter filled the great space and made the hall ring and there were thumbs up everywhere. It settled down and he continued, "My Dad was a bit of a rebel. He was supposed to go to Harvard. He decided to go to the Naval Academy instead, no doubt frustrating and confusing his parents. Then I came along and I suppose I was expected to go down to Annapolis for my education." He looked around, paused, "and I went to Harvard." The crowd gasped and again fond laughter filled the space. Lodge finished, "I'd like to think I'm a chip off the old block."

Three days later, Nancy and John were writing the last of the cards and thank you notes, when he looked through the book of condolences and caught the name, Crowninshield. He noted the address and wrote it down and put it in his pocket. "Mom, I have somewhere to go just now. I'll be back in a bit." He took the keys to the car and found the address on his note. It was in one of the best neighborhoods. The thought had occurred to him that maybe he should have called first, but he decided to take his chances that they'd be home. It was not yet suppertime and he was thinking frontal assault.

At quarter to six he pulled up at the residence. Parked and went to the front and rang the bell. A tall stately lady who looked a lot like her daughter came to the door, peered through the glass and unlocked the door. "Come in, Commander, I recognize you from your Father's funeral."

"Thank you so much for seeing me without notice, forgive my manners."

"Not at all, it becomes very busy at a time like this for families. You are welcome." Just then her husband came into the foyer, shook his hand and introduced himself, "Samuel Crowninshield, Commander, I take it you know my Daughter, Lydia. It was she who invited us to your Father's funeral."

"Yes sir, I first met Lydia at Admiral Fitzsimmons' home in Makalapa, Pearl Harbor." Mrs. Crowninshield spoke up, "Won't you come on in and sit down, Sir?" John turned to her and asked, "Please call me John." "Of course, John," and just for a moment he thought she was going to say, 'And you may call me Ma'am,' because she had a hint of Lyd's mischievous look on her face. "I'm also Lydia, as our daughter was named after me at Sam's insistence."

They moved into the sitting room and all sat down, and the two of them just sat and looked at him. Sam looked serious and apprehensive. Lydia looked. She just looked at him hard because she knew her daughter and also suspected she knew the type of man she would choose. John stood and crossed the room to Crowninshield. Sam stood too. "Sir, I request your permission to marry your Daughter, Lydia."

Before Sam could answer, Lydia stood and moved close. They both looked at her. "I have only one question, John, do you love her?" "I love her with all my heart, I love everything about her." And the look of a smitten man was all over him.

Then they all looked at Sam and he said, "Does she want to marry you?"

"Sir, I haven't asked her yet." And Lydia laughed out loud, just the way her daughter did. "I wanted your permission first and now seemed like a good time to ask."

"You mentioned at the funeral that you're from Harvard, yet are in the Navy, same as our Lydia. Do you intend to make a career of the Navy?" "Sir that is my intention. I have just been promoted to Commander." "How long have you known each other," he asked. It was his final question. "Sir it seems like a long time but honestly has been only," and he paused to think, laughed and said, I think we've known each other for about ten months, eight maybe." And he succeeded in not looking sheepish.

Lydia spoke up, "There will be times of separation in the Service and they can be hard on a marriage." Yes Ma'am," thinking of the three month time apart, only *three months* "and I know this too: I love her and she loves me. With your permission," he asked as he turned toward Sam, "I intend to propose." *He's bold and strong with a bit of a stubborn streak,* she mused, a bit of a smile playing across her face, *He'll need all of that and a hell of a constitution to handle our Lyd."*

Sam at last smiled and grasped his hand again, "And you have my permission to ask!" Lydia hugged him, knowing he would've asked whether or not he had 'permission' but still appreciating the gesture and they went into the kitchen to find something to eat, chatting like old friends and future in-laws.

The next day John went to 'Revere's' and looked at engagement rings. He picked out a stunning and large, perfect diamond, worth a year's salary at a fresh caught Commander's pay, ordered it set in a gold band with the diamond ringed in aquamarines and rubies and said he'd call for it in three days.

Having done all the damage he could or could afford he left four days later after spending the rest of his time in Boston at home, talking to Nancy about Hawaii and Lydia and telling her that he was going to propose.

CHAPTER 24

ON THE TENNIS COURTS

Lodge stepped down from the side hatch of the PBY, his ride back to Hickam Field, yawned and looked around. The place was practically deserted as his flight had landed at 0200 Saturday morning. He lifted his Valpak and a jeep took him to the parking area behind Base Ops where his car was parked. As he got into his car he noticed an envelope, opened it to read a short note from Lydia.

"I have been staying at your place in the valley. If it's after work as you read this, that's where I am. I've missed you. Please hurry home!

Lyd"

He took the drive up Nuuanu slowly, in the dark. After the trip and burying his Dad he was reflective, thinking it was time to get busy with living and making new memories. He pulled up to the cottage, doused the lights and went around to the trunk to fetch his Valpak. The kitchen light came on in the house and the door opened and there was Lydia in her nightgown, holding her arms out to him. They hugged, standing there in the doorway and tears welled up and dropped and they kissed for a long time.

Finally she said, "Tough trip." He set his luggage down inside and she went to set the coffee pot on the stove. He took off his uniform tunic, loosened his tie and sat at the table as she did the same. "I met Sam and Lydia." She looked up, "At the funeral?" "No, actually at their home." She cocked her head quizzically, waiting for the explanation. "Your Mother reminds me of you, same laugh, and also beautiful." Her eyes started to mist again. He stood up, straightened his tie in front of her and slowly got down on one knee as she continued to sit there. "Lydia Darling, will you marry me?"

She made as if to get up from her seat and he dropped all the way to both knees, leaned forward and put his arms around her waist, holding her where she was and put his head in her lap. "Oh Honey yes I'll marry you." And she lifted his head to see his smile and his tears as well. They more or less swapped positions with John sitting in the chair and Lydia in his lap. He reached into his pocket and withdrew the velvet box and handed it to his lover. She took in her breath at the magnificence of the diamond surrounded by red and blue stones. "John I love you with all my heart and I always will." My ring is beautiful. They slipped it on and it fit perfectly.

The neglected coffee was perking madly and about to boil over, as was John. He turned the stove off, swept her into his arms and took her to bed where they also fitted perfectly together.

Ten o'clock in the morning, after maybe only two hours of sleep and John staggered into the kitchen, cleaned the mess on the stove and started a new pot of coffee. He heard Lydia in the shower, smiled happily and started some bacon in an iron skillet while he checked the fridge for some eggs. Had he checked in the mirror he'd have seen dark circles under his eyes, tousled hair and the bleary look of a night without sleep. She came smiling into the kitchen in her robe looking radiant and gorgeous, hugged him, "Good morning, Hon," and put some bread on a cookie sheet and in the oven for toast. "Gotta' say I love a man in the kitchen, but this is my domain" and she bumped him with a hip away from the stove and poured them both a cup. He took the opportunity for a quick shower and run of a comb through his hair and returned in his robe for breakfast.

They both ate ravenously hardly looking at their food while efficiently putting it away. Then it was gone, plates wiped clean with bits of toast, coffee finished, and Lydia said, "How did your visit with my parents go?" "Your Mom caught on right away, wasn't particularly surprised and was very gracious. She's a lot like you and she made me feel very at ease. It'll take Sam a little longer to get used to the idea, I think. Maybe more to the point is, what do you think, big wedding or intimate and small? What might your parents want?" I think they will want only for me to be happy," she replied. "And what will make you happy, Sweetheart?" "I'm thinking not a long engagement, but enough time for perhaps my folks and your Mom to get out here, spend a bit of time in the Territory and with us and then a small wedding with the people who matter the most to us standing up with us."

After a week in Hawaii, the Crowninshields, Nancy Lodge, RADM Cochrane and SN1 Dantes made the trip to Makalapa. They were welcomed at the door not by a steward but by Jane and Fitz, all smiles and the girls all aflutter as they swept into the formal dining room. The Bride had stayed the night in the guest room, had been given a garter by Jane, a pink one to go with the pakemu that John had given her. There had been no fittings of an elaborate gown as the happy couple had decided to do it in their uniforms, perhaps an acknowledgement that they were marrying each other and yet both remained married to the Service.

John had engaged the base Chaplain, who although employed full time and therefore not expecting a payment had been given $200 for his services. The wedding party were all in starched Full Dress Whites with large medals, the tunics coming up to high collars with long sleeves, a very formal uniform and perfect for a sparkling Hawaiian day. A small band had been offered, almost turned down with thanks and then they remembered the one who would not be attending, so at Lydia's suggestion they included the quartet and requested the Navy Hymn, "Eternal Father," in honor of John Cabot Lodge, John's Father.

The ceremony took place on the tennis court, a special place for John, remembering her in her tennis costume, entrancing him and oddly enough the place where he started "courting" Lydia. All of the hibiscus and orchids were in bloom amongst the lush ti leaves and tropical foliage surrounding the courts. The brilliant sunshine in a cloudless sky flashed off of the gold stripes of the men's shoulder boards as well as their unsheathed swords when they came into play. Rod Kinney had organized the arch of swords, with all of the tennis invitees from that first time at Makalapa participating. When it was time for the rings Dantes came forward with them and handed them to Lodge, receiving a fond glance from Lydia. It was another touch in the wedding that had been requested by her. John's choice for Best Man would have been his Father; instead he had his 'Uncle" Fitz and they had asked Dantes to be the bearer of the rings.

The Chaplain gave a short homily and asked those attending to stand with this new couple and strengthen their bond as it was known that there would be separations when the Naval Service required them to be at different parts of the globe. "Eternal Father" was played to the accompaniment of stricken looks and tears of shipmates remembering lost friends and classmates. Vows were exchanged and the rings put on and the groom kissed his bride. The sword bearers formed up in two files facing the pulpit and at a soft command turned center, facing each other in two ranks. Another command had the sound of naked steel scraping against scabbards and all swords placed at parade rest. As the couple made to approach, another command called the detail to attention and then formed the arch, four swords rising in military precision. The couple entered the arch but were not stopped at the end of it. Civilian brides were customarily halted and given a swat on the fanny with the flat of a sword, 'welcoming' them to the Navy. It was a nice touch that they did not do this to Lydia, as she was already a member of the Service.

The reception was well attended, a parade of vehicles arriving on schedule and every Commander on the Island as well as all of their friends coming to congratulate the newlyweds. Inviting Dantes had been LT Crowninshield's idea and she also set him up with a young nurse's assistant from work as a date for the occasion. Lodge had approached Aku and asked if it might be possible to purchase the cottage in Nuuanu Valley. The skinny Kamaaina raised an eyebrow and a small frown, "That'll be a tough one, John." But when he approached the owners and explained that it was to be the first home for the newlyweds, the Bishops relented. They also offered the use of their retreat near a secluded waterfall on Maui for their honeymoon. It was a place where in ancient times young couples had gone for their honeymoons.

After their honeymoon on Maui they threw a luau at their new home up Nuuanu way and invited of course the Bishops, the Fitzes, everybody they knew including the Mayor of Honolulu. It was their coming out party as a couple and everyone they knew showed up and had a grand time.

Eventually as the days and weeks passed he asked her why she didn't just come home, leave the Navy and enjoy their home. In reply she asked him the same question, "Honey, why not just leave the Navy and live here in Nuuanu Valley?" He answered, "Because I want to serve." She just looked at him. "And that is why I became a Nurse and a Commissioned Officer, Dear; I too want to serve. And I know that you have the financial resources to afford for me to stay home. Well I also have the financial resources to afford your staying at home or painting or writing or any other hobby you might want to pursue." And he just looked at her. "We are not taking any precautions to avoid getting pregnant," he said. "No, and that's the way I want it too. If and when I get pregnant I will want to come home to stay and care for our children, if we are lucky enough to have them."

With that decided they settled into a happy married life, tried like the dickens to have babies and did it in a carefree joyous manner.

In the meantime the intelligence that Lodge and RADM Cochrane had gathered was being sifted and compared with other sources. Reports of the movements of Isoroku Yamamoto and the Imperial Japanese Navy and Army were sought and pounced upon as analysts did their jobs trying to see into the future and into their likely enemy's mind. Assets were being shifted to anticipated pressure points and supplies, though scarce, were being placed in depots within range of the Fleet units that would eventually require them. Finally, new leadership was being identified and long range plans made to install key players where they would be needed, not if, but when the Emperor's forces made their moves.

CHAPTER 25

RACE PREPS

Two knocks on the door of the Detroit Commanding Officer's inport cabin, with the armed Marine guard standing in the passageway, looking Dantes over even as he returned the favor. "Come," is heard through the thin bulkhead and Dantes stepped into the CO's presence, stopped two paces from his desk at attention, cover held at his right side, eyes in the boat and focused about two feet above the Captain's head as the Marine sentry softly closed the door. "Seaman First Class Dantes reporting as ordered, Sir!"

Captain Phil Ryan looked up with interest, if not irritation at this Seaman whose name kept coming up, seemingly involved in significant event after event. Yet the reports are all good, it's just that it's unheard of for an enlisted man, *any* enlisted man and non-rated at that to be spoken of by the senior Officer in the entire Pacific theater. If the scuttlebutt is to be believed, he'd actually been to Makalapa, some said he played tennis with CincPac, himself! *He's sharp looking, perfect uniform, where in hell does he get that confidence?* "At ease, Sailor." And Dantes relaxed his posture slightly, a sort of loose parade rest and let his gaze drop to that of the CO.

Ryan fingered the sheets clipped to the manila folder that was Dantes' Service Record. He'd been reading its contents and the record was thin; he was but a Seaman First, after all. "Says here you were your Company's Honor Graduate in Boot Camp," looking up at Dantes. Dantes remained silent, he was not being invited to chat. *Hmm, he is waiting for either a question or an order.* "Also says you had the best qualifying scores on the range in rifle and pistol firing, and I happen to know that you are on our pistol team. Aaand you're from Beaumont, Texas, also made the whaleboat crew and if what I hear is to be believed you're responsible for our win in the recent regatta." Still no visible response, but the look was not that of an automaton. Respect, certainly, but not any sign of awe or discomfort. Dantes simply waited to see what this was all about. He figured that Officers got interested when any of their subordinates were in the company of their bosses, might even want to know what was discussed and how it came about. He expected his Division Officer and Department Head were as curious about this summons to the CO's cabin as he was.

"Why'd you join the Navy, Dantes?" "Sir, same as most I suppose. Jobs were scarce and I wanted to better myself." "Like it?" "A lot more than I expected, Sir, yessir. Of course there is a lot to learn, but I do enjoy standing the watches and I am proud of the Navy, Sir." "How'd you get to know the Mayor of Honolulu, Dantes?" "Sir, it was after the whaleboat race. He was one of the dignitaries aboard the Admiral's Flagship, watching the race. My boat crew was invited aboard and congratulated. He was in the reviewing party, Sir." Ryan tossed the service record into his out basket and eased back in his chair, holding a communications flimsy received that morning from CincPac, UNCLAS. "Says here that Detroit's whaleboat is to participate in some races in Honolulu and that you and your crew are to be given time to prepare and that you are in charge of this evolution. Do you know how this came about, Dantes?" "Yessir, when the Admiral suggested we race the Battleship champs I thought it might not look so good for a cruiser to beat the battleship winner." "Did, huh?" "Yessir, I thought it might be more fun to mix it up with the Hawaiians, where we both could win, do it for fun." "Were you so sure that you'd beat the heavies?" "Sir, with the way the wind was blowing and our method of steering it was likely that we'd beat them, so long as the wind held out." "You modified the oars, too, didn't you." "Sir, Chief Locker got me some help and the shipfitters did a good job. We needed every advantage we could get."

Ryan was smiling now, he liked sailors who dodged the credit. "One last question, Dantes," and he chuckled, "did you really play tennis with CincPac?" "Oh, no sir. He just gave me a job, chasing down the balls that went past the screen." "Well, good luck in your race with the Hawaiians. I'm putting you on temporary additional duty on the beach, with your crew. You'll billet with the Shore Patrol at the Royal Hawaiian and get your chow there but you won't be making tours with them. Dismissed, oh and one more thing, I am proud to have you representing Detroit." "Sir. Thank you Sir." And with that Dantes came to attention did an about face and smartly left the CO's cabin.

In the First Division berthing compartment, Dantes and his crew sat at a mess table waiting for Hicks to show up, "Daughter, are you sure Hicks understood where we were meeting?" "With Hicks, who's sure of anything? You want me to go looking for him?" Just then Hicks shows up, sits down and says, "What's up?" "Okay, ship's Office is cutting TAD orders for the whole boat to cover two weeks of practice time, the race and what I expect will be a mighty fine party after the races. Recreation is outfitting us with special jerseys and shorts with neat lettering. We're going to be billeted at the Royal Hawaiian, free of charge because we are starting and ending the races at their beach, right at the hotel. I'm going over on the beach today to check in with the hotel and give them our names and get our room assignments. I'll take Daughter with me and we'll visit with our buddies at their boat yard. We'll need to set up some practice sessions for ourselves in their canoe and for them in our boat. I've requested that the ship include Chief Locker in our detachment, to be in charge of it and he and the XO have agreed. So, if there was any question, the Chief is in charge and I know he will have high expectations of our conduct ashore.

Now, for the Races themselves. The outrigger canoe is much narrower and lighter. It gets its stability from the outrigger. To propel it we will use paddles instead of oars. We're getting two weeks to get used to paddling instead of rowing. It'll be a different set of muscles but I think we'll at least be in shape from our rowing training so it ought to be a really fun time. The first race will be from Waikiki to Diamond Head. I want to start out with us in the whaleboat. The Hawaiian team should beat us handily on that leg of the race. At Diamond Head we will swap and it'll be us in the canoe, the Kanakas in the whaleboat. We should easily come across the finish line first at the Royal Hawaiian. But it will still be the Hawaiian canoe that wins the races, both of them. He looked around the table and saw excited faces and lots of smiles. "Who knows why we're getting to do this?" "Because we won the cruiser division." "Nope. Who else thinks he knows why?" Somebody said, "Because you have pull with the Admiral?" "That's ridiculous," Dantes replied as they all laughed. Daughter said, "Because the Mayor and CincPac see a chance to form better relations with the locals and the Navy." "Exactly right. Our job is to make a good impression for the Navy; we get to have a good time doing it. Let's be sure we don't mess it up."

Dantes also had use of a ship's vehicle, making it easy to get the crew back and forth from the boat yard to the hotel. They pulled up to the Kekoa brothers' boat yard and got out to be greeted by a hugely smiling Kaikane and Holokai. "Hey, Bruddah, Daughter *really* good to see you! You know, our business has really picked up since you got us invited aboard after the race. The Mayor has visited us and started steering business our way. We are now offering souvenir paddles like the one we made for Moku Lahaina!" "That's great, Holokai, I'm really happy for y'all." "We going to start calling you laki kekahi. Means lucky one," said Holokai. Mo beddah we call you akamai kekahi, means smart one," Kaikane laughed. They all laughed at that and Dantes said, "I'd like to see if we can set up doing our practices out of your yard, for my crew in your canoe and for your guys in my whaleboat." "We wouldn't have it any other way, Bruddah, besides I think lots of people will come here to watch us in our boats and maybe enjoy some of the practice sessions. Who knows, maybe even some wahines might be interested in some good lookin' sailors." And Daughter and Dantes both grinned at that. So, it'll be okay to store our boat with you and you'll have paddles and everything?" "You bet and there's another little detail that you might not yet know about." They looked at Holokai. Remember that we had two VIPs on our canoe on race day? They looked at each other, "ahh maybe. Was it a large Hawaiian woman and a man seated next to her?"

That's exactly correct. The lady is directly descended from Princess Lili-uokalani, the last Royalty in the Islands. Actually she became Queen as our last ruler. Although we no longer have royalty we still have great respect, ka mahalo, for our heritage and our old ways. It is that respect that keeps us in business, making these canoes the old way for those who still respect our traditions. Anyway, Akela Ailani, the honored descendent wants to be aboard the canoe for the races, along with her husband," and Holokai looked at them with the question on his face that said, "any problem?" It will be our honor, Holokai, and a supreme one at that." Everybody relaxed at that and they agreed to start tomorrow. Before leaving, as they turned to go, Kaikane said, "We have something for you guys," and he went back into the shop and came out with plumeria and Vanda orchid leis, one of each for both Daughter and Dantes. The sailors thanked them profusely but Dantes said, "I don't think we can wear these in our uniforms." Holokai said, "No problem, Bruddah, we also got civvies for you" and he brought out pairs of shorts and a couple aloha shirts and some flip flops. You gonna' race in a Hawaiian canoe we gotta' make Hawaiians out of you. At that they decided to stay for the rest of the afternoon, and were brought into the shop to change. The brothers brought out some bottles of beer and they sat down to while away the afternoon bathed in the sweet smell of frangipani and relaxing in laughing wisecracking brotherhood. It was the best...

That evening the boat crew and Chief Locker moved into the hotel. Chief got them together and told them there would be a loose curfew, be in your rooms by ten, each night. He and Dantes had talked about it and Dantes thought they should observe some kind of taps if for no other reason than to not detract from their training. After two days of training Dantes went to see the Chief, knocking at his room. Locker came to the door, "What's up, Dantes?" "I need to bounce some thoughts off you, Chief. I think we may have a problem." They went down to the beach and found two beach chairs and sat for awhile. "Chief, I've noticed some surly looks by some of the tough guys down by the boat yard. I mentioned it to the brothers and didn't get much from them, but I think I can figure it out." Locker just kept looking out to sea, nodded and asked, "What do you think, Dantes?" "Well, the Kanakas have a name for us, haoules, and anybody with anglo blood in them, even if born out here is called hapa haoule, half white." Locker stayed silent, waiting to hear the rest of it. "I think there is still resentment of Americans coming in here and taking the islands. I don't know if it's a big problem but there must be a reason why the Mayor of Honolulu jumped on this as a chance to "improve relations."

At that Locker looked directly at Dantes, truly impressed with his mature thinking and inquisitive mind. "What are you worried about, Dantes?" "Well, it occurs to me that some of them might like to throw a wrench into the works right before the race when there's almost no time to do anything about it. They could damage one or both of the boats, for instance. The Mayor is a white guy and they may resent him, too. Maybe he has political opponents who would like to make him look foolish. I don't know but I do know that I was sent over here with a job to do and I don't want any of that egg on the Navy's face or for Detroit to get a bad reputation for not getting the job done." "What you say is interesting and hard to believe, coming from a sailor whom I had to pull out of a shack in Tijuana just a year and a half ago. I agree totally that you have identified a possible problem. Now, what do you recommend that we do about it?"

"Chief, I figure that they know we could replace a whaleboat pretty easily, but the canoe would be a big problem. If anyone were to try to damage a boat it would be the canoe." "I agree." Dantes continued "I'd say we approach the Kekoas with our concerns and see if they know of a substitute canoe that is available. They have the most to lose if something goes awry and would want to help us avoid a last minute emergency. We could also increase security for the boatyard with some sort of fencing and put some tough guys of our own on the premises every night. One more thing is that we could gather the materials needed to make a patch in the hull or reinforce a hull strake and maybe bring a shipfitter or two in with the tough guys, just in case."

Chief sat back in silent amazement at the thought processes of his young protégé. "What's our next step, Dantes?" I'm thinking *your* next step, Chief. I asked for you to be in charge and of course there would be no one better to handle this." Locker came forward with his forearms on his knees, emphasizing his points with his hands. "I say you approach your friends, the brothers and broach your concerns. I will be glad to back your play. You're the one who spotted the problem and I think you are perfectly capable of solving it. I'll see about getting people and materials ashore from the ship if you recommend it, but this whole deal is yours." "Thanks for your confidence, Chief. Although the last thing we need is violence I think we need to be prepared for it. I think we need a couple of pistols, a .45 or two ought to do, and that you and I should be the ones who have access to them."

The two went straight to the boatyard and found the Kekoas there, working on some souvenir paddles. They could tell right away that this was no social visit, put down their tools and said, "What is it, Bruddah?" Dantes told them what he'd noticed and what he thought they should consider doing about it, finishing with, "Of course this is your property, your canoe and your livelihood. I can't just come in here with demands, but I do have some responsibility for ensuring that we get to complete our mission. What do you think we can do together to prevent or counter any deliberate "mishaps?" They both turned and looked at Chief Locker, who in turn just looked at Dantes, letting him carry the ball. Holokai said, "I think there's no way that something like this would happen." Dantes didn't reply but turned to Kaikane. "And I think that this is entirely possible and that we need to prepare for it as though it is going to happen," Kaikane replied. Holokai thought for a moment, "It would be foolish not to take precautions, wouldn't it? He asked with an unpleasant look on his face. Finally Locker spoke, "how many men might you allow here on a nightly basis?" "I guess that depends upon how many we are preparing to repel," Kaikane replied. "Also how many we could put in place without making it obvious," Locker said. They settled on four able bruisers and two shipfitters to be added for the last two nights. They would not put any measures in place this first week but would do so with two days left before the races. In the meantime they would keep their eyes peeled for any suspicious activity or increased attention.

Locker went back aboard, briefed the XO and checked with the Gunny for four volunteers. He checked in with the Chief Master at Arms and got two .45 pistols and some spare magazines, fully loaded. The CO was briefed by the XO and said only, "Violence is the last resort, use those guns only if you absolutely have to." Then he got hold of CDR Lodge, invited him aboard for lunch and told him what was going on. Lodge was very appreciative and forthwith briefed the Admiral. There was the chance, after all, that he or the Mayor might prefer to call it off. CincPac went calling on the Mayor and they chatted. It was the Admiral's thought that they should not cancel on a fear but should just be ready for it. The Mayor was a bit more nervous, suggested no pistols and the Admiral agreed. The Mayor sat down and wrote a couple of press releases for his use if something did occur and the pistols were put back in their locker aboard Detroit. The races were on.

For the second week of training Dantes procured some pig iron and placed it in the canoe right about where the VIPs would be sitting. He had gotten a total weight estimate for the special guests and it came to 300 pounds. They practiced with this additional weight in order to get an accurate feel for the ride of the canoe and how she would handle in all sea conditions with the VIPs aboard. At the shop there was nothing amiss, no loiterers, no nothing. Kaikane was going around saying I told you so and Holokai was saying we just scared them off. It was three days before the race when Holokai said it again, "We just scared them off." That's when it clicked for Dantes. He said nothing to the brothers, but found Locker, again in his room.

"Chief, we're making a big mistake." Locker looked at him. If something is going to happen it will be at the turnaround point, in the vicinity of Diamond Head. We have had no protection there and it is wide open to anyone who might want to disrupt things, maybe sink the canoe or the whaleboat. Locker got a grim smile on his face and nodded, "I think that you've got it figured out, Dantes. It's bothered me that there had been no activity, none at all at the shop." Dantes said. "I have a suggestion." "Let's hear it." We go to Gunny and have him go out to Diamond Head for a pistol practice. As part of his normal routine he can take all the pistols he wants out there. Instead of pistol team members he takes his Marines; we can depend upon them to handle firing at people if it comes to that better than sharpshooters who only shoot at paper targets. And we don't wait until race day, but do it the day before as well as race day, if necessary. It's my guess that they would pick the day before, when the VIPs would not be aboard and there would be no spectators. The plan is to do it where we ain't, and *when* we ain't." Without further ado, in the time honored manner of Chief Petty Officers throughout the Fleet the resources were put together and put in place, including a motor whaleboat loaded for bear that would stay on station until the end of the race. No one was informed and no permission was asked. After all, it was just a pistol team practice, right?

In the meantime, Mayor Wright was having some thoughts of his own. With no fanfare five days before the races he went to the Kaikoa boatyard, pulling up in a plain Chevy coupe. The brothers welcomed him effusively but with an air of what's up. They went into the kitchen where a couple of beers were brought out and they all sat down to talk. The Mayor turned toward the two brothers earnestly, "Really nice shop you guys have here." They both thanked him and thanked him for the new business he had created for them. "My pleasure, totally," he said and then got straight to business. "I have some pretty sharp detectives on the island and we've put out feelers in the usual places to see what we could come up with for suspects." Both brothers said, "And?"

"And I'm coming up with blanks, nobody bragging what they are going to do, nobody making any threats, no obvious preparations for some kind of violent mishap that we can find." Kaikane turned to his brother, "I *told* you I thought it was nothing!" "Yes and you also said it was a good idea to take precautions," Holokai said. "Precautions is what I do, as a politician", said the Mayor, holding his hand up for attention. "Tell me what you can remember that set this sailor Dantes off. Can you remember what was going on at the time?" "Now that you mention it, I recall a couple of the bruddahs poking their noses in and looking none too happy about things," Holokai said. "Yea, Kaikane added, it was Kimo and his guys from the boatyard down Ewa way." "Another boatyard? Competitors of yours?" The Mayor leaned forward and asked. "Yessir, we end up taking business from each other from time to time." At that Mayor Wright sat back, comfortable for the first time, asked for another beer and told them what he thought they might do about this situation.

Three days before race day. Holokai turned to Kaikane, "I guess we'd better go see Kimo and Kavika." "Yeah bruddah let's head to Ewa." It was a smaller boat yard but busy just like theirs. The two Hawaiians looked up with suspicion on their faces, and hostility. A couple workers also stared at them and one of them reached for a hammer. "We ain't looking for no beef with you guys," Holokai said. "Nah, we got an invitation," Kaikane added. At that everyone relaxed a bit and drew closer. "Look we talked to the mayor and he suggested maybe we make the race a little bigger. We want you guys to enter a boat, one of your canoes, for the leg from Diamond Head to Waikiki." Kimo and his men just looked at them suspiciously. Hey man it's a big ocean, room for everybody." At that smiles broke out and they went into the shop, sat down and talked about the details.

Back at the boatyard, sitting in their own shop, Kaikane turned to Holokai, "What we going to tell Dantes?" Holokai replied, "I been thinking about just that very thing. This whole race is really his idea, even the Mayor is just trying to take advantage of it." Kaikane nodded. Holokai continued, "I say we tell him nothing." Kaikane frowned, "Why? There is no more problem; I think the Mayor had a good idea." "Yes it was a really good idea but we don't know for sure that what Dantes is worried about isn't still going to happen." Kaikane scoffed, "I knew all along there was nothing to this." I know that's what you *thought* and I hoped and still hope that you're right. I say we let things go along the way they are. It'll be safer. Besides, when you look at it, this could be a really big thing in a few years. I can see villages putting up big war canoes representing their heritage, and the race taking place between Molokai and Oahu, bruddah. It's a few years off, but when it happens I want us to be building those boats and racing. With the Mayor behind it I expect there will be a big push for this and we can ride the wave."

Race day dawned bright and warm and there was a large crowd at the Royal Hawaiian to see the two boats, the Navy's Moku Lahaina whaleboat and the Kekoa brothers' canoe, the newly named Moku USA, beached on the sand just beyond the place where the hula shows were held. The starter blew his whistle and the two crews ran to their boats and pushed them into the water and started rowing and paddling to get them through the surf and out to sea far enough to turn left and head for Diamond Head. It was a good four miles once you got the boats out past the surf, nothing these crews couldn't handle, both ways. As expected the Moku USA got out to a quick start through the surf and headed for Diamond Head. Dantes had his crew moving smoothly through the surf, as they'd practiced it several times; but also as expected they quickly fell behind. He told his crew not to worry, just keep going steadily, this was more of a workout than a race. And he checked for the third time the .45 pistol he had wrapped in a piece of oilskin, still wondering if they would run into any trouble this afternoon.

Diamond Head was in view from the very start and although they couldn't yet see who was at the turnaround point, Dantes knew that the motor whaleboat with several Detroit Marines and Chief Locker in it was certainly patrolling the area and ready to handle anything suspicious. In about an hour as they were approaching the finish line for the first leg Dantes noticed an additional boat, a large Hawaiian canoe and it was headed toward the race course, seemed to be headed toward them. As the Kekoa's boat slowed, finished and sat rocking in the gentle swells, broadside to the approaching Moku Lahaina the mystery third boat joined up with the other canoe. Then Detroit's motor whaleboat also joined. Dantes brought his boat up and stopped as the motor whaleboat embarked two men, one each from each of the two canoes and headed toward Detroit's whaleboat. Dantes could see Chief Locker holding a thumb's up for him, telling him it was alright. As they pulled alongside, Holokai reached out and took hold of the gunwale of Dantes' boat. Dantes looked at him for an explanation.

"Bruddah, we got a request from another Hawaiian boat that wants to join the race. I told him dis was your race, your idea and you had to make the decision." Dantes looked at the Chief and the Chief said, "Your call, Dantes." Dantes gave a huge grin of relief and stood up in the boat, motioning to the Chief. As they drew fully alongside he handed his oilskin package to the Chief and then turned to the other Hawaiian and introduced himself, "Hod Dantes." "I'm Kimo, and we have a boatyard in Ewa and thought this was such a good idea that we wanted to join your "Navy" and join the fun." Dantes reached across and they shook hands and Dantes said, "Of course, the more the merrier. And, uh, I have a request of my own." "Sure, Bro, what you thinking?" "I think we should mix up the crews, making all of them part Navy and part Hawaiian." Kimo split a huge smile of his own, readily agreed and all three boats nested together while Dantes told off who would transfer and to which boat while the motor whaleboat assisted as required to do it quickly. Dantes and the two Kekoa brothers ended up in their canoe and Daughter and Hicks went to the other canoe. When it was all settled Dantes pointed toward Waikiki and shouted, "Let's *GO!*

Chief Locker and the Gunny kept pace with the boats and kept an eye out as well. As the Moku USA pulled ahead and at the halfway point, where the Moku Lahaina was pretty far behind, Dantes turned to Kaikane who was steering and told him to turn the boat around and circle back to the whaleboat. Kaikane looked at Holokai who nodded and smiled in admiration, and they did exactly that, dropped back alongside the whaleboat and kept it company, heading for Waikiki. Meanwhile the two honored guests were delighted with it all and kept up a happy conversation, pointing and laughing. The third boat caught on and it too circled back and joined up on the other side of the whaleboat, putting her in the middle of a tidy little flotilla rowing and paddling toward Waikiki. And that's how they finished the 'race', a dead heat or as close to it as they could manage. They turned in unison toward the beach and rode the same wave into the shore where a huge crowd awaited them. There was amplified slack guitar music and a line of swaying hula dancers and the Mayor and the Admiral waiting for them along with a buffet that seemed a hundred feet long, tables groaning with luau pig and pineapple. The photographers were there, shooting for their papers and the crowd cheered lustily each time a flashbulb went off.

At last the music died down and the Admiral stepped up to the mike. "Alooooha!" he said. "This is the most fun and best liberty a sailor could possibly have." And he turned to the Mayor and stuck his hand out to be shaken, "Thanks for putting this on, Mr. Mayor." And he turned to the hotel Manager and thanked him as well. The Mayor thanked the Royal Hawaiian, the two boatyards and the Navy for having the brilliant idea for the race. "This is a great display of the friendship between our Community and the United States Navy." And with that he thanked the Admiral for his leadership and said, "Let's eat!"

At the tables, when they'd gotten their chow Kaikane brought the honored guests, Ailani and her husband up to the tables and they sat and joined Dantes and the rest. Holokai brought up two heaping plates of food for them and they all sat down together. Ailani looked up at Dantes, "That was a very generous thing you did, today," she said. Dantes looked back with the greatest respect, "Ma'am, is was truly a pleasure and an honor to have you aboard." A servant or retainer came up behind her and handed her a lei. It was plaited of bright green Ti leaves and not a loop but instead made like a scarf and about five feet long. With it was a matching headband. She got up and went to Dantes, who also stood, as he realized he was about to be honored. "This is an old Hawaiian custom, and the green lei symbolizes appreciation, admiration and respect." With that she put the lei around his neck and tied the headband in place across Dantes' forehead. Then she hugged him and kissed him and whispered in his ear, "No Hawaiian can deny you anything on this day. That is our custom." People from all of the tables were standing and clapping and cheering and Dantes was blushing. Clapping hardest of all were Commander Lodge and Lieutenant Crowninshield. The Mayor and the Admiral came up along with a photographer and pictures were taken. Overwhelmed by it all Dantes turned to look for his Chief, found him and they both broke out huge grins. Dantes merely pointed at the Chief who shook his head and pointed back at Dantes. Holokai said to Dantes, "You are invited to stay at the home of Akela Ailani tonight and for the weekend. They are hosting a luau tomorrow and everybody will be there." And with that they all sat down again and ate and drank until the sun went down.

Late that night as they were saying their goodnights, Dantes took Holokai by the arm and pulled him aside. "Bro, I have a question or two." "And the answer is, I don't know." Holokai said even before he could ask. Dantes stared closely at his Hawaiian friend. "I will say this, they had a canoe all equipped and ready to go and they had no problem getting a crew put together on very short notice." "Tell me the whole story, Dantes replied." Kaikane and I had a visit from the Mayor and he had searched high and low to find any plot or potential attackers. He could find none so he asked us if we had any ideas. I thought of our competitors, Kimo and Kavika. He suggested we invite them to join the race. Kaikane and I went over there and did just that. I decided not to tell you because I didn't want the Navy to pull the protection. We didn't actually *know* that we had shut down a possible problem and Kimo hasn't said anything except to thank us for the invitation. They may have had something in mind, I don't know. I'm sorry for not telling you but I had confidence that you would understand and handle whatever might come up, and you did. Perfectly." As Dantes took all of that in, Holokai added, "By the way, you're invited out to my Mom and Pop's place tomorrow afternoon when things die down. We hope you'll stay the night. My Sister, Kuulei will be visiting home, from Saint Andrews Priory School. I'm sure she would like to meet you."

At their home out in the country, the next morning after breakfast Akela Ailani showed Dantes around the place, a beautiful setting of cliffs and waterfalls. There were cattle and a garden, some plantings of pineapple and sugar cane and lush stands of koa trees, hibiscus and frangipani. A stream ran by the house and under a short bridge that took the drive out to the highway, a mile and a half away. The bright colors amazed him and he felt great gratitude just to be here amongst so much beauty and so many friendly people. "Here is where we are cooking the pig," Akela said. "We put it in the ground the night before the race. First we build a great fire and use it to heat lava blocks. We get the dense kind, the pahoahoa and we heat it up before we even go for the pig. We also dig the hole and cut banana leaves with which to wrap it. We have a trapping pen out in the woods where we usually have some wild hogs. When we know we are going to roast a pig we generally pick the best one and turn the others loose. Sometimes we will feed that pig for weeks or months. When it's time we slaughter the pig and cut it up into roasts and wash it all down with salt and water. Then we wrap it in the banana leaves and immediately put it in amongst the heated pahoahoa blocks. We put some more hot rocks on top of it all and then put the dirt back on top, to hold in the heat. For this luau, since so many are coming, we killed a wild hog and bought two more from the butcher in Honolulu. We ordered them ahead of time and he is able to keep them refrigerated until we pick them up, or he delivers them. They are whole hogs and we decided to roast one on a spit and do the other one in the ground. We also put bananas and pineapple and chicken in the hole with the pig. If you like you can try them all and tell us which you like best!"

People started arriving at noon and all were met with leis and cool fruited rum drinks. A trio of three singers had also arrived and set up close to the cooking area with a ukulele, slack guitar and drums. Soon Hawaiian tunes were heard and they blended with laughter and excited talk as the crowd gathered. Akela Ailani took Dantes over to meet a woman of some fame as a hula teacher, Mama Bishop. They chatted for quite awhile and Mama showed him the sign language used in hula, the birds fluttering and soaring, the waves and wind over the Pali. She finished her tutorial with the laughing rejoinder to "Watch the hands, not the okole." Mama Bishop wore her customary muumuu which hid her own natural curves. You only noticed the okole when she thrust her hips from side to side as she "went around the island." Dantes was totally enchanted by this smiling and impressive Hawaiian woman and he introduced her to Lieutenant Crowninshield and Commander Lodge as they strolled up, drinks in hand. "Good to see you, Ma'am, Sir," Dantes said respectfully. Lydia replied, "We understand that you are the guest of honor, Dantes. And I very much like the unusual green lei and headband you are wearing." "It is a gift from our host; she gave it to me right after the race and said that as long as I wear it no Hawaiian can refuse my request," he smiled. "Oooh then I do hope you will ask Mama if she will teach me the hula," and turning to Mama Bishop she said, "You are very well known among the ladies at Pearl Harbor; I understand they clamor to be included in your classes. Lodge shook his hand and told Dantes he was mightily impressed with his leadership. Then he added under his breath, "and your alertness to a probable incident was noted and appreciated." When Dantes reacted with a surprised look, Lodge took him aside, bent closer and told him that in their investigation the Navy had determined that indeed a likely attack had been avoided at almost the last minute. "Is there going to be any further action or is the investigation closed," Dantes asked. "I believe that the Mayor's office is going to keep a local boatyard under loose surveillance for awhile," Lodge replied. "I have just one question, Dantes. To your knowledge were the pistols returned to the ship before the race?" "Sir, the original sidearms that were drawn from the armory were returned to the ship before the race." Lodge looked closely at him. "However the pistol team was in the area and they did have their firearms with them, naturally. We practice in the crater at Diamond Head, actually, Sir." Lodge smiled in admiration, "No more questions, Sailor, and thank you for your candor." Dantes in turn was grateful for the information and appreciated the trust shown in him by the Commander; but typically he was not about to say so. It was the Admiral himself who put it in his mind that there were confidences you just automatically protected. Some things you just didn't talk about. For his part, having his suspicion that Dantes was armed during the race confirmed added to Lodge's overall confidence in Dantes as an outstanding and capable seaman. He would not repeat his information to anybody either. This was a normal process, the adding of seemingly disparate bits of information until they formed what was known as a service reputation. You tended to dilute your own service reputation if you divulged too much or did so unnecessarily. Both Dantes and Lodge appreciated that truth.

Akela Ailani had asked Dantes if there were any friends of his whom he wanted to invite to 'his' party. He had responded that he would not want to put her to expense or trouble, but asked if it would be okay to invite The Admiral and Mrs. Fitz, Lodge and the Lieutenant, his Commanding Officer and the XO and his Division Officer and Department head. And he added, "Of course the Kekoas, as well. And two Chief Petty Officers from my ship, Chief Locker and Chief Grundy. "May I call you something besides your last name, son," she asked. Dantes blushed deeply, "My apologies, Ma'am. I have been forgetting my manners. At home in Texas they called me by my middle name, Howard. My little sister shortened that to Hod when she was very young and couldn't say Howard. It would honor me if you were to call me Hod, Ma'am." "That's settled, Hod and if you would you could call me Kupunawahine, it means Grandmother." Hod repeated it twice with her correcting his pronunciation until he had it right. With that they hugged and laughed and Hod rejoiced to have not one but two grandmothers. They came in handy when you had already lost your Mom and your Dad.

As the afternoon wore on the luau fare was steadily consumed and the musical troupe had played all the songs they knew and the sun was sinking fast behind the mountains when the Kekoas made their appearance, and Dantes, standing with Chief Locker was introduced to Kaikane and Holokai's parents and their grandparents and their little sister, Kuulei. They stood there, smiling and talking about the race, when Mr. Kekoa mentioned that they would be honored if Dantes would come to the house, spend a weekend or longer if he could. Chief

Locker spoke up, "Dantes, now might be a good time to tell you, sorry I forgot to mention it earlier, but the XO and CO have endorsed and approved a request for meritorious leave for you, one week." Dantes looked totally surprised. "But I made no such request, Chief." "One was made for you, Dantes and may I add my congratulations. The rest of the boat crew got a weekend and there are rooms at the Royal Hawaiian for all of you for the duration of your liberty."

"Ohh how nice," Kuulei chimed in and they all turned to look at her. "You *will* come out to the house, won't you, Dantes?" And they all laughed and looked back at Dantes who once again had turned a shade of red. He looked directly at Mrs. Kekoa and thanked her and Mr. Kekoa for inviting him into their home and said he was honored. The rush of friends and family, dignitaries and neighbors had wended their way to their cars, thanking Akela Ailani on their way out. Dantes and the Kekoas were among the last to leave. Once again he thanked her and she replied that he was now a Hawaiian in her eyes and she truly appreciated the pride and recognition he had made possible for her people. It seems she was Kupunawahine for all Hawaiians and Dantes was one of them. The Kekoa brothers slapped him on the back and they all piled into the last vehicles still parked and headed to the Kekoa homestead.

CHAPTER 27

KUULEI

Driving to the Kekoa home, with the brothers, the Kekoa parents and grandparents and Dantes and Kuulei, took three cars. "Holokai and Kaikane have spoken of you so much!" Kuulei said. "Finally I get to meet you. Did you really get them invited aboard the ship with the Admiral of the whole Pacific? Tell me about that!" "Well there's really not much to tell," replied Dantes. "They say that you already knew him, the Admiral, and that you just invited them to go aboard with you." "Well that's not quite true. Yes I had been up to their Quarters in Makalapa but just as a driver for a Commander on the Commodore's staff, he just chose to befriend me because we had been on the bridge of the ship at the same time and had a chance to talk and discuss things." Her eyes dancing as she sat in the backseat of the car across from him, she kept him talking. She didn't get too many chances to talk to sailors or to any young men for that matter. On the bridge, huh? I bet you get to steer that huge ship, don't you?" "Well yes, but…" "Kuulei, give our guest a chance to catch his breath!" her mother exclaimed from the front seat. And she cast a sidewise glance at her husband driving them. He had a slight smile on his face, listening while still paying attention to the road. He was thinking of a time when his wife had peppered him with questions, too, only nobody stopped her and see where it had gotten *them*.

Dantes picked up the conversational ball, "I take it you go to school, College maybe?" Kuulei smiled, "Not yet but next year, yes. I go to Saint Andrew's Priory School for girls. It's a private school founded by Queen Emma Kaleleonalani, the wife of King Kamehameha the fourth in the late 1800s. It was with the help of Kupunawahine that I got a scholarship. Dantes took notice, here she was again, his new grandmother, wielding influence at many levels of Hawaiian society. In a few minutes they pulled up at the Kekoa home, a modest place sitting to the side of a county road. As they got out and headed to the front door, the others also pulled to a stop and debarked, all of them congregating on the front porch while Dad just opened the door. It was unlocked.

They went inside and Mr. Kekoa went into the kitchen and got some beers and brought them into the living room. The women stayed in the kitchen making sandwiches and frying some chicken, while Kuulei edged toward the living room where she could listen. And watch Dantes. She was fascinated. The grandfather, the kupunakane, sat in the best chair and mostly just listened while the brothers and Dantes talked about the race. Kuulei was startled when Kaikane, her volatile and standoffish brother stood and walked across to stand next to Dantes. As Dantes stood up Holokai noticed Kuulei eavesdropping and went to the door and apologetically but firmly closed it in her face. He knew what Kaikane was going to say and it was man talk.

"Bruddah." Dantes looked at Kaikane with interest but not fear or apprehension of any sort. "I got to tell you sorry." Dantes just stayed quiet, figuring it was best to let him get whatever he was stirred up about off his chest. "Man, I was wrong about those guys from Ewa, they meant to do us harm. You were right all along." Dantes' mind was racing, "What do you know? Why are you saying this?" "Simple, bruddah. Did you notice who was not at the party today?" Dantes made a show of thinking it over, not wanting to belittle his excitable friend. "No, I didn't know most of those there today and I hardly missed anyone who was not." "Two things, Dantes. You were the guest of honor and the gang from Ewa was not there. They were in the race but they were not invited to the party." As it hit Dantes exactly what Kaikane was saying, Holokai added, "Any Hawaiian would instantly realize the meaning of this snub. When Akela Ailani did not invite the participants it had to have been deliberate; she would absolutely not make a mistake like that. Did she not ask you who you'd like to invite?" Dantes nodded. "See, the grandmother knew exactly what she was doing. They don't give out those green Ti leaf leis every day, you know. Those are almost a national award when bestowed by the Kupunawahine, a direct royal descendant."

Dantes flopped down into his chair, taken aback by all of this. He looked up at Kaikane and shook his hand. "It's okay, Kaikane, I was probably way too sure of myself. I doubted my own observations when nobody came around the shop." Kaikane responded, "And you don't have to tell me, but that was a gun you had wrapped up and next to you, I think, and you turned it over to your Chief." "Yes, I didn't want anything to happen to the honored guests, in case it suddenly got rough." "Kupunawahine knew that too, and she appreciated your consideration and bravery. No other explanation."

As Kaikane sat down the grandfather spoke up, "You do our family honor by joining us. Everything Kaikane said is true. What the Grandmother said is true also. If there is anything you would like from a Hawaiian you have but to ask." Dantes looked up and grinned and said, "Then I'd like another beer, how about you, Grandfather?" The tension and apology over and accepted they all trooped into the kitchen and began munching on the goodies and getting their hands slapped. Kuulei barely had time to get back from the door, where she had heard everything.

After the late night snack as they were all finishing and the women were cleaning up the kitchen, Holokai cocked an eye at Dantes and said, "My bruddah and I are going to head home and let you catch some rest. It's been a long day. My parents, and Kuulei I'm sure, have plans for you for tomorrow. Probably hit the beach, one of the small ones around here, feed you and make you feel welcome. When Kuulei goes back to school we'll come and fetch you, take you wherever, maybe spend some time at the shop. That sound good?" "That sounds mighty fine, bruddah." Dantes was picking up on some of this Pidgin English that the brothers liked to toss around. And with that they kissed their Mom and Kuulei goodbye, rounded up the grandparents and took them out to their car for the ride home. Mrs. Kekoa showed him to the bathroom, gave him a towel and showed him his room, the one that the boys had slept in, growing up. Mr. Kekoa went around turning off the lights and locked the doors, bid him goodnight and he joined his wife in the bedroom.

Dantes treated himself to the luxury of an actual shower, though he limited it to a very short one, Navy style, wrapped his towel around his middle and made his way quietly to his room. He stepped inside and turned on the light and closed the door behind him. As he did so, Kuulei swiftly stepped across the room from the closet where she had been hiding and turned the light off. Dantes held his hands up, palms out silently giving her the stop sign in the dim light from the window until his towel started to slip and he had to reach quickly to keep it from falling to the floor. He went to the door and stood there motioning silently for her to leave. She was dressed in a modest nightie that came to just below her hips and though made of flannel and not clingy, left little to the imagination. Instead of leaving she sat down on the bed and did a little pout as she crossed her legs. She was a fully developed and beautiful young woman and they both knew it. Dantes didn't want a fuss so he sat on the other side of the bed and whispered, "You'd better get off that bed and back to your room before your parents hear us and come in here." "I'm just here to ask you if there's anything you need," she whispered back. And she did her best to look winsome and sultry at the same time. Dantes had to guffaw at that one, but he did it quietly. "Look, I am of course very flattered that you have thought of me this way but I am a guest in your parents' home and of course I would do nothing to insult them or betray their trust. Now either you leave on your own or else I go and knock on their door." At that she said, "They are already asleep and I would be very surprised if my Mom didn't suspect that something like this would happen." "Suspect it she might but welcome it she would not. Now you go back to your own room." "Fine. But first

I want to hear you say my name." "Okay, Kuulei. What does it mean?" "My flower, or my child. As you can see I am no longer a child." "No comment, and let's say goodnight." "Alright, if I can call you something besides Dantes." "You can call me Hod." She leaned across the bed and smiled a "Good night Hod" and kissed him gently on the cheek. And then she was gone, leaving a scent of frangipani, and he wondered if he had imagined it all. It had been a long day.

And in the bedroom down the hall, Mom smiled next to her snoring husband and turned over and went to sleep.

Next morning and everybody had been to the bathroom and cleaned up and put on some clothes and appeared, one by one in the kitchen. Mom and Kuulei were rustling some bacon and eggs while Pop sat at the table drinking his coffee and reading yesterday's paper. The atmosphere was anything but electric; it was completely normal and relaxed and Dantes felt as though he was in his Grandma's house at the farm only there wasn't work to do and his Grandma wasn't making pies and fussing over him the way she did. The way he loved. He pulled on his coffee and mulled his answer. Mom had just asked him about his home, back on the mainland. A sleepy smile crossed his face and stayed there. He started telling them about Texas and a little town called Lockhart and a boy on a farm who had already lost his Mother and his Father by the time he was fourteen. Kuulei sat down across from him with a plate of eggs and bacon and sausage for both of them and asked if he had any brothers and sisters. Before he could answer she also asked if he had a girlfriend. Mom and Dad looked at each other knowingly, small smiles on their faces and also waited with interest to see how he answered. Dantes grinned, "Oh, there was a girl in Beaumont, where I worked at the movies…" "But I thought you said you lived on a farm," Kuulei quickly replied. "Well, yes but the family decided that I needed to go to a better school and I went to live with my Aunt and Uncle in Beaumont for my eleventh and twelfth grades." "This girl, you write to each other?" At that her parents laughed out loud, "Kuulei, let Dantes eat his *breakfast!*" And Kuulei smiled to herself because he hadn't said yes, but she also said, to no one in particular, "And his name isn't Dantes, Dantes, it's Hod." "And Kuulei means my child or my flower," Dantes responded, looking at her across the table, "and whose flower are you?"

At that both parents laughed, delighted with the light tone the conversation had taken and impressed with Hod's quick wit. Pop spoke up, "We thought maybe a beach trip this morning?" said with a questioning look in Hod's direction. "Why that would be super," he replied. Just as Kuulei was about to pull a glum face, as she had other thoughts in mind, Mom spoke up, "I think I'll stay home. I have things to do around here." And she didn't quite nudge her husband though she reached with her foot under the table and gave him a small kick. Which turned into a sliding stroke up his leg. Pop quickly got the message that there was going to be some fun for him if he stayed home. He suddenly remembered that he needed to catch up with work out in the yard and he returned to his paper while Mom refilled his coffee and squeezed and rubbed his shoulders while she was there. It seemed that having these two young people in a normally almost empty house had excited both of them a bit. Kuulei openly smiled at the two of them. They were still in love and they showed it.

After cleaning up the kitchen Mom brought Hod a pair of Holokai's old swimming trunks while Kuulei, who had already changed into her one piece suit, made some sandwiches, two for each of them and tucked them into the family wicker picnic basket. Pop brought Hod the keys to the family sedan and Mom gave him a smile, drew close and said simply and quietly, "Thank you, Hod." And that's when Hod knew that she hadn't been asleep last night. Kuulei noticed too. And she kissed them both on the cheek and thanked them for the use of the car and said they'd probably be back for supper. Mom said, "you'd *better* be back for supper!" And with that they were off, with Kuulei giving directions to a beach that she said was her family's favorite. Actually the thing they liked most about it was that almost no one knew about it or went there and they usually had it to themselves. As Hod drove she kept scooching closer to him until she was sitting right next to him with their thighs touching. He put an arm loosely across her shoulders and she kept her hands to herself. But no mistake, the atmosphere in the car was electric and both of them were tingling.

They drove for maybe thirty minutes and finally took a turn to parallel a stream that ran down into the sea. "This is it," Kuulei exclaimed, "our family place where we've come ever since I was a little girl." They got out and took a blanket and the picnic basket with them and strolled a hundred yards or so away from the stream to a copse of coconut palms. Dantes was astonished to see that the sand was inky black. Kuulei explained that it was broken up lava and this was one of three or four such beaches she knew about, but the others were all on the Big Island or Maui. Dantes tried to slow things down a bit by asking her about school, what it was like to be in a girl's school. Kuulei put down the blanket and he put down the basket. She thought for a moment, "I'll show you one of the things I learned in a girl's school." And she turned toward him and held her two hands pointing left at right and right at her left and then slid them together with the index finger and middle finger of the left hand rigidly extended and nestled into the same two fingers of the right, which were equally stiff. It formed a bundle of four fingers and she held it out to Dantes, saying, "hold it, it's what we girls do in our rooms at school." He did and she said nothing, just stood there a little closer to him while he held on to her girl's school 'handshake' for want of a better term. He wasn't embarrassed, and though it was a new thing for him, he had had the feeling of holding something quite similar in his own hands, only bigger he thought. He let go and put his own hands together in the same way and held them out to her. She looked into his eyes and slowly grasped his four fingers. They filled her hand. She went a bit further, slowly stroking, sliding her hand back and forth. Then she pulled his hands apart and kissed his palms and said, "That's what girls in school think about and talk about. Let's go in the water."

The swim did little to cool them down, though the water was a bit chilly. They took refuge in splashing each other and he chased her and dunked her and she at last climbed onto his back and he walked around with her legs wrapped around his waist and her arms around his neck. Back on the beach she spread their blanket and remarked the absence of tattoos, "I thought sailors had tattoos." Hod laughed, my Grandma made me promise I wouldn't get any. How about you, you have any tattoos? I know that many Hawaiians do." As they lay down on the blanket she pulled her straps off of her shoulders, leaving her suit still covering her breasts and looked downward, "nope, I don't see any." And there they were, alone as she had schemed to do and still she wouldn't make the first move. It wasn't that she was particularly shy, it was more that she didn't really quite know how to go about it and was perhaps losing some of her bravado. Hod was past thinking about it. He reached out and tugged her suit a bit lower and she moved closer to him to snuggle and he pulled her suit all the way down to her hips. And at last they kissed. After awhile she pulled his trunks down and finally held him and not just his fingers. They spent most of an hour like that, caressing and kissing and breathing heavily. They rolled around and she had her back to him and he spooned her. She would reach back and tease him with her hand until finally he did the same for her, through her suit. She pulled it aside, giving his hand access and they continued doing what was natural until both of them relaxed and Hod pulled the blanket over them. Hod and Kuulei both had enough time to realize that they were glad they hadn't gone "all the way" before they fell asleep together.

They awoke with a start, realizing it was getting late. She could feel him poking her from behind. Already feeling more like a woman she turned toward him and her look said, should we take care of that. "You remember, Kupunawahine said that no Hawaiian could refuse you *any*thing." So they did it for each other, a second time and then straightened their suits and got up to go back home. At the car door she paused with her arms resting on top of the car and swayed her hips, letting him enjoy, and enjoying herself, the display of a bit of native talent. Of course it felt different, driving back to the house. She was sweetly possessive, supremely confident and very, very happy. They walked in the door and her Mom took one look and she knew. She also knew, by looking at Dantes and the natural respectful way he still carried himself that her daughter and Dantes were most likely boyfriend and girlfriend and were certainly enjoying it. As they sat down to dinner Mom set a bowl of vegetables in front of Hod and while she was there she gave his shoulders a bit of a squeeze, "You two look like you had a good time at the beach!" "It was beautiful," he said. And what he meant was, she was beautiful, and that's what both Mom and Kuulei heard. Pop missed it all, eating his steak.

Later that night, as Mom shook the blanket out and folded it, she put it to her face and breathed in a bit of the scent of love making. It was the same scent in their bedclothes, left by her and Pop that same afternoon. She knew that the Kamaainas, the old ones, were loving and active people. Their heritage celebrated sexuality in dance and song. Women were often seen partially clothed and they did it naturally, with no shame. She, herself, had had sex with one boy before she met her husband to be and had done so when she was only sixteen. Kuulei was now eighteen, and she had always been a beautiful child, a precocious and natural one when it came to showing affection. It was one of the reasons why they had accepted so quickly when Akela came with the scholarship to Saint Andrews. It was a chance, she had thought, to perhaps extend her daughter's childhood. Mom smiled at the thought, *it must have been like confining a volcano, my goodness it's in her heritage, it's in her blood!* She had a quick few tears through her smile, sniffed and wiped them away and put them in with her memories for the day when she would be an old woman and have only her memories.

The next morning the brothers showed up to take Hod to the shop and drop Kuulei off at school. The brothers rode in the front and the two lovebirds in back. Kuulei reached up and kissed him as soon as they were out of the yard and they kissed all the way to school, not caring if the brothers looked, after the first kiss. For their part, Holokai and Kaikane kept up a running conversation in front, overhearing the passionate sounds coming from the back seat but keeping their eyes mostly to themselves. About two blocks from school they sat up and kissed one last time while the car idled at the curb and she asked him when she would see him again. "I'll let your brothers know, maybe next weekend, if I don't have the duty." They waved goodbye as the car pulled away.

Back at the shop nobody said anything until Kaikane brewed some coffee and brought a cup to Dantes, set it down on the table, looked totally seriously at him and said, "I think she likes you, Bro." He blushed and they all laughed good naturedly. And they waited for his response. "Look, your sister is just totally beautiful and I've never met anyone like her and I wonder what your parents must think." "What you mean, what they think, they invited you to their home, didn't they?" "Well, yes and I made sure that I respected that in the way I treated Kuulei while we were there." "Yeah, we can tell by the way Mom treated you this morning that nothing upset her, nothing at all. She seemed happy to us, right brother?" Holokai drained his cup and put it down. "Dis is nobody's business but yours and Kuulei's, brother. If it happens for you

I'm happy for you both and if it doesn't I am still your friend. To the end."

With that talk turned to business prospects for the shop and again thanks to Dantes from the entire family for having given them an enormous boost. Eventually the guys needed to get to work and Dantes told them he had leave for the week and was staying in a room at the Royal Hawaiian. "Maybe we come and see you this week sometime. What room you in?" "Uh, it's room 220, on the second floor facing the beach." So they drove him to the hotel, left him at the front portico and he took the elevator up and crashed on the bed and slept for several hours, his dreams populated by a beautiful Hawaiian maiden.

CHAPTER 28

GOODBYE

In room 220, of the Royal Hawaiian Hotel in Waikiki, the phone sounded almost angry. Ring…ring…ring. Hello, hello, who's this? And Dantes settled back in his chair as he heard coins being deposited into a coin telephone. Ding, ding kachunk, kachunk and Kuulei's voice came on the phone. "Hod, is that you?" "Yes, my flower, what are you doing up so late. You have classes tomorrow." "I know but I was thinking about you. Are you thinking about me?" "You know I have been, almost constantly." He could almost hear her smile over the phone. "I want to see you so badly. Is it bad of me to be calling you?" "Of course not, but if we are still talking when the operator comes on the phone, ask her to reverse the charges." "Thank you, Hod." "Listen Kuulei, I need to talk to you too, but I want to do it in person." She smiled at that, "Ooh I would like that." "Maybe so, maybe no, but there are some things we need to talk about and the sooner the better." She thought about that for a moment. "How do you want to do it?" "I can use the staff car while I'm here on leave, and I could come to the school and pick you up. Is there any time that you could get away for a couple of hours, anytime soon? I will be back aboard ship in less than a week," he explained. "Hmmm I do know that some girls have gone out at night through the window and snuck back in the same way. Do you want me to do that? And sometimes girls get signed out to their parents' home for special occasions."

"Here's what I think. If you think it will not get you in trouble I will come by the school tomorrow night and wait at the road where it joins the turn into the school. We can either talk right there in the car or we can come back to my room. Let me know with a phone call by eight tomorrow night if you can't make it. If I get no call I'll be there by nine thirty." "Alright, if I can't make it or chicken out I will call you. At eight." Thanks, Kuulei and see you tomorrow night, I hope."

As it turned out, she got out through a window after lights out at nine thirty and made her way to the car. He was waiting for her and they hugged and kissed and he held the door for her to get into the car. "We can talk right here, Hod said." "Alright," she replied. "This sounds serious." "Well it is serious," he said.

"You know I have feelings for you and at this point they are mostly physical and affectionate. You are the most beautiful and wonderful woman I've ever met. I know I want you more than anything." She just smiled happily. Hod expected some guff at some point and was already surprised at her patience and composure. Before he could continue she replied, "You are worried about me when some day you have to leave me, when your ship goes away and the Navy doesn't let you take me with you, if you even wanted to do that." His jaw almost dropped as he stared at this beauty talking total sense to him. "You are also worried about what my parents will think if we become a couple and then you leave. You worry that they will feel betrayed." "Yes, yes of course you are totally correct." "Hod, of course I want to make love with you. We could use the back seat of the car this very instant and do it until the sun comes up. I think. I don't know if that's possible." "But I think it is very unlikely that we will become married," he said. And she interrupted, "And you think I should save myself for my husband, right?" By now Hod was totally deflated. He didn't feel like a noble lover giving his girl an out, he felt like an amateur who was more out of his depth than he had thought.

She looked him over, still liking what she saw. "Don't you think I should be the one to decide who will be my first lover? Don't you think that I've thought of nothing else but my first time, for a long time? At the age of eighteen I have already waited longer than almost all of my friends; I can wait a little longer. The question is, can you? I know that I will not be your first. How do you feel about taking my virginity from me without giving me yours?" And with that she unbuttoned her blouse and opened it up a bit, letting a bit of a breeze blow across her through the car window and he smelled the frangipani flower she had pinned there. "I think I don't mind that you have had women before. It is not necessary for me to be *your* first, it is only necessary that you want me more than anything you can imagine, the way I want you."

This was not going the way he had imagined, at all. "Anything else you want to talk about, Darling," she asked sweetly. He smiled at her, wanting her more than ever, "No, I don't think so," he said. "Then I do have a bit more to say. For me, when you touched me at the beach and I touched you we had already become lovers. That was the first time anybody had touched me there. You are the first whom I've seen and touched that way as well. On the way back in the car I felt more like a woman than a girl. A man does that to a woman, I guess. I'm proud of you and I have these strong physical feelings and affection for you, too. But I want you to think about all of this for a few days and then let me know what you think.

And then she took her blouse off to reveal that she had no bra on and started unbuttoning his shirt. She smiled, "nothing wrong with another sample. For both of us." An hour later she was dressed again and walking toward the school. He stood outside the car, watching her go. She reached the back of the dorm, turned and waved and she was gone, again leaving behind the faint scent of Frangipani…

Three weeks passed while Detroit went out into the local operations area and Hod was thinking about Kuulei a lot. He was finding out that when out of her presence he settled down and regained control of his emotions and thinking. *There is no way that I can see to be together with her,* he thought. *Her Family trusts me and think that I am an honorable person. We are both too young, just starting out. Kuulei deserves to have her own man, one who will be home every night.* Then, the night before pulling back into Pearl, the Skipper got on the 1MC and announced that the ship was detaching from Hawaii and returning to her homeport. They would be headed to San Diego within a few days!

Hod was wearing his best whites when he showed up at the Kekoa Brothers' boatyard. "Hey, Bruddah! Good to see you again!" in chorus from Holokai and Kekane. They slapped each other on the back and the brothers looked at him knowing, because it was already written on his face. Dantes was a stricken, tortured young man, barely out of his teen years and though he was unusually self-controlled he didn't bother to hold back his emotions. "It's true, then, your ship, Detroit, is leaving the islands?" Unwilling to trust his voice Hod nodded. "Yeah we heard, small article in the Advertiser. Told Kuulei yet?" He shook his head. "Want us to take you out there, to her school or the house? Better yet, if you remember the way we can loan you the car." Hod nodded his thanks and took the keys gratefully.

First he drove out to the house and found Kuulei's Mom there, with her Husband gone to work. She hadn't seen the article in the paper but she invited him in and they sat at the kitchen table. As he told her her face crumpled up, just the way Hod's did. She hugged him and kissed his cheek and thanked him for coming to tell her in person and Hod's back heaved with choked back sobs. She passed him the kitchen towel and they both used it. "You haven't told Kuulei yet?" "No Ma'am. I think I would like to go out to her school and see her there, tell her goodbye." She nodded. "And I have something to tell you, as well," he said. Kuulei and I think we are in love with each other and if I were to be able to stay here I would want to be together with her. I want you to know that although both of us wanted more, we stopped, Kuulei and I, and it was her decision as much as it was mine. She is such a wonderful young woman and someday she will find the one that is meant for her." He left her softly weeping at the table and quickly headed to the school.

At the Saint Andrews Priory School for Girls, they called her from her room, where she had been studying, daydreaming really. One look and of course she knew. They went outside and sat in a small flower garden on a bench and they were surrounded with clouds of frangipani scent. "You're leaving?" she said. He nodded. They hugged and kissed and cried. "I hate the Navy," he said. "No you don't, you love it and you love me too, I know. I love the Navy also because you're in it. Without your being a sailor I would have never met the love of my life," she said. "I love you, My Flower, and I will never forget you." "Oh, Hod, I love you too. So does my whole family. We will all miss you." And she snapped off a whole branch of the plumeria growing there and put it against his chest, leaned into him and kissed him one last time and left.

Back aboard Detroit, enroute San Diego at a respectable twenty knots, fantail bouncing just a bit as she left her wake bubbling and tossing astern. Dantes is there, holding on to the lifeline. Chief Locker came up and stood beside him, saying nothing for awhile. "Peaceful place, the fantail," Chief said. "I don't want to be here," Hod said; "I'd a lot rather be back there." "The goodbyes are a lot tougher than the homecomings," Chief replied after a minute or two. "Chief, did you ever have a girl, a woman that it just tore your insides out to leave?" "No, son. Ummm, I can remember three, maybe. Or was it four?"

And Dantes turned toward the Chief, his Chief, and laughed his first laugh in several days. They grabbed each other by the forearms and laughed and laughed as the very last bits of Dantes boy-childhood bobbed and spun into nothingness, left behind with their wake in the vast reaches of the Pacific.

CHAPTER 29

THE DEBRIEF

At CincPac Headquarters in Pearl Harbor, Admiral Fitz was following a career-long habit of checking how things were going by walking around and ambled into Dick Cochrane's outer office, a pleasant word to his Secretary and, "May I go in?" She of course was standing and smiled and nodded an invitation to "just go right in, Admiral." Cochrane had heard the deep bass and the excited response and was standing, himself, as his Boss and friend of some twenty five years poked his head in and said hi.

They went off to the side to the visitors' twin couches, and sat as Barbara came in with coffees for both, receiving their thanks as she quietly closed the door on her way out and rescheduled Admiral Cochrane's next two appointments. Fitz cast a glance at Dick's desk, cluttered with papers with much scribbling and erasures, along with a notebook or three and said, "How's it coming along, Dick?" "Sir, it was an interesting trip and I'm trying to be accurate and at the same time give you more than numbers." "Dick, you're an old China Fleet Sailor and it's your impressions that I sent you for. Those numbers will end up not being very different from the ones that I have that are updated every year. By all means take your time with the official report. We'll classify it as SECRET and that'll make it hard for anyone to even get a look at it, myself included. Of course it'll go to DC and eventually find its way to the War Department and who knows, maybe the President and by that time it'll likely have my name at the bottom. I want to know the guts and the feathers, who's scared of whom and what they're doing about it and how much help we can expect when the balloon goes up."

This was the Admiral Fitz, Cochrane knew and loved. They were as alike as two peas in a pod and had known each other for so long they could have finished each other's sentences but they were too polite and respectful of each other to do so. Cochrane cocked an eye at Fitz, "I still have a few bottles of the Black..." Fitz grinned, "come on up to the house for dinner. I'll have Jane set an extra plate, make it 1830." Cochrane stood at a respectful attention, not rigid but comfortable as CincPac got up, spent a minute chatting with Barbara on his way out, leaving smiles in his wake as he always did, unless he was pissed.

Jane reacted with genuine delight when she got the call from Fitz; she thought her husband could use more such time with his long-time friends and she especially welcomed Dick Cochrane. "Do you think you might also like to invite John up with him," she asked. "Not this time. We'll probably be talking about John as part of this debrief and he doesn't need to be there for that." Jane's eyes danced at that because she loved John Lodge as a son and knew that what Fitz would be talking about would almost certainly include where they would use him next. A word to the steward and it was done, steak dinner for three and a little time on the lanai before they started.

It was an annual exercise, pulling together updates from all of his subordinate Commanders and it would soon be drawing to a close. Cochrane's cruise was different, though, this was the first time that Fitz had sent out one of his staff to look at all of the potential hotspots. He was in no rush to get the final product but he very much wanted the chance to question his chief investigator and get some of his personal observations. With Dick it would be the next best thing to being there, maybe better in fact as it was his experience that many times he got nervous and ill-considered answers as people tried to figure out what he wanted to hear. And that was something Fitz could not abide. And again, Fitz reflected on that astonishingly accurate and direct interview he had conducted in his study at Makalapa. *A Seaman First! Dantes,* he recalled. And he looked forward to settling in with some scotch and getting briefed by Dick Cochrane.

Meanwhile, in the First Division Compartment, USS Detroit, San Diego Naval Base: "Mail Call! Here's one for you, Dantes." Hod looked at the envelope and it had foreign stamps, he recognized the likeness, it was Manual Quezon. It impressed him that he actually was somewhat acquainted with someone so famous. Actually this was the third letter on the subject he had received. Quezon had offered the services of his personal lawyer and Dantes had accepted. Then Dantes had heard from his Attorney, Ricardo Verdad and they had agreed upon the services he would provide and Dantes found out that Quezon would be paying the required funds into an account in Dantes' name upon which Verdad could draw. The meaning of his lawyer's last name was not lost on the boy from so close to San Antonio. Today's letter ought to be an update on his requests. He opened the letter eagerly to see.

Dear Mr. Dantes,

Your deed is filed and a copy with the required stamps and signatures is enclosed. I have been to your property and am happy to report that there are retainers living there and a list of dwellings and other buildings is attached. The people using your land are not paying rent but they do turn in an annual accounting and a record of incomes and disbursements is also attached. From now on all disbursements will go through me, and essentially they will be reduced to zero. Your funds will be allowed to accumulate and earn interest. You have some cattle and goats and a few small crops. It's enough to keep the retainers alive but with a little extra. They were very glad to learn that you would be continuing the arrangements and look forward to serving you.

On the other, more personal matter you asked me to pursue, I did in fact find a Miss Rosa Vasconcellos working at the establishment you named. She did remember you. If I may say so, vividly! We met privately at her home in order not to arouse any unnecessary interest from Mrs. Rosario Gabangabang. I acquainted her with some of the facts concerning your recent acquisition and it seems she has a few relatives in that area, so she is familiar with the property and also with the Calderones. She has great respect for the Calderones and now she evinces great respect and appreciation to you, Mr. Dantes. I assured her that your offer of a place to live and work, on your property was genuine. She was emotional. What can I say, these Filipinas are warm, emotional creatures. I told her that there was one stipulation and only one; that she could work and live there but not in anything even remotely resembling her present employment. Mr. Dantes, she leaped out of her chair and threw her arms around me. Indeed I weep at the memory of her total joy. She messed up my suit! I jest, Mr. Dantes, but it is true that you are venerated for your generosity and even more so for your bravery, about which people are only now starting to learn. We require only your signature on the enclosed contract which lays out all of the conditions for her use of the property. As you asked, the initial contract is drawn up for a period of ten years, to be automatically renewed unless you desire not.

Sir, if I may be permitted, this is truly one of the most admirable and satisfying experiences of my professional career. God bless you. I will make another report after the contract is executed and let you know how things are going. For now I am keeping communications with you private, as you'd expect, but will forward any from Miss Vasconcellos as and if you desire.
Sincerely and with great admiration,
Ricardo Verdad, Esquire.

Dear Ricardo, thank you for your services, you have done a fantastic job! If you would please continue your loose supervision of the property I would be indebted to you. In particular I desire that people not be allowed willy nilly to live there, but only as approved by you. My goal is not to make money but to provide for Rosa and her family. We need to perhaps control the numbers of people living there until we are sure we have the necessary funds to support them. Other than that, again my thanks and I look forward to hearing from you again.
Horace Howard Dantes.

PS. Ricardo, the real bravery was Rosa's as it was her warnings and willingness to part with dangerous information that in fact saved my life. Please tell her that I am in her debt and that she has my admiration and thanks.
Hod

Hod licked the envelope and the stamps at the ship's post office and paid for registered mail. He figured that was that and he'd likely not hear about it again until Verdad chimed in with an annual report. *If I'm lucky I won't find I'm in arrears for some new taxes or something.* He promptly put it out of his mind.

Admiral Cochrane drove himself up the hill to Makalapa, no need to have some poor driver sitting out in the car waiting for him, he'd thought. He eased to a stop, grabbed his briefcase with the notes in it, and the scotch and went up to the door. Jane and Fitz were both there with a handshake and a hug. Both men were dressed in khaki trou and aloha shirts and boat shoes. Dick also had a side arm in his briefcase, just a little extra protection for the information he carried. Inside he unlocked the briefcase from his wrist, rubbed his wrist and was handed a glass of iced tea by Jane who then went into the kitchen to check on their meal. It was nearly ready and she dismissed the stewards for the night and joined the gentlemen out on the lanai. After watching the start of nautical twilight for a few minutes they went inside and sat down to excellent steak and potatoes. They finished with a bit of espresso and some cake and then excused themselves into Fitz' study. Fitz brought two old fashioned glasses in with him and Dick broke out the scotch. After lighting up a couple of Cuban cigars from Guantanamo Fitz turned to his sidekick and said, "How much trouble we in, Dick?"

Pouring two stiff ones over ice, Dick said, "Down and dirty?" Fitz said, "You know the answer to that." They both took a swallow, let it chill them all the way to their stomachs and Dick said, "It's worse than anyone thought. I'll tell the tale in chronological order, pretty much as we performed the cruise." Fitz noted that Dick hadn't made a move to unlock his briefcase, much less break out his notes. The P.I. thinks they have a savior in Quezon and so does Quezon. Furthermore, Manual talks of Arthur MacArthur as though he were there only yesterday and can't wait to get Douglas out there, the sooner the better. I wouldn't be surprised if he offered him some grand title like Field Marshal of the Philippines and of course MacArthur would just eat that up, as his due of course. Their Government is in flux as they make their way incrementally from colonial status through commonwealth status until they eventually gain full independence and statehood. At some point either Quezon or his successor will undoubtedly demand we relinquish Clark Field as well as Subic. One can't really predict which way Quezon will go next and that's dangerous in a region that values personal politics so highly. He is a very powerful man. US policy is even more changeable than Quezon's, bouncing back and forth between beneficent and peremptory, depending upon which US Governor we have there at the time and how serious he is at pursuing good policy. On the one hand the Filipinos want us out and Americans largely have a bad reputation while on the other they know that they can't even rule in their own country against insurgents, much less foreign players, without massive American assistance. Quezon walks a fine line between dependence upon the US and the need to satisfy the hunger for independence in order to stay in office." "Got a prediction?" Fitz asked.

"Yessir, I think they will get MacArthur out here and he will do a good job of ferreting out the weaknesses and making solid recommendations for fixing them. But he will not get the needed funds and Quezon will not get the numbers of volunteers he needs, either. I think by the time the Japs get ready to take the Philippines it will not take them very long. That they will absolutely make it one of their goals is certain because the P.I. sits across their shipping routes, the ones they need to control for shipments of oil and other materials." "Do you think they will make it their first target?"

"No Sir. I agree with the Dutch and the Aussies that the first target will be the oil fields and refinery and storage facilities of Royal Dutch Shell, in the Dutch East Indies. The Dutch of course want to retain their possessions in Java and Borneo, but not badly enough to fund naval construction or to re-deploy their assets from the North Atlantic to the Pacific and give themselves a decent shot at it. They are too cozy with the Germans, selling them their submarine technology and their strategy is frankly ludicrous and certainly not supportive of the US. Their plan, if it can be called that, is to let the US and Japan duke it out and destroy each other's major capital ships, such as battle-ships and then simply to prevail, like vultures over the leavings of the Japanese fleet, using heavy cruisers they don't even have and refuse to fund.

Australia knows this and are similarly dependent upon our good offices for the survival of their fleet units, such as they are, and for their very existence when their own military must necessarily fail them. None of this is for want of fighting spirit in their Commanders, either the Dutch or the Aussies. It just amounts to a matter of priorities. The priority is defending the European homeland, not the colonies. That's where the money will go and that's what is going to determine victory here in the Pacific."

"My questioning has gotten you out of geographical order, we skipped the Brits." "Sir the Brits are aware that they didn't handle Jerry so well in the At-lantic in the War and you can detect their lack of confidence in their bravado, referring to themselves as the largest Navy in the world. Again it's homeland over far flung and shrinking Empire. Their ships are showing wear and their best units are back home, not here. It seems everyone is counting on the good ol' USA to save their bacon this time around, especially in the Pacific." "And finally the US Fleet, my Fleet, how prepared are we to be able to contest suc-cessfully with the Japanese?"

"Leaving out our units that are based here in Pearl, not so good. My assess-ment of the China Fleet is that it is worn thin, aged and out of practice. With the movement of IJN units I see, I know they are every bit as aware of those facts as are we. They know we depend upon our battlewagons. They have the results of Fleet Problem Thirteen. Isoroku Yamamoto will soon, if he has not already done so, be planning the demise of our major fleet units at Pearl. They have a history of surprise attack and they have never been beaten. If they can take us out at Pearl they have a chance, given that they have the oil to keep their war machine running, which means given that they also have the Dutch East Indies.

"Finally, before we dive into your briefcase and look at individual strengths and weaknesses, if you had my job, how would you prepare for what you have just described as coming?" At that Cochrane sat back and relit his cigar which he'd let go out in his impassioned description of the situation. He poured himself another scotch and one for his friend. "Sir, we would need to keep our major units in Pearl somewhat scattered and largely at sea, conducting training and surveillance and joint operations with our allies and reducing their vulnerability to a Japanese attack. Regarding the China Fleet, recognize it for what it is, our eyes and ears in the forward areas where things are happening that will warn us of the enemy's specific intentions and capabilities. We will be faced with the same shortages that plague our allies and we must take every step to preserve them and sharpen them to their maximum capability. If we are to lose a major portion of our fleet it must be the ones at the boundaries, our trip wire as it were, saving our more modern heavies until the time that we can slug it out successfully with the Japs."

"Do you see any way, any way at all, that we can avoid or preempt this expected Japanese aggression?" "Sir, even total abject appeasement would only be a delay and that's because of the Japanese national character. They feel that they are superior racially to all others and that they are only taking that which is rightfully theirs. They hate and have contempt for Gaijin and take it as their job to subjugate us for their own use and benefit. There is only one way to beat them and that is to be as brutal as they are and to serve as their executioner. They will respect nothing but power and the will to use it, Sir."

Both men looked at their watches and saw that it was approaching ten. "Dick, I know that you have the detail in that briefcase that backs up your presentation to me, just now. I want to give it over to my analysts and see what they come up with as a plan for following your recommendations, or see if they differ with any of your major conclusions. I will tell you that the plan we develop for enhancing our China Fleet and positioning it to give us our best chance is the plan that I will nominate you to carry out, as CincAsiaticFlt."

Most of the First Division was seated at mess tables swung down from the overhead of the berthing compartment. Dantes and Daughter sat together, chatting quietly and waiting for the mess steward to bring the noon meal in tureens to the table.

Two of the more senior Seamen Firsts of the Division, Houlihan and Raney came sulkily into the space, looking angry and stared at Dantes. Dantes looked up with an eyebrow cocked, silently asking what was up. Houlihan said to him, "Ricketts wants to see you, said he'd be at the…" "Gun turret?" Dantes finished for him. "Yeah, he said there's no rush," Houlihan said. Daughter taking all of this in turned toward Dantes about to speak when Dantes shook his head almost imperceptibly. The food came and Dantes quickly finished his chow: navy beans and pork. He pushed back from the table and told Daughter, "See you later," and went over to where his seabag was stowed and got out his best pair of shoes, a clean shirt and sparkling white hat. Then he went into the head and checked out his appearance in the shiny back splatter surface mounted by the steam outlet and headed topside forward to the six inch turret of which Ricketts was the Gunner's Mate First and in charge. He was mount captain during all firing exercises and responsible for its mechanical condition, correct operation and the training of assigned personnel. Ricketts was of course well known aboard Detroit. His reputation was as a thorough-going professional.

Dantes came up to the mount, stood before Ricketts and nodded, not standing at attention and not slouching either. You see Dantes had something of the same sort of reputation aboard ship. He too was respected and while there was a vast difference in their ranks, one a First Class Petty Officer the other an increasingly experienced Seaman, in the crew they were both men of substance who had proved their worth. In Navy lingo they had what was called service reputations. Dantes knew almost as soon as Houlihan and Raney had come into the compartment, what was up. You see, those two had service reputations, too. It was of the other sort: lazy, careless and tending to take short cuts. They were well into their second tours without making rate. This was not all that unusual, as the coveted job slots for petty officers were few and there was not a lot of opportunity for advancement. Still, if what was about to happen was what Dantes suspicioned it was, it was either an outburst of temper in which he was to be the temporary beneficiary or else it was an opportunity. Dantes always looked for opportunities and usually turned even nasty situations into something far better. He was called lucky, but it happened too often to be luck.

Ricketts looked Dantes over, noting his spotless appearance and knew that Dantes had taken pains for this meeting, for that's what it was, every bit as important as a job interview. "What did Houlihan and Raney tell you," he asked. "Just that you wanted to see me, Ricketts." "I've kicked them out of my turret," he said," they probably were pissed, I know I am." Dantes said nothing in reply but continued confidently looking Ricketts in the eye. "And I ain't taking them back," he continued, "so if you want the job you can replace them." "How many are you taking in," Dantes asked, because now they were into a sort of negotiation and he needed to know the details. "Just one, Dantes, so it'll be one man replacing two and that means twice the work," and he peered closely at Dantes, trying to read his expression. For Dantes that meant twice the opportunity, no matter the work and he didn't pause even to think about it, "When do I start, Ricketts?" "So you ain't interested in striking for Signalman? I heard you was learning semaphore, flashing light and picking up all sorts of topside skills on the bridge." "I enjoy standing watch on the bridge and I enjoy learning all I can," Dantes replied. "Besides, gunnery sort of runs in my family." "Yeah, I seen you made the pistol team. Okay, I'll see the Gun Boss and he'll make it official with the XO." And with that he gruffly reached out and sealed the bargain with a hand shake. "Go back to the berthing compartment and put on your working dungarees, you are now my striker." "Thanks, Gunner," Dantes replied, I will do my best and I appreciate the opportunity." There it was again, the temptation to say 'Sir' but he was after all a quick study and there were other ways to show his respect. Changing into a cleaner uniform was one of them and they both knew it.

Dantes' life changed in many ways, large and small. Instead of swabbing decks and chipping paint and holystoning the patches of decorative wooden deck he was keeping the turret clean, doing all of the work of two men, as Ricketts had promised, and doing a better job than the two of them had. He still stood watches but his time in the pilothouse and on the bridge was more seldom. They used him as the helmsman for special sea and anchor detail, because they wanted the very best controlling the ship when in close quarters or restricted sea room, headed up a narrow channel. In an environment where the best was often like the worst and there was not much in the way of benefits or promotion, Dantes had achieved a sort of status. Privilege was sliced thinly because there was so little of it to go around; Dantes had finished only two years of his first tour and it was practically unheard of for a seaman to make rate in his first tour. Here it was only halfway through his first tour and Dantes was already a striker. He knew his chances were slim, but it was a chance, one that was prized and already muffed by the two seamen he had replaced.

After a couple of months, when by his hard work and attention to detail Dantes had already convinced Ricketts of the wisdom of his choice, Ricketts took over Dantes' time off, too. Every Wednesday afternoon was 'Ropeyarn Sunday', personal time off for the crew to mend torn uniforms, write letters home, that sort of thing. Instead Ricketts and Dantes would repair to the turret where Dantes would take apart a Browning Automatic Rifle, a Springfield thirty caliber rifle and a .45 caliber pistol. Dantes had to name all the parts and explain their function and put them together again. Then he had to disassemble them and reassemble them again against the clock and he was expected to do it faster each time. As the months passed and he got incredibly adept at this exercise, the Gunner would mix the parts up in a big pile before Dantes could again race the clock to put them together again. It was a sort of professional humpty dumpty drill only with cold deadly steel instead of eggshells. The professional regard between the two men had increased as Dantes had progressed; indeed there was an easygoing manner, neither walking on eggshells around the other, instant obedience on Dantes' part and recognition on Rickett's part that he didn't often have to give Dantes orders of any sort. Dantes knew that "Gunner" had things he could be doing with his Wednesday afternoons, too, and it became a game, a pursuit of excellence with it becoming harder and harder to challenge Dantes, forcing Ricketts to become inventive. Like blindfolding Dantes with the parts in a pile, both of them laughing as he unerringly found parts and set them aside into piles for each weapon to be reassembled. Hilarity ensued when Ricketts would hide a part and tell Dantes to tell him which one it was.

Ricketts would also write up sheets of questions every Friday having to do with everything from descriptions of powder grains in the raw silk bags to use of special tools for mount maintenance, to procedures for clearing a defective round from the mount after an unsuccessful firing attempt. Questions on specifications for fluids used for cleaning, or for hydraulics and on detailed safety practices and the reasons for them were all written out, usually twenty to thirty questions per sheet. Dantes was expected to write out all the answers and turn them in on Mondays. So, Ricketts took not only Dantes' Wednesday afternoons but also his weekends. Dantes was fascinated, knew it was an opportunity and in a way they continued to compete, one against the other. Ricketts was showing his charge how much there was to safely firing a six inch turret on a man of war, and Dantes was showing his professional mentor that he was worthy of the Gunner's time and effort. He had to dive into the operating and repair manuals for most of the weekend to find the information required and then take the time to write out reasoned and detailed answers. He found himself becoming proud of his knowledge and of his role aboard Detroit, for what was the purpose of the whole ship if not to bring naval gunnery to bear in situations for which the very ship and its crew were intended?

Dantes' mount of course got the "E" and kept it throughout his time aboard Detroit, and he continually drew his bonus of five dollars a month and sent it plus some of his base pay home to his sister, Loraine every month. After a year had passed in the mount Ricketts told him that one position for gunner's mate third had opened up in the entire light cruiser fleet of nine ships. Just one slot was all and an examination was scheduled. All of the strikers for GM3 sat for the exam at the same time under supervision on their individual ships and it took the entire morning. Hod had prepared but he knew the odds were against him. It had to be close to a hundred strikers like him spread throughout all the mounts and turrets of nine men of war, all competing for that one slot. A week later the results were in. It took time to grade the exams as they were written essay answers and fill in the blanks questions and it did take time to grade so many tests. Then the word was out; the results were in!

Quarters that morning were a bit odd. Chief Locker was standing next to the ship's Chief Gunner's Mate. Mr. Smythe read the Plan of the Day until he got to the part that said, "Congratulations to GM3 Dantes, who has gotten the highest score on the examination for GM3 in the cruiser fleet and is promoted." The whole division cheered and they started pounding him on the back when Chief Locker stepped in and said, "Hold on a minute." He produced the rating badge for gunner's mate third along with some safety pins and tacked the 'crow' to Dantes' right sleeve, saying "Now you can tack it to him." And every man in the division slugged his crow, tacking it on for him, Dantes not letting his grin slip as they hammered him until the Chief gunner called a halt to it and the Division Officer administered the oath. Locker turned to him, "Son, that is one *hell* of an accomplishment; I expected nothing less." Dantes knew how hard he had worked for his crow and he thanked "Wall" Locker and then turned to look for Ricketts and found him looking his way. He went up to Ricketts who held up his hand, "You earned that crow, Dantes, I've never had a striker like you who worked so hard and learned so fast." "Gunner thanks for busting your tail for me. I owe you. We did this together." Ricketts nodded, "It's been a lot of afternoons and weekends for you but worth it. I never heard of anyone making it on their first tour and you still have a year to go. Well done."

It took all of three weeks for the bruises on Dantes' right shoulder and arm to shrink and turn black, purple and yellow and fade. It was the hardest promotion to make, that first one, except Chief. With his pay increase Dantes ordered a set of custom made blues from Charlie the Chinese tailor, in San Diego. He got them with the oriental style embroidery on the inside of the cuffs, a dragon on one and some Fu Dogs on the other. It never ceased to amaze how Charlie could get these tailor mades delivered to the ship, no matter what the deployment schedule was or how many times it changed. There were thirteen button trousers with a sweet flare to the bell bottoms and everything fit to a T. With his stretched and rolled white hat on the back of his head, in a bar with his sleeves turned back one half turn, shoes shined to perfection he was a head turner. Three years of life aboard Detroit had sculpted him to a muscular torso and a slim waist. He had a scar on the left side of his face like a permanent grin line that swept down his cheek and ended in a small mole-like rounded bit of flesh. Women liked to touch it. His eyes were a deep and bright blue and his smile was confident and easy. Eventually in bars they liked to count the thirteen buttons, pretending they didn't believe that many buttons were there. It was one of the benefits to getting 'tailor mades' over Government issue. If Hod knew anything he knew how to create opportunity and then take advantage of it.

Aboard ship with increased rank came added responsibility and the expectation of leadership on his part. He had already been leading without the crow by force of his personality and ability, but now it was formalized and he picked up a couple seamen seconds whom he supervised and he no longer had to participate in evolutions for non-rated. It was a chance to practice giving orders and instruction and to become the person for whom others would gladly do the difficult and dirty. He approached it the way he did everything, with thought ahead of time and with a manner that drew respect from everyone, up the chain of command and down. He was generally pretty quiet so that when he did speak others quieted down to hear what he had to say. He always knew what he was talking about, so that garnered him instant respect. He'd been taught by Grandma to treat others the way he wanted to be treated himself, so that's what he did. And he didn't want to disappoint her so he never got a tattoo and he avoided dirty language. Still he had to tell *some*one so he wrote to Loraine.

Dear Loraine,

I've got some good news! I've been promoted to third class gunner's mate. I made the highest score in the GM3 examination of all the cruiser sailors who took it and

got promoted right after the results were announced. To
make it to Petty Officer in your first tour is practically unheard of, and I am glad to be starting on my way up.
The work is hard but satisfying and it feels good to be
a gunner's mate on a Navy warship. A lot will depend upon
how we do our jobs and I am working hard to be sure I
learn mine. I bought a set of tailor made blues with some
of the pay increase and had a picture taken in town which
I enclosed to you in my new blues. I should be able to
send a bit more money home after I pay off the bill for
my new uniform.

How have you been? I haven't received a letter in a
few weeks. Tell the folks hello for me and I will write
them soon. Study hard and it will pay off for you.

Love,
Hod

CHAPTER 31

LEAVING DETROIT

In 1935 after only three years of his first enlistment had elapsed, Dantes became a Petty Officer Third Class, a Gunner's Mate. His new status had given him a space on the second deck for a cot, a more comfortable place to sleep and a coveted privilege that came with seniority. Hod bought his cot from another sailor who had received orders and was leaving the ship. He no longer stood watches on the bridge and no longer had to participate in some of the backbreaking evolutions such as loading of stores which usually featured all non-rated. Older and wiser hands watched to see what rookie Petty Officers would do with their new found status. For Hod it was not possible to see much difference. He didn't slack off, just changed the type of work that he did. As Ricketts had said, Hod was a quick learner and an extremely hard worker, but as a new leader in a new division his ingrained personal habits now had a better chance to flourish and spread. Younger sailors admired him and his new crow and there was an uptick in small ways that in aggregate amounted to a pretty big improvement. The newly arrived boots wore their white hats like him, they were quick to anticipate what was needed, or at least displayed energy as they went about their tasks. Another thing the old hands noticed was that Dantes was with his growing following, working alongside to show the correct way or pointing out, quietly, where an improvement could be made. Some Petty Officers were stingy with their knowledge, seeing it as power and holding it close rather than sharing it, but not Hod. He was constantly studying and then sharing what he knew. As a result his popularity continued to grow and his turret shone and Detroit, at least Hod's small part of it, was a happy ship.

On liberty in San Diego Hod never went back to Tijuana. He and Daughter had their favorite hangouts, some of them with dartboards and every now and then Dantes would put on an exhibition or take a free round from some unsuspecting new guy. With other sailors his manner was easy and unassuming, with the ladies it was devastating. His eyes had a twinkle that set their minds to imagining things. His stories were fun and his smile was easy but he was not. Easy, that is. A girl had to be someone really special to catch his attention. One look at him and you knew he would never pay for it, and he never did again. He pretty much forgot about his good fortune in the P.I. and in any case kept the information to himself. As the last year of his first hitch was drawing to a close he got inquiries about his plans. It might have been a big decision for some but not for Hod. The Division Officer, and even the XO had asked him if he was shipping over. With what they were calling the Great Depression still in effect world-wide the navies of the world suffered, were tough to get into and had little money to spend. But Hod knew he was established and had a position. He felt lucky to have a job, especially one that allowed him to advance and be a part of defending the Country.

Daughter, too, was coming up on time for a decision. The Navy didn't want to let go of you if you were any good, figured they had an investment in you. Daughter had been listening to Dantes talk about going to DC to ship over and he thought it might be a good idea. Besides, that's what Chief Locker had done, on more than one occasion: take a trip across country, visit the DC area, do a little negotiation and get his pick of what was out there. As the time to sign up or temporarily get out got closer, the ship's office told both men that Detroit would be at sea when their time was up, and they were going to have to transfer to another ship that would be in port in order to be discharged. That set off a round of parties ashore as their buddies bought them drinks and wished them well until the day came.

And finally, that day came. Standing on the fantail, inport San Diego, Chief Locker and Dantes, with his orders and his seabag beside him, made the most of a bit of privacy after knock off and before chow went down. "It's been one heck of a first hitch for you, son. And I think you're smart to take your chances and go see the detailers; with a record like yours they'll give you what you want, for sure." Thanks for the tip, Sir and thank you for everything you've done for me." Chief looked to correct Hod, calling him 'Sir' but Hod held up a hand. "You've called me son for awhile and I've never called you Dad. We all only get one Dad, one real father and I find I'm proud of mine, proud to be his son and hope I can be the strong man I know he was. But I also have a "Sea Daddy" and that person is you and always will be. I call my Sea Daddy Sir, Sir." Locker coughed to cover his emotions and Dantes looked away at the gulls circling. After a time Locker responded, "You were a boy and an orphan when you came to boot camp. You may have needed a father then but as a man grows up he outgrows that need. Son you are a man in your own right and I would be proud to be your Sea Daddy." Dantes came to attention, did a left face and rendered his Chief the finest salute he had ever received, and he'd received a few, as a Boot Camp Company Commander. He too came to attention and returned Dantes' salute, Dantes cutting away after Chief dropped his. And just like that, Dantes left Detroit with the requisite honors to Quarterdeck and colors, his heart full and looking forward to the next adventure.

CHAPTER 32

SHIPPING OVER

Dantes rendered snappy salutes to the colors and then to the OOD, at the Quarterdeck, USS Pruitt (DD-347) pierside San Diego Naval Base. "Request permission to come aboard, Sir." "Granted." "Gunner's Mate Third Class Dantes reporting for duty, Sir." "Very well, Messenger, take Petty Officer Dantes down to ship's office." "Aye, aye Sir." In the ship's office the Yeoman took his orders and his service record, logged him into the ship's muster roll and put a copy in the XO's basket. He looked up at the Messenger and told him to take Dantes to the XO's stateroom before handing Dantes back his Service Record. "The XO likes to see all personnel reporting aboard, he'll want to see your service record." "Understood, you'll see that I'm to be aboard for only thirty days, long enough to discharge me." The Yeoman nodded, said the XO will want to see you anyway."

Leaving him in the passageway at the XO's stateroom, the Messenger returned to the Quarterdeck, Dantes knocked twice, heard, "Come," and entered and sounded off, "GM3 Dantes reporting for duty, Sir." The XO looked up briefly, nodded to the single extra chair in the space and invited Dantes to sit. He held out his hand for the Service Record and scanned his orders clipped on top and perused the rest of his records also permanently clipped to the top with a two-hole keeper. Looking up with more interest, "This is highly unusual, making your crow in three years, Dantes, usually this happens on a second hitch, especially in a rate like Gunner's Mate. Almost never on a first tour of duty. Any idea how many made it when you took your exam?" "Yessir." And when the XO looked at him to continue, "One, Sir. In the light cruiser fleet at Pearl, nine ships." "Also says we are to discharge you. That because Detroit will be at sea, then?" And Dantes replied that the Detroit was scheduled to be at sea, had gotten underway this morning.

The XO sat back in his chair and smiled, "And you came straight over here, didn't take a liberty in Tijuana first?" Dantes smiled back, "Sir I've been down there once, right out of Boot Camp. Not planning to go back." "That good, huh?" And they both chuckled a bit. "Do you plan to ship over, or take your chances in the civilian world?" "Planning to re-up in DC, Sir." "Know some detailers there?" "No Sir, not yet." "Well, we can save you the trip, Dantes, ship you over right here." "Sir I'm planning on taking a month or so and visiting with relatives in Texas." "I like a man with a plan." The XO flipped a couple more sheets and was about to close the folder when he saw a commendation for one SN1 Dantes. That was unusual enough, but the signature of the originator brought a low whistle. He looked at Dantes again, "This is a very nice commendation in your jacket." Dantes sat and listened. "You actually *know* CincPac?" "Sir, I wouldn't say that." "He evidently thinks he knows *you*. Has some very nice things to say, in a general way, about you. Care to say what you actually did, in the P.I.?" "No, Sir. At the time it was classified." "Okay, Sailor. We'll make good use of you while you're here with us. Come by and see me before you go." "Aye, Sir." And Dantes went out into the passageway hoisted his seabag, hit ship's office and got sent to the Gunnery Department Office, was assigned a berth and a job and he shifted into dungarees and found the Chief and was in turn handed off to the First Class in charge of the five inch mounts. They put him on the inport watch bill and gave him a duty section and a GQ station and welcomed him aboard.

Dantes had the roving patrol on the four to eight one night, two weeks after he had reported aboard. One of his duties on this watch, which was brand new to him, was to light the fire under the galley stove. It was an oil burning stove, a large one and on this cold morning the oil had thickened and was slow to flow. As a consequence he allowed way too much oil into the stove and as it heated it grew less viscous and the flames billowed almost to the overhead, bubbling green paint on the backsplatter and turning the stove a cherry red. It was too hot to get close enough to try to control it and it just continued to burn. Dantes watched it for a while until the Ship's Cook came into the messdecks and saw the blaze. One look and he just threw up his hands and left the messdecks. He came back two hours later and breakfast was finally served, two hours late for the whole ship. Everybody knew whose fault it was that breakfast was late and Dantes was mightily embarrassed and pretty disgusted with himself. But Dantes never heard anything official about it. Two weeks later his time was up and he went by the Ship's Office for his discharge papers, got them and was told to go by the Exec's Office. Inside and standing this time, the XO grinned, learn anything while you were with us, Dantes?" "Sir, Yessir. A little oil goes a long way." "And a commendation from CincPac carries an inordinate amount of weight, Dantes. You're a good sailor. Good luck in DC and enjoy your trip to Texas."

From the train station in Luling, Texas, Dantes caught a ride to the farm, located between Luling and Lockhart. He got out of the truck with his hearty thanks for the lift and paused just a bit before going up the dirt path to the house. It was Mr. Crowell's place and he and Grandma lived there. All of Mr. Crowell's sons had grown up and moved out, that's what had made life on the farm so hard on Hod. He did the work of several men at an early age. He did see Joe, the mule, out back but the place looked, well, different. It had to have changed in six years, but it looked a lot smaller than he remembered it and kind of run down, too. He glanced and saw the smoke house out back, wondered if his Dad's jacket was still there, decided that on one of his trips to the outhouse he'd check.

He climbed the cracked and warped steps to the porch and knocked at the screen door, making it rattle. He heard some motions inside and the door opened on squeaky hinges and there was Grandma, grayer but still slim and fit and with a rapturous look on her face and her arms wide open, HOWARD! YOU'VE COME HOME AT LAST!!! She kissed him half a dozen times and kept pinching him as if to make sure he was really here. Hod held the old woman and smiled and smiled as old man Crowell came up and stuck his hand out. Grandma said, "You should have let us know! I'd have had something special for you when you got here." "Grandma it's special just being here."

They stood back and took a look at him, a close look for the first time since tenth grade at Luling High School. "Oh, Howard! You've become a man, my sweet Howard is a man." She took his hands, both of them and examined them closely. Hod grinned. He knew what she was doing. She squinted up at him, "No tattoos? None?" "None at all, Grandma, you know I promised." Take off your shirt, your jersey there. I want to see for myself." Hod pulled his tailor made jersey over his head, folded it carefully and put it over the back of the rocker. He stood inspection, turning slowly around until she was satisfied. "Where'd you get those enormous arms, Hod?" "Sir, it comes from tossing around hundred pound six inch projectiles." "How long can you stay, Hod?" "Long as you'll have me, Grandma, or three weeks, whichever comes first." She had an apple pie hot and in the pie safe that very afternoon and there was fried chicken for supper that night. Hod shifted into some old work clothes and asked Mr. Crowell what he needed done around the place. He made a list out and Hod started tackling it the next morning, before sunrise. He would work all day except for meals and he and Grandma would talk into the night until she fell asleep and he pulled a blanket over her in her rocking chair. Finally, one morning before he started in with his self-appointed chores as he came out of the outhouse he went into the smokehouse and with the first breath he took in, the smells and the memories came flooding in. He was driving that old Model T and couldn't reach the pedals. Or diving off of Joe's back or Prince into Plum Creek, skinny dipping. In the gloom he felt for the nail and found the jacket, still hanging there. One last time he poked a finger through it. His hands were bigger but he still got his finger through the two holes made by the bullet that had passed through without hitting his Dad. He bowed his head, "Dad, I know you loved us and I know how brave you were. I love you still and hope to be just like you."

He closed the door and closed a chapter with the same motion. He would make a stop in Beaumont and mention it one more time, with Loraine. That noon after lunch he handed Mr. Crowell his list with every item crossed off and thanked him for the visit. Grandma was on the porch saying, "Come back every chance you get." Mr. Crowell had pulled the car around to the front and gave him a lift into town to catch the train. It was a sharp looking and tanned Sailor who boarded the train to DC, with a stop at Beaumont.

Hod caught a cab to Uncle Bill and Aunt Leta's house down by the railroad tracks. Aunt Leta was home and she exclaimed over him and made his bed in his old bedroom. Soon Uncle Bill came in from work and Loraine came home from school. After the excitement died down Loraine wanted him to put his uniform on and walk with her to school the next morning. He did it and also went into the Principal's office and said hello to everybody there. Loraine was so proud she almost burst. He was invited back for lunch and of course he did it and again Loraine couldn't show him off enough in the cafeteria. The girls were practically swooning and the boys looked envious and admiringly at him at the same time. Then it was a Friday night movie at the place where Hod had worked, more smiles and excitement until they went home and had some pie and tea.

Bill and Leta had gone to bed and it was Hod and Loraine at the kitchen table. Loraine made another comment about how good he looked in his uniform. Hod said, "This is just my work clothes, Sis." Then she said, everybody envied you, admired you." And Hod said they were the lucky ones, still in school with a chance to learn at home before having to work for a living. And Loraine said but you go to all those exotic places that almost no one gets to see. Hod said they are all on edge there, worrying about what will happen when the Japanese come. She looked at him quizzically, wanting to make a hero out of him and he steadfastly turning it all into humdrum reality. "But you love the Navy, I know you do!"

"Let's talk about love for a minute because that's what Grandma and I talked about, night after night on the farm." Loraine hadn't seen Hod like this before and she sat back and listened. "Grandma said that Dad loved you to distraction and me and John, too. She said that I looked and sounded like him, that I had turned out just like him. Again and again she would tell me stories of Dad doing this and Dad doing that, and about his kindnesses and his strength and bravery. I wished you had been there to hear her because I think that you loved Dad in a way that a son never could. You are his only daughter. Here's my point, I believe we *did* turn out to be just like him and we have turned out alright. We love each other and have been taken care of by our larger family. *We* are the kind of family Dad would be proud of and we're just like him. I have no fears that we are some kind of monsters in hiding, waiting to burst out and kill loved ones. I know that Dad wasn't either. Our Mother dying was a terrible thing for us and especially for him. In a moment of weakness he had decided not to live anymore and he didn't want to leave us as orphans. Problem was, for his plan, he also raised brave fighters, just like him. In the Navy I may be called upon to kill. I think when that happens I will be able to do it and do it with skill. But I am not afraid that I will also turn around and try to kill the ones I love. That simply is not possible."

"I liked to smell his hands and make him laugh, and I liked it when he tickled me 'til I almost peed my pants," Loraine said. "Those were special times and they meant that he was happy and that he loved you, loved all of us," Hod replied. And Loraine got a funny look on her face and grabbed one of Hod's hands and sniffed it and they both laughed out loud. Aunt Leta heard their laughter in her sleep and smiled a soft smile. Hod left the next day for Washington, DC.

Hod found the YMCA and got a room there, took his best uniform to a cleaners and had it back the next day. Then, well rested and with his belongings locked in his seabag and locked in his room he took a taxi to the Navy Department and found the area in Personnel where the detailers were located and walked up to a window like a ticket window and showed his orders and said he was there to ship over and could he talk to a detailer. They had him take a seat in the large anteroom and he had waited for an hour or so when a second class personnelman came to the door and called his name, mispronouncing it, of course. Dantes answered up and was waved inside the large office with maybe ten or twelve desks. He started reading signs and realized that they were organized by rating. He saw the one with the Gunner's Mate symbol and that's where they went, Dantes being invited to sit down. Chief Gunner's Mate Hollander looked up, "Says here you were discharged from the Detroit, Dantes. I know a couple of Chiefs there. Did you ever run into Chief Gundy or Chief Locker?" He laughed when he saw Dantes' response, the look on his face. "I apologize, Dantes, I knew the answer before I asked the question. I know them only by reputation, service reputation, but they thought enough of you to send letters to me to be sure I took good care of you. That doesn't happen very often, not very often at all. Even if they had not said anything about you, your record of making your crow in three years on your first tour speaks for itself. The question is, what do you want for your next tour? You can have a tin can, either coast, cruiser, anywhere you like or a battlewagon out of Pearl, if you want.

That last choice really hit Dantes hard. Did he want to go back to Hawaii, to Kuulei? "Chief, I think I like cruisers, I'm used to them, not too big and not too small. I'd like to go where I will have the chance to learn a lot and get the chance to make second class. Where she's homeported is not as important." The Chief sat up a little straighter, *this is unusual. Many times they want a location before anything else.* "I also think that a new ship would be better than an old one. It would be more fun operating than staying in the yard all the time, trying to get to sea." Hollander smiled, "Then I have just what you're looking for, a cruiser, the Brooklyn, still being built and not yet commissioned. You'll be a plank owner, part of the first crew to ever board her and get to sail her brand spanking new out of the shipyard." Dantes leaned back in his chair for the first time, smiled. "That sounds great, Chief." And we'll send you on Temporary Additional Duty on the East Coast and get you some really good experience in schools and such while you're waiting for Brooklyn to come out of the yard." The Chief took to the typewriter on his desk rattatat tatted some rapid fire personnel abbreviations into a compact set of orders directing him to proceed to thus and so, report for duty as umptysquat and thence to another place with it seemed some sort of weapon mentioned at every stop. Whipping the carbon set of orders out of his typewriter he took it for signature to a Lieutenant at another desk, returned and got Dantes' signature acknowledging receipt, entered the orders number into his bound log and stood at attention telling Dantes to do the same. The Chief recited the oath by heart and it seemed his recitation was heartfelt. Dantes stood with his right hand held up and repeated every word. At the end he said, "So help me God." The Chief reached out and shook his hand and gave him a set of his orders in a folder inside a large manila envelope. Dantes held up his hand, Chief Hollander paused, "Chief, did you happen to see a Seaman First, named Daughter, come through here?" The Chief picked up his log, paged through it, hmmm, yes, here he is, shipped over a week ago." "And Chief, where did he go?" Chief smiled, "Why it looks like he's headed to the Brooklyn, same as you!" Dantes smiled his thanks, made a quick visit to the pay office for an advance on his travel expenses and just like that Dantes was set loose in DC for a weekend before having to travel to his first destination. Instead he went back to his room at the Y and deciphered all the gobbledegook and personnel speak and figured out his next move.

CHAPTER 33

BROOKLYN NAVAL SHIPYARD

Hod heard at the YMCA about the new electric train service from DC to New York and boarded at Union Station, changed trains in Philadelphia at the 30th Street Station and debarked at Penn Station in New York just over three hours after boarding in Washington. He checked bus schedules and soon found his way to Brooklyn Naval Shipyard, where the USS Brooklyn was under construction. At the pre-commissioning detail office he reported in and got his orders stamped, asked about berthing and was given a list of approved places where his per diem would cover the cost of lodging, and confirmed that his first three assignments were aboard Badger, Taylor and Decatur, all Destroyers, and all located at the naval shipyard in Norfolk, Virginia undergoing overhauls. It was expected that he would find berthing aboard. He was being sent there to overhaul their 4"/50 caliber guns.

On board Taylor he had to mix up some liquid for the recoil cylinders. It was a mixture of glycerin and water with an alkali substance added. It had to have a certain specific gravity and alkalinity. As he mixed it he put in too much water, whereupon he added glycerin and then more alkali. It was too much so he added more water and then the specific gravity wasn't right so he added more glycerin. By the time he got it right he thought he had enough recoil liquid to supply the whole Destroyer fleet. *This is almost as bad as incinerating the galley of Pruitt,* he thought, but at least it wasn't a case of the whole ship knowing he had messed up and delayed breakfast.

After the last tin can went to sea he was transferred to the U.S. Naval Academy at Annapolis, Maryland. While there he kept ancient Lewis Machine Guns operating while the Midshipmen fired them, simulating anti-aircraft fire. Along with five other gunner's mates on this detail, it turned into very choice duty for the summer. With time on his hands one Saturday morning he decided to swim across the Chesapeake Bay to a beach on the other side. Making it to the other side after almost being run over by a ferryboat he was surprised and relieved to find that one of the other gunners found out what he was doing and a couple of them took a rowboat across, found him on the beach and rowed back alongside Dantes as he swam back across the bay.

At the end of the summer training for Midshipmen Dantes was transferred to the Naval Gun Factory in Washington, DC for training on the 5" anti-aircraft guns. While there he took the examination for Gunner's Mate Second Class. After completing his training at the Naval Gun Factory he finally went aboard Brooklyn. She had just been commissioned and was in the Brooklyn Navy Yard undergoing extensive modifications. Of course, since he had just finished training on the 5" anti-aircraft guns, he was assigned to the Number Four turret with 6"/47 caliber triple mounts. Shortly after going aboard Brooklyn he was promoted to GM2.

With so much time in port and the ship in the yard it was a case of liberty almost every night and Hod took advantage of it. He would hit the beach and it was but a short stroll to the bars in Brooklyn. One night in a beer joint on Sads Street he saw a stunningly beautiful woman across the smoky barroom. She was like a movie star, maybe a cross between Ginger Rogers with her dancer's lithe body and the sparkling manner and beautiful features of Katherine Hepburn. A light brunette with masses of wavy hair who smoked like a stack, she was a working girl with an eighth grade education. But when she smiled, Dantes melted. The first time he saw her he was too shy to even go over and talk to her. She was there with a girlfriend, seemed on friendly terms with everyone and quite a popular attraction.

A week later he saw her again, in a different bar in Brooklyn. She was actually looking at him, as though she might have recognized him. Hod laughed, *how could I forget her, no chance. No chance she'd even give me a second look.* And as he nursed his beer he was startled when she came up behind him and asked "Is this seat taken?" Dantes jumped up out of his seat, stammering, "No, no not at all." He seated her and she brought a pack of cigarettes out of her purse and put it on the table, tapped one out and leaned forward for Hod to light it for her. Dantes of course did not smoke, had no earthly idea what the ritual was but quickly figured it out when she picked up a book of matches from the table and expertly lit her cigarette, and with an upraised eyebrow asked if he wanted one, too. Hod shook his head, no thanks and just took in this ravishing and confident figure *sitting with me.* Hod did go to another table and came back with an ashtray into which the Goddess put her smoke and then smiled her thanks at him.

He finally said, "Are you from Brooklyn?" and immediately cursed himself for his dull comment. "No, I just work in Brooklyn, I'm from Jersey. I'm Hazel Moore." He sat there, uncharacteristically tongue-tied, just staring at her. He had never seen a woman this flat out good looking. He even liked her Yankee accent. She smiled again, "What's your name, Sailor?" He said, "Dantes." She said, "What, Dantes." He finally replied "Dantes, Dantes." What, you've got a first name just like your last name?" And he looked down at the ashtray, turning a bit red in the neck. She said, "Actually I'm Hazel Frances Moore. I have three names, but I go by Haze, Dantes. Did I pronounce it correctly?" Dantes knew when he was being teased and he loosened up a bit, "Except for that Yankee accent, you did just fine." There was a jukebox in the bar and Hazel took Dantes by the hand and they looked over the selection: Cheek to Cheek, Lovely to Look At, Isle of Capri and Red Sails in the Sunset. Dantes put a dime in the slot and punched the button for Lovely to Look At and Blue Moon, thinking she was certainly lovely to look at and someone like her came along once in a blue moon.

"I'm no Fred Astaire, but if you'd like we can give these a try." They were slow and he liked slow dancing, and it would give him a chance to get close. She kept looking at him, he liked the way she moved. After their two songs had finished one from the 20's came on. It was "The Charleston." Hazel immediately threw her hands up in excitement and started in, doing a very professional looking version, Ginger Rodgers-like in her grace and athleticism. Hod, of course, just looked and liked what he saw. When they sat down, he said, "They don't do the Charleston in Texas." She smiled there's another one on the jukebox, did you notice, "I Want to be a Cowboy's Sweetheart." She went over to the jukebox and put a dime in and pushed the button to hear Patsy Montana and the Prairie Ramblers sing a sweet melody.

Over the next several weeks Hod took up smoking; later he would say it was in self-defense. He also learned the Charleston and they spent time at Ebbets Field, watching the Dodgers on Saturdays. She wormed his actual first name out of him but it took her almost a month. He finally told her to call him Hod and explained where that came from. Finally one night as he walked her to the front stoop of her mother's apartment house in Ridgefield Park she popped some Sen Sen into her mouth and gave some to Hod. They had a long kiss and Hod was in heaven. So was Hazel. She said, "That's to hold you until you get back." Brooklyn was at last getting underway.

Hazel was the baby in a single Mom household. Her Mother, Mildred "Dinty" Moore, a switchboard operator had been abandoned by her husband when Hazel was twelve. He just left town and there was no help for Mildred in the raising of her two girls, Genevieve and Hazel. At the age of thirteen Hazel up and got on a bus to Chicago and went looking for the man whose name was never mentioned. Word had gotten back that he was somewhere in Chicago and Hazel was determined to find him, and find him she did. She banged on a tenement door until a blowsy bleach bottle blonde answered and let her in. He had put on some work trousers and beheld this tall for her age spitfire of a scrawny kid who was berating him, using words of some imagination, all of them profane. There ensued a one sided shouting match with the blonde looking on in amazement. When she'd had her fill Hazel turned on her heel, slammed the door on her way out and never spoke of him again.

She quit school after the eighth grade but became a lifelong reader, educating herself with all sorts of books from the Carnegie library in the next town over. At the age of fourteen she had a full time job in the City's Garment District. Though slim enough and tall enough to be a model, she worked at first at cleaning up the floors, and then became a machine operator, whatever paid, and what she earned helped Mildred to put food on the table. As she filled out she developed into a magnificent young woman, aware of her looks of course but also painfully defensive about her lack of formal schooling. You did what you had to do to get by but that didn't mean you weren't as good as anybody else. And along with her natural beauty and fierce Irish temper she developed an attitude. The smoking was part of it but being loose in her affections was not. On the outside she was a tough cookie, and on the inside still a little girl who wanted to trust a man but who would find it hard to do so. She was used to being chased and flattered and proficient at fending that type off. Perhaps that was the initial attraction that Hod held for her, the fact that he didn't immediately chase her. That and his equally astonishing good looks. And his obvious intellect. He just had this understated way about him and was well spoken and had funny stories and had already been to so many places.

Jen was married to Jack Kaulfhold, a mechanic who labored in a garage, repairing automobiles. Jen worked too, but in her time off, on weekends and the occasional week night she and Kaulf would join Hod and Hazel for a beer and a meal. They would often find a bar, usually one with a dartboard and Hod would occasionally get up and demonstrate the art of pinpoint accuracy with darts. They liked his stories of being taught by an Aussie in Hong Kong, or Kowloon, whatever that was. He could do this imitation of an Aussie accent but they had to beg him to do it. To them he was a world traveler, to him they were creatures from another planet and the shine of the City shone in them, for him. New York was the center of the Universe and they knew their way around. It was a symbiotic relationship. It worked for all of them; they got along. There were no stories of killings in Manila or Admirals in Makalapa or a fight for life at the age of twelve. Haze knew that Hod had been orphaned and felt an odd sort of kinship and never mentioned running down the Father who had left them.

For his part, Hod was perfectly content to let their relationship grow slowly and naturally. The initial attraction to the flashy tough girl was gradually replaced with an easy comfort as Haze grew confident in Hod and sure of his affections. He was a goner, and like no one she or Jen had ever seen. They held hands everywhere they went, were comfortable with their arms around each other. They were a couple. When Jen would ask the questions in the powder room, the gently probing ones about "how they were" together, Haze would just smile softly and say he was a good kisser. "Nothing else," Jen would ask. And Haze would just shake her head, pat a bit more rouge in place and say, "Ready to go back?"

Standing on the stoop of Mildred's building, giving each other one more kiss goodbye, it suddenly seemed a kiss was not enough. They held each other fiercely, pressed together head to toe and both were wanting more when Haze broke away and took a deep breath. There was Hod with lipstick smeared all over his mouth and he was breathing hard too. She looked at him, "I'll write." "I will too, he said." And she turned slowly toward the stairs and he headed for the bus stop.

Haze was not there on the pier, where the dependents were crowded, waving goodbye as Brooklyn, with two tugs in assistance singled up all lines and then took them in and turning South in the East River made her way into the open sea. But she knew when they were getting underway and she listened for the ship's whistle that Hod told her she might hear. And there it was, a mournful faint sound in the distance, and three more beeps down at the Navy Yard. Haze got up from her seat and went into the restroom and had a short cry. She was already missing her sailor and would write to him that very night.

CHAPTER 34

LETTERS BETWEEN LOVERS

The special sea detail had just secured and the brand spanking new light cruiser Brooklyn was underway for Guantanamo Bay, Cuba with her full complement aboard. Hod and Daughter sat at a mess table, "Ha, writing a letter already?" Daughter said, "I wonder who?" Dantes looked up, "Never mind, don't you have something to do?" "Tell her hi for me," as GM3 Daughter went to his berth in the Gunnery Department spaces.

```
30 October 1937
Dear Hazel,
    We've just cleared the channel and are underway for
Cuba on our shakedown cruise and I miss you already. I
hope you miss me, too. As we backed away from the pier
and sounded our ship's horn I hoped you heard it. The
long blast said Haaaaze and the three shorts were I.
Miss. You.
    Usually when I get underway it is exciting and I'm
looking forward to what comes next. This time is differ-
ent. What I look forward to is not on Brooklyn, or where
she can take me; she's in Brooklyn and I wonder where
you'll take me next. Take care of yourself and I'll look
forward to seeing you when we get back.
Love,
Dantes Dantes
```

October 30, 1937
Dear Hod,

I heard that mournful whistle that you told me to listen for. I had to go to the ladies room and cry where no
one would see me. Maybe I will be able to get some overtime to keep me busy while you are gone. Stay safe and
come back to me. I miss you.
Love,
Haze

---

30 October 1937
Dear Haze,

I'm sure I won't be able to write every day; we stay
busy with either watch standing or training. Today we
learned that we'll be going to Haiti and Trinidad on this
cruise, and not just Gitmo. I think they don't tell us
some things until we get underway so that the information
doesn't get out to the public. There's a lot going on
in Europe, Germany in particular, and I heard that even
letters get censored during wartime. That hasn't started
yet. I don't know how that would feel, knowing someone is
reading my letters to you before you get to read them.

We're expecting some weather, the seas are starting to
kick up. I have to go and make sure my spaces are bat-
tened down, that the turret is secure. I imagine some in
the crew will get seasick, it always happens after a long
stay ashore. It's fine being on a brand new ship out of
the yard. But things will pop up, rattle loose and break.
Maybe that's why it's called a "shakedown" cruise.
Missing you,
Hod
PS Daughter says hello.

2 November 1937

Dear Haze,

I bet that when you get my letters you will get them all at the same time. Mail won't leave the ship until we get to Gitmo. I don't know when we'll get any; it won't be waiting there for us. When it happens it'll be like Christmas. I hope mail call isn't like Christmas, though, coming only once a year.

On our way down to Gitmo the whole crew is going through all of our evolutions. There are graded exercises and only one correct way to do them. The Engineers practice recovering from a boiler being put out of commission, for instance, while we have to clear a round from the bore that misfired or else suffer some other malfunction in the turret or hoist or even the magazine. Every single part of the ship has to work together and we train in order to make that happen without even thinking about it. With enough training we will function automatically, even when there are casualties in battle. We are told, though, that no matter how good we are that we will fail and fail horribly in Gitmo. They are the experts of the experts and we will learn the "Gitmo way" before we pass.

I'm looking forward to it.

Love,

Hod

November 3, 1937

Dear Hod,

Do you remember how funny you were, not willing to say your first name! It took me _forever_ to get that out of you. Your eyes told me you liked me long before you said so. A girl gets used to being looked at, and it's not always a welcomed thing, when men stare. But I love your eyes, your deep blue eyes. And you can stare all you like when you get home. And I'll stare, too. Can't wait to see you again.

Love,

Hazel Hazel

---

8 November 1937

Dear Haze,

We took our time, getting down here, doing a full power run, lots of man overboard drills, and managed to rendezvous with another ship, an oiler, and practiced going alongside and refueling. The full power run was at night, and I went topside and back on the fantail and watched the wake glow and dance in the moonlight. There was enough of a breeze coming across the ship to carry the stack gas clear, so it was really pleasant. Those four screws kick up a powerful rooster tail at full speed. I like the way it all comes together on a ship. The engineers get us to where we need to go and give us power for our weapons. Supply keeps us fed and in spare parts and paint and pay. And all of it is so that we Gunner's Mates can fight with our weapons. It all goes to waste if we can't hit what we're shooting at. So we launched some rafts and some helium filled balloons and got in some live fire practice with all of our weapons. I get the feeling that the whole ship exists so that we can do our job, which is to put rounds on target, on time.

During my time in the Pacific I learned quite a bit about our likely next enemy, the Japanese. A couple of Officers spent time telling me about the situation out there. The Japanese are brutal and confident and have a big navy that has never been beaten. They are in need of resources to keep their navy at sea. I think before too long there will be a mighty struggle in the Pacific with the Japanese going against all the other countries with navies in the Pacific. We'd better be ready.

On a more pleasant subject, I went back and numbered all my letters with a circled number on the back of the envelope. Hopefully you'll find the numbers as the date stamps will all be the same date. I kept my letters to you in my locker until we reached port. Yes, we're in Gitmo and we are as ready as we can be. Now starts something like three weeks of "the Gitmo way." Maybe by the end of it we'll get some mail before leaving to go to Trinidad and Haiti.

Miss you,

Hod

November 14, 1937

Dear Hod,

Boy is it dull around here without you. My Mom and Jen and Jack say Hi. I've been seeing a lot more of them, with you gone and catching up on my reading in the evenings. Going over to the clubs in Brooklyn isn't where I want to be. Hopefully there will be some mail of mine that gets to you when you get into port. I've written a bunch of letters and hope to get some in return. What I really want is you, back home with me.

Love,

Haze

----

25 November 1937

Dear Haze,

We finally had a mail call, about the time we're wrapping up at Gitmo. Guess who had the most letters at mail call! They kept calling out Dantes, Dantes… almost like me, that time in the joint on Sads Street. I am so glad to have your letters to read; they'll keep me company on our way to Haiti and Trinidad. I'll read them over and over until we get back to Brooklyn. The ship has put out a schedule and we are due alongside at the Brooklyn Navy

Yard pier at 0900 on December 20th, in time for Christmas. Can't wait! This will be in the mail, maybe you'll get it before I get back.

We've done very well in our training, the crew is sharp and ready for anything. I'm ready to get home!
Love,
Hod

November 25, 1937
Dearest Hod,

I keep looking in the paper, there's a section where they put the news of ship arrivals and scheduled port visits. I don't want to miss it when Brooklyn returns. I will try to be down there on the pier when you get back. Mom says hi and you should plan on coming over when you get back in port. She thinks we should have a party and she'll make an apple pie and a fruit cake we'll celebrate Christmas a little early!

It's past the halfway time now. You'll be back soon. Can't wait!
Love, Haze

---

14 December 1937
Dear Haze,

I'm writing from Port Au Prince, Haiti. We'll soon be leaving here for home as this is just a "showing the flag" visit. It was only three years ago that our occupation of Haiti ended and the last of our Marines left. There is a strong German influence in Haiti and with the way The Great War ended, all countries are keeping an eye on what they are up to. As far as I am concerned it's not worth fighting over and the Germans could probably make something of this place. We get information on every place we visit, a little about the history and of course a list of places to stay away from. We don't want any

trouble, just the chance to remind our hosts that we're
big, powerful and friendly and that they want to keep us
that way.

Trinidad was, by comparison, really nice. It was pretty warm there, just like Gitmo, but so are the people.
I never saw such a mixture of races and people. I think
when conquerors come they leave a bit of themselves behind and Trinidad has had a lot of visitors and conquerors. I went on the beach and found a place with these
strange drums made of the bottoms of steel barrels. They
give off an eerie sound. Some of the drums have more than
one section hammered into a dish-like shape and they can
make different notes by themselves and in combination.
The better bars have what they call steel bands and they
play Calypso, a really neat local music. They get drunk
sailors up and have them do limbo contests. Maybe I'll
teach you the limbo to go with your Charleston. Ha ha.

You won't get this letter until after I see you at
home. A party at your place sounds great. Probably you'll
already know the limbo by the time you read this. I'm
guessing that by now you might have some of my letters.
Love,
Hod

December 12, 1937
Dear Hod,

Hooray, I finally got a whole bunch of letters from
you! Halfway through them I got your note about the numbers on the backs of the envelopes and went back and
sorted them all out. And then I started all over. I
thought of saving them and reading one each day. Needless to say, that idea was dropped almost immediately!
Now I'll read them all, every night before I go to sleep.
Maybe you'll do the same with mine.

I'm proud of you for becoming good at your job and
proud of my sailor man. Come home to me soon.
Love,
Haze

As the USS Brooklyn (CL-40) closed to the last few yards approaching the pier at the Brooklyn Navy Yard, the Bos'n's Mates threw their monkey fists arcing to the pier on lightweight messenger lines, there to be swiftly picked up and hauled in as increasingly larger diameter lines also snaked their way ashore until the shore party is hauling the actual heavy manila berthing lines with their spliced loops at the ends and throwing them over bollards and cleats. The Officer of the Deck skillfully used the engines to put the bow close to the pier at the right position and after number one was secure he kept slight pressure on that line as the tug gently pushed the stern alongside. He and the Captain both knew that he could have berthed her without tug assistance. It was a matter of pride to be able to go to sea and return on your own, a matter of safety and regulation to use the tugs when available.

The pier was fairly crowded, though all of the women and dependents had been kept back until the monkey fists had been thrown. The old timers knew the drill and were patiently waiting and pointing to the sailor they had come for, waving and smiling. The crew was manning the rail to port as she was portside to, all of them in their blues and at attention until 'at-ease' was given.

A beautiful brunette dressed in her finest dress and heels searched the line, then looked more closely near the turrets and found him. She waved and he waved back and tears of happiness messed her make up. It would be an endless half hour before they started coming down the gangway. More than a few aboard had picked her out and followed her gaze back to the ship to try to see who the lucky sailor was. Many of those aboard would have no one there to greet them. Many had agreed to pull standbys for the lucky ones, single or married, who had family or loved ones ashore waiting for them and would take their watches and duty for the first day or two. Hazel had enough time to get her compact out of her purse, turn her back to the ship and do a bit of a repair job.

Shortly after she turned back, Hod appeared next to her and took her into his arms. It was a long kiss and a tight hug. Hod had a small handbag with a few things in it and after things settled down they headed to the bus station, almost bumping into things and people as they walked because they could not take their eyes off of each other. They were an exceedingly handsome couple and many others gave them lingering glances as they strolled. They caught the bus and both of them were a little tongue tied, not finding it easy to just talk.

Finally Haze said tell me some stories about Trinidad and Gitmo. And yes she listened, but mostly she watched the play of enthusiasm across his features as he talked. She took in his physique and squeezed his biceps from time to time. And every now and then she touched his cheek as though she couldn't believe he was really there. She couldn't keep her hands off him.

Finally Hod noticed her looking at him, slowed down and stopped talking. With a look around at the next stop he took her to the back seat of the bus, seated her in the corner and sat next to her and they kissed the rest of the way into Jersey and until two stops to go, when Haze again broke out her compact, shook her head and just put it back. Hod took out a handkerchief and wiped his face clean and hers too. Finally, looking a bit more presentable they walked up the stoop at 101 Mount Vernon Street and arriving at Mom's apartment, went in. Mildred and Jen and Jack were there and they had already started with the beer and they handed Hod and Haze one. It was a big welcome home for the returning hero, all tanned in the middle of winter in New York and looking fine in his tailor mades.

After dinner and a big slice of Mom's apple pie, coffee was served and Hod brought his handbag into the living room. With no fanfare he went over to Mom and gave her a package wrapped in white tissue paper with a tag that said Mom. Everybody stopped and watched as she opened it. It was a beautiful lace tablecloth from Trinidad. Mildred oohed and ahhed and immediately went to the table and spread it. It was a perfect fit and she said Hod didn't need to do that and beamed her thanks and pecked him on the cheek. Next out of the bag was a set of doilies in white lace for Jen and she too got up and kissed Hod thanks. Hod looked into his bag and came out with a bottle of rum for Kaulf, which he tossed to him with a smile. Jack caught it and returned the smile. Hod looked into his bag, looked up and said, with a totally serious expression on his face, "That's it!" Everybody caught their breath and looked at Haze, who said, to relieve the embarrassment, "I got the best present of all!" And then Hod brought out a beautifully wrapped present and gave it to Haze. The note attached and folded so that only Haze could read it said: To the woman I love. She couldn't help it, she cried when she read it, and then she opened her gift. It was a beautiful gold bracelet, a stylish large hoop with a charm attached to it, a sea turtle, to represent Trinidad. She put it on and stood and put her arms around him. The rest went into the kitchen and started clearing away the dishes and they sat together on the couch, maybe wishing they could lie on it together instead.

Christmas was good, really good and spent mostly at Kaulf and Jen's place except for the turkey at Mom's. They were easy together, Hod had a place to sleep on their couch on a Friday night and they generally got together at Mom's sometime on Saturdays when it was a weekend. In late February, on Hod's Birthday, he asked Haze to marry him. She said yes and he gave her a brass anchor with the explanation that he could not afford an engagement ring, but that this anchor would mean that she belonged to him, if she would wear it. He explained that it was a Chief Petty Officer's rank insignia and that he hoped to be a Chief some day and then they would both have one. Haze wore it proudly from that very day, wore it for years. The date was set for April 26, 1938. It was a civil ceremony with Daughter standing up with them as best man. Haze wore the dress she had worn to the pier, and Hod wore his tailor mades. There was no wedding dress as they were saving their money for their own place, an apartment on 96th Street in the City. The day before the wedding, Hod took her to their apartment for the first time. It was sparsely furnished but it had a bed. They tried it out.

CHAPTER 35

A PLAN IS APPROVED

Admirals Fitz and Cochrane had conducted a round of briefings in DC where they had presented to the War Secretary and Chiefs of the Army and Navy at the War Department. With their approval, a visit to the White House was laid on and the Secretary of War and the Admirals did a formal briefing in which the situation in the China Fleet and in the entire Pacific was described, albeit at a high level. The President stopped them from time to time with questions, all answered to his satisfaction. They broke for lunch, saving their conclusions and recommendations for an hour set aside in the afternoon.

During lunch, with Fitz seated at his right side and Cochrane to his left President Roosevelt talked politics for a bit, mentioning that the public was very much against getting involved in any foreign war. Then he turned to the situation in Europe and this fellow Hitler, who was stirring things up. "You know I don't get very much or very good intelligence on Europe, not at all. The Army and the Navy have their own intelligence and code breaking operations and the State Department had one but it was shut down nine years ago. Admiral, you are commended for your initiative in bringing me the most and most in depth information I have received since I've been in office. I look forward to your conclusions and recommendations." Roosevelt was wheeled from the Executive dining room into his quarters where he freshened up and then to the Oval Office. One minute later the Secretary, Fitz and Cochrane were admitted and took seats around the President's desk.

Roosevelt turned to Harry Hines Woodring, former Governor of Kansas and said, "Harry, I take it you approve the conclusions and recommendations I am about to receive." "Yes, Mr. President, I do." "Well then, let's hear it, gentlemen," and he turned toward Admiral Fitz. Fitz started to get up, looked at Roosevelt, "Sir, if I might stand, I'm not used to sitting so much." Woodring looked stricken and at Roosevelt but Roosevelt laughed, "Fitz, I'd stand up if

I could, too; make yourself comfortable. Have a smoke?" And while CincPac turned bright red as he realized his faux pas, Roosevelt broke out his cigarette holder and lit up. With a deeply satisfied sigh and his famous smile he handed Fitz a box of cigars, "they tell me you like a Cuban cigar every once in awhile, Admiral, when your wife lets you." Deeply grateful at being let off the hook with such grace he thanked the President, lit up the cigar and started pacing back and forth. "Sir, if you'll permit, the President has better intelligence than I do. Who told you, one of my Stewards?" They all laughed and Fitz stopped in front of the desk.

"Not all of the Navy's battles are fought with a foreign enemy, Sir. We have differences within our own ranks and sometimes the battles are fierce." Roosevelt nodded, "Then things haven't changed much since I was Assistant Secretary of the Navy for Wilson." Fitz continued, "The current fight is over battleships versus aircraft carriers with a lot of careers riding on the battlewagons. We ran a Fleet Problem in Hawaii just four years ago, Sir and the carriers waxed our battlewagons. The Japanese Imperial Navy Staff are well aware of the results of our exercise. They are covering both sides of that battle, with new super heavy battleships on the drawing boards and a rising star as one of their Carrier Skippers, Isoroku Yamamoto. He is a gunnery expert and is getting into aviation with a will, Sir. I'd say that the Japs are putting their chips on their carriers. As the President well knows, the IJN is expanding, highly motivated and have never been beaten. Our Fleet assets in Pearl Harbor are certainly competitive with the Japanese. The Japs will have to move first against the Dutch in the Dutch East Indies. They need their oil. Our China Fleet assets are useful in their role as intelligence gatherers but are old and tired and will not stand up to a battle with first class Japanese units. I believe the Japanese will do their best to neutralize our Fleet at Pearl in order to achieve their aims elsewhere. There is no doubt in my mind that they will attack us and they have a history of using surprise attacks."

Fitz took a puff, reflected and tapped his ash into a tray on the President's desk. "Sir, with the depression on world-wide the only ones currently expanding in the Pacific are the Japanese. The Dutch and the Aussies are depending on us. The Brits have the numbers but are not what they were in terms of fighting ability just prior to the Great War. And the situation, materiel-wise, is not likely to change as Colonial powers are pulling resources closer to home and letting the Pacific go begging." Roosevelt leaned forward and said, "And that's why if and when we get into this the priority will be and must be in the Atlantic and the Med. Whomever runs the show in the Pacific will have to make do with less than he wants for training and for fighting."

Still talking to Fitz but looking directly at Cochrane, Roosevelt continued, "And your recommendations, whom do you have in mind for carrying this fight to the Japanese? Might it be Cochrane here, the one whom you sent out to WestPac to gather the intelligence?" And Fitz said, "Yessir, I'd go with Dick for CincAsiaticFleet. Admiral Yarnall is due to be relieved and we're also due to put a Rear Admiral in there." Want the job, Admiral?" And Dick Cochrane thought for just a second or two. He hadn't expected things to move quite this fast. He turned to Fitz, "Sir, thank you for your confidence," and turning to the President, "I'd be honored, Mr. President."

Roosevelt said, "Make it so" to his Secretary of War and to Cochrane, "I never saw a man so eager to carry out what may be his death warrant. Dick, I will depend upon you for more good intelligence and to make do the best you can with what you've got, to give us an early warning." With that his secretary came in and announced that the Foreign Minister from the United Kingdom was in the outer office. The President turned to Fitz and said, "One more thing, Fitz, keep those carriers on the move and not in one place for very long. I want them to be better at their job than the Japs are at theirs and I will need them when the Japs attack." He handed the rest of a full box of Cuban cigars to Fitz on his way out.

A few days later, at the Lodge home in the Nuuanu Valley, Oahu, Hawaii, John and Lydia were discussing their future. "Admiral Fitz got back from DC to-day. Though it's not yet for public release, Admiral Cochrane is slated to command the China Fleet; he'll relieve Yarnall." Lydia came over to John in his overstuffed chair and leaned over him from the back, with her arms around him. "And whom do you think he might be taking with him," she asked. He looked up at her and got a kiss for his efforts. "There is a command coming open, a Destroyer out of Subic," he said. "And, has he mentioned anything about it to you?" "No. But he is certainly aware that I will soon be available for assignment. Perhaps now is the time to revisit whether you should continue on active duty" "Honey you could retire and live here with me and I could continue *my* naval career. My reasons for staying on active duty are much like yours, dear. I love my Country and I like to be a part of protecting it. I have thought that if we were to get pregnant it would change everything and I would want to be a full time mother. But that has not happened, though we are doing our best in that department," and she giggled. "You know, there *is* a medical facility in the Ship Repair Facility in Subic Bay. I actually already checked into it. The Commanding Officer is a Lieutenant Commander and the billet is currently up for assignment, will certainly be filled in the next year or so." "A lot could happen in the next year or so," he smiled and he pulled her into his lap and they started undressing each other.

Later, in Admiral Cochrane's Office at CincPac Headquarters. "Ahh, John yes come in." "Sir, congratulations on your new assignment as CincAsiaticFleet." "Well, if you stay around long enough they eventually find something for you to do," he replied. "One of our missions with the China Fleet will be to provide fresh and in depth intelligence by probing at our many ports of call and bases. I say "our" because I have requested that you join the Asiatic Fleet as Commanding Officer of John D. Ford, a Clemson class Destroyer. The Asiatic Fleet has responsibilities for supporting our open China policy as well as defending the Philippines and Guam. To do that I have 13 Destroyers, a Submarine Squadron, Tenders, Minesweepers, PBYs and a seaplane tender, and Motor Torpedo Squadron 3 plus a couple of yachts. The China Fleet has been the neglected step-child of the Pacific Fleet, waxing and waning and generally ending up getting more to do than resources would allow." He looked up to allow Lodge to comment. "Sir I look forward to continuing to serve with you."

Cochrane nodded, "I think our recent experience in Manila and with Quezon gives you a leg up on what will be an increasingly important mission: tracking IJN units and pulsing the support communities where they conduct port visits. We need to know more about their movements and their capabilities. On the other hand, our presence in the P.I. is a large one, with bases at Olongapo, Manila, Corregidor, Miraveles and others. This will ultimately require the Japanese to attempt to take the Archipelago in order to secure their lines of communication. Any network we can build there will have potential use when, as I expect, the Japanese attack and make landings. I intend to homeport Ford at our Olongapo Naval Base. We'll talk more about this later, but the more contacts you can develop in the P.I. the better." He looked up with a twinkle in his eye, "There is a Medical Facility at Olongapo with a branch in Manila as well. Know anybody who might be interested in running that shop?" Lodge replied, "Sir, you amaze me." "Well, she *is* coming up for promotion to LCDR, Lodge, ought to fit right in, I expect." Cochrane watched Lodge's head spin for a moment, "Well, Lodge, what do you think? You get about as much time to think about it as the President gave me," he chuckled, "and I'll give you the same warning he gave me. He said that by taking this job I could be signing my own death warrant, as undermanned as we'll be and as far forward as we'll also be, when the Japanese come calling." That night up Nuuanu Valley, Lydia had news for him. "Honey, that billet, the one in the Philippines, the Medical Facility? I think it's already been filled. It's no longer listed… What is so funny about that? I thought we thought or agreed at least that…" "Sweetheart, I have something to tell you."

Three months later in the Manila, P.I. Army Navy Club, Manual Quezon had attended both Change of Command ceremonies, the one for CincAsiatic-Flt in Manila and the one for Commanding Officer of Ford, held in Subic Bay. A new member of the crew was its Chief Master of Arms, Chief "Wall" Locker, who had more or less been shanghaied from Detroit to Ford, the one pick the new Skipper was allowed as he accepted his orders and left Hawaii for the Philippines. He and newly promoted LCDR Lodge, Nurse Corps had flown together to Manila by PBY and before leaving had turned over the keys to their place in Nuuanu Valley to Admiral Fitz and Auntie Jane. They'd agreed that they could use a getaway honeymoon spot and would do their best to hold the fort until the Lodges could return, even if in retirement.

Cochrane, Quezon and Lodge were seated in the same small room they'd used before, with Chief Locker holding the chained briefcase. After the iced tea was served and before they got started, it got quiet, each of them suspecting what the other was thinking, as they all were thinking back to that night at the Manila Hotel. It had been a fateful and violent night, with untold consequences that had never happened, all because of a sharpshooting Sailor who snuffed out an unthinkable attack before they even had time to fully realize what had happened. Admiral Cochrane stood, "A toast, gentlemen." They all raised their glasses of tea and Cochrane said, simply, "To Dantes, without whom we most probably would not be here today." Chief Locker toasted too and had a hard time swallowing.

Cochrane had a handwritten agenda in front of him and he swiftly went down the list, explaining to Quezon, or Manual as he called him, what his mission was, how it affected his interactions with the Government and tied into his responsibility to defend the P.I. and Guam. They discussed the various minefields that had been laid and were operated by the US Army, as well as Cochrane's plans for the defense of likely landing spots if and when the Japanese would come. Quezon mentioned that he hoped that the Admiral would also be coordinating with the former General Douglas MacArthur, to whom the Government had offered the position of Marshal of the Philippine Army. MacArthur had recently retired from the US Army and had accepted his new position and was already making a pest of himself, cajoling and wheedling and demanding resources and more resources. Quezon had none to give and was mounting a full frontal assault on Washington to get aid of all sorts. His requests of Cochrane was but one of a host of ongoing conversations. Lodge looked on with interest to see how his Boss would handle this one. He knew of the longstanding relationship between Cochrane and MacArthur, as both had been baseball players on their respective Academy teams and had played against each other. Lodge knew or thought he knew that the relationship was a prickly one.

"Manual, I have been in touch with the President on this very subject. He is extremely interested in having the help of Filipinos and Filipinas in accomplishing a part of my mission here. We will be building a network of informants and intelligence operatives here in the Philippine Archipelago. Given that the quality and quantity of information that we get with your help is deemed valuable and helpful I would expect that Washington would find helpful ways to express their thanks. Hopefully your Marshal will be cooperative and helpful. I personally find that our relationship, Manual, yours and mine is very helpful. *"I'll be damned,"* Lodge thought, *"Close my eyes and I'd swear that was FDR giving that answer, For sure politics is a big part of my Boss' job."*

Chief Locker walked into the Bar of Rosario Gabangabang before the regular crowd had started to build. He ordered a Kirin. Dantes had something after all, with his preference for the beer with a dragon on the label. There wasn't a lot of interest in him: too early, too old and experienced and maybe too white, as they didn't get that many of them as customers in this part of town. After awhile the Proprietress strolled up to him, smiled and asked if she could sit down. She believed in doing as she trained her girls to do. Chief noticed the bit of byplay, appreciated the leadership inherent in such setting of the example. As one professional to another he turned to her but before he could speak she had to do it, she had to flash a bit of her expertise, for she knew that it was the reason a man like Chief Locker would be coming in here, to her place. "Chief Locker, will Dantes be coming in here next? Oh, that's right, he's now on the Brooklyn and the Detroit is still in Long Beach, probably you're on the Ford with Commander Lodge." Her eyes danced with merriment and Locker let her have her triumph. After all he was here for her cooperation and that would require many nights of gradual and increasing trust for what he had in mind.

For her part Rosario was keenly observant of the Chief. She knew it was something important, probably something extremely sensitive and most certainly something profitable. She also knew that to gain the upper hand she had to let the Chief bring up a request and in his own time. As a result nothing of seeming consequence was discussed that evening. Except that by the time he left she knew, deep in her bones that Locker loved Dantes like a son. Locker was sniffing for politics and knew no more than he did, walking in. He suspected she liked Americans, but it would be a close question for many if not most Filipinas. Americans made up a small percentage of the population and they were mostly in business, government or agriculture. The Military were different. They fit into no category as residents. You were either fighting with them or you were fighting for them. With Locker she very much preferred, she thought, to be on the same side. She decided that next time he visited she would let him find that out. She knew there would be a next time. She appreciated the courtesy when Chief left a twenty on the table for her. It wasn't the money as much as it was the respect. If she wanted more money she could have moved out of the shadows and into the tonier parts of the city. What she didn't want was the attention she would get. She required her independence.

It was on the fourth visit when Rosario declined the money that Locker suggested that they repair to her office. Once seated in the tiny space behind the bar, with cigars lighted up and beers, Locker saluted her with his, "Thank you, Mamasan." Rosario smiled in return, "How may I be of service, Chief?" "I am concerned for the future of the P.I. and all Filipinos. The US is committed to defending the P. I. but I fear the Japanese are very advanced in their preparations for war and it will be difficult to catch up." Rosario considered for a bit. "Sometimes we think that the US hasn't made up its mind about her former colony and we also wonder about you. We need your help and yet we want our independence. It's not an easy situation." "No it's not," Locker replied. "What we have in mind is a way for your country to help my country help you. The Japanese are brutal, ambitious and on the move. What we need more than anything at this phase is information. Actually I should refer to it as what it is, intelligence."

Rosario's eyes glittered as her mind raced, "We have heard the stories of the Japanese and we do see them from time to time in our bars and places of business. I think what you want is to know more about them and perhaps to identify as best we can who their supporters are, in the P.I." "Yes, Rosario, we need that and we need more. We need to have a network of trusted supporters and patriots upon whom we will be able to depend when things get really rough. Such a cadre would not be doing what we need for money, Rosario. They would be doing it for their country and their freedom." "Then you are talking to the right person, Wallace." And they reached across the small table and shook on it. They went on to discuss scope and matters of control and command. Locker volunteered that the Navy would supply a small number of radios to be distributed to the other major islands as the network grew. As their meeting drew to a close Rosario mentioned that she had not spent any of the money that Wallace had been leaving. "I will be keeping it against expenses," she said. "And I will secure funding from time to time to support things like necessary travel." Then Rosario said, "Thank you for choosing me as your partner in this, Wallace. It feels good to be doing something for our independence." "I look forward to our continuing association, Rosario;" and he smiled as he added," I think we should call our network, Mamasan."

CHAPTER 36

LYDIA TAKES COMMAND

There had been a short but formal relieving of duties at the SRF Subic, Medical facility by LCDR Lodge after she had checked the property book against everything listed in it as to location, security and soundness. The small supply of drugs and medicines was inventoried and secured and then she went over all of the medical jackets in the shelves. There had been patients from the Submarine, Destroyer and Aviation units as well as some from commands that made port periodically for repairs and the repair facility itself. Finally she studied the service jackets of all assigned personnel: two medical doctors, five nurses, a pharmacist and a yeoman. There was also an office that she maintained in Manila, with a Chief Hospital Corpsman in charge and three nurses who performed the functions required for accounting for medicines and medical instruments as well as medical care. The Subic facility had ten beds, the one in Manila had but four, two of them cots. She reviewed the medical quarters assignment and watch bills and over two twelve hour days felt she knew her facilities, her people and her responsibilities. She formally saluted and said, "I relieve you, Sir" and wished that John had been there for at least a small celebration. The Ford had been underway for a week and would be at sea for another before returning.

The Naval Base at Olongapo was tidy, fenced and had a twenty four hour roving security guard. A Marine contingent was barracked aboard SRF Subic and they maintained security at the Main Gate. They also built a range for rifle and pistol practice and maintained their proficiency in small arms. There was a base housing area with one and two bedroom cottages for assigned personnel. As a relatively senior Officer at Subic, Lydia rated one of the two bedroom furnished units. One of her first orders was to establish what she called "liberty hours" service. This was a nurse on duty at the facility to handle injuries and wounds suffered by military personnel while on liberty. She met with the Commander of the Marine Contingent and made him aware of this service and suggested she be allowed to train the Marines who stood the main gate watch. He readily agreed and at the end of a week Lydia felt pretty good about their readiness to handle drunks who would show up at the main gate around the expiration of liberty. For the next week she made the rounds of all tenant commands and left a brochure that listed the medical capabilities at her facility. While there, at the seaplane tender, or the submarine tender, for instance, she asked to see their medical facilities. Maybe they had a sickbay, maybe not. It might be a wardroom dining table that converted to an operating table with lights in the overhead or it could be something more substantial. She left a list of "to do" items that would improve their medical capability and offered to provide training and any assistance they might need in bringing their sickbays up to snuff.

She'd been in charge for less than a month when one afternoon she had a visitor. It was a Marine Gunnery Sergeant and he looked vaguely familiar. He was escorted back to her office where he announced himself, "Gunnery Sergeant Clancy," Ma'am. "Come in, Sergeant, forgive me if I'm mistaken, but you look familiar to me." Gunny smiled, "Yes Ma'am, thank you for remembering. I believe it may be the party on Oahu after the canoe race, where we ran into each other. I was on the Detroit, Ma'am, along with your husband, Commander Lodge." Recognition flashed across her face and she invited Gunny to sit down. "As I recall you were holding a tryout for your pistol team and Seaman First Dantes was meeting up with you for that. How did he do," she smiled. "Ma'am he is the best I've ever seen, especially at rapid fire. I've never seen such accuracy. He's a natural." "Well I'm glad to hear it and not surprised at all. What brings you here?" "Ma'am I'm in charge of the detail at our Embassy in Manila and when I heard that Captain Lodge had assumed command of Ford and then heard that there was a new CO at the Subic sickbay I thought I might welcome you to the neighborhood." "Well, thank you, Gunny, I do appreciate that. One can never have enough friends at a new duty station." "Yes Ma'am. Also, I get to see the traffic at the Embassy and am aware of the threat levels as they rise and fall. In particular we keep an eye on Japanese movements and stay aware of the locations of our countrymen. You may rely on me to pass along any urgent alerts and should it come to it, to provide an armed escort to safety, should the need arise, Ma'am."

For some reason, the offer struck the Commander emotionally. Here this big brawny Marine was, saying he would be looking out for her. She stood, and extended her hand, "Gunny I view this as personal and not official and that makes if even more meaningful to me. Of course I gratefully accept your chivalrous offer and will rest more easily knowing that you're watching the situation and watching over me. Thank you so much. He shook her hand then stepped back a pace, stood at attention, said, "Ma'am," did an about face and marched out of her office. Ford made port two days later and John was home that evening for supper. After cleaning up in the kitchen Lydia joined him in their small living area.

"Honey?" "Yes, Darlin'." "I had a visit the other day at the Medical Facility. Very nice man, Gunnery Sergeant Clancy. He reminded me that he had been aboard Detroit when you were there and I recalled seeing him at the party on Oahu after that fabulous canoe race. You remember, the one that Dantes suggested to Admiral Fitz. It was a great success." "Umm hmm. I do recall that race and the party. What did the Sergeant have to say?" Lodge looked up from the stack of Manila Heralds that Lyd had saved for him while he was at sea. "Oh, it was the sweetest thing. It turns out he is in charge of the Marine Detail at the Embassy in Manila and he was dropping in to welcome me to the neighborhood, as he called it. He also said that he was kept in the loop as to threat level and wanted me to know that he would be keeping a watchful eye, and that he would notify me if things were about to get a bit dicey and also that he would furnish safe escort for me if it ever came to that. I think he was thinking in case you were at sea, something like that. I took it as a personal favor and told him it meant a lot to me." Lodge grunted, "You have to love the Marines. No better friends, no worse enemies."

"When I was trying to place him I recalled that night of our first date, that Dantes had to turn down a beach trip the next day because he was going to try out for the Detroit's pistol team, the Gunny's pistol team. I mentioned it to the Gunny and asked him how he'd done, Dantes. Did he make the team? And the Sergeant said that…" She stopped her story as her husband was laughing, almost out loud. "All right. What's so funny?" "Nothing Darling, nothing at all." "No, I want to know. What's so funny about Dantes and this pistol team?" "Well, what did the Gunny have to say about Dantes and his shooting?" "He said something about Dantes being accurate, the best he ever saw, and a natural." John gave a small smile and said, "The Gunny is a master of under-statement." "Alright, you've really got me curious now. What's funny about any of this and how would you know anything about how good Dantes is with a pistol?"

Lodge sighed, put aside his paper and motioned her over to his lap. Look-ing at him with interest, Lyd got up and joined him, squirming around in his lap for good measure and maybe a little encouragement. When he didn't say anything, perhaps enjoying what she was doing in his lap, she stopped and said, "Give." "It was never classified, and it came out later but was suppressed onboard Detroit and by Admiral Cochrane. I suppose I can tell you if you can keep it under your hat." She stared at him in some exasperation, wondering why he was dragging this out. "Of course I can keep it to myself." "Dantes and Chief Locker and the Gunny were serving as security for Admiral Cochrane and me during our port visit to Manila on our WestPac cruise. As a matter of fact it was I who suggested to the Commodore that we could use them during and after our talks with Manual Quezon."

This was getting interesting. "Go on, what happened?" "A group of insurrectionists known as the Tayags had gathered information on our visit and unbeknownst to us made plans to assassinate Cochrane, Quezon and no one knows how many others. There was an attack at the Ball on the roof of the Manila Hotel, three men armed with knives and a machete. Two of them had women as hostages, ready to slit their throats, while the leader of the group made directly for the Admiral and Quezon with a machete. Everyone was totally surprised except Dantes; he was moving immediately toward the noise while the rest of us were frozen into place. In an instant he shot both of the men holding the women and then turned toward the Admiral. He shouted STOP and the assailant hesitated and Dantes fired probably the rest of his bullets into the last attacker. He pitched forward into a pool of his own blood at the Admiral's feet." In her amazed total silence he continued, "The shots were continuous, one after the other as though he hardly had to aim. I've never seen that kind of marksmanship before, expect I never will again." As she started to protest, he put a finger over her mouth, kissed her and then took her into the bedroom.

The next morning she knew not to make a big deal over how much danger John had been in, but she had questions. John coughed up that Dantes had come under scrutiny earlier in the evening by the very same rebel leader and that he had been befriended by a bar girl who warned him about the Tayags. "In his own words he had been warned and also told by me to stay out of trouble, so he came back early and was there just in time to foil the attack. He refused to take any credit, said he was lucky. After the attack, the next night we added the Gunny to the security detail and sent Dantes and Chief Locker and Gunny back into the bar to see if we could get more information on the Japanese who were funding the Tayags. That ultimately turned out to be successful as well. Listen, darling. I am more than thankful and grateful to Gunny for his offer. I will rest easier while I'm at sea knowing he has your back. Probably you will want to drop in on him when you make your visits to your medical facility there."

"I have a bit of news, as it turns out, Lyd." "Mmmm?" Admiral Cochrane is making an effort to cooperate with Marshal or General, whatever his title is, nowadays." Lydia knew exactly whom he was talking about, MacArthur was generally not a favorite with Navy types. "With the situation being what it is with the Japanese and the necessity to get as much out of every dollar we spend in the Pacific, the Admiral and the General are familiarizing each other with their commands, capabilities and requirements, to see if there's any way we can get a synergistic result, you know, something more than the simple sum of its parts." Lydia tossed her head, "Fancy words for cooperation and eliminating duplication where we can without losing a political battle between the services over turf, or responsibility. That about cover it?," she asked sweetly.

Lodge laughed out loud in a bit of astonishment, "Yeah, that about covers it. They've been to look at the sub squadron and the seaplanes and patrol boats and the tin cans will be next week. Then MacArthur is going to show us how the Army operates the minefields and be certain that we can serve as back up for that duty, turn it on or off and maybe move the mines around a little. It'll be no surprise at all that they will talk about intelligence operations in the P.I. as well as arming and training the various armed and semi-armed groups that serve as a military defense force out here. Most of the weapons are from The Great War and most of the stuff is basically useless. Cochrane says that FDR is not going to spend any more money out here, that it'll be a defensive posture and a delaying action that we'll have to prosecute if and when we finally take on the Japanese. MacArthur understands all of this and is still fighting like the good soldier he is to make the most of what he's got."

"So, what does any of this have to do with me, your roomie with benefits?" "Darling we are invited to El Supremo's HQ and private residence atop the Manila Hotel. You know Quezon pointedly asked Cochrane awhile back to get together with MacArthur and to be a friend of the Philippines, said that as long as he was a friend of his homeland Quezon would be a friend to him. In fact said to please call him Manual." "So let me guess, we're going to a reception of some sort this weekend in Manila?" "Better than that, Cochrane remembered me being invited up to Makalapa to play tennis with Uncle Fitz, he has requested that we be prepared to play some tennis in the gardens and courts of the Manila Hotel. MacArthur has a newly remodeled penthouse and I'm given to understand that there is a suite reserved, one floor down, for the weekend for us. It would not be surprising to me to find Quezon there and others of the ruling class as well."

At the event, on Saturday afternoon, some of the General's Junior Officers were down at the courts, banging away with a sort of languid ferocity that at once showed their foppish elite status and cutthroat approach to just about everything. There were a couple of wives and drinks and the games which went on too long to be called fun, were too inconclusive to declare an out and out winner. Lodge had played for fun, ruefully acknowledging at least to himself how out of condition he was, while at the same time pulling off some spectacular shots that made the Majors whistle in appreciation. Lydia rescued him, with Jean MacArthur in tow, looking regal and charming and entirely covered from the sun's rays in a colorful summery garment that could generously be called colorful. There was bright conversation and brittle laughter and the occasional buzz of an errant insect that hadn't gotten the word that the courts were off limits. Everyone manfully ignored the insects and trooped off to their rooms for showers and a pick me up before rejoining on the dance floor adjacent to the penthouse.

In the shower. "Having a good time, Darling," she asked. "I am now," he answered. Mmmm you like it wet and slippery, don't you? "Yes I mmmff." And that was the end of the talking until after their nice relaxing nap.

Topside there was a receiving line and they went through, having already deposited their calling cards on the silver tray. There were the Calderones, the MacArthurs and their son, bravely dressed in coat and tie, followed by the Quezons. A quartet struck up and there was dancing and drinks passing freely through the dancing area, served by choker white clad servants. A gentleman introduced himself to them as Ricardo Verdad, and Lodge remembered him from Dantes' surprise business dealings. At the head table were the receiving party, Admiral Cochrane and Senor Verdad, Esquire. After a while MacArthur invited the Lodges up to his table, where a pair of chairs magically made their appearance. It was a total charm offensive that was not in the slightest bit offensive. The General gave his full attention to Lydia and Jean did the same with John. Cochrane sat there and chimed in when called upon.

MacArthur leaned in and said, "You know, my Father commanded here, some years ago as the Military Governor. He set up at the old Price Castle. I can arrange a tour of it for you if you like. By that time I had been off to school and back to the Philippines as a young Engineer." Lodge also leaned in, "Sir, I believe I saw his portrait in the foyer as we were coming in." "Yes, indeed," and the General sat back and took a bit of a sip of his drink, lost in his memories for the moment when Lodge said, "Medal of Honor recipient, Sir. I know you're proud. Missionary Ridge, I believe it was." At that MacArthur positively beamed and slapped Lodge on the back, even handed him a box of cigars as he tried but failed to hide the sudden tears that had sprung at this generous mention of his decorated Father. Cochrane, who had told Lodge about this bit of family history before the party, leaned in and topped off a drink or two while the General blew his nose and Jean looked fondly at him and at Lodge for being so, well, admiring.

Before the party was over MacArthur professed his undying love for the Philippines and profusely thanked Cochrane and the Lodges for their friendship and being a part of it all, here on the Archipelago. He made it a point to tell Lydia, "I hear that you have been providing free medical services to civilians in the community. I can't tell you how much it affects me to know that you are taking care of my people. I feel a part of this Country and I am sure that the Filipinos accept you as a part of their Country, as well." With that Cochrane also beamed, rose and made his manners and the Lodges did the same. The next morning at breakfast there was a note from "Douglas" and a bouquet of roses at their table in the restaurant. Cochrane looked at it all, looked at Lodge, and said, "You must play a mean game of tennis." And they all laughed, drawing some attention to their merriment from the others at their tables.

And on the way home, Lydia wondered to herself how the General knew that about medical services to civilians. She hadn't even told John, yet.

CHAPTER 37

FIRST CLASS

Married life for an Enlisted Man, and a second class at that, wasn't easy. In addition to the expenses of living in New York, the unexpected always seemed to pop up. On March 14, 1939 Hod and Haze had a baby boy. The Baby was ten days old before Hod found out that he was a father, as the Brooklyn was in Gitmo at the time. Hazel insisted that he be named after Hod, so he was stuck with Horace Howard Dantes II, as Haze didn't want it to be Junior and have him called "Junie" for most of his life. But he also got a nickname, sort of a shortening of his last name, Dant or Dants which sounded like Dance. So the busy little family was three" Hod, Haze and Dance.

About three months after Dance was born, the Brooklyn got orders to change home port to Long Beach, CA. The Navy didn't pay transportation for sailors rated at second class. So, the couple needed a couple of trunks to pack pots and pans and linens for the move to the West Coast. They went to Hackensack one day to shop for trunks and found a store that had some very nice ones. One was for $20.00 and a slightly smaller one for $16.00.

The couple didn't have much money and hated to part with it. After arguing with the salesman for a while, Hod was ready to leave. He told him he wouldn't give him more than $20.00 for both of them and started to walk away. The salesman said, "I'll take it." Oh, how Hod hated to let go of that $20.00 bill. The two trunks were delivered the next day, no charge and they were ready to make plans for their trip. Hazel was to take the train from New York to New Orleans, transfer to the Southern Pacific for the rest of the trip to Los Angeles. They chose this route so Hazel could stop in Uvalde, Texas, where Loraine and her husband lived. Hazel and Dance were to get off the train there and stay two days to rest and wash clothes. Then they would get back on the train and arrive in Los Angeles about 1700 on Sunday evening.

The Brooklyn was to arrive in Long Beach on Saturday morning. That would give Hod time to find a place to live, and he would meet Hazel and Dance the next day. The Brooklyn arrived in Long Beach about 1000, and Hod didn't wait for the mail, but went ashore in the first liberty boat. He found a real estate agent, and she had a car and drove around Long Beach until they found a place to rent that Hod could afford. He went to a store and bought food. Everything was set, and it was only about 1300. So he decided to make a dummy run into Los Angeles so he would know exactly what to do the next day to meet Hazel at Grand Central Station.

Hod got off the P.E. train in Los Angeles and walked to the first beer joint and had a couple brews. He left that place and walked down the street to the next bar and had a couple more beers while watching the floor show. Leaving that place, he saw a streetcar with "Grand Central Station" on it, got on and rode it to the station. The track made a big circle in front of the station and back out. Hod had decided to stay on the street car and go back to catch the P.E. train to Long Beach. But he changed his mind and got off the street car to look around the station. As he walked by the waiting room he heard a baby crying, looked around and there were Hazel and Dance! He couldn't believe his eyes.

"Darling, what are you doing here?" "What am I *doing here*? I'm out of formula, Dance is starving, no more clean diapers and he's howling his head off and you say what am I doing here?" And angry tears of disappointment flowed down her cheeks. This wasn't the welcoming she had been anticipating. He made to kiss her and she drew back at the smell of beer on his breath. Hod nonetheless took the baby, sopping wet and held him in one arm as he screamed even more and gently pulled Haze to him and at last got her, at least, to stop crying. Passersby were giving him dirty looks as the three of them made for a noisy, smelly hazard to navigation for hustling passengers. Finally Hod said, "You were due in here tomorrow, I am only here on a dry run, to be sure there wouldn't be any problem in picking you up tomorrow. I got off the streetcar at the last second, just to have a look around." "But I wrote you a letter, telling you of the change in plans; I only stayed one day on the ranch in Uvalde." "And I caught the first liberty boat to come ashore and find a place for us to live, before mail call. I had no idea you'd be here today." Hod knew it wasn't the time to ask why she would change the plan that was already a very tight schedule. In fact it would not be a point he would ever bring up. They walked to a store not too far away and were lucky to find diapers and formula. With Dance cleaned up and Haze settled down they caught the trolley and then the train and that evening wound up in their apartment in Long Beach. Hod was able to fix a meal while Haze put a clean, sated and sleepy Dance to bed. Finally they had a home warming of sorts as Hod mixed a rum and coke for the two of them and Haze fell asleep in his arms. Needless to say,

Hod handled the feeding for Dance at 0200 and 0600 and he and Haze finally laughed about it over breakfast of toast, coffee and eggs, whipped up by Chef Dantes.

Hod was promoted to GM1 while the ship was stationed in Long Beach. After a few months operating out of Long Beach, the Brooklyn was sent to the Bremerton Navy Yard, Bremerton, Washington, for 3 months overhaul. Again, the Dantes packed all of their belongings in the two trunks and shipped them to Bremerton. Hod rode up on the ship, Hazel and Dance rode the train. They skimped to save enough money to get back to Long Beach, but had a good Christmas: a tree, a few presents and a turkey dinner.

Soon after returning to Long Beach, the whole Pacific Fleet went to Pearl Harbor, T.H. for maneuvers. But, trouble was brewing with Japan, and the fleet was kept in Hawaii.

While on the Brooklyn, in #4 Turret, Dantes got the reputation as a problem solver. They were having trouble with the catapults for launching small sea planes, so they transferred Dantes to the aviation division to maintain the catapults. Gunner's mates had this job because a charge of gun powder was used to catapult the aircraft into the air. Dantes soon had all the problems solved and trained another gunner's mate to take over. There were so many problems with the 5" anti-aircraft guns that Dantes was transferred to the 6th division. The Chief who had been in charge was transferred to the armory and magazines, leaving Dantes as de facto leader in place of the Chief. Lt. Downs, the division officer told Dantes that the chief couldn't get the rammers to work properly, and had made out a job order for the Navy Yard to fix them, when and if the ship got to a Navy Yard. Dantes found that there was too much air pressure for operating the rammers and had the engineers reduce it, and there were no more problems. Lt. Downs brought up another job order that the chief had submitted. One of the 5" guns couldn't be fired because a small shaft that operated the safety feature of the firing mechanism was broken. The chief had convinced Lt. Downs that the gun mount would have to be lifted to get the broken shaft out, a navy yard job. Hod found a way to get the broken shaft out, sent the two pieces to the ship's machine shop and had another one made. It fit perfectly, the 5" gun was back in commission. Dantes' stock was going up by leaps and bounds. The hoist that brought ammunition from the magazine to #3 mount was inoperative. Dantes studied the operating manual for the hoist one morning and found out how it was supposed to work and fixed it in the afternoon. Dantes was steadily reducing the backlog of delayed repairs. The telescope sight setting mechanism on #2 mount was inoperative and the chief had convinced Lt. Downs that the ship would have to be in dry dock in order to disassemble the sight mechanism and get it realigned properly. While the ship was at sea Dantes had disassembled the sight setting mechanism when the chief happened to walk by and see him. He blew his top and said he was going to tell the Gunnery Officer what Dantes was doing. Dantes went ahead and fixed the mechanism, and never heard a word from the Gunnery Officer.

One day in Port after all the minor problems had been fixed, Lt. Downs sidled up to Dantes. He caught him with a cup of coffee in his hand. "Dantes, you've proven to be a wizard. But now I have the ultimate challenge for you, the loading machine." The loading machine had never worked properly, and there was no way to train eight gun crews without the loading machine breaking down. Again, Hod studied the thing and found out exactly how it was supposed to work. It was impossible to keep the three way air valve operating properly. The valve controlled the air pressure to the rammer and breech plug. So, Hod devised a way to operate the valve by a system of levers attached to the rammer handle. Then he drew pictures of the levers he wanted, and the machine shop made them.

In a couple of days Dantes had the parts in hand and modified the three way valve and then told Lt. Downs that the loading machine was ready. Downs called the #1 gun crew and went through a good loading drill. The machine worked perfectly. All eight gun crews went through a good drill, and there were no problems with the machine. When the last crew had finished, Dantes walked around to the other side of the loading machine. He had been watching the operation of his levers. Dantes saw a bunch of strangers. The Brooklyn was moored in a nest with three other sister ships, and as the gunners mates on the other ships saw, or heard, the loading machine operating for so long, they started coming aboard to watch. No one had ever seen the six inch loading machine operate that long; usually it was CLANK, CLANK quit.

Lt. Downs was pleased, but said it was an unauthorized modification and ordered another 3-way valve. With the new valve installed the machine broke down before the first gun crew had finished their loading drill. Dantes put his rig back on the machine and it was still operating when he left the ship. When Brooklyn got back to Long Beach the Chief who had been banished to the Armory and magazines shanghaied to the China Fleet. He didn't tell Dantes good-bye when he left. Dantes was growing in reputation and maturity. Now he knew that all Chiefs were not created equal.

Lt. Downs was training pointers and trainers for short range battle practice and was discouraged because the sailors he had selected were not doing very well. One of the GM3s and Dantes started practicing a little and the third class told Lt. Downs that he and Dantes were the only good pointer and trainer he had. Finally, the day before the firing practice, Downs said, "OK wise guys, you two are to fire #4 mount." As it turned out, #4 mount was the only mount out of the eight that made an "E". Dantes continued to draw the $5.00 extra each month.

When Dantes' and Daughter's enlistments expired in October 1940 Daughter decided to ship over for the Houston, another cruiser, and tried to talk Dantes into going with him. Dantes, however decided again to go to the Navy Department for reenlistment. Hod and Haze had talked it over. Hod thought that it wouldn't be too long before the US and Japan would be at war and if it happened anytime soon Mildred's place in Ridgefield Park would be a good place for Haze and Dance to stay. Houston was a Pacific Fleet ship and the Dantes had decided to try to get assigned closer to home. Something on the East coast, if they could get it, would fill the bill nicely. Once again, Hod and Haze packed their two trunks and headed for New Jersey to stay with Haze's mother.

CHAPTER 38

VIXEN

The Navy Department, Washington, D.C. was just as Dantes remembered it, the wait in the outer area just as long. When he was called in he went straight to the desk that handled Gunner's Mates and was surprised to see the same detailer he'd seen four years earlier. *That's a lot of shore duty, maybe they detail one another to stay right where they are.* Dantes took a seat while Chief Hollander perused his jacket. *No telling what he's looking at, for sure he doesn't remember me.* Chief Hollander was looking at a steady progression up the ranks after an extraordinary jump start at boot camp and Dantes' first ship. "So, what sort of duty do you have in mind to start this hitch, Dantes?" "I'd like a ship that is in the shipyard, preferably one in New York," Dantes replied. "It could be any type of ship at all, mainly I want one that is in pre-commissioning or overhaul, in New York." "Don't want a cruiser? You've been a cruiser sailor for both tours." "Size and type of ship don't matter to me, Chief. I'm interested in a duty station that will have me staying put for awhile and in New York." Chief Hollander's eyes flicked over to the personal data section of the file and noted that Dantes had two dependents, a wife and a son. Then he checked his list of billets for first class and found the Vixen, a yacht undergoing modifications to bring it into the Navy as a warship. It was in the yard in Brooklyn and would be there for months, completing her outfitting. Dantes was an easy sell. He knew what he wanted and figured he could make the most of any situation once he got aboard. *Vixen, huh? Sounds interesting. Haze will be happy and so will I. It's not quite shore duty but it's the next best thing.* Vixen was a luxury yacht that the Navy had just bought from German-American woolen manufacturer Julius Forstmann and was converting into a gun boat with three inch guns and depth charges at the Sullivan Drydock and Repair Shipyard, Brooklyn. Dantes was assigned to the pre-commissioning detail and could go home every evening. Vixen was a beautiful ship before the

Navy started remodeling it. There were winding stairs between decks, heavy carpeting and French doors opening out on deck. There was a swimming pool on the third deck. The water could be heated to the desired temperature and lights could make rainbows. There was one big room on the third deck that was completely lined with cedar where the owners stored their winter clothes. The fittings in the bathrooms were gold plated. She was powered by two huge Krupp diesel engines. The ship was built in Kiel, Germany in 1929.

Vixen underwent a five month, $1.2M conversion from pleasure yacht to warship. Ripped out were the gold-plated plumbing, swimming pool, cedar closet and winding staircases, to be replaced with four three inch guns, two depth charge tracks, seven .50 cal machine guns and two .30 cal machine guns. Instead of a small deck force and engine room crew plus cook, stewards, full liquor locker and guests, Vixen in her haze gray and deck gray paint job was manned by some 279 Officers and crew.

On 5 March 1941 she got underway for her shakedown cruise, calling at Saint Thomas, San Juan and Guantanamo Bay, Cuba and before ultimately arriving at her new home port in New London, Connecticut where she assumed duties as flagship for ComSubLant. Vixen was kept busy in Fleet maneuvers off New River, North Carolina and various ports of call, fairly routine if not humdrum duty until on one occasion she was tasked to participate in a test.

Vixen was operating with another ship to test hydrophones. The other ship had the hydrophones, and the Vixen was to drop two depth charges, set to explode at 30 feet. She was dead in the water when Dantes asked permission to let the depth charge roll down the rack into the trap to be ready for dropping. The Gunnery Officer said "go ahead". Hod operated the release handle, but when the 600 pound depth charge hit the trap, it jerked the handle out of his hand, rolled out of the trap, and fell into the sea. When it exploded, it raised the Vixen's stern out of the water. But, she was a sturdy ship, and no harm was done. It was an accident due to a poorly designed release mechanism, which was soon modified. The Captain was fairly calm about the whole incident, which is more than could have been said about Hod. At the time all he could think about was the two ships he came close to destroying, Pruitt and Vixen. Vixen returned to New London on 6 December, the day before the Imperial Japanese Navy attacked Pearl Harbor. The USS Augusta (CA-31), which had been vacated by Admiral Ernest J. King upon his promotion from Commander Atlantic Fleet to Commander in Chief US Fleet was still at Newport, Rhode Island where Vixen went alongside to bring on board King's papers and belongings. Admiral King had flown from Quonset Point to Washington, DC to commence his tour as Commander in Chief, United States Fleet.

Once, while Vixen had been operating with the Atlantic Fleet, Admiral King had come aboard and said that if she could make 30 knots, he would take it for his flagship. At that time King was commander of the Atlantic Fleet and Vixen was flagship of the Commander Submarines, Atlantic Fleet, based in New London, Connecticut. As it turned out he settled for a flagship that would do just half that maximum speed when underway. Vixen tied up at Washington Navy Yard as Admiral King's Flagship and Admiral King moved aboard. Because of her extended time in port she became known as USS Paradise.

During the time the Vixen was in the Washington Navy yard, Hod's daughter, Loraine was born. The family lived in Ridgefield Park, and accumulated furniture, and had their own apartment. They could no longer pack everything in two trunks, but they still had them.

"Hey, Chief, the word's in." *Chief! Who's he talking to?* Dantes looked up at the yeoman from Vixen's ship's office, glanced around the space, nobody else in the passageway where the yeoman had stopped him. He also saw the beginnings of a look of awe and respect on the yeoman's face and dared to think, *he means me, and he came looking for me!* But as was his habit he kept silent and waited for the development if it was going to come, to come to him. The ship's yeoman just stood there with that silly grin on his face, looking at him. For some reason he couldn't or wouldn't just call him Dantes. The yeoman reached out and handed him the UNCLAS message board. As he started down the list he realized it wasn't in alphabetical order. It was the list of those promoted to Chief Petty Officer, alright, and it was a pretty long list, the names of everybody in the Fleet who'd been tapped, knighted, given the ultimate in respect and there it was, Dantes, Horace Howard, GMC.

The first picture that flew to his mind was of Chief Locker at Boot Camp, as he handed him his Seaman First stripes. When you had a couple tours in you started looking for these bits of news, knew when they were coming. Dantes reflected on the fact that Chief Locker was probably looking at this same list, looking for his name and finding it. Maybe he was remembering a fight in a shack in Tijuana, or a young man sobbing his heart out. Or a deadly sharp-shooter on a hotel roof in Manila. There were most likely two Chiefs smiling from ear to ear at this very moment, one a Sea Daddy, the other a brand new Chief.

There was a crackle of sound on the 1MC as the familiar voice came on, "This is the Captain speaking, now Chief Petty Officer Dantes report to Chief's Quarters." Hod looked at the yeoman in a daze, tried to hand him back the message board and the yeoman refused to take it. "Your souvenir,

Chief. It's an honor to have been the first to call you Chief." The Chief continued to stand there so the yeoman grabbed his hand, shook it and pointed him forward in the direction of the Goat Locker. "They're waiting for you, Chief."

It was a suddenly gathered gauntlet of shipmates that stood aside in the passageway, lined his progress as he made his way forward. Hands were thrust at him, and over and over he heard, "congratulations, Chief." And in truth as was customary, he had lost his last name. Every Enlisted man on board was known by his last name. Except the Chiefs. When you achieved the pinnacle it seemed only that title was used. Or if your last name was used it always came after that singular title, earned and not bestowed.

He went to open the door to Chief's Quarters, *it's jammed,* he tried again and the door wouldn't budge. He put his shoulder to it and it gave a little but slammed back. Hod was no dummy, with a huge grin on his face he then knocked on the door. He heard muffled laughter on the other side. Then, "Who's there?" "Dantes." "WHO?" and it was in unison and loud. "DANTES!" Again the response, "WHO?" "CHIEF DANTES!!!" And at that they pulled the door open and he almost sprawled onto the checkerboard black and white tile deck. They grabbed him and somebody put a Chief's bonnet on him, a brand new one. He looked up and it was the Skipper. The C.O. and X.O. got in front of him and pinned his anchors on. They sat him down roughly at the end of the table and held a kangaroo court on the spot and told him he had been guilty of impersonating a First Class Petty Officer and it had also been reported that he'd been out of uniform. The CMAA polled the jury, "What say you?" GUILTY came back with a roar. "I hereby pronounce sentence, you are to hold a wetting down party at the Chief's club at our earliest convenience where your stripes will be appropriately wetted down! Welcome aboard, Chief!"

But first he gave Haze the news at home and told her how he'd found out. Haze was no boot, either. She gloried in his happiness and in her pride of him and how far he'd come. She had similarly been elevated to the sorority that was the wives of the Chiefs, which was neither here nor there but somehow she knew the absolute best and only real way to celebrate this achievement and they went to bed to do that. Later that night as she nuzzled him one more time, just before they both fell asleep, he heard or dreamed she'd said, "Dantes Dantes, now you're my Chief Chief."

Within a month a package was delivered to the Vixen, addressed to GMC Dantes, USN. In it was a Chief's hat and insignia with a note from Chief Locker.

"I'm not sure the hat will fit but I am sure if not it won't be because of a "big head." Welcome to the greatest fraternity in the Navy, if not the world, Chief. Wear these signs of professional excellence with pride and know that you've earned the privilege.

You earned my respect long ago.
Wallace Locker"

The Chief retired his tailor mades with the dragon and the Fu dog on the cuffs, and after he had bought his new rig with the gold hash marks and Chief's rating badge and had two blocked his tie and gotten the grommet in his Officer's style billed cap with the anchor just right, and after they had celebrated with friends from aboard Vixen the reality settled in. The Country was at war and he was about to be assigned to a seagoing destroyer, not the pier-bound flagship of the Admiral of the Fleet. It was sobering for Haze, a Chief's wife with two kids about to say goodbye to her husband while she stayed at home with the ration books and a Blue Star in the window.

Before reporting to Ellyson Hod had talked with a yeoman in DC who assigned gunner's mates to school at the Naval Gun Factory. He asked the yeoman to get him transferred from the Ellyson to the school and the yeoman said he would. When he got aboard Ellyson he found that they already had a Chief Gunner's Mate. The yeoman had assumed that Hod was the only GMC aboard and just ordered "one GMC to school." The Gunnery Officer decided that he would rather have Hod and sent the other one to school. It felt like a fateful moment in Hod's career. He never heard whether the other Chief survived the war or not, but so began Hod's long cruise on the "Elly Mae", which became known as a very lucky ship.

There's a saying that the biggest demotion in the Navy is from First Class Midshipman at the Naval Academy to Ensign in the Fleet. Conversely it is also true that there may be no greater promotion than that of a sailor from First Class Petty Officer to Chief. The change in uniform was striking and it conferred universal respect in all who saw it. In the case of the brand new Chief there is some trepidation, knowing what is expected of a Chief in the Navy and perhaps a bit of nervousness about whether or not he is going to be exposed as a charlatan. Chief Dantes thought back over the chiefs he had known and respected as well as the ones who had not measured up. There were good Chiefs and bad. There were also good and bad aspects to being transferred to a new ship upon making Chief. The new crew would not have to get used to seeing him in his new position and he would be accepted as a Chief Petty Officer from the day he reported aboard, no lingering thoughts of him as a First Class. On the other hand, Chief or no, he would have to prove himself professionally to his new shipmates. Of course Dantes had thought about it and thought he preferred the new ship with no preconceived notions except possibly positive ones. He figured it would not take long to demonstrate his prowess.

With Haze and Dance and Loraine safely ensconced at 101 Mount Vernon Street in Ridgefield Park for the duration, Hod moved into Chief's Quarters aboard Ellyson. He laughed, remembering when he had moved from his hammock aboard Detroit to the cot of a more senior Seaman First. Now it was still a tight fit, as space for anything but weapons aboard a Destroyer was at a premium. Still it was an aluminum frame with a tightly laced piece of white canvas serving to support the bunk's owner, the whole frame one of a stack of four high bunks swung at all four corners to chains that were fitted to weldments that projected down from the overhead and to rings on the deck. The bunks could be pulled up against the bulkhead to give more space if and when required. The same seniority system applied, wherever you went in the Navy. With almost no privileges to hand out they were sliced exceedingly thin and appreciated all the more for their scarcity.

There was one very special extra that the Elly Mae had that very few ships and probably none of her small size had. Ellyson was given the gift of an ice cream maker by the shipyard workers at Federal Shipyard. The crew had ice cream from time to time and the Chiefs always had ice cream. Elly Mae was generous in sharing her bounty with smaller units such as patrol craft, and they usually were able to find a bowlful for the occasional visitor. The Elly Mae might have received superior mail service, at least they thought they did. For after she had received mail at sea as one of the last slings to come across by highline, when alongside for supplies or fuel, the ship would usually send a tub of the frozen delicacy back across before taking the connection down and pulling away. Ellyson was known not only as a lucky ship bit also a generous one.

Life on the messdecks could be brutal and always was rough and tumble. In the Wardroom it could be tense and uncomfortable, a place where sometimes you had to endure the presence of the C.O. and meals could be eaten in silence and a feeling that you couldn't get away from things. Anything. But Chiefs Quarters had the feel of freedom, hilarity and comfort. Chiefs were at the top of their particular food chain and respect for them, or at least most of them, was universal and profound. There were no pretenses in the Goat Locker and no uninvited guests. Not even the Captain would go there without being invited. Of course the whole ship was his, but anybody who was anybody knew that there was something special about Chiefs Quarters and that was true aboard every ship.

The impartial observer, if such could be found aboard a man o' war, would readily recognize that in a sense Chiefs were like every other group: some were very very good, most were damn good to good enough and a few were absolute slugs. The outstanding ones could be found amongst the crew in their duty stations, on watch in the beastly heat of the engineering spaces, or sharing the freezing cold of a rough arctic sea passage. They were free with their knowledge and expertise, sharing always the secrets of their trade and accepting nothing but excellence. In their turn they could be depended upon to accurately assess that other group aboard ship, the Wardroom. In fact the proven COs depended upon his Chiefs to know who the weak performers were and to guide them in ways that would make them more successful. This treatment could be subtle, overt, and even hilarious but it was always respectful. The vast gulf between the Chiefs and everybody else was maintained by them as appropriate and contributed to their mystique. The lucky junior Officers landed with good Chiefs in their Divisions from whom they learned. Sometimes a JO would only learn the hard way or would not learn at all. It was a Chief's job to make the system work no matter who was placed over him in the chain of command.

Ships themselves had their own reputations and it all started with the CO. A ship could be known as a happy ship, a fighter or a rust bucket that was always a day late and a dollar short. And every ship, at least the ones that survived combat, took on an armor that was made up almost entirely of attitude; that and a significant portion of superstition. For example on D-Day at Casablanca in the North African campaign, Ellyson had just pulled away from an underway refueling alongside the oiler and was replaced in turn by Hambleton, another destroyer in DesRon 10 when she took a torpedo in her engineering spaces. Ellyson had pulled smartly away having finished her refueling in record time and was steaming at twenty five knots to a screening position on the carrier when the torpedo hit Hambleton. Elly Mae instantly turned in the direction of the casualty at General Quarters, bristling for a fight and ready to render assistance to her sister ship. Had she been either sloppy or slow at taking on their fuel it would have been them that took the fish in the guts, Ellyson that would have limped into port and spent the next ten months trying to get back into the fight.

That fighting attitude expressed itself as anger at an enemy and love for each other. It was pride in their ship and affection for their Skipper. It was a no nonsense lethality and pure love of Country. There was no room for fear. Had you asked them they would all have told you that when your number was up it was up. For Hod it went deeper than that. Since his fight for his life on the kitchen floor in Lockhart he figured it was all gravy. He had reasoned long ago that by rights he should already be dead but he wasn't and it was because he was tough enough and now was ready enough for anything that might come his way. If it was good he was ready to take advantage of the good, after all you only went around once in life. If it was bad he was free of fear to an extraordinary extent. Again, by living life to the fullest at every turn when you got to the end there would be no regrets. A lucky ship was more often than not one that was always leaning forward looking for a fight. If there was no fight to win then they would win the party, win the girl, leave them laughing and dazzled in their wake.

CHAPTER 40

ROSARIO GABANGABANG

Rosario had become a shrewd businesswoman without becoming hardened. She cared about her people, her employees and received in return the loyalty she showed her "girls." That's why she was concerned when Rosa, one of her workers, simply disappeared one day without an explanation. It had happened after the shooting of the three Tayag insurgents at the Manila Hotel and Rosario suspected Rosa was perhaps frightened because she, Rosa, had been involved in the altercation at least to the extent of warning a young sailor, Dantes about the Tayags that had been paying him attention. Rosario waited for word from or about Rosa but none was forthcoming. She worried.

There was some information that eventually became known about that evening, even young Dantes' name was briefly mentioned as the shooter who had killed the assailants and then the name forgotten. Rosario recalled the night because it was unusual, when Dantes had bought Rosa out of the bar very early and seemingly without a care about the amount of money required to do it. That same evening Chief Locker with his sidekick, the Marine Gunny along for obvious protection, had sought her help in identifying Tayag members currently working for the Japanese. But Rosario didn't like loose ends. They could turn out to be fatal in a covert operation such as the network that Chief Locker had subsequently dubbed "Mamasan."

Rosario started locally, signing up people she knew who had connections and in whose loyalty to the Philippines she had no doubts whatsoever. Then it was relatives who were smart and self-confident and who could keep a secret. Some of them were on other islands and the radios that had been promised by the Chief had made their way into the Mamasan network, delivered by runners or even by herself when she combined Mamasan business with vacation visits to relatives. After about a year of putting in place her skein of informers and communicators she decided to try it out. She would use it to try and find

Rosa. Her first steps a year ago had been to inquire whether she had been arrested or turned up dead somewhere. Within six months of making her inquiries she felt that Rosa was alive and not in jail. She checked with other Mamasans and drew a blank there, too. No one of her description or name was working for any of her competitors and if her family knew they were not saying.

Her couriers had a picture of Rosa and they fanned out over the countryside, showing the picture. There had been a couple dead ends until the word came back that she had indeed been found, healthy and well, living on a landholding in somewhat mountainous country near Baguio on Luzon. The search had concentrated on Luzon as Rosario thought it unlikely Rosa would have had the means to go to one of the other islands in the archipelago. Rosario decided she would make a visit, after all Baguio was one of the most beautiful spots in the country known for its cool climate and lush tropical pine forests.

Her contact escorted Rosario into one of the folds between mountains known as the Calderone place. It looked to be an isolated fertile valley some twenty five miles from Baguio City. They arrived at an orderly encampment of huts, a stream and some fields under cultivation. Rosa looked up and her face was a mixture of expressions: joy, shame and guilt until resolution showed itself and stayed and she walked up to Rosario and they hugged as Rosa cried and smiled and invited her erstwhile boss into a humble hut and they sat on a mat to talk. "It is so good to see you, Mama," Rosa said. "I was very worried after you didn't return and had to find out if you were alright." "I am sorry I did not keep you informed or even say good bye. When the lawyer came things happened so quickly." "The lawyer?" Rosario asked. "Yes, Mr. Verdad came to see me at my home with a story and a contract." Rosario looked at her with great curiosity. "It seemed that this property here, some five thousand acres, had been given to that sailor, Dantes, you might remember him, in thanks for having saved the life of Luz Calderone, the wife of the previous owner." "Actually I do remember him and quite well. The rumor is that he was the one who shot and killed three attackers one night in Manila. And this contract, what sort of contract?" Rosa said, "It says in writing signed by Mr. Dantes that I have the right to live here for ten years and to use this land to support myself." "So, he was given this land and it must have been immediately that he made arrangements with the lawyer to settle you here in order that you might be able to make a living." "Yes, and the contract will be renewed for another ten years unless he changes it."

The two women walked the valley and toured the property and got comfortable with one another. With gentle probing Rosario learned how many people were here and that Rosa was looked upon as the head of this group; that had been one of the stipulations in her contract. As she was told about the yearly accounting and Rosa's goals for the place, Rosario's immediate thought was that the Calderone place could produce so much more. Rosa asked her how long she could stay and Rosario said maybe a couple days and she stayed a week. During that week she formulated a business plan that would expand the irrigation system, bring more fields under cultivation, add livestock and establish business ties with the markets in Baguio. They discussed her ideas and before she left she was invited to return and help Rosa put her ideas into practice. Two years later she had become a regular visitor and had her own hut and the yearly accounting of excess funds had mushroomed. Still Rosa, following Rosario's advice had followed the terms of her contract exactly and had also held down on the number of people that the place supported. They hired workers from the next valley over and were turning in a very tidy annual profit.

Ricardo Verdad, Esquire, opened the envelope with a yawn. This was fairly pedestrian business, overseeing a sleepy and barely profitable enterprise up Baguio way. The figures this time astonished him. There was a substantial increase. He decided then and there to make a trip to Baguio. In fact it became a very pleasant annual visit to the resort and a side trip to the valley. Verdad would convert the annual cash to investments and then it was necessary to make the trips more often as they didn't want the money to be accumulating and lying fallow for so long. He and Rosario worked together to gather the funds and feed them into the growing and growing numbers of accounts. For her part as supervisor with authority over the whole farm, Rosa Vasconcellos from time to time would pay Rosario for 'supplies' most of which were plowed into the Mamasan network. Rosario insisted that they also build an underground hideaway on high ground just below the ridge. It was reinforced with timbers and covered with soil which soon grew a natural cover. An emergency supply of food and water was put into the hideaway. The intelligence Rosario was getting was telling her that such a place of refuge could come in handy.

CHAPTER 41

LYDIA AND ROSARIO

Lydia Lodge hung up the phone at her Manila auxiliary medical facility and sat back to wait for Gunnery Sergeant Clancy to come by. She had something she wanted to discuss with him and had invited Gunny over to her small clinic just a few blocks from the Embassy where Clancy was stationed. When she heard his voice in the outer office she went to the door and invited him in. They sat at two folding chairs to the side of her desk at a table with a pitcher of iced tea and two glasses. After pouring their glasses full and settling back, she said, "Good to see you again, Gunny." "Always a pleasure, Commander, how may I be of assistance?" And he took a healthy swallow of his tea as she framed her response.

"Gunny, my husband, who commands the Ford, homeported in Subic Bay, told me a very interesting story from the time you and Chief Locker and then Seaman First Class Dantes were together here, in Manila and aboard Detroit. In fact Chief Locker is aboard Ford as Chief Master of Arms. It seems everyone is back in Manila either stationed here or homeported except Dantes." Gunny returned her gaze with interest, "Yes Ma'am. I'd heard that "Wall" Locker was on board Ford. Good troop, one of the best and Ford is lucky to have Captain Lodge as their Skipper." "My husband told me about a Ball that occurred during Detroit's port visit and an incident that occurred there." Gunny raised an eyebrow, "Although that story was never classified we were told at the time to keep it quiet, Ma'am." "Yes, that's the same thing Commander Lodge said."

Clancy continued to sit there, respectful but not volunteering anything, waiting to see what this was all about. "It's my understanding that a woman from one of the bars in Manila was key in giving a warning to Dantes about the danger, in fact I heard that Dantes refused credit and said that the successful outcome of that evening's festivities was directly attributable to that woman." Thinking back over the evening under discussion, Gunny had a wry look on his face, "Yes Ma'am, I'd say that that's exactly true; if it had not been for the help of that young lady things would have turned out very differently." "In fact, not to put too fine a point on it, but my husband's life may very well have been saved by that young lady," Lydia replied. "Ma'am, I certainly can't disagree."

LCDR Lydia Crowninshield Lodge leaned forward over the small table, "Gunny, do you think you could find that lady, that bar again?" "As to the young lady, I couldn't say. But I do remember the bar and I could find it again. If the Commander has in mind some sort of reward or acknowledgement for the person we're discussing, her name is Rosa Vasconcellos; I think the way to go about that would be to approach her boss, the Mamasan of the bar. She owns it and no doubt would appreciate our going through her on any approach to Miss Vasconcellos. If you'd like I can look into this for you, see if Rosario Gabangabang would be willing to cooperate. It would most certainly not be a place for a lady to go, Ma'am." "Gunny that would be perfect; thank you so much."

Gunny had gone straightway to the bar from the sickbay office and was the only customer in the place when he walked in. Most of the girls were not in attendance; that would happen as it got closer to the end of the workday. Rosario looked up and thought she recognized the sergeant, drew two beers and joined him at his table. "I have been here before, Mamasan." "Yes, I believe you were here with Chief Wallace Locker, more than a year ago, maybe closer to two." Gunny leaned forward and introduced himself, "Gunny Clancy, Ma'am." "Rosario Gabangabang, Gunny. Glad to meet you. Tell me, how is "Wall" Locker doing these days?" It was her little way of testing him. She had seen her friend and partner in the Mamasan network the last time he had been in port, only a week ago, when he had delivered to her three more radios. "I haven't seen the Chief for maybe six months or a year. You know how that goes." Rosario laughed, "Yes I do. Tell me, how may I help you?"

The Gunny recalled the events of that fateful evening and how Rosa had helped Dantes and actually been instrumental in warning Dantes and thereby saving the lives of many. Rosario put in, "The rumors say that even Quezon and the Admiral themselves were about to be under attack and this very special sailor, Dantes, saved quite a number of people that night." Gunny was listening very closely and was pleased to note that she did not expand upon her further dealings with the Chief. The fewer who knew about the Mamasan network the better. "Rosario, I have just come from a meeting with an extraordinary lady, the Lieutenant Commander who runs the Navy medical facilities in Subic and Manila, Mrs. Lydia Lodge. Her husband…" "Was also on the rooftop of the Manila Hotel that night," Rosario finished for him. "Yes he was and he has told her about the brave actions of Rosa Vasconcellos and she is deeply grateful to Miss Rosa and would like to show her appreciation in some way."

With that Rosario leaned back in her chair, smiled a soft smile of remembrance with something else, fondness maybe, as she held counsel with her thoughts. "I believe Miss Rosa feels very rewarded already," Rosario said at last. "But I would be privileged to talk to Commander Lodge." Gunny smiled at that, suggested a meeting at the medical facility in town for the next afternoon and they agreed upon a time. Gunny said if anything changed he would get back to her.

At 1300 on the dot the following day, Rosario Gabangabang was granted entrance to Lydia Lodge's office where the desk had been overlaid with a sheet folded to serve as a table cloth and between the desk and the table they had laid out a pretty nice feed of chicken and rice and iced tea. Both women took each other's measure and apparently liked what they saw. After a friendly shaking of hands and excited friendly chatting over the "small lunch" put together in Rosario's honor, the guest put aside her fork, dabbed at her lips and said, "How may I be of help, Commander?" "If you would like, you could call me Lydia." Rosario laughed, "My honor, and I am Rosario Gabangabang." Lydia said, "I understand from my husband that someone who works for you was instrumental in saving the lives of many, some two years ago, including I suspect, that of my husband." "And I would say that the one who saved all of those lives, including those of Manual Quezon and Admiral Cochrane, was Seaman Dantes." "Do you know Dantes, Rosario?" "He is truly an outstanding young man," Rosario replied. "Not everyone is the sort to deflect praise or to be so decisive in moments of what would be sheer terror for most of us."

Lydia turned serious for the moment, "Rosario, I wish to do something for Rosa, the name I've heard as the one who warned Dantes on at least two occasions of a possible attack." Rosario took her time, looking deeply into Lydia's eyes. "Rosa left town sometime after that night and I eventually found her. I would need her permission to disturb her privacy, but I think that should not be a problem. She is living in a small community of poor Filipino families, living the life of this small farming community's leader, is responsible for their welfare." Lydia reflected in her turn, took a sip of her iced tea and wondered aloud if this community might be in need of health services. Rosario gave an angelic smile, this she understood. Their discussion covered the sorts of services that Lydia could supply, the medical supplies that she might be able to make available. With a promise to get back in touch within a month or less, Rosario was waved good bye from the front door of the small clinic.

The way it happened was that Lydia convened a meeting in the sickbay a month later and a plan was made for the Gunny to escort Lydia to the location given to Lydia on the map by Rosario. They planned to take a bag of medical supplies and to stay overnight, perhaps for the entire weekend. The Gunny provided tarps and line, ground cloths and water cans to go with the Embassy vehicle which he'd checked out for the weekend. Rosario was to already be at the site to welcome them.

They drove up to the tidy huts and people working in the fields that comprised Estancia Calderone in a cloud of dust, brakes squealing to a halt and piled out to a welcome from Rosario and a smiling greeting from Rosa. Rosario pointed out to Gunny where they could put up their shelter and as he went to do that the ladies went into Rosa's hut and sat on a clean woven mat and sipped water from a gourd that was passed around. Rosa didn't react much to the name Lodge, but as soon as Dantes' name was brought up the reaction was instantaneous. "You know Dantes?" Rosa asked? "Why yes, he was in my wedding. My husband knew him aboard ship." "Dantes is the bravest, most wonderful man I have ever met," Rosa responded. "I understand that he gives all the credit for the rescue of that night to you, Rosa." Rosa smiled, "That would be just like him, giving credit to everybody but himself. Also I don't know any man who is so generous," Rosa said. Lydia filed that away for later, wondering what that could be about.

Later that afternoon, after dinner over the cook fires and with people relaxing in their huts, Rosa sent the word for all of the mothers and their children to come to the shelter that had been set up. Lydia had on her white jacket and a stethoscope and a clipboard. Rosa explained to all of them that this was Doctor Lodge who had come at her own expense to check on their health. Lydia said she was not a doctor but was a nurse and that she would like to do a quick inspection of all of the children. She started with the oldest of some thirty five children, not counting the ones carried by their mothers. Lydia did a standard and quick exam for blood pressure, pulse, joints, lungs and limbs, head for lice and general cleanliness. She asked the name of each patient and wrote it down and then recorded against the names what she had found. The little kids watched the big ones and knew what to do when it was their turn. She picked out one of the woman who seemed particularly interested in what she was doing and soon included her into the routine, having her hand things to her and before long writing down the findings. At the end of the day she asked Rosa if it would be alright to designate the woman as the village 'nurse'. With Rosa's approval it was made official and Lydia doffed her white coat and gave it to her assistant, knowing it would serve as her badge of office. It was also decided to leave the tarp and line for the shelter at the village to serve as a place for medical supplies and as a place for Lydia in the event of further visits. The next day was largely taken up with the unloading of the medical supplies from the vehicle to the medical shelter and the instructions and cautions to the village nurse as to things to look for and things not to attempt. Proper wound cleaning was demonstrated as well as the placement of bandages and a sling and splints. The few bottled medicines were explained and a list made up that described their usage and dosages. With that they offered Rosario a ride back to Manila which she gladly accepted.

All of the kids were outside to wave them off on their drive to Manila, Gunny driving and the two women seated in the back, in the stern sheets. "Rosario," Lydia asked, "isn't it unusual for a woman to be the one in charge of a village, even a fairly small one as this?" "Well of course you are correct." "I would also think it unusual for someone so young and female to be the owner or proprietress of a working farm out in the countryside like this." Rosario smiled, "Rosa is not the owner of the Estancia," she said. Lydia looked at her with interest and the Gunny perked up his ears, too. Rosario turned to also include Gunny and said, "You both know the owner." They waited to hear the rest of the story. "The whole place, five thousand acres of it, belongs to Mr. Dantes. He had his lawyer draw up a contract giving Rosa a place to live and work for ten years, renewable every ten years." Gunny guffawed and slapped his knee while driving, but Lydia just got sudden tears in her eyes and turned toward Rosario and they hugged for the first time, became an odd couple, a pair of sisters on that ride back to Manila.

CHAPTER 42
TRANSITIONS

The Chrysler sedan pulled up in front of the CincPac Residence in Makalapa on a Saturday at 1300, John holding the door for Lydia and handing her out of the car, both turning resolutely toward the entrance where Uncle Fitz and Auntie Jane stood smiling and waiting for them. This was the place where they first met, probably where they fell in love if you believed in love at first sight. And it was the place where they were wed in their Service Dress White uniforms with Seaman First Dantes as their ring bearer. They were greeted with hugs, kisses and laughter, all of them in shorts and aloha shirts. Each of the Lodges carried a small gift. John had been given a bottle of Johnny Walker Black for the Admiral by his new boss, Admiral Cochrane and Lydia had a small package in her purse.

All of them had received their orders, an ongoing ritual in the Navy for anyone who stayed in past their first hitch. You were either leaving, yourself, or else your Commanding Officer was, every year and a half to two years. It made for interesting times and many goodbyes. The Fitzes were sailing off into retirement and this was but one of a series of parties and ceremonies that attended the change of command of a major command or new orders for close family friends. They moved out onto the lanai and there they shared a lunch and topped it off with scotch neat after the dishes had been cleared.

Lydia reached into her purse and brought the gaily wrapped package out and placed it on the table in front of Auntie Jane. Jane's look said, for me? John said, "It's for both of you, Auntie Jane, please open it." The Fitzes looked at each other and then she opened it and looked up at John and Lydia as if to ask, "What's this?" Admiral Fitz took it from Jane and looked at it thoughtfully. He knew without asking and his Adam's apple bobbed a time or two as he swallowed. Lydia said, "We hope that you'll start your retirement here, in Hawaii and do us the enormous favor of taking care of the place up Nuuanu way. Jane said, "The key to your honeymoon paradise in the valley?" "Yes, it's used to being the home port for a loving Navy couple and we hope you'll live there as long as you'd like." Jane was a tough albeit graceful bird, but this caught her totally unprepared. The four of them stood and hugged and there were tears all around.

So the Fitzes happily settled-in in the Nuuanu valley and loved the waterfalls and lush tropical flowers and misty rainbows caught in the spray of the falls. He had felt his responsibilities lightly, joyously when he'd had them, worried for his fleet when someone else was in charge. Fitz had left a one sentence note in the desk drawer at headquarters for his relief. It said, simply, "Keep the carriers moving, FDR sends" and was signed Fitz.

The goodbyes felt like benedictions, Cochrane, John and Lydia knowing that they owed their new assignments and opportunities for service to Admiral Fitz and determined to do their best not to let him down. In truth the Fitzes were not yet ready to go back to the mainland, they had found a niche in the Islands and a place in Hawaiian society and in the hearts of their many friends. The Nuuanu place became a much visited home by shipmates passing through, stopping at Pearl on their way to or from WestPac. And on occasion CincPac and his wife made the trip to the valley and gave Admiral Fitz an update. As the evening wound down and the honored guests were saying their thanks and goodbyes until next time, CincPac would answer the upraised eyebrows, the unspoken question, "We've got 'em moving, Fitz, the carriers are staying at sea as much as we can keep them there." Admiral Fitz would thank him for the update and his mind would turn toward a crippled man in his wheelchair with a silent salute and an *Aye, aye Mr. President.*

Then came the Japanese attacks at Pearl Harbor, repeated eight hours later in the Philippines, the loss and near destruction of the Pacific Fleet at Pearl, except for the carriers, the fuel depot and the repair yards. Even with eight hours of advance warning, MacArthur's air forces in the Philippines were mostly surprised and destroyed on the ground. The Japanese largely overran the island of Luzon in the first month and then, believing they had won there, took their best troops to the Dutch East Indies in order to secure vital oil resources. As the U.S. and Filipino forces withdrew into defensive positions in the Bataan Peninsula they were able to hold on for another four months as the U.S. Asiatic Fleet shifted toward the Dutch East Indies in an effort to deny the Japanese those very same resources. It seemed the Japanese were successful everywhere and the Asiatic Fleet was effectively erased, either sunk in actions as part of the ABDA (American, British, Dutch and Australian) force in the Dutch East Indies or else absorbed by CincPac into the Pacific Fleet as he consolidated his remaining assets in the theater.

At home on the mainland, headlines blared the news of the attacks at Pearl Harbor and families gathered in shock around their radio sets. Hod's sister Loraine worried about what it would mean for her brother, soon to be at sea again, with so many submarines at sea and sinkings occurring daily. Young men were volunteering and being inducted into the services in large numbers. There were reports of German U Boats off the East coast and occasional explosions and sinkings that lighted up the night sky off the Florida Atlantic coast as U Boats feasted on easy pickings cruising up the Gulf Stream. There was a war on and no one was certain of victory. The near total destruction at Pearl Harbor showed that the war was off to a very bad start. People of Japanese descent on the West coast were being brought in for questioning and confined then interned and kept as prisoners, entire families, for fear of sabotage and spying for the enemy.

MacArthur was ordered by the President to evacuate from Corregidor and escaped in the dark of night to Australia with the aid of Lt. Bulkely and his PT boat. There was not much room for staff on board the PT boat, although MacArthur was able to take his family with him. Not enough was known about the fate of those left behind except for the garrison at Corregidor. There the noose had tightened and General Wainwright was forced to surrender to General Homma. General Homma threatened execution of some 10,000 prisoners unless in his surrender of Corregidor Wainwright also surrendered all American and Filipino forces in place throughout the archipelago. This set up a situation in which thousands of yet undefeated and poorly armed troops were cast adrift without a chain of command and expected to surrender. As for the smaller commands such as the Ship's Repair Facility and its medical offices in Manila and Subic, almost nothing was known. What was feared, by virtue of reports of Japanese atrocities such as rapes and summary executions, was that women were not safe.

Eventually in May of 1942 with the Battle for Manila ended, the nurses were rounded up and interned in separate facilities, while undergoing the same privations of short rations and illness that the rest of the captives endured. Names were hard to come by and communications were mostly nonexistent. Ford had survived the Japanese offensive and was now part of the U.S. Pacific Fleet. Her Commanding Officer had heard nothing to indicate the fate or whereabouts of his wife. What is known is that he cursed himself for a fool for not having insisted that Lydia resign her commission and stay in Hawaii or else go back to be with her folks in Boston. Instead at their home on Oahu there resided a fretful retired Admiral feeling out to pasture when he ought to be fighting and his wife, trying to keep his spirits up when she, herself, felt the same weight of terror, worry and anxiety for loved ones and the Country.

In short order the Navy did what it always does, it assigned responsibility to the Commander and CincPac was relieved of command and replaced by a brilliant naval tactician, Admiral Chester Nimitz, himself from the same Texas hill country that had birthed and formed Chief Dantes. It was felt that Admiral Cochrane had positioned his forces as best he could and though he lost his Asiatic Fleet Command he still held a nominal position in PacFlt intelligence and was taken on board Nimitz' Staff and valued for his knowledge of the Mamasan network he had set up as well as his in depth knowledge and understanding of the Japanese culture and key military figures. There was another little known reason that Nimitz kept Cochrane aboard. He knew that Cochrane had a relationship of sorts with MacArthur and he suspected that knowledge of the man who carried himself as a veritable American Caesar might be more important than intimate familiarity with the Japanese. Sometimes you had to win the fight against the opposition within before you could fight effectively those who had waged war from beyond your borders.

The contrast between the two Commanders could not have been more striking. One the scion of a famed military family, son of a Union Civil War General who was a Medal of Honor winner and past military Governor of the Philippines. MacArthur had been first in his class, First Captain at West Point, Superintendent of the Military Academy and the youngest Chief of Staff of the Army. Nimitz was raised by his grandfather who had been a Texas Ranger who fought in the Civil War for the Confederacy. Nimitz wanted to go to West Point but no appointments were available. There was one appointment, though, to the Naval Academy and it was awarded competitively. Young Chester applied himself to his studies and got the appointment. He graduated near the top of his class at Annapolis and went to sea for two years as a Passed Midshipman. When commissioned as an Ensign he soon found himself in the Asiatic Fleet and on one occasion as Officer in Command of a Destroyer ran it aground on a mud flat. The ship was hauled off the bar the next day, Nimitz was court martialed and given a reprimand for dereliction of duty. How ironic that later in his career he would head the Bureau of Navigation. At one point in his career Nimitz commanded Augusta, a cruiser then serving as the flagship of the Asiatic Fleet. In fact he and Cochrane had come into contact with one another in the Pacific over the years. Nimitz may have been stuck on a mud flat but he was not stuck on himself. The very opposite of flashy, he was quietly brilliant, innovative and active. He would find a soul mate in Cochrane, his Intelligence Chief.

CHAPTER 43

CORREGIDOR

Under duress from the Japanese attacking forces of General Homma since the 8th of December, General MacArthur and the Philippine Government withdrew from Manila and made the island of Corregidor their Headquarters. Corregidor sat just off the southern end of the Bataan peninsula and was fortified to protect the entrance to Manila Bay. The Allies were determined to deny the Japanese the use of Manila Bay. It and Subic Bay on the other, western side of the peninsula had been heavily mined and these minefields were operated by the U.S. Army. Thus with the remaining assets from the Asiatic Fleet still in the area, a submarine squadron and some patrol craft, they were able to protect and maintain at least intermittent lines of communication to the sea.

On December 30, 1941, outside the Malinta Tunnel, Manuel L. Quezon and Sergio Osmeña were inaugurated respectively as President and Vice-President of the Philippines Commonwealth for a second term. Less than two months later on 19 February they were evacuated to Australia as the government in exile. The Japanese had quickly established air control upon landing in the P. I. and were making rapid progress to the south on Luzon Island, driving the allies before them. Soon the Japanese had emplaced heavy artillery on the northern end of the Bataan Peninsula and were steadily advancing southward, turning the tables on the occupants of Corregidor. Instead of the U.S. denying the Japanese the use of Manila and its bay the Japanese had stopped supplies from reaching the island from the north by investing the peninsula and slowly advancing, closing the range to the island.

MacArthur had his critics for the performance of Allied forces when under the initial Japanese attack. In spite of some eight hours of advance warning furnished by knowledge of the attack on Pearl Harbor, the air forces in the Philippines were mostly caught on the ground and destroyed before they could get airborne and offer resistance. The battle for Luzon was the largest land battle loss in United States history, yet the Commanding General was deemed important enough to save, to fight another day. On a moonless night he and his party were brought out from Corregidor and thence to Australia to set up his Headquarters, leaving behind some 10,000 troops under LTGEN Wainwright with orders to defend and not to surrender. The feeling on the rock as the last PT boat left was not unlike watching the rats leaving a drowning ship.

Still, Wainwright conducted the best defense he could as the noose drew tighter and tighter around their necks, on Corregidor. Caught up in that self-same noose was LCDR Lydia Lodge. As the evacuation of Manila was ordered, and while the Embassy staff were burning documents and destroying coding materiel, Gunnery Sergeant Clancy, true to his word first checked the Medical Facility Annex in Manila then went to the main facility in Subic Bay, to find the Commander. Indeed she had already stripped the Manila Annex of its supplies and personnel and consolidated her facilities and was continuing to offer medical services at Subic Ship Repair Facility.

Saluting with a grim smile, "Ma'am, Gunny Clancy reporting for duty." With a huge sigh of relief the Commander returned his salute and asked if he had any news. "Yes, Commander, we have evacuated the Embassy and are shifting colors to Corregidor, the new Headquarters. I am here to offer you assistance in getting your command to the island. The Commander looked distracted so the Gunny continued, "Communications have been spotty, Ma'am, you may not have heard that there has been an order for all personnel to report to Corregidor. I did stop by your facility in Manila and noted that you have already closed it down. Are you ready to so the same here, Ma'am?" "Gunny, that would be so helpful, would you please work with my Chief?" "Yes Ma'am," and he sought the Chief out and they discussed loading the available vehicles and getting them down to the pier where watercraft were waiting in a makeshift boat pool to make the necessary runs to the island. The Commander's last act at Subic was to report to the Base Commander that she was embarking her staff and supplies and transferring over to Corregidor. Then she sent a SECRET message, using the Base Communications shack, to USS John D. Ford (DD-228) that simply stated that the SRF Health Facility and staff were shifting their location to Corregidor. That done she made her way to the landing and was the last of her command to board and make her way with Gunny to Corregidor. They had a patrol boat with two manned .50 cal machine guns in company and to shepherd them out through the minefield, around the peninsula and again through a minefield into the receiving pier at the island. It had taken three loaded craft to haul all of her personnel and their equipment and supplies.

First had come the air attacks and landings to the north on Luzon. After handling the local casualties that resulted from the initial air attacks things settled down except for the fact that the Japanese were steadily advancing to the south, toward Manila and Subic. The daily reports were not good and it was soon apparent that their isolation was to be complete. When MacArthur left it was with a sense of impending doom, soon to be replaced by daily attacks that drew closer and closer to those left to defend Manila and Subic and Corregidor. There had been speculation about who would be accompanying the General; some thought that he would take women with him, as many as he could. Lydia had been summoned into Malinta tunnel and reported to Wainwright who said that if there were room he intended to put her forward as medical staff to go with MacArthur. She didn't take it as an order and her response left no doubt in Wainwright's mind what she would do if ordered to leave. "Sir, my place is here. There will be plenty of medical capability in Australia." In any event, MacArthur left without her.

As General Homma's heavy artillery moved onto the Bataan Peninsula the attacks increased in violence and intensity. The US mobile hospitals closed and reestablished further south under pressure from Homma's forces, finally running out of land and time and all medical personnel were evacuated to the Malinta Tunnel on Corregidor. There was not room inside the tunnel for everyone and the troops were dug in as best they could manage and still there were daily casualties to be triaged, aided and somehow put under protection where available. Stores and supplies dwindled and they held on until Wainwright sought surrender terms. He still had some 10,000 defenders and they were all aware of Japanese atrocities and greatly concerned about the treatment they could expect from their captors.

By this time there had been three evacuations other than the PT Boat escape of General MacArthur. Two PBYs had loaded up evacuees until they could barely fly, a submarine had taken a few and a merchant vessel had been the only other escape for some medical personnel, Officers and other officials. Gunny Clancy went into the tunnel, braving the noxious smells, filth and crowding, sought out Commander Lodge and asked her to accompany him outside. Knowing that the Gunny had been manning a machine gun emplacement on the north shore she had been looking for him and hoping not to see him arrive on a stretcher. Lydia looked at him in some relief and inquiringly but did as he asked. "Ma'am, the scuttlebutt is that we are negotiating terms for surrender to the Japs." "That's true, Gunny." "The really hot skinny is that General Homma is demanding that we surrender all troops, US and Filipino, throughout the islands or else he will execute all prisoners, some ten thousand of them." Lydia did not comment and Gunny went on, "Ma'am, I have taken the liberty of laying on a patrol boat and obtained the necessary charts and information to make a safe passage out through the minefield. You are probably not aware, but your husband and Chief Locker have set up a network throughout the archipelago which has been used for intelligence gathering. The leader of that network is Rosario Gabangabang and we call the network Mamasan. They have been supplied radios and undertaken various missions as requested. I expect that although we might indeed surrender all troops throughout the country not all will be walking in to be imprisoned. There will be a resistance. The headquarters of this Mamasan resistance is at Dantes' place up by Baguio, where we set up a first aid and medical capability." Lydia started to speak, but Gunny held up his hand, "Ma'am we could use your services in Baguio and I am prepared, with the help of the network, to get you there. If anything this will probably be more dangerous than staying here and waiting to see what the Japs do to everyone. In my opinion it is far better to be able to carry on the fight than to await almost certain atrocities. We can't go to Wainwright to get his permission because he is restricted in his actions as a negotiator. I will be going to Baguio and I am asking you to join us, to come with me and help in the resistance. We will be in uncertain circumstances but it is already certain that we will need medical help in our resistance network."

"How much time do I have to decide," she asked. "Tonight is a new moon, Ma'am. We go tonight if you will come." "You are leaving shortly after dark?" "Yes Ma'am." Looking at her watch, "So then, I have maybe four hours to think about this and decide?" Gunny nodded and continued to look at her. "It's not exactly abandoning my duty station if I go in order to continue the fight," and she looked searchingly at him. "It is about to get totally uncontrolled here and many will die after they surrender, Ma'am." She frowned and a steely look came over her, "I will go with you, Gunny. Thank you for giving us this opportunity. I must talk to my Staff and initiate a change of command, informal though it will be." Gunny hesitated just a moment, looked at the determination in her expression and let it go. He understood matters of chain of command. He would have been disappointed at any other outcome. She was relying on his judgement and now he would have to rely on hers.

That night the two of them walked down to the pier, put on dark jackets and smeared their faces with a camouflage paste to cover the white, stepped into the patrol boat and put on ammo belts and took charge of a pistol and a carbine, each. The boat took in its two lines and backed down slowly and softly, then turned into the minefield. Gunny took bearings on illumined ranges on shore, guiding the coxswain into the middle of a generous channel and out to sea. Once clear of the minefields they looped south around the Bataan Peninsula, stood out to sea and headed north with the coast of Luzon to starboard. In six hours if all went well they would raise their contact on shore, exchange flashlight signals and put in to the beach. The boat had enough fuel cans to fuel the trip back to Corregidor. Gunny prepared a place for Lydia to sleep and suggested she rest and sleep if she could as it would be a likely two or three day hike into the hideout in Baguio District.

With two hours of darkness left they turned toward the shore at a small inlet and made their signal. It was returned. Gunny turned to the Cox'n and thanked him. "You'd do best if you can find a place maybe a few miles from here and pull close to shore and cut some branches to cover the boat, then continue at nightfall on your way back to the rock." The Cox nodded, they shook hands, "Good luck Gunny, Ma'am." And with that the two of them waded ashore and together with their guide sought cover away from any trails to wait for darkness to cover their first night's march. Lydia regretted not being able to communicate with John and did not feel good about leaving the way she had, without permission. But she had weighed the possibilities and decided and she was comfortable that she had made the best decision, given the circumstances. Like a marriage, she was committed to making the best of this situation, one she had chosen.

Their guide, a middle aged Filipino named Juan, briefed them on the likely location of Japanese forces and said, "We are okay to move today in daylight to our first stopping point. There we will get an update on Japanese locations. If it is safe we will travel in daylight, if not we have time to move slowly at night. We will also pick up food rations and water at our stops. Any questions?" There were none so they headed out in single file, Gunny bringing up the rear. Four days later they raised the hideout, were passed through the security line and kept going past the original tiny village, all the way up to the ridgetop underground spaces.

When they first saw each other Rosario and Lydia hugged. "How was your trip, Lydia?" "It was very well guided, thanks to Juan and your Mamasan network, Rosario. I believe I owe you my life." "Lydia you have done so much for the lives of those of us here. Welcome. We have been able to escape notice and we observe pretty strict radio silence in order not to attract attention." "Then that answers my first question, I can see that I will not be able to communicate my situation by radio to the Navy or any of our military. You see, my husband knows nothing about my fate or that I'm even alive." "Of course the reverse is true as well, Lydia, you know little about your husband and how he is faring. It's part of how we live, until this war is won and we get back to peacetime routines." And with those realities understood they quickly fell into their routines for getting food, water and information. Lydia picked up the responsibility for medical care for the commune dwellers and network resistance members. Gunny melted away into the jungle on periodic patrols with couriers, gathering intelligence and offering reassurance to the resistance. When he came back to camp he was the source of all of the news they had from the outside. Sometimes Lydia would accompany him, carrying her medical kit, and render medical aid to men and women who were part of the Mamasan network. It was how she kept her conscience at bay for having left Corregidor. She was beginning to feel she didn't deserve to live and so she sought out dangerous work and longer range missions and developed a hardened outlook. She was adapting.

CHAPTER 44

USS JOHN D. FORD

CincAsiaticFlt ordered all of his able assets to sea to defensive positions upon learning of the attacks at Pearl Harbor. Ford came through the initial Japanese air attack on Manila Bay on 10 December unscathed and then headed south to patrol the Sulu Sea and Makassar Strait, staying there until just before Christmas and then setting sail for Balikpapan and Soerbaja in the Dutch East Indies. It was tacit recognition that the Philippines were lost and at least an effort would be made to keep the Dutch oil out of Japanese hands. Failing that it would be an attempt to slow down and defeat any Japanese thrust toward Australia.

She joined a Destroyer striking force of four tin cans and proceeded off Balikpapan to conduct attacks on Japanese shipping. The protecting Japanese Destroyers were in the Makassar Strait chasing a reported American Submarine while the four American Destroyers conducted an attack with shells and torpedoes. Four Japanese ships were sunk with the Ford sinking the Japanese Navy transport Kuretake Manu, sending it to the bottom. She also fired on the Asahi Maru causing minor damage to the Japanese hospital ship. With Japanese advances and air strikes hitting Soerbaja, Ford steamed to the south coast of Java and the Japs landed at Bali. Ford and other Destroyers then conducted a running engagement with a couple of IJN Destroyers without result except that the Japanese could claim successful landings at Bali and a Dutch Destroyer was sunk.

After replenishing with the last of the available torpedoes from the tender at Kiritimati, the Ford rejoined the shrinking and tired ABDA Striking Force. There were now only four remaining U.S. Destroyers. When joined by five British ships the enhanced Striking Force steamed to meet the enemy off the northern coast of Java. What ensued was the Battle of Java Sea, which lasted for more than seven hours. Five Allied Cruisers and nine Destroyers took on four Japanese Cruisers and thirteen Destroyers in a furious running battle with gunfire and torpedo attacks. It was a victory for the Japanese with the Allies losing five ships but the Ford again undamaged. Ford joined up with three American Destroyers and steamed for Australia. On the first of March they encountered three Japanese tin cans guarding the Bali Strait. With little to no ammunition and no torpedoes with which to defend themselves the American Destroyers made a run for it at 35 knots, steaming for Fremantle, Australia.

Lodge gained a healthy respect for the IJN and valuable experience in maneuvering in concert with other ships and pressing home attacks. But the China Fleet was tired and joint operations are never as well run as those involving a single Navy. The Japanese had trained well and were lethal and effective. The Allies were neither; they were older ships, less capable and out performed by the Japanese. But then Lodge had been reporting these very same facts to Admiral Cochrane and this information was forwarded and acknowledged by CincPac in Pearl. Lodge knew that they had been the tripwire, the ones sent to fill the gap while America rebuilt and re-manned. Their mission in the end had been to provide warning, which they had done, and to provide time for the defense of Australia, which they had also done.

If there was another, albeit personal, benefit for Captain Lodge it was that as the single Officer responsible for his ship and crew he had almost no time to fret about the whereabouts of his wife, Lydia. Of course there had been no mail either going out or coming in. Lodge continually drove his crew and his ship to sharper performance, better maintenance, and quicker rates of fire. If his ship wasn't fighting it was training to fight. In the escape to Fremantle he had had his engineers gag the safeties on the boilers. They hadn't needed it but it was there just in case. Perhaps the Japs were out of torpedoes and low on ammo, too. Or they may have entertained thoughts that they were being led into an ambush. More likely they had bigger fish to fry and could afford to let these remnants of the old China Fleet go.

In the evenings the radio shack would tune in to the Zero Hour radio show out of Tokyo, Japan. It was American pop music mixed in with English language news and it was intended to hurt the American servicemen's morale. There were several women announcers in addition to the original, but the G.I.s referred to them all as just Tokyo Rose. If he had thought that his men were being negatively affected by the broadcasts, Lodge would have turned them off. But they at least had music and were considered a diversion from the grinding existence aboard a man of war. But disquieting information of another sort was reaching headquarters, CincPac. They were hearing that many had died on the Bataan Death March and it was suspected that prisoners were being shipped to the home islands of Japan to perform slave labor in the factories there. Finally, though not yet confirmed with actual decapitated bodies, there were rumors that the Japanese were beheading their American prisoners. This did nothing for Lodge's morale and he avoided thinking about it. But he had not yet learned how to control his dreams, actually his nightmares. In them Lydia or someone enough like her in appearance was being tortured, raped and he would wake up just as she was being killed. The result was not enough sleep and a Captain who would often fall asleep in his chair on the starboard side of the pilothouse. He grew haggard, tired and hardened to his existence. He kept up a good front for his men, as they did for him. There was one seaman aboard who vaguely reminded him of Dantes, and on the few occasions when they were in close proximity he would think of that outstanding sailor and better times.

There were the occasional liberties in Australia and the stories of welcoming Aussie women were true. A Destroyer Skipper would have no trouble finding company, none at all, and that was with the women knowing that they were likely married. Lodge, however barely noticed and in any case he was not about to tumble into the sack with anyone but Lydia. He put it from his mind and would accept the occasional invitation to an Aussie Officer's home for a relaxing evening and a good meal and conversation away from the ship. Shifting to escort duty between the California coast and Pearl Harbor he had occasion to drop in on Auntie Jane and Uncle Fitz. They had all of the good news that was available and they always repeated it to him on his infrequent visits. Jane seemed as haunted as he did and he knew she was worried about Lydia.

There was an ASW exercise off the coast of California in which Ford participated, getting sharpened up on detection and identification of subs, running the patterns and delivering her weapons, refining the teamwork between Sonar, Combat, the Bridge and Weapons Control until they could run a submarine ragged and maintain contact through evasive action and in heavy seas. Then Ford got orders to proceed to duty in the Atlantic.

One of the ships lost to the Japanese in the battle of Sunda Strait was the U.S. Cruiser, Houston, the ship that Daughter, Hod's best man had shipped over for. He had tried to get Hod to go with him, even appealing to his Texas roots, but Hod had been bound and determined to ship over in Washington, DC and as for his Texas roots, he would take the time to visit his Grandma, on the farm while he made his way across country. So it was that as Hod was making Chief and about to board Ellyson on the East coast, Daughter, a First Class Gunner's Mate, had found himself a China Fleet sailor on board Houston part of the ABDA Task Force sent in to do battle with the Japanese who 'til that time had never been beaten in a major fleet action.

Houston got the nickname of "Galloping Ghost of the Java coast" because she seemed to have multiple lives, as the Japanese had claimed so often to have sunk her. There would be a bit of gallows humor on the messdecks when one of the Tokyo Roses would claim yet again that the Houston had been sunk in battle with the mighty Japanese Fleet. Yet here she was, still steaming albeit some the worse for wear after close engagements with the Japanese in the Java Sea battle. Her luck was running out, however. Scout plane reports had located Houston for the Imperial Japanese Navy and she suffered repeated bomber attacks as well as Destroyer torpedo attacks and heavy shelling from Japanese cruisers. The 500 pound bombs, even when they missed, did more than send up mountainous geysers as they straddled the ship. They also loosened Houston's plates and weakened her not unlike body blows in a heavyweight boxing match. Illumination flares would show Houston to her attackers, moving slower and slower, taking hit after hit of eight inch rounds from the Jap Cruisers until finally the bugle call for abandon ship was sounded. The Skipper had already been killed and several of the men were pushing float plane pontoons loaded with supplies overboard to be used as rescue craft and for their supplies. Daughter had been the gunner's Mate in charge of maintaining the catapults and their shotgun charges, so he knew of the advance preparations for just such an emergency as this.

Before the ship sunk beneath the waves Daughter and several of his shipmates had shoved pontoons into the sea and clung to them, swimming away from the ship in order not to be sucked down with her when she made her plunge. They sung out to locate themselves to others in the water and eventually they were alone in the dark except for Japanese Ships patrolling with searchlights and rifles and machine guns, shooting survivors as they found them. Daughter spotted a smaller bit of flotsam, a broken up raft with hand lines looped along two sides and he left the float to make his own way from the more noticeable pontoon, which had been punctured and was sinking.

He woke up the next morning to the sound of a motor whaleboat approaching him with armed Japanese sailors and marines. He held up his hands and instead of shooting him they roughly pulled him aboard their craft. They tied his hands behind his back and made their way to a large auxiliary ship. A ladder had been rigged over the side and he was prodded up the ladder until he got to main deck where he found several other American sailors sitting on the deck in a group. All of them were covered with fuel oil and missing parts of their uniforms. The last craft was swung inboard and they were frog marched forward to a brig like structure, a compartment three decks down with no lights and no bunks. Within probably three hours the door opened and they squinted in the blinding light as they were removed, one at a time, and interrogated, given a cup of cold watery soup that tasted something like sweet potatoes and then put back in the hole, as they had come to call it.

"My name's Daughter, USS Houston" he said to another prisoner. "Tromp," answered his brig companion, and he named a Dutch Destroyer, Piet Hein, that he had been attached to. "We were sunk in battle in the Java Sea, and I've been a prisoner aboard this ship since then." "Any idea where we're headed," Daughter asked. "Scuttlebutt is that we are to be put to work on some island building an airstrip." "They were shooting us in the water after the Houston went down," Daughter replied. "I suppose we're lucky to still be alive." Tromp grimaced and vouchsafed that they'd soon enough have a better idea of their luck when they got to the island. Daughter lasted for two years, getting weaker and weaker under the hard working conditions and short to non-existent rations while crushing coral by hand and spreading it to form a packed runway. When they could no longer work they were executed. In Daughter's case he was given the 'honor' of having his head chopped off, as he had in some twisted way earned a modicum of respect from his captors. A wiry Japanese Colonel stood to the side of Daughter, read something in Japanese, handed the proclamation to an aide, unsheathed his sword and positioned himself before raising the weapon high over his head and bringing it crashing down on Daughter's neck. Daughter had been warned by other prisoners not to move or resist, as if he was lucky it would only take one blow. He indeed held perfectly still and as his blood poured out onto the sand his body fell to the side. The troop drawn up in ranks to witness the execution shouted BANZAI! And then it was over. Daughter was dragged to a grave and pushed into it and covered. His war was over.

CHAPTER 45

INTELLIGENCE

The Allies had taken their licks at Pearl Harbor, and the Battles of Manila, Java Sea, Sunda Strait and Coral Sea. It was now nearly six months since the disaster at Pearl Harbor and the US had struck back with a swarm of mosquitoes under Colonel Jimmy Doolittle, dropping low level bombs on Tokyo with B-25B bombers launched from the aircraft carrier Hornet. But it wasn't enough, not nearly enough. Nimitz and the nation needed something more; it was time to seriously engage the Japanese. The problem was how to catch the Japanese by surprise, their favorite tactic, against a numerically superior force, again something the Japanese were used to doing to others.

Upon joining CincPac's Staff as Intelligence Brass Hat Cochrane was read into the code breaking system the US Navy had been operating against the Japanese since the late 1920's. The Germans used mechanical machines to encode and decode their transmissions while the Japanese used code books. Many nations had had some success against the Japanese, but it only went so far. Within the message traffic the Japanese used alphabetic letter groups to identify locations, so that even if you could decode the basic message content, such as intentions to attack, the actual location of such an attack was encoded within the already coded message.

Cochrane spent a lot of time with the codebreaking section and was able to view the traffic and results of analysis and gave Nimitz frequent briefings on the latest intelligence estimates and trends. The volume of traffic pointed to an attack and a large one. It seemed that the target was to be "AF." But the navy didn't know what AF stood for. The best guess was that the Japanese intended to attack at Midway but Cochrane couldn't go in to Nimitz with a guess; he had to have more than that. The US had an undersea cable between Pearl Harbor and Midway, which was not subject to eavesdropping by the Japanese. They used it to instruct the command at Midway to broadcast a report in the open to CincPac that their desalinization equipment was down and they were short of fresh water. It was done and soon the code section at Pearl decoded a Japanese message that said that the desalinization equipment at AF was inoperative.

Cochrane knocked once, softly before being invited into Nimitz' office. Looking up from his desk and a pile of papers, Nimitz grunted an invitation to sit. His upraised eyebrows said, "What's up?" "Sir we have pretty good confirmation that the Japs are planning to attack us at Midway." "Midway, huh? That's been our guess for awhile now, what makes you so sure it's going to be Midway, Dick?" "We sent instructions to Midway via our undersea cable network to go out in the clear with a report that their freshwater equipment was out of commission. They did it and then we intercepted a Japanese message saying that "AF" had suffered the casualty. We put two and two together and figure they are going to hit us at AF, their designator for Midway." Nimitz cranked back in his chair and his eyes glittered and a small smile played across his features. Then he leaned forward and hit his bitch box to his Secretary, "Senior Staff meeting in five minutes in the conference room." Swiveling toward Cochrane, "Stick around, Dick, you can tell it to the rest in five minutes."

Feverish activity ensued and plans were laid by staff for an ambush of the Japanese Imperial Fleet, at Midway. The result was the greatest naval victory in US history with the sinking of four Japanese carriers and loss of one US carrier. It was exactly the tonic the Country needed, only six months after Pearl Harbor and it validated Roosevelt's choice of Commanders and solidified Nimitz' Staff. They knew that they had earned their victory but they also knew that they had enjoyed a spot of luck as well. Indecision by the Japanese, once they had discovered the US carriers caught them with returning aircraft from Midway in the midst of refueling for another attack and undecided whether to employ torpedoes to attack the enemy carriers or bombs to continue attacking Midway. Though they were successful in downing all of the US torpedo bombers, their fighters had been brought down in altitude and that left the US dive bombers virtually unopposed in pressing home their attacks.

Cochrane also searched all of the intercepted traffic and the US' own reports for any mention of the fate of the people trapped at Corregidor. He had not heard from Mamasan and he had also not tried to pulse it as he didn't yet have enough reason to risk their detection by communicating with them. In his occasional trips out to the Nuuanu Valley he would give Fitz and Jane an update and always it was no news about Lydia or any of the other medical personnel from Manila or Subic. He was able to keep them informed in a general way about John and his command, the USS Ford, but all three of them took the deliberate attitude that no news about Lydia was still good news, though it was grinding at them, particularly Jane. At night after going to bed she would pray and always John and Lydia were in her prayers, and always a few tears would glide softly into her pillow.

Fitz and Jane opened up the place where they lived to people whom they knew at the hospital and at Fitz' old command. They did their best to keep morale up with gay occasions at the valley hideaway and never asked for information. Their discretion was noticed and as a result they often got bits and pieces of information about their loved ones and former comrades. Unbeknownst to them CincPac had approved a roving patrol that looked over them and the approaches to their hideaway. He did it at Cochrane's suggestion and nobody talked about it. The couple never knew but they would not have been surprised; the Navy always looked out for their own.

Operations in the Pacific continued apace but now more in the Allies' favor; Midway had been the turning point, there was no longer any question whether battlewagons or carriers had the upper hand. The same was true of the overall effort in the Pacific. Yamamoto's quote, fearing that all they had accomplished at Pearl Harbor was to awaken a sleeping giant, had proved to be prescient. America's industrial strength was flooding the theater with weapons and supplies and it seemed only a matter of blood, sacrifice and time before the Japanese would be defeated.

Also after the pivotal victory at Midway, Nimitz took to spending more time with his Intelligence chief. It wasn't a lot nor was it of an official nature; it was, if anything, social. One noon Nimitz' steward showed up at Cochrane's office bearing two lunches. To Cochrane's amazement he asked permission to spread out a meal. With alacrity Cochrane readily agreed and shortly after that CincPac stepped in and closed the door behind him. With a grin he asked, "Hungry?" And Cochrane laughed and said, "You bet!" Of course Cochrane knew it was just a case of the Admiral getting away for a few moments, using his lunchtime to be with a friend. They talked on the first occasion about the 1902 Army Navy baseball game in which Cochrane had an apparent inside the park homerun, only to be thrown out at home plate. The ball was hit so deep to right field by Cochrane, a lefty, that the left fielder for Army came over to serve as relay for MacArthur, who was running down the ball in right. MacArthur hit his relay and the relay threw a perfect pitch to home, barely catching the sliding Cochrane for the out. At the time both had been Plebes at the Naval Academy, Classmates though not in the same Company. "So, tell me about your visit with Fitz to D.C." Nimitz prompted. "Sir it was just the annual briefing given by CincPac to the Commander in Chief and I was along for backup on details." Nimitz gave him a knowing look, "Yeah, I know all about who does the work on those reviews. Your impressions of FDR," he said with an inquiring look.

"Admiral Fitz had made the worst possible faux pas in the Oval Office, saying he had to stand up to give his presentation. The President was utterly charming in putting all of us at ease, lit up a cigarette in that holder of his and offered Fitz a cigar. He is an exceptionally quick study, picked up the essence of the entire brief and then delivered his strategic assessment of how he would divide our forces between theaters and why. Then he essentially offered me the job of CinC, Asiatic Fleet. With Fitz' concurrence I accepted. He wound up giving Fitz the whole box of Cuban cigars and told me not to thank him for my new assignment as I was probably signing my own death warrant by taking the job." Nimitz nodded to himself, taking note of his Classmate's fine manners in seeking his boss' approval. "You ever hear the story about how I got *this* job?" Nimitz asked. "I didn't get a trip to the Oval Office, I got a call at a local movie theater in D.C. on a Sunday, was told it was the President. He informed me of my promotion and told me to get out here and take over as CincPac. I think it really helps when the Commander in Chief has had some military experience, in FDR's case, Assistant Secretary of the Navy. I figured my career was over after running that tin can aground, as an Ensign," he laughed.

On the occasion of their next impromptu lunch, Nimitz brought up Yamamoto. "You've studied him, haven't you? Ever meet him?" "It was in '24, I believe. He was a Captain and visiting the Naval War College. I was back there as a student so it wasn't a lot of interaction. There was a reception and I got to observe him and we did meet, albeit briefly. My recollection is that he spoke American English like a native, enjoyed a good game of poker and you could see, just barely, the wheels turning behind his poker face." Shifting in his chair behind his desk, with his boss sitting across from him, Cochrane swiveled his chair around, reached for his iced tea and took a swallow while he ordered his thoughts. To give him a little more time "Chet" chuckled and said, "Not going to be a quiz, Dick. I know that you probably have forgotten more naval history than I ever knew. I'm just trying to get to know my enemy a little bit better. I figure he currently has, for the Japanese, my job and Ernie King's, combined." "You want the one minute summary or the full run down," Cochrane asked, turning again to face Nimitz across his desk and putting his tea down. "Let's see where it goes and start with all you know. If we run out of time we'll get the rest another time."

"Let's start with the misconceptions. He could not have said that he intended to dictate the terms of surrender to us in the White House in D.C., the way it was reported. He is too smart for that. He likely did say that it would not be enough to take Guam and the P.I. and Hawaii and maybe San Francisco, but that they would have to actually march all the way to Washington in order to defeat us. Yamamoto spent many years in this country and got to know us as a people with two years at Harvard and two tours as a naval attache. Although a noted warrior he is not a headstrong or careless one. His presence here for so many years was an obvious attempt by the Japanese to get to know us, their enemy, as well as they know themselves. They studied Sun Tsu and learned their lessons well."

Cochrane leaned into the space between them and Nimitz was transported back to the Ensign Factory where the professors encouraged questions and were energized with the desire to get the facts out and create understanding among their pupils. Indeed, Nimitz felt like a student and he listened intently as though if there *were* a quiz it would be he who would be taking it. "He was born as the son of an intermediate level Samurai and named Isoroku because that is the word for fifty six, his father's age at the time of his birth. The family name was Takano, not Yamamoto. As a rising young person with prospects in the Navy he was adopted by the Yamamotos, a family with no sons. They were of higher Samurai class and could provide the connections that Isoroku would need while also, themselves, basking in the glory of his anticipated career. He graduated from the Imperial Japanese Naval Academy in '04, just a year before we graduated from the Naval Academy in Annapolis. He is no doubt beloved by his navy and there are reasons for this."

"Yamamoto fought in the Battle of Tsushima, a great victory over the Russian Fleet which established Japan as a naval power of the first rank. Aboard a cruiser that was struck several times in battle he was wounded, losing two fingers on his left hand. Isoroku, like many of the upper class in Japan, enjoyed his time with the geisha girls. They had a nick name for him, "80 sen". You see, a manicure in a geisha house cost 100 sen, or the equivalent of one yen. With two fingers missing he would be charged only 80 sen. In this way he made light of his wounds with humor and his legend grew. Whether eighty sen or fifty six, Yamamoto was known and loved within his service but that love did not extend to the Army."

"Yamamoto fought against Army policy. He opposed the invasion of China. He was not satisfied to merely serve as transportation for the Army, he believed in gunboat diplomacy. And he had his enemies, receiving many death threats and hate mail from Army supporters and Army members. It is thought that he was promoted to Admiral in charge of the Combined Fleet as a means of keeping him alive, the thought being that if he was at sea he was safe from assassination attempts from political foes. He has an inquiring mind, loves games of chance and is absolutely fearless, believing and saying so in writing, that there is no higher honor than to die in the service of the Emperor.

In his career he became an expert in gunnery, then switched his specialty to aviation. He developed the aircraft with which they go to war and commanded his own carrier strike group. He could read the writing on the wall before many of us here in the States could. He knew that aviation would be decisive over battleships. He opposed the building of the Yamato and Musashi or any battleships, for that matter. Instead he developed ordnance and tactics for air attacks on opposing forces. He read the lessons of Fleet Problem Thirteen and put them to good use in preparing the attack on our Fleet at Pearl. He believes in quick strikes in overwhelming force and leads with his aircraft, every time. The Japanese as a culture are known for their contempt for all Gaijin. Yama-moto is the exception. He certainly believes that Japan's rightful position is at the top but at the same time he has a healthy respect for our strength as a people and our economic strength. In closing he is a well-educated, thorough and dangerous man, this enemy of ours. He does indeed know himself and also know his enemy."

Nimitz stared into the distance, not breaking the silence, the spell, until at last he said, wryly, "You had me going there, Dick, could've sworn I was back at the Boat School and in a class on Naval History. When this is all over you ought to look into going back there and running the place. Look, I want you to know everything there is to know about his movements and actions and I need to know what you think his motivations are, every step of the way. Let me know if anything pops with Yamamoto."

Two weeks later, Cochrane has been cleared in to see CincPac. Nimitz looked up and must've seen the excitement in Cochrane's face. "What, Dick? Something hot?" "Yessir, we have an opportunity." Nimitz relaxed back in his chair, "You know that I refer to problems as opportunities, Dick. That kind of opportunity? Another problem to add to the stack here?" and he pointed to an untidy pile of flimsies yet awaiting the Admiral's action. "Sir, we have a chance to bag Yamamoto, if we want him." Nimitz' face came alight with sudden intensity, "You bet your ass I want him. How much time to pull this off?" Sir, if it follows the schedule we have, it'll be in less than a week; actually it should fall on the one year anniversary of Jimmy Doolittle's raid on Tokyo, 18 April." Nimitz held up one hand and with the other flipped the lever on his intercom. "I want a senior staff meeting in forty minutes, at 1630." Then he turned to Cochrane and made the motion for 'give'.

Cochrane handed over the red bordered folder with the TOP SECRET flimsy inside. As his boss looked at the contents he explained, "This is a fresh intercept and we have high confidence in its accuracy as we picked it up at three different listening posts. Of course their plans could always change, but if they don't, we have most of a week to plan an intercept of Yamamoto's inspection party. He's proceeding from Rabaul on New Britain to the Balalae Island air strip off of Bougainville. We have his departure time and arrival and can assume a straight line course from takeoff to landing. Our initial assessment is that we task aircraft out of Kukum Field on Guadalcanal.

"If we do this, we'll let the tasked unit do the final planning and logistics. It's our job to figure out if we really want to do it. What are your thoughts, Dick?" "Sir, we need to think through the consequences of success as well as failure of the mission." And he referred to a set of handwritten notes. "What are the consequences if we succeed? If Yamamoto is killed we will have to learn the tendencies of a new commander. Sometimes it's a case of better the devil you know than the one you don't. We know that Yamamoto leads with his air forces, every time. We may also have to deal with an extremely violent reaction from the Japanese, as he is a revered leader. If we succeed the Japanese will probably assume we have broken their code and we could lose the incredible advantage conferred upon us by our "Magic" code breaking operation. On the plus side, they lose a near genius, one whom many think is invincible. Also on the plus side for us is a likely nosedive in morale for the Japanese, as Yamamoto is a national hero. Along with that will be an upward spike in our morale as we get pay back for the attack on Pearl. Coming on the one year anniversary of the Tokyo raids it will be a forceful reminder of our successes in attacking them. They will start to realize that they are not so invincible. We ought to consider also that this will be viewed as an assassination, something we have not yet done in our nation's history of warfare. Finally the Admiral must consider whether he has the requisite authority to conduct this operation or whether he must first go up the line for permission.

Nimitz dropped his head as he thought about that one. "Well, it won't be as bold as Nelson turning a blind eye toward the signals to him from his Commander. In this case of course I have the authority to commit the resources. The question is do I also have the responsibility to inform my seniors before I do it, if that's the decision. He thought for another minute or so and then turned to Cochrane, "I believe I'll settle for the blame if this is frowned upon or criticized afterward. We will prepare an operation to kill Yamamoto on 18 April and we will also prepare a cover story that they were observed by Australian coast watchers who tipped us off.

Dick's look, a sober one, was saying, "Are you sure you really want to do this." Nimitz caught the look and said "I want to kill this bastard." And running through his mind was the saying of Davy Crockett's, taught to every Texas schoolboy, "First make sure you're right and then go ahead." We owe him for Pearl and all the rest of our ships, Marines and shipmates that we've lost in this war."

With cooperation from Admiral Bill Halsey, Commander South Pacific the planners on Guadalcanal plotted a four leg track out to the west and then closing on Yamamoto's destination. It would be 600 miles out and four hundred miles back. A larger spare fuel tank was installed on the participating P-38 Lightnings as well as a ship's magnetic compass for dead reckoning navigation. Messages were written up at CincPac headquarters with the cover story that coast watchers were involved. The day came and Operation Vengeance launched, much as Doolittle's doughty warriors had done, a year ago to the day. The flight intercepted the two Betty transport bombers, fought off the escorting zeros and delivered killing fire to the two bombers, one of which crashed into the sea, the other on Bougainville itself. Vice Admiral Ugaki, Yamamoto's Chief of Staff, survived the crash of his Betty into the sea. Yamamoto, however was hit by two .50 cal. Machine gun bullets, one taking him in the shoulder, the other going in through his left jaw and exiting through his eye. He was dead before his aircraft crashed into the jungle on Bougainville. Three days after the attack Japanese news was broadcast confirming the death of their naval hero, Admiral Isoroku Yamamoto. For his part, Nimitz waited with interest to see if he would catch any flak from DC. As it was a win, it was of course all congratulatory. His only public notice of the event, other than congratulatory messages to the participating units and signing off on recommendations for decorations was to pop into Cochrane's office, reach out and grasp his hand and shake it and say, "Well done, Dick, well done. I knew what I was doing when I took you on board." Cochrane stood up and said, "Chet, you saved me from an untimely end after the loss of my Fleet. I'll never forget that." Nimitz cocked his head, "Well, FDR was entirely correct in his assessment of that job; you knew you were not at all likely to survive it, that it was a stacked deck against you when you took it. You, sir, are a fighting Admiral and I could not let such a man go to waste. Besides," and here he paused, showing rare emotion, "What are Classmates for?"

Time passed and the lunches in Dick's office became fewer, petered out. Cochrane missed them but made allowances. Then one morning Nimitz popped into his office and said, "Come with me, Dick," and they went outside and hopped into Nimitz' Staff car and got in the stern sheets, the driver already instructed and heading down to the piers where the subs tied up. There was a Navy band arraigned in gleaming white ranks with shining brass instruments, standing at attention and with the Band Leader rendering the salute as the car drove up. There were dependents there as well for this was the return of a ship from its war patrol; Nimitz tried to send them all off and to greet them upon their return, and the information of their whereabouts was closely held, though the dependents were kept in the loop.

"Dick, I'm sending you out on one of these boats, the next one to deploy. I'll dedicate some of its very valuable mission time to getting you safely to Australia. I want to loan you to MacArthur for as long as you think it is working and the best place for you to be. This is neither a firing nor a hiring. I need better trust with MacArthur and we need more cooperation and I simply can't go there myself." Several emotions flitted across Cochrane's face as he absorbed this. He made as if to reply and Nimitz held up his hand, "We've never blown smoke up each other's ass and there's a reason for that. We know each other as only Classmates at the Ensign Factory can, and have been through a lot, together. Our Country is going through a lot, too. The jealousy and mistrust is too great and entirely inappropriate. Your job is to 'sell' me to him and on your return to explain him to me. With your help we will build a bridge that joins us, preferably at the heart, if not the hip. I swear I can't spare you but I must. When you go there you go with authority to speak for me. It'll be the same thing as me saying it and I want him to know that. You might start with baseball but you absolutely must meld us, intelligence-wise; in that way, with the trust over Intel, we might get on to the more operational matters. To the extent we can erase the divisions between us without being seen as usurpers we will succeed. We have the bit in our teeth, Dick, and our cooperation is paramount if we are to save lives and bring our people home as we finish this."

Dick drew himself to attention, looked his Classmate in the eye and said, simply, "Aye, aye Sir," accompanied by his very best salute. Nimitz, too, stood with starch in his spine and snapped one off in return. Then they turned to the boat approaching and got ready to welcome her and her crew home. There was a broom lashed to a 'scope in the conning tower and a serious looking Skipper bringing his command slowly and safely to its berth. With lines over he turned with a huge grin to CincPac and rendered his salute, again returned. Nimitz didn't hold up the crew, stood aside as the gangway was put in place and stood by watching sailors bouncing ashore to hugs and kisses. It got to him. Always did. These were the reminders, the reasons why we fought and Nimitz knew it. There weren't any dry eyes at times like these and the Admiral was no exception.

CHAPTER 46

MACARTHUR

The trip from Pearl took a bit over three weeks with time divided between cruising on the surface while charging batteries, or snorkeling or running on batteries, submerged. It was tight, packed is what it was, and the times allowed topside were welcomed for the fresh air and sunshine or stars, whichever was offered. Cochrane tried to stay out of the way, insisted that he not be given the CO's quarters and wound up sharing the XO's bunk, a hot bunking sort of sleeping by shifts. The XO volunteered to take some night watches in order to make it work and make it work it did. Cochrane was extraordinarily impressed with this time with the Silent Service. It was true, he knew, that a crew takes its personality from its Skipper, but it seemed that all of the Skippers and all of their men took after a quiet, hard-nosed Texan from the Hill Country. He reflected on the difference between both Commanders, Nimitz and MacArthur and shook his head. He was being trusted to bridge that gap! He wondered if he would be equal to the task.

Having made his initial courtesy calls to the Navy in Sydney he returned to his hotel, the Lord Nelson. It was a Friday night and he thought a visit to the bar in the basement was in order. He changed into his civs and eased into the place, first standing at the bar while he looked around, taking the place in. It seemed mostly a younger crowd and there were several piling up to the bar so he asked for a beer, one the house made in their own brewery, pointed at a table that was empty and went over and took a seat. He took in the yeasty smell, the sandstone walls and the historical feel of the place. He'd been thinking of his assignment, the time to come when he'd be sizing up MacArthur and his Staff and trying to find a way in, past The General's Palace Guard. It was making his head hurt so he deliberately turned it off and settled in for perhaps an interesting time, at least something *less complicated*, he thought as his beer arrived at the table.

Across the room but in the front rank of tables nearest to the small dance floor were two young ladies at a table, no one with them, just the two and they were drinking beers. They were also being almost aggressively ignored by the Australian men in the place, all of them seemingly captivated by their "mates' and perhaps their sea stories. In his last stop through, when he made the rounds of the Dutch East Indies and Australia, he'd become aware of this reputation of the Aussie men. With a bit of a grin he thought, *makes it easier for we Yanks, eh?* The two women seemed to be looking at him too, wasn't sure because he couldn't quite catch them at it. Looking down at his beer he could have sworn he heard the word, *Dantes*. There was a bit of a buzz of conversation going on in the room so he couldn't be sure. He pulled a sardonic smile, *that guy's name keeps popping up!* Then he heard it again, or at least thought he heard it. Now his head snapped up at their table and there was no doubt. They were looking at him. One of them turned to the other, "I think I saw him, or else it was his picture in the newspaper, that time when Dantes and Daughter were here, remember?" "Remember? How could I forget?

They looked up just as Janie was saying, "Maybe if he were in uniform it would bring it back..." And there Cochrane was, smiling urbanely at the two of them but concentrating on the one he was sure had used that name. "Pardon me, ladies, I didn't mean to eavesdrop, perhaps it's the acoustics in here, but, and I apologize, this is not a pickup line, I thought you mentioned the name of one of my Sailors, Seaman First Class Dantes, from some time back." At that Janie squealed, "Oh! Do you know Hod?" Cochrane looked a bit perplexed, so Janie stuttered, "Y-yes, Dantes. We both know him, I met him here in this very bar and we spent some time that weekend together." Cochrane was picking up on the gist of this quickly, actually he was lightning fast on the pick up and said that he'd known Hod for quite awhile, that they had sailed together, they were both in the Navy and he didn't actually know anyone quite so brave as Hod. "By the way, I'm Dick Cochrane, and you are?" looking directly at Janie. "I'm Janie and I rather think I know who you are, Admiral." Cochrane was actually crestfallen and looked it. Janie quickly added, won't you join us Dick?" She was no slouch in the lightning fast department, either. Cochrane smiled in relief and quickly took his seat across from Janie. Mavis saw what had already started to develop and made her way to the powder room. "Another beer or would you prefer some wine, something stronger?" He leaned back and summoned a waiter with just a look, ordered scotch for himself, looked inquiringly at her, she nodded and he said make it two.

"I haven't noticed the recent arrival of any Navy ships, Dick, unless you count the one by a submarine, was it only yesterday? I believe it has already gone." Cochrane chuckled, "Actually that is how I arrived here, and I'm impressed that you were so observant. It's the same in Subic Bay, Hong Kong, the world over; want to know anything about our ships' schedules, go to a local bar, they'll know." And they both chuckled, "So, does that mean that you'll be here in Australia for some longer period of time, Dick? I mean, without giving away any classified information, of course." Now Cochrane knew his leg was being pulled and it had been a long time since anyone had done that to or with him. Janie was finally relaxed, was enjoying herself at the same time as she wondered if her lipstick was on straight. I mean what a coincidence he knew Dantes but he was so, well, *old.*

It had been awhile but Dick knew how to recognize the opening exchange of rounds in a naval engagement and this had all the earmarks of turning into one, engagement that is. He looked at his watch, allowed as how it was approaching time for dinner and would she care to join him? She smiled and said that would be soopah and would he excuse her while she freshened herself. Cochrane got the waiter to call a cab to the front, visited the head and was back out when she returned to the table. He smoothly rose from the table, took her by the arm and they proceeded to the waiting cab where they were whisked away to a very nice place with a stunning view of the Harbor. From their conversation Janie learned that he was single, no kids, had never been married. Dick learned that Janie was the oldest of the siblings in her family, thought the world of Hod Dantes and was not nosey, not at all. She laughed easily and was a stunningly good looking woman who was a working girl and supported herself, thank you very much. Oh, and she absolutely adored Yanks and Navy men. The conversation kept coming back to Dantes and Cochrane was feeling his age and not sure he should tell her the story of what had happened on the hotel roof in Manila

There was dancing at the restaurant. A trio did their best imitation of the Andrews Sisters. The music tended toward patriotic as did the conversation. They danced and their embrace went from loose to quite a bit closer, the music slow and dreamy. She could feel his excitement from time to time as they brushed together, one of those times caused by her. There seemed every reason to do the "I'm going off to war or am just back from war" routine, but neither of them brought it up while both of them thought of it. Back at the table they were now sitting side by side and his arm was around her waist and it seemed her drinking had gotten the best of her. Cochrane was winding down, a bit tired of talking about Dantes, feeling more than a little bit old for this situation and thinking it was time to bring what had been a fun evening to an end.

He paid the bill and he supported her as they made their way to the taxi line. They got in back and headed for the Lord Nelson when Janie quietly vomited on her blouse. The driver wound his window down and passed back a towel which Cochrane used to wipe her as clean as he could. When they got back to the hotel he realized she was in no shape to drive herself back home, so he had the driver pull around to a service entrance and together they carried her up the stairs to his room, without being noticed. He tipped the driver very well and thanked him profusely then let her gently down on the bed, while he went in to the bath and showered. When he came out she was snuffling softly, sound asleep. He removed her blouse, went ahead and undressed her completely and tucked her into bed, then washed out her blouse and hung up her clothes to dry. Then he took a blanket and made himself a bit crowded on the couch and was soon asleep.

In the morning she awoke a bit disoriented to a hot cup of coffee, toast and poached eggs. Cochrane gave her a hotel robe and she went into the shower and came out looking none the worse for wear. "I'm sorry, but I don't remember anything past getting in the cab, last night." Dick looked up from his eggs, grinned, "Oh, other than the little accident brought on by a bit too much scotch and champagne you were fine, utterly beautiful to the last inch in fact." Janie had the good grace to blush down to her chest, at which they both looked and she pulled her robe closer, covering herself up a bit more. He could see her wheels turning so he volunteered, "No, we didn't do anything last night except dance. And it was a wonderful time."

She dressed in the bath and he escorted her back out the way they'd come in and he got her address and phone number as he handed her into her car. There was no talk about the rest of the weekend and that was that. But Cochrane had been shaken alive and made aware of his own needs and desires. And he was glad he hadn't made a total fool of himself with that wonderful young lady.

An hour later, down at the front desk he had decided to spend his weekend in one of the hotel's cabins at the lake in Royal Park. He was inquiring about a rental car to go with that when the Concierge looked up from his phone, "Admiral Cochrane this call is for you, Sir. You may take it on the house phone. Cochrane excused himself from the front desk and went to the phone, "Hello?" "Dick, this is Janie," and she hurried on, "I still have no plans for the weekend and I wanted to see if you have any." Dick smiled, frowned and finally said, "Actually I do." And he imagined a deflated Janie at her end of the line. "I've just taken a cabin at the lake in Royal Park for the rest of the weekend. Why don't you join me there, if you like?" The laughter was back in her voice, "I can do a bit better than that, when can you be ready, Dick? I'll drop by and furnish the transportation and a packed picnic lunch to get us started!" He laughed, "Make it in one hour and we'll take it from there. See you soon."

At the cabin the food was put in the icebox and the windows thrown open and the place aired out. They were both uncomfortable so Cochrane suggested a walk. When they got back to the cabin Dick poured a couple of beers. The cabin was pretty rustic, no radio or music and she said, "I really enjoyed our dancing Dick." She put her beer down and went over to him and sat in his lap. And then she wriggled around in his lap. Before long they were kissing and they enjoyed themselves and each other all weekend with no regrets. They knew it for what it was and it was lovely. Strangely enough it would have been hard to know which one of them gained or regained the most confidence out of their encounter. It wasn't something they would analyze; it was something they would never forget.

On Monday morning a Staff car from Naval Headquarters arrived at the hotel and loaded his cruise box and gear into the back and took him down to the airport. He flew Space available on a military flight into Brisbane where another car waited to whisk him off to the Flag Officers apartments. Settled in by noon he had his first appointment to meet with the many Flag Officers, all senior to him, in the barroom of the building that had been commandeered and was now serving as a conference room. It was a lot to remember, all in one meeting, especially since these new faces and names were competing for his attention with the random pictures of Janie that kept flicking through his mind. He didn't meet MacArthur, not yet. He was too busy doing things on Mount Olympus to attend this group session. No, he would, it turned out, meet the great man at a reception being thrown by the Governor of Queensland, the province in which Brisbane was found. It was to be held at the Governor's Residence, a more intimate setting than one that would hold them all. MacArthur seemed to prefer the smaller groups and others vied to be on the invitation list. Cochrane didn't know any of this, he was just informed of the time, place and uniform for the shindig and knew it was but a short drive to get there.

He spent the afternoon catching up on all the sleep he'd lost in the cabin at Royal Park, bragging of, definitely not complaining of his soreness and actually a bit cocky and proud of himself, unusual for him in recent years. It was with a spring in his step and a gleam in his eye that he was admitted to the Residence in his Dress Whites with large medals and sword belt, gold shoulder boards with the white stars gleaming, competing with the dazzling smile from his tanned face. He cut a dashing figure normally, and he was conscious of it this evening. Like all of them, he'd commanded large numbers of men and material. Except for the Staff types, that is. The line battle unit Command Officers cut a bit of a wider path, were given special deference, and it was earned.

MacArthur, when he and Jean showed up, was dazzling in his blue-rib-
boned, star bedecked Congressional Medal of Honor, depending down from
his neck. Every Officer stole a look at it, never having seen one in person
before. Most of them, though they would never admit it, wondered what he
had actually done to earn it. A photographer, the General's, took a round
of pictures in the foyer before they proceeded into the hall and down to the
receiving line. Cochrane was surprised to be introduced to the others in the
short line and to find out that he was in the line itself and had been placed
right next to and before the Royal Couple, Jean and the General, who were the
last in the line. Several of the others who had yet to go through the line were
looking at him curiously, never having seen him before.

When all was ready a string quartet started up softly in a far room and that
evidently was the signal for the other guests to wend their way to the line
and go through it, giving their name to the first person they met and being
introduced to the next, in turn. There grew a silence, starting from the end of
the line. Just a gradual lessening of the buzz and it seemed to be attached to
the figure approaching him now. The person to his left, the Prime Minister of
Queensland, spent an extra bit of time talking to her before turning to him
and introducing "Dame Sandra Tweedsmuir Wilson, may I present Rear Admiral Richard Cochrane, United States Navy. It was a lot of formal frippery,
done with precision and totally dismissed by Dame Sandra's smile, disarming
rather than imperious, her posture perfect and perfectly natural, for her. Her
eyes were locked on his and for him the whole room went silent as it seemed
several were looking in their direction as if to see something special, even for
this occasion. He took in the badge and star of her GCMG, which of course
was not announced, even as she took in the man before her, in his totality.
She reached out her hand and Cochrane took it, said, "Dick Cochrane, Dame
Sandra." She took him in for just another second and said, "My friends call me
Sandy." The grip was strong, very strong and the look supremely confident.
For her this meeting was already extraordinary, measured in seconds as it
was, for there was no awe, no obeisance, nor intimidation, an effect she had
had with all men, since a young age. She was now forty eight but moved with
the grace of youth, a mature beauty, breathtaking in her presence and confidence. And Cochrane stood there like a young stud, minding his manners
before he went out and killed the enemy or made love to someone just like
Sandra.

The moment and the heat from her presence faded as she let go of his hand
and moved to Jean MacArthur. Jean jumped right in, thanking Sandra for
inviting them into her home for this occasion. Dame Sandra was, in fact, the
sister of the Governor and by rights could have been receiving, but she often
preferred to just pass through the line instead, staying conscious that the position was her brother's, not hers. She was as straight as a string and not every-

body called her "Sandy." She was the last one through the line and MacArthur the last greeter. He engaged her in some amusing bit of conversation and they both turned to Cochrane.

MacArthur said, "It's been a long time, Sir." Even though they had met not that long ago in Manila. Cochrane responded, "Indeed it has, General," for he too was thinking of that play from right field and his home run denied. A challenging grin started to spread across both faces as Cochrane threw one of MacArthur's own quotes at him, "Upon the fields of friendly strife…" And MacArthur picked up, "Are sown the seeds that on other days, other fields will bear the fruits of victory." They had each other by the upper arms with both hands, as close as a military man could get to a hug, and MacArthur deliberately stood there, prolonging it, for he knew if he knew anything the value of the noble gesture and not just the gesture but also the recording of it. Dame Sandra took all of this in, of course, as did it seemed the entire room. In case anybody missed it there was a picture of this greeting in the local papers, that very afternoon and the next day. As a matter of fact, a personally signed copy of the paper and the photo arrived on Chet Nimitz' desk less than three weeks later. It was signed, "With all respect, Douglas"

As the mass of people moved on into the main quarters of the Governor's residence, the Governor had been the very first person in the receiving line, he caught up to Cochrane, the General and his sister. "I was just reliving a very special memory with an old foe from our days at West Point and Annapolis. We were opponents on the baseball field, fierce competitors for there is no competition, not even warfare, that can rival Navy Army," MacArthur said. And here all turned toward Dick. "The General knows that it is always Army Navy that we at the Naval Academy follow in Army's steps. Besides," he hastened to add, "Army won that game and it was your throw, hitting the relay man that caught me at home plate, sealing the victory for your team on that day." Here it came again, that eerie ability to let his emotions rise, for MacArthur's eyes welled up just a bit as he put a hand across Cochrane's shoulder, almost as if it were a King's sword and he was dubbing Sir Dick, "Ahh, but you know, as only Midshipmen and Cadets do, that after the game, after our mock battle we come together in Brotherhood, welded together as members of the same *team*." And there it was, the first demonstration that MacArthur was always a step ahead and absolutely knew how to draw those he respected in and claim their loyalty. Cochrane was on the team, always had been and those of his Staff who were present knew for a certainty that this upstart Rear Admiral from Nimitz' Staff, probably here as a spy, was to be given access, bypassing even the Chief of Staff, should it come to that.

They broke into small gatherings and the busy noise mounted again as the two of them found themselves together, Sandy and Dick. "I rather like your name, but I think I shall say it my own way, Richard. Sometimes it shall be

Richard, but pronounced as the French do it, Ree Sharrrr. Or maybe just
Sharrrr and she growled it deep in her throat in that feral way she had when
she chose to show it. She always showed it in the bedroom and those were the
thoughts she engendered in Cochrane right now, only seconds after meeting
her. This woman was extraordinary, but just as extraordinary was the fact
that he was totally comfortable with her, that way. She led him out onto a
balcony of the Residence, itself situated on several acres, the stars out and the
privacy total. There was a soft glitter from her badge and star as Cochrane
remarked he GCGM, "I read several of your assessments and summaries in
Hong Kong when I was briefed by the Governor there, on a previous swing
through the theater. I am glad to have the opportunity to tell you that they are
outstanding." "Yes, that was shortly before you took Command of the China
Fleet, I believe. God, I'm glad we've done with *that!*" He knew she meant the
exchanging of credentials and pissing on fence posts.

A waiter brought out a tray with Champagne flutes and offered them.
Cochrane took two and handed one to Sandy. They clicked the crystal together and spent another hour on the balcony. Sandy didn't flout tradition, she
just surmounted it or created it. She was deliberate in practically everything
she did and she did practically everything she wanted, got everything she'd
ever gone for and had most likely emasculated all men with whom she came
in contact. Until now. "Why did you not marry," she asked. "Never met the
right woman," he responded. He did not ask her the same question, rather
it came out, "Do you like men, Sandy?" She knew what she was being asked
and appreciated the confidence of the man who could ask her that. For an
answer she placed her champagne flute carefully on the balustrade and slowly
put her arms around his neck and kissed him for about a minute and a half."
Cochrane just as slowly put his arm around her waist, the one with the champagne in his hand, raised it while they kissed and poured the rest of his champagne down the back of her dress, let it run until the bubbles had popped
amongst the goosebumps raised there and all the way down to the end of its
travel, that nether region of her body which had of its own volition already
crushed itself against him, bringing him to attention and quickly. "Mmmm,"
as she broke their kiss, I can tell that you like women, Sharrrr," she growled,
"but never just one woman," she added, "Until now." And then she did something entirely foreign to the nature she had shown one and all to this point
in her life. She dropped her head on his shoulder, lessened the heat of the
contact and turned it into a familial hug. "I'll call you whatever you want me
to call you, Dick." She still used her feminine wiles, but gone was the impe-
rium, gone the deliberateness. It was as though she had finally met someone
who could dissolve all of that. That fearful aloofness and control had served
but one purpose and served it well; when it came down to it, it had saved her
for Dick. When they rejoined the others it was with loose arms around each

other's waists, loose but unmistakably proprietarial. There was one leader and they both knew who it was. Dame Sandra was out of circulation.

The party was winding down, with the MacArthurs making their manners to the Governor and his sister, Dame Sandra. MacArthur turned toward Cochrane, "You all settled in, Admiral?" "Sir, just fine at the Flag Officers' Apartments." "Why don't you drop by my HQ sometime tomorrow? I should be available after lunch, say for the rest of the afternoon?" Cochrane nodded, "Aye, aye Sir," the others smiled and the august couple made their way to the door. For his part the Governor couldn't imagine anyone getting a full afternoon with the General and Cochrane was wondering, himself, why he had been so open with the information and free with his time. Cochrane waited until the MacArthurs had been driven off and turned to Sir John and started thanking him. The Governor was offering him a ride back to town when Sandra jumped in and said that she had that covered, smiled and took Cochrane by the arm and they strolled back out onto the balcony, leaving several guests in the foyer making their way out to their vehicles, wondering knowingly and no doubt setting tongues wagging the next morning.

They picked up a bottle of champagne from a bucket of mostly melted ice, the beads of condensation having run down the bucket and made a wet soggy sponge of the damask napkin. Cochrane had the bottle and Sandra picked up the napkin. At the balustrade they both sat while Dick opened the Champagne expertly with a soft pop and managed to get all of the sudden frothy eruption, frosty cold, into the two flutes. There they sat, quickly downing the first drink and then as Dick poured another, Sandra reached over and pulled on his waistband and squeezed the napkin directly onto his crotch. She smiled sweetly, "Thought maybe you needed cooling down." "Not fair, Sandra, you were probably already wet when I poured my drink down your dress." She chuckled, "Sharrr what am I to do with you? I do have my own cottage here on the grounds; you didn't want to go back to those lonely Flag Quarters tonight, did you? The General isn't expecting you until after lunch," and she just took him by the hand and they walked in the dark to her cottage, went in and closed the door.

At about four they rolled onto their backs and took a bit of a breather. "Have you figured out how this is going to work," Dick asked. "Entirely up to you, Darling," she replied. "We have some time to figure it out, he answered." "Exactly," she replied and threw a leg over him and they fell asleep that way until about ten and then after a delightful shower they sat in the kitchen and talked intelligence, her experience with the General's Staff and with MacArthur, himself. She had worked with all of them, had received advances from most of them and in general (no pun intended) knew what made them tick. Cochrane was amazed at her in-depth knowledge of the various personalities and her suggestions for handling all of them, especially MacArthur, himself. They worked their way through a pot of coffee, looked at the clock and she took him back to his Quarters, dropping him off to change and get ready for his first meeting with the General. She was to pick him up afterward, back at his Quarters, when he would join her for dinner out on the town. "Be sure to bring some civvies," she said, "and a toothbrush."

The General and Sutherland had rooms 808 and 807 in the nine floor AMP Building on Queen Street in Brisbane. It was a neat arrangement where to get into MacArthur's Office you generally went in through Sutherland's. Cochrane showed up in his working uniform, a set of short sleeved Khakis with only ribbons for his personal decorations. He was tired and a bit creaky in the back but it was a dazzlingly happy junior Flag Officer who arrived and talked with MacArthur's Chief of Staff in 807 at about 1230. Sutherland knew of the appointment, of course, and though curious didn't ask too many questions of Cochrane. "Heard you arrived by submarine in Sydney. Nice town, that. Where'd you stay?" "Lord Nelson. Nice brew bar in the basement." Sutherland was thinking *that's a dive for young people* but he just grunted. The little green light over the door to the General's Office glowed and Sutherland got up and took him into the inner sanctum. It was a very spacious room with a huge desk, paintings and maps on the walls, along with the portrait of his Father. MacArthur came around his desk, beaming and took Cochrane's hand, "Dick, join me over here in the sitting area." To Sutherland he cocked an eyebrow. Sutherland coughed and said, "Will that be all, Sir?" He'd obviously expected to be invited to stay. "Ah, yes, Chief. I don't think I'll need anything else for the day, why don't you secure and lock up on your way out? Tell the sentries that I'm still up here, will you?

Now Cochrane *was* impressed. This was top drawer, nothing but. *What's he got going in that Machiavellian brain of his,* he wondered. A steward in starched whites came in and poured some iced tea and also put a bottle of scotch on the sideboard with a pitcher of ice and two snifters. MacArthur thanked him and he let himself out of the suite. Both of them took a pull at their teas, MacArthur staring into the carpet then abruptly saying, "They all think you're here to spy on us on me. They've been running around like a bunch of chickens with a fox loose in the hen house ever since we got the message that you'd boarded a submarine to come here." And he looked up with an unfathomable smile at Cochrane, to see the effect of his performance. Getting no response, he said, "Sutherland is excellent, very protective and perhaps slightly concerned that I didn't keep him in here, as part of the meeting. He runs a tight ship." Cochrane only took another swig of his tea and put it back onto the napkin, exactly in the circle it had left and let the silence grow. He was comfortable with it.

Last night during one of the times they'd rested Sandy had said, "Everyone snivels before him, you know. They think he requires it but it's just the opposite. He will make all the right gestures and say all the right things, but if he doesn't respect you, you will get nowhere with him." As he had hesitated she had said, "I know because I am exactly the same way." Cochrane knew of her deep background in intelligence and respected her work. Now in his office he was listening with interest as the General had said or done just about everything she had predicted. When the silence was interrupted only slightly by the creaking of the General's overstuffed chair as he reached for the scotch, Cochrane spoke. "Sir, the quality of your Staff is legendary, you attract only the very best and brightest." MacArthur's gaze narrowed just a fraction. "Admiral Nimitz and I are Classmates, as I think you know. We often have lunch together and I am his Intelligence Chief as I am also sure you know. Chet asked me to tell you that I represent him, that I come empowered to make decisions, if circumstances require it. In short I can commit assets and resources and conclude agreements in matters that will have the effect of drawing your Command and his closer together." With that he chugged the rest of his tea and got up and got the scotch and topped off the General's snifter and poured a smaller one for himself.

MacArthur said, "You and Dame Sandra… you seemed to hit it off spectacularly," he smiled, with a mischievous dance in his eyes. "That introduction alone has put me in your personal debt, General." *Sandra said he places great importance in personal loyalty, the problem with the General was that his loyalty ultimately was to himself.* Cochrane had countered to her last night that with Nimitz it was loyalty to our Government and her supreme effort to defeat her enemies. The rest just didn't matter. He'd wondered how he would be able to serve two such different masters: one from the Silent Service the other a showman and self-promoter. Cochrane continued. "Sir, I do have a personal goal for this assignment of mine." MacArthur looked with interest, waiting to hear it. "I want there to be complete honesty between us, for it to lead to an unbreakable trust and for us to measure the worth of the relationship we build, to be the results we get in accomplishing my Boss' objective."

MacArthur immediately said, "And, Dick, precisely what is that objective and please give me an example of what that might look like." "It's disarmingly simple, Sir. Chet thinks we need closer cooperation if we are to succeed quickly in defeating the Empire of Japan. He sees jealousy and mistrust and he wants synergy, wants the two commands to be more than the sum of their parts. We want to start by giving you something, sharing an asset and working to share all of it. I am talking about intelligence, Sir. We have a small but fairly widely spread network of intelligence operatives in a network in the Philippines. You have many more assets and connections to them in the P.I. than we do. We think that they need to be integrated so as to be able to share all of the information, all the time. To that end we are suggesting you start receiving copy of our Intel product to include all of Magic as well as all of Mamasan, our system that operates just in the P.I.

MacArthur took his own turn with a sip on his scotch to think and finally said, "You mentioned the ability to commit resources, do you have anything specific as an example?" Cochrane said, "If I may?" And he got up and took down a chart that was pinned to the wall and brought it to the low table at which they sat. Sandra had reminded him how important the Philippines were to MacArthur. "Sir, if you were to establish secure depots here, here and here," pointing to small islets strategically placed on the outer borders of the archipelago, we could include, as part of most if not all of our sub patrols, an operational requirement to pick up, say, medical supplies at these depots and deliver them ashore to our Mamasan coastal positions, here, here and maybe two dozen others. You'd provide the supplies and their storage, we'd put them ashore where they'd do the most good, keeping the Scouts, guerillas and people like Fertig in the fight. Sandy had identified these very islets as some that she knew were already under consideration for use by MacArthur. The proposal was a natural, knowing of his love for the Philippines and his desire to support them. To do so there would have to be intelligence sharing, a critical element of teamwork.

The General smiled and leaned in, "That evening in Manila, at the penthouse, remember it?" "Yessir." He already knew what was coming, had felt it at the time. "That fellow, that Destroyer Skipper of yours and his wife, Lodge, was it?" "Yessir." "He made a very nice speech about my father's Medal of Honor, and." "And it was I who fed it to him, Sir," said Cochrane. MacArthur smiled broadly and in triumph, "But don't you see? I knew and it still worked! The emotions it engendered were real, regardless of the motivation. I respected the use of the information even as I knew the motivation behind it. My question to you, Dick, is can I respect the motivation behind the things you will say as well as the content of your suggestions?"

Here it was, the moment he knew he had to have and it was a make or break moment, for sure. "Sir, I have been deeply concerned that I will have to serve two Bosses who on the surface appear to be so different. Nimitz comes from the Silent Service while you are a creature of great accomplishments that are very well known and come with the glare of publicity. My Navy Boss works quietly whereas you make speeches, speeches such as few have ever heard much less been able to give. You seem diametrically opposed in style yet both are blessed with substance. It is my job to help fashion a partnership between two such different Commanders."

"Dick, you've hit upon it, the essence of the conundrum. I use this gift, if that's what it is, of oratory as a weapon with which to hopefully inspire a nation's people to fight and to believe in our ultimate victory. You will have to get to know me well enough to judge how sincere that effort is. I suppose that by my own actions you will either be convinced or not. We will succeed together or will not." And here he paused for effect, "I approve the sharing of intelligence, all of it. Work with my Staff to identify all of the products on both sides that we have and come up with a plan and embedded procedures for doing the transfers as well as safeguarding the material. I will set my Logistics people to work on the depot and resupply system, starting in the morning."

"Aye, aye Sir." MacArthur said, "And if I understand you, your personality is more like Chet's than mine." And here Cochrane merely nodded. "Dick, I won't worry over for whom you're working, though my Staff will; I'll just know it is for the ultimate victory of our nation against Japan and trust that in spite of my modus operendi you will believe the same of me. How you report that back to your boss is entirely up to you. As I see it our relationship is but a stepping stone to the one between Chet and me.

Douglas' eyes had welled and Dick's had, too. It would have been more convincing if Sandra hadn't predicted it last night…

Sandy was waiting outside Flag Officer Quarters at 1600 and he hopped in her car. "How'd it go?" "Time will tell. It took my breath away to see how prepared he was and how quickly he could come up to speed and make a decision." "You're no slouch in that department yourself, Dear. Dinner out or at my place?" and she looked at him with a leer and they both broke out laughing. They were comfortable, they were excited and they were totally in love. They dined in, again.

In the weeks and months they settled into a routine; weekends were spent away from everybody, usually at a beach or in the mountains. Dick usually slept over at Sandy's cottage and he continually fed her reports of the day's events at Headquarters and she would offer her insight as to how Staff dynamics had influenced the response he'd received and they would come up with a different approach. She was the reason he didn't get bogged down in Staff politics. Macarthur took to inviting Cochrane into his Quarters for lunch, about once a week, figuring if Nimitz could do it and profit, so might he. During these times MacArthur would admit that his admiration for Sandy was for her insight and not so much for her other accomplishments. "I think she knows my Staff better than I," he said "and I swear sometimes I don't know with whom I'm talking, you or her," and he'd laugh but it was because he knew that he'd just scored another point. He liked surprising Cochrane. Because if anybody had a better intelligence network than Dame Sandra it was El Supremo; he had always made it his job to know all there was to know

"You know, Nimitz was at that game all those years ago and he suggested to me that I use it to get into your good graces." MacArthur laughed, "And then it was I who beat you to the punch!" "We've certainly gotten beyond those games." Cochrane thought it and MacArthur said it. "Did you know that it was FDR who gave me my job as CincAsiaticFlt? He told me my job was to gather Intel and that I'd be lucky if I survived the assignment, once the Japs started things up And, of course it was my Classmate, Chet Nimitz who saved my butt after I lost my Fleet in the early months of the war." "That was an impossible situation, Dick, and Nimitz was wise to bring you on board. You know, back in DC they are again deciding how to split up the baby, between me and Nimitz, between the Army and the Navy. It's probably going to be something we'll do in order to get ready to attack the Japanese homeland. While I think we'd be better off with one Commander overall, it may be that it's simply too big and too complex to do it that way." "Sir, it's a few steps above my paygrade, and the first I've heard of it." "Ahh," he laughed, you mean FDR didn't consult with you? Roosevelt understands strategy, unlike the haberdasher from Missouri," MacArthur replied. "The word is that The President fancies Harry Truman for his next Vice. He was an artillery Captain in the last war, so that should count for something," and he sniffed. "He seems to run through them with little care, Garner, Wallace and now, it seems, this fellow Truman. And that's how many of their lunches would end, with an informal joke or a laugh. MacArthur knew he was going to miss this Naval Officer when he went back to Pearl and it wouldn't be too long before it would happen.

On their next to last time together he sked Cochrane, "You going to make an honest woman out of her before you go? And take her when you leave?" "Sir, we've been talking about it and that's the plan." "I support that and I'll lay on a flight to get you both there." The tears that didn't quite fall were there again, again both men. Real, for both men.

That night in Dame Sandra's cottage at the Governor's Residence, Sandra, with her back to Cochrane, spooned from behind and a very nice behind it was. Their breathing had slowed though his hands were still busy. She put her hand on his and stopped him. "Dear?" she made her voice sound sleepy but her eyes were wide open. "Mmmhmm?" "Have you figured out how this is going to work?" while she backed into him even closer, reaching for his reaction. His smile was as secret as her look. He rolled her over so that they were facing each other, hair mussed, the scent of their lovemaking warm and rising between them. He reached in and kissed her tenderly on the mouth and now she had to restrain her own hands. "Yes, my dearest. I will be the Captain of our wee ship and as you know there can be but one Captain." Saying nothing for once she just nodded, her head against his chest. "In matters of professional excellence you lead; there is no one better able to keep me out of trouble, to keep our ship off the shoals." Tears started their way down her cheek and he felt them on his chest. "The reason I probably never got married was because the Navy came first with me and all of them knew that and didn't want to be in second place. There's still a war to win and it has priority for both of us but you will not have to be concerned about where my loyalties lie. I think that probably covers it except for one more question, darling, Will you *please* marry me and make my happiness complete?"

Her answer was a growling "Sharrrr, you know I will." They celebrated their new status until they were both sweaty and exhausted and asleep with faint smiles on their faces. MacArthur was true to his word, he not only set them up with air transport back to Pearl but he hosted an intimate party of some five hundred after the wedding, rented a whole hotel to do it. Though MacArthur was sad to see them go, not so his Staff. Ahh well, there was still this war to win with the Japanese, the one with the Navy was over.

CHAPTER 48

THE WHITE ANGEL

Upon her arrival at Dantes' place in Baguio, having escaped from Corregidor, Rosario and Rosa took her immediately to the underground hideaway to rest up. Rosario stayed with her and over the time of two days briefed her on their situation. Gunny stayed in camp for a day and then moved out to join a small group of guerillas that operated in the area.

"How are you feeling, Lydia," Rosario asked," recovered your energy?" "Much better, Rosario. I'll probably be sore for awhile is all." "There are naturally some precautions we must take, for our own safety. For your information I was engaged by Chief Locker, on behalf of your husband to form a network here in the Philippines. It has been running, now, for about a year and a half. We are an intelligence gathering organization, using persons who are known to me personally. We have radios in many parts of the P.I. and had been communicating fairly frequently until the Japanese attacked, three, almost four months ago. Gunny Clancy knew of the network, "Mamasan" and used it to contact us here and arrange for your escape. That must have been a frightful experience for you," looking concernedly at her friend.

"I think it must be dangerous for you to keep me here." "We are all in some danger, though we have set up a warning system which is working so far. Of course you are more than welcome and we are in great need of your medical expertise. If we are caught it will mean execution by the Japanese, perhaps after they interrogate us. We are considered enemy combatants and spies and part of the resistance and there are several organizations out there looking for us. Regarding news, most of what we get is Japanese propaganda with questionable 'news' mixed in. We hear of their victories, of course. The last instructions to the network, Mamasan, were that we are not to transmit but are expected to do our best to be available to receive instruction or information and we have a schedule of certain days of the week as well as time periods during which we are to listen for messages or instructions." Lydia nodded and Rosario could tell that there was something she wanted to say. "Tell me, Lydia, have you heard from your husband, Captain Lodge, or were you able to get any sort of word to him about your situation?"

"Thank you for asking, and yes, I did send a message to his ship when I went to Corregidor but nothing since and I have not heard anything back from him. He does not know I'm here or whether I am dead or alive." "None of the propaganda from the Japanese has mentioned his ship, the USS Ford, so I suppose that that is good news." Rosario replied. "You know it could be a very long time before this is over; we must take the long view and do all we can not to come to the notice of the Japs. At the same time we must continue to grow our own food and trade amongst ourselves for the things we need but cannot provide for ourselves." "Rosario, thank you for taking me in and giving me a chance to join the fight. I believe that we will ultimately defeat them and probably within two or three years."

On his next visit to Mamasan headquarters Gunny Clancy brought news of some badly wounded resistance fighters who were in hiding within a day's march. Lydia immediately volunteered to treat them. The decision was made not to try to bring them to Mamasan but instead to see what could be done for them in the field. Lydia had already inventoried her supplies and had a kit packed for just such an emergency. It was agreed and the next morning she and Gunny pushed off headed south. They used a Mamasan equivalent of an underground railway, known paths not frequented by much traffic and out-posts to keep them informed of what they were headed into. A one day trip took two days but the wounded fighters were still alive when they got there. Using a practical approach she assessed all four of the fighters and undertook to treat the least endangered one first and then the others. If the worst of the lot died before his turn, then so be it. What was important was to get men back into the fight.

Indeed the last of the lot had an infected arm which needed to be amputat-ed. She looked at the Gunny, "I'm trained as an operating room nurse but I'm not a Doctor, myself. I've assisted in many surgeries but have never done one; the very thought in normal times would be preposterous." "Yes Ma'am." Lydia looked at him, "But I'm the only one available, right?" "Yes Ma'am. Either you operate on him or he dies." She nodded and requested they find something with which to deaden his pain, some foul smelling homebrew was the best they could come up with. Gunny and two others held the patient and got him semi-drunk while Lydia requested a bolo knife and it had to be a sharp one. Then they started a small charcoal fire to cleanse the blade, it was the best they could do. In her kit she had rubber tubing with which to fashion a tourniquet, bandages, Merthiolate and mercurochrome and some hydrogen peroxide; what she didn't find there was the confidence or experience of a surgeon.

Her thought as she washed her hands and pulled on a pair of gloves was, *God please help me, use me to do your work of healing.* Before she started she asked, "What is this man's name?" "Jose, Ma'am, Jose Aguinaldo." She nodded and began. A bit of sponge collected the initial spurt and compresses slowed the bleeding. It would have been much, much easier with a saw but the bone was not particularly large and she straightened her arms and pressed down to break and sever the arm, using pressure as well as a bit of a sawing motion. With tweezers that had also been through the fire she picked out the fragments, then trimmed the flap and sewed it into place. Looking up from her work she saw the men gathered around her, in addition to the ones still holding her unconscious patient down. They were looking at her with respect, she heard the word, "angel" and they called her Doctor as they left shortly after. It did not pay to stay too long in one place.

One day, not too long afterward a package arrived at Mamasan "for the Doctor." It was a bolo which had been filed into a saw with three different sizes of teeth: fine separation, medium and larger still. The whole instrument shone of polished steel and there was a handle at either end. It was her pay and her thanks. A note said simply, "Jose lives." Months passed and she got better and better at her diagnoses and ability to treat injuries and wounds, though she mightily wished for more disinfectants. She sent out a call through couriers to Manila with lists of medicines she needed. After a week several of the items on her list came to Mamasan. Patriots had broken into pharmacies and stolen the items. Along with the potions, powders and salves came a note that they had taken the entire stock of medicines and hidden them, would have more when she called for them.

Yet, even these stocks dwindled or spoiled and one day Lydia asked Mamasan if it might be possible to communicate with any allies to seek more medications. A council was held amongst the network by Rosario and it was decided to set up a transmitting station on a relatively tall peak. They had a bicycle powered generator and transmitter along with a Morse code key and wire for an antenna to be strung in the trees. After about a month of periodic trials they did raise a Coast watcher who said he would pass their request along and they also set up a listening schedule for any reply.

None of these activities was without risk, both personal and deadly. Japanese occupiers in Manila had tracked down some of those who had worked to steal the drugs and some of those divulged information under torture, others went to their deaths under torture without talking. Yet still there were volunteers who were vetted and used in the resistance to pass messages, provide escort and move material from place to place. Then one day there was an unusual communication. It came with a practiced fist on the radio system and swiftly set up a rendezvous on the coast. A submarine would be bringing medical supplies ashore there during the new moon and at high tide. An offer to embark any downed fliers or others stranded from the fight was also made. This set a buzz going. It was new and the first serious contact with an Allied fighting force. The information had to be kept closely and it was exciting. Names were not used, never were, for security reasons, but this seemed to start a more hopeful phase of the resistance for those working in the Mama-san network.

A year passed quickly as she adapted to her new environment and her responsibilities. Everyone was hungry and horses disappeared as they were eaten, crops such as the long skinny green beans and taro root were stored in the root cellar or saved for their seeds. Lydia lost weight and was gaunt and tired with her cheekbones and hip bones prominent. He skin grew deeply tanned and her menstruation periods stopped. She no longer felt like a woman but instead saw herself as a guerrilla, with one exception. She would not kill. When questioned about it by Rosario who had no such compunctions she said that she was still a woman and the job of a women was to give life. She was still a medical practitioner and the job of nurses and doctors was to preserve life. She would leave the taking of it to the others, the warriors.

Rosario had seen the cruelty of the Japanese and thought that they needed killing. She saw their occupation as an enormous affront to Filipine dignity and was ever on guard to kill before being killed, herself. She worried that Lydia's refusal to carry a weapon would someday bring them to a hard situation and she always had an armed bodyguard assigned to accompany Lydia. Unknown by Lydia were Rosario's instructions to the bodyguard in the event of extremis, or the likelihood of capture and torture. The situation was not made any easier by Lydia's apparent unconcern for her own welfare.

One night in the sleeping pallet they shared, Gunny, who had been watching this situation develop over the months, said to Rosario, "I don't think I like the way you look at her." Rosario said, "Lydia?" "Yes." "I don't like the way *you* look at her sometimes, either." He smiled in the darkness, "You know I don't look at her that way." "Well, you had better keep it that way, too," and she jabbed him hard in the ribs. Still a few days later it was Gunny who became the more or less constantly assigned muscle and armed guide for Lydia. He tried to bring up the matter of weapons, said he had a small pistol that would be just her size, he could teach her how to use it and. And she always cut him off, finally in exasperation showed him a capsule and knowingly hinted that she would know when and if to use it. When he told Rosario his lover that, she stopped her worrying about the situation. And Gunny started. She was very, very good in the field and she was also an ongoing concern.

Stories kept filtering into camp of Japanese atrocities. They had no effect on Lydia, she just kept on making her rounds, doing the job on short notice and little food. Gunny thought about it and mentioned it to Rosario. "The Doc is taking more and more chances," he said. "I noticed," Rosario answered. "It's all she thinks about, these "boys" of hers; she's totally devoted to them." "Yes, and she talks in her sleep about it, too. She may not be a killer but she has a pretty deadly or dead look in her eye," Rosario mused. Lydia, after two years and still alive had a nom de guerre. The native fighters called her the white angel. It was not good to get a name like that, a name of any sort. With a name to start with the Japs could attach other bits of information and come up with a pretty good description, making a target out of the "White Angel."

Rosario received a request for some intelligence on a camp at Cabanatuan. It was a POW camp within a two or three day march. The Allies believed that those who had survived the Bataan Death March were being held there. They wanted an intelligence estimate, wanted to know roughly how many prisoners were being kept there and anything that could be learned about the condition of the prisoners. Rosario and Gunny decided to undertake the mission, themselves, with a small armed escort. Learning of their plans, Lydia asked to go. Rosario demurred until Gunny reminded her that Lydia had become his charge. The fact that she could give a medical assessment if the opportunity arose was the clincher. In the event they made their way to the settlement and sent in a teenaged boy to act as a local. He was to beg for food from the locals and in the process find out what he could. He knew it was a very dangerous assignment; they all did. They were close enough to the camp to smell it, as they were also downwind from the huts and open sewer pits. Lydia watched the men moving from maybe half a mile away and was moved, herself. They could just barely make it out when someone fell and was beaten. It was like watching an old time silent movie, with the subtitles provided by the watchers; no sound but a horror movie with fuzzy, out of focus violence played in pantomime to the background of buzzing insects and shimmering heat waves.

The boy returned and he had stories of summary executions and beheadings, an almost daily ritual of shoving bodies into lime pits. They counted the huts and crosschecked with the information brought by Jesus and arrived at a number of somewhere between 800 and 1200 prisoners, but dying fast. New arrivals, mostly Filipinos would be trucked in from time to time to serve as Camp workers. That slowed the attrition rate some but it was obvious that the camp at Cabanatuan was a dead end. Gunny stole a look at Lydia, she was not emotional but there was a soft look in her eyes for the prisoners. "I think you actually want to go down there," he said. "Some of my boys are in that hell hole, I need to be with them," she replied. They made their way back to the Estancia by a circuitous route, doing Mamasan business at every stop, and again Lydia was mentioned, pointed out in place after place as the white angel. Gunny could see nothing good coming out of such notoriety and he worried about how it would end.

CHAPTER 49

NORTH SEA OPERATIONS

August 1942 saw Elly Mae escorting a cargo of army P-40 aircraft to Africa. This became standard duty until D-day landings at Casablanca when Ellyson screened the carriers. On his daughter Loraine's first birthday Hod and the Elly Mae pulled into Naval Station Argentia, Newfoundland for a period of operations with the Royal Navy. With a Squad Dog aboard Ellyson as well as a new Skipper they patrolled the coast of Newfoundland and then joined up with the South Dakota for duty with the British Home Fleet. They joined with battleships shepherding convoys from Archangel to Murmansk in foul weather and fair, always on the lookout for the German U Boats. Between convoys they were anchored in protected anchorages, one of which was located at Scapa Flow, the Orkney Islands off the coast of Scotland. Scapa Flow was a vast area of relatively shallow water enclosed by the mainland of Scotland as well as the Orkneys. In these protected waters with the submarine nets up and patrol craft tending the nets they were relatively safe and there was time and opportunity to get to know the Brits, also resting up for the next patrol or escorting duty.

Knock, knock on the door to Chiefs Quarters and the Messenger from the signal bridge stepped in and immediately looked for Chief Dantes. Finding him playing a game of acey deucey at a table with the board pattern painted onto the surface, he waited until the Chief had rattled and thrown his dice. Acey Deucey! Hod called out with a satisfied smile as the Chief Boatswain pulled a long face and grumbled under his breath. "Ain't never seen anyone with your luck, Chief!" Dantes rapidly made his moves, filling in a block that prevented most of Boats' checker pieces from moving and paused before rolling again to look up at the Messenger. He handed Dantes a message slip made out by the signalman, "If you think you'd like a rematch in darts you're invited over to HMS Active. John Shands sends." Hod looked up and the Messenger said, "They contacted us asking if anybody named Dantes was aboard. After a few flashing light messages we got this one which the Signalman wrote down for you, Chief." Hod looked at his watch, thought for a second and said, "Tell them I'm coming for chow, about 1700." Then he dropped by the Gun Boss' rack in the JO's area, knocked and the Lieutenant looked up, then sat up asking, "What's up, Chief?" "Sir, I have an invitation to visit HMS Active, a Royal Navy tin can here in the anchorage. With your permission I'll catch a ride over there in the motor whaleboat, be back by 2400." "Pergra, Chief. Somebody you know, huh?" "Yessir, we met in Sydney after I'd had some dart lessons in Kowloon. I think he wants some revenge for Sydney, Sir." The Lieutenant looked up at him in some admiration, these Chiefs seem to know someone in every port!

Hod caught a ride in the MWB and as they pulled alongside the Jacob's ladder Chief Shands called down to the Cox'n, "Shove off, we'll get him back aboard Ellyson!" Hod scampered up and over the side and was well and fairly greeted by Shands along with a couple of the other Chiefs. They repaired to Chiefs Quarters and inside he was introduced as that Yank I was telling you about, Hod Dantes from Texas and one hell of a lucky darts player. Hod didn't rise to the bait and was given the razzberries by Shands' shipmates as he sat down to a huge mug of rum. Hod looked up at John, head cocked, "What, you want to get me drunk before we play?" Shands laughed along with half of his messmates. "Nah, you don't have to play for your drinks or your chow. You're our guest, Mate. We've saved up from our grog rations for just such an occasion as this. So you just relax and we'll see who can tell the biggest lies." Dantes gave a lazy grin and opened his duffle to pull out a large tub of vanilla ice cream. "That being the case, I thought we could do with a bit of ice cream." He was given three cheers and that started a rollicking evening of drinking and sea stories.

They got him back aboard with drunken company in Active's Captain's Gig, standing by at the foot of the ladder up to the quarterdeck, in case he fell. The Chief saluted, got permission to come aboard and careened down the passageway, bumping and banging from side to side until he found the door to the goat locker in the garish red light of the battle lanterns and went inside. He relieved himself in the head and crashed in his bunk, jostling two other Chiefs in their bunks climbing up to the one with his name on it. He giggled to himself, those limeys know how to drink! And had just enough time to think that he really ought to write to Haze soon when he was asleep. Even faster than that night in Manila. What about that night in Manila? Something happened in Manila. Ahhh yes and he had started to dream and it was Rosa and there she was in her nighty but not for long. And the rats, rats she said that were making a racket in the rafters. And soon they were making noises down below and the rats were not heard anymore. The rats…

Duties for the ship varied and never got boring. For one thing there was the constant threat of U Boat attacks. Mixed in with the convoy duty were attempts to lure the Tirpitz and other major German units from their Baltic ports. On 7 July, Elly Mae left Scapa Flow to participate in a mock invasion of southern Norway as a diversion from the invasion of Sicily. Hod grew to appreciate the size of the Detroit and the Brooklyn. Often there were passages with terrible Atlantic storms. Freezing storms. Times when Ellyson's bow and superstructure were submerged under near-freezing "green water" and had to struggle to get back to the surface. At times the bow would hold high out of the water on a mountainous swell and shake from side to side like a dog yanking on a line at play. Then she would plow low again, decks awash and no one allowed topside on main deck lest he be washed overboard. To fall overboard in weather like this could mean death by freezing before the ship could circle back and make an attempt to pick you up. That's if she made the attempt at all, it being by no means certain that the ship could make it through a trough with seas of this size on her beam instead of her bow without turning turtle. Headed back to Iceland the ship collided with an ice floe that slashed a four foot by twenty foot hole in her bow during a sham battle between the forces of the "Blues" and the "Reds." Repairs by Navy Seabees at Hvalfjord fitted the ship for sea again. It was the ship's excellent Damage Control teams that limited flooding and enabled the ship to proceed to port for permanent repairs, another instance of the Ellyson making her own "luck."

Hod was accepted by the crew aboard Ellyson without a fuss, it was a little more complicated getting to know his shipmates, as this was the first time he was on a first name basis with Chief Petty Officers. For instance there was the Chief Bos'n, Joe "Knucks" O'Reilly. Knucks had the moniker because of his predilection for handling every problem physically. When they were introduced it was as Hod Dantes and Knucks O'Reilly. Knucks just matter of factly said, "Call me Knucks, Chief." It was only two days later when Hod had his first demonstration. In Chief's Quarters and it was late but several Chiefs were up when the messenger from the bridge came in looking for the Bos'n. Knucks looked up, "What's up?" "Chief, they are having trouble getting Hanson to come up on watch to the bridge." Knucks looked at his watch, it was close to midnight and Hanson should have already been up there early and getting briefed and assuming the watch. "He's already punched out another messenger who was waking him up to go topside."

Knucks gave a bored and somewhat tired sigh, "That miserable SOB." And he got up from the table and went straight to First Division's berthing compartment, slamming the watertight door on his way in. He went over to Hanson's bunk and called his name. Hanson answered with a fist thrown in the direction of the voice interrupting his sleep whereupon Knucks uncorked a flurry of short powerful shots to Hanson's head, mouth and nose. He then hauled him bodily out of his rack and stood him up while his head cleared. "Get your uniform on and do it quickly, Hanson," he said almost sweetly. Hanson shook his head to clear it and soaked up some of his own blood in his towel, hanging from his rack. The Chief stood patiently waiting, "I don't expect to see a liberty chit from you for about a month or two." Hanson nodded. "Now get your ass up there on the bridge and I don't want to hear any stories about this and I don't want a repeat of this either. Got it?" Hanson mumbled something in return. Boats grabbed him by the stacking swivel and put his face in Hanson's. "I said, got it?" "Yes Chief." Boats escorted Hanson topside to his watch station, watched as he relieved and then went back to the Goat Locker. The Chief Radioman looked up and asked, "Problem, Boats?" "Nah, you know how these young sailors are, no respect for their shipmates and lazy about standing their watches. He'll be just fine, no problem."

Hod's relationship with Knucks was easy and mutually respectful. Knucks caught the glint in Hod's eye and the way he carried himself along with his large biceps from years of throwing around six inch shells. For Hod's part, he just took life as it came, genuinely interested in everyone and everything and fearing nothing. Boats was covered in tattoos and Hod had none. Neither remarked to the other about this, but the next time there was liberty it was Knucks who looked up Hod and took him in tow to go on the beach together. It was absolutely certain that nobody in the bars that they would frequent would want to tangle with either one of them. Knucks liked Hod's slight Texas drawl and Hod liked Boats' scowl. And his sea stories. Knucks had them by the hundreds but he liked to hear about life down on the farm and rats in the rafters in 'Po City. There was cachet in having been a China Fleet sailor for a Med sailor, and Boats was a veritable fount of knowledge of all the liberty ports in this neck of the woods. They became fast buddies.

Before long the Radioman Chief started joining them in card games and at the Ace Deuce table. Of course he went by Sparks or "Tiny." Tiny was about six foot six and as mild mannered as they came and somewhat of an intellectual. He'd read most of the classics and had some aboard ship. He also had the most up to date scuttlebutt as he read all of the traffic that came aboard in Radio Central. Three more different men you could not imagine and yet they fit together seamlessly. Interestingly the leader of the trio was Hod largely due to the fact that he spoke softly and never raised his voice, which caused the others to quiet down to hear what he had to say. About him it was said, he might not always be right but he was never wrong. The Ellyson was all about attacking with her torpedoes and guns and that was another name the Chiefs had for Dantes, "Guns." On a lethal war machine Hod was at the epicenter of what she was all about. He was tapped as Chief Master of Arms within six months of reporting aboard and the whole ship looked up to him and sought him out when they had any sort of problem, before it went official. In a sense he was the XO's right hand man and the lock between them was absolute. You could see it in the way they stood together, laughed together. Ellyson was a happy ship and one of the reasons was the respectful and accurate flow of information between the XO and his CMOA. The XO protected the Old Man and the CMOA protected the crew. Hod had never had to say it to an Officer but his credo was that the Officer gave the orders and the crew carried them out and Hod personally felt delinquent if he actually had to receive an order for a situation he should have already handled.

The night before Ellyson was due to get underway, headed out on an operation that would likely see her no more at Scapa Flow, Shands and his bunch had Hod over for one last visit. They picked him up, no ice cream this time, and they played darts and drank into the wee hours of the morning, Hod finally falling asleep at the table. They woke him with a start, "C'mon Mate, yer ship is already underway." They sent a flashing light asking for you." Hod leaped up and headed straight for the Jacob's ladder and waiting at the bottom was the Active's Captain's Gig. The Old Man himself shook Hod's hand and gave him a "Godspeed," and then he was in the gig, standing and looking anxiously out to sea to see if he could spot Ellyson. They had gotten underway but he thought he saw her and pointed. The Cox'n had the gig going flat out and nudged her over to track the fantail of the ship Hod showed him. On the signal bridge of Active one signalman was talking to another on board Ellyson by flashing light. He let him know that their Chief was enroute in the gig. The Skipper received the message in his chair on the starboard side of the pilothouse with a grin. "Tell them thanks, Ellyson sends. See you in the next port."

Hod didn't know for sure it was the Elly Mae and he didn't know they were in contact, he only knew that he was the CMOA and he was AWOL unless he got back aboard before she got into heavy water. It was a sheepish Chief Dantes who at last and just barely got aboard ship before she rung up twenty knots, and a relieved one who was razzed in the Goat Locker for the rest of the day. He didn't know that the Skipper had held the speed down but not so slow that it would be easy for him to make it. He and the XO finally stood watching from the wing of the bridge as he came aboard, looking up at them.

They both laughed and waved him aboard. Hod shook his head, gave the Coast Guard salute, arms spread, palms up and shoulders shrugged in apology, then saluted the two of them, long distance. It was returned and his last liberty at Scapa Flow was never mentioned. He did keep his job as CMOA and finally was able to laugh about it when he wrote home to Haze and told her the story.

Hod didn't get off totally free, however. Within a week the Chiefs got around to holding a Kangaroo Court. It was right after noon meal and all the Chiefs were there and by special invitation the Captain and the XO. Hod was seated rather roughly in the witness chair while Knucks read the charges:

```
To wit:
1. One Chief Gunner's Mate Hod Dantes had been noted ab-
   sent from Quarters without permission.
2. Subject Chief Petty Officer has missed a ship's move-
   ment, was AWOL from his duty station when the ship got
   underway.
3. When discovered, trying to sneak aboard ship he was
   observed out of uniform, failing to set the example
   for the Crew.
4. Failure to request permission to come aboard.
5. Compounded by a sloppy Coast Guard salute when he did
   come aboard.
```

The charges read, the President of the Court, Tiny stood and said, "We don't need to know how you plea, Chief." Turning to the Jury he raised his voice, "Verdict?" "Guilty came the roar back from the rest of the Chiefs, with the CO and XO laughing. Whereupon Tiny pronounced the sentence, "The next liberty ashore the prisoner will pay the penalty of a round or three for his ship mates, gathered here! Does the guilty party have anything to say?"

Dantes rose with a rueful look on his face and a barely covered smile. "I thank the Court for its indulgence," he said. Drinks on me the next time ashore." They all roared in laughter and affection and everybody crowded around to slap him on the back, including the Co and his sidekick, the XO.

CHAPTER 50

ATLANTIC OPERATIONS

After her time at anchorage in Scapa Flow, a welcome time of respite, Elly Mae got underway with the Squadron Commander aboard, as always. The ship worked in concert when she could with the other Destroyers of her Division and Squadron. It was an advantageous element in their operations, they could operate as a task element, or independently, although with the Squadron Commander aboard it was less likely that she would be steaming independently. Like the frigates of old, Destroyers ranged far and wide, generally looking for trouble but fast enough to break off contact if the opposition was too powerful. Ellyson was equipped to hunt and destroy submarines, shoot down attacking aircraft, conduct shore bombardment and rain fire and torpedoes on enemy shipping. She was thin skinned and vulnerable to fire from, say, cruisers and battleships but given enough warning she could turn tail and outrun her pursuers while leaving a smoke screen behind.

Life at sea was inherently dangerous and destroyers were among the denizens of the sea that made it that way. There was a saying that constant vigilance was the price of good navigation; the crews of most ships felt that way about pure survival. To a man, if they thought about it at all, they knew that their very lives depended upon that constant vigilance. Care in avoiding disastrous weather or knowing how to steam in it when it caught you and smooth professionalism in carrying out simple skills like loading and firing the ship's weapons were what was going to keep you alive, to tell your sea stories in foreign ports, and when you got home again. In Chief Dantes' case it was a wholly different frame of mind.

He believed in excellence and being the best; at everything, whether it was a game of acey deucey, or racing in a whaleboat or winning a game of darts. As for life expectancy he figured he had already beaten the odds in that department when he and his siblings had subdued their father in a fight for a loaded shotgun and their lives. That one experience early in life had given him the attitude that it was all gravy from here on out. He felt like he was already into overtime in the game of life and he intended to live it to the fullest and that included, to some extent, at least until he got married, the enjoyment of women. He attracted women. They couldn't help themselves. He was good looking, smart as a whip and genuinely adored women, starting with his own grandmother who had raised him after his mother died when Hod was only five.

Coupled with his own feelings of a certain invincibility was an implacable and resolute readiness to destroy the enemy. If anyone understood kill or be killed, Hod did. He didn't hate, but he was constituted to act quickly and without hesitation. After a life on the farm in Texas he found life aboard ship to be relatively easy. The hardships were easier than back home during the depression. Hod felt lucky to be alive, lucky to be in the Navy and definitely excited to be aboard a ship that was also called "Lucky." And, as you'd expect, a leader who was called Chief and "Guns" had a mighty influence aboard ship. His mates felt they were part of a very special crew and the Chief, "Guns" was a big part of that.

On 9 August 1943 Ellyson returned to Norfolk, Virginia and screened USS Iowa (BB-61) during her shakedown cruise off Argentia, Newfoundland, returning to Norfolk in late October, then sailed in the scouting line for Iowa, carrying FDR to the Teheran Conference. She returned in Iowa's screen touching port at Bahia, Freetown, Dakar and Port Royal, SC then returning to Boston on 19 December. After a rare and much appreciated Christmas at home, on 14 April 1944 Ellyson set sail for Oran, North Africa.

Though Churchill had met personally with both Marshall Stalin and FDR, Roosevelt had never met Stalin. He had traveled 7,000 miles to meet the other two leaders at the Teheran Conference conducted in the Russian Embassy in Iran, a tough trip on an old man not in good health, necessitated by Stalin's unwillingness to fly to the meeting. He was growing frail, his time running out, whereas Stalin was fresh from a massive victory over the Wehrmacht at Kursk and used his power and prestige to bully Roosevelt. The meeting was necessary to order priorities in the global struggle, apportion resources and forces and put in place a rough schedule for the next strategic moves against Germany. Churchill had long favored attacking from the Mediterranean as he knew that the shipping was not available for an attack in northern France. Stalin had been pressing for a "second front" against Germany and complaining that Russia was doing the lion's share of the fighting and dying. Churchill read the situation clearly and finally weighed in, agreeing to a major thrust across the Channel in May.

The meetings were not without their tensions and histrionics. At one point Stalin proposed executing 50,000 to 100,000 German Officers so that Germany would not be able to plan another war. Roosevelt joked, "Don't you think that 49,000 would be enough?" But Churchill theatrically left the meeting, storming out amid a refusal to execute prisoners of an Army fighting for its country. He was indeed outraged. Stalin retrieved him claiming he was only joking. In the event a pattern was repeated that has been honored through time: The rulers set the policy, objectives and strategy, the Officers plan the operations and give the orders and the enlisted sailors, soldiers and airmen carry out these orders at the risk of their lives, hardly aware that a comment made over tea in a Persian Palace caused them to go where they went and do what they had to do.

German U-boat Operations in the Med were not a plum assignment. Admiral Doenitz considered them a waste to the war effort and the fate of his U-Boats was uniformly bad. Once committed to this almost totally landlocked body of water, no German boats ever made it back to the Atlantic; they were either sunk or else scuttled by their own crews. Passage through the British controlled Straits of Gibraltar was dangerous with nine boats sunk in the attempt and ten more having to turn back as a result of damage. Also, living conditions aboard the Type VII boats were terrible. It was hot bunking without a shred of privacy, there were no showers, no laundry, you could not get comfortable or get clean, and in the Med without air conditioning there were electrical failures and foul air caused by diesel fuel, body odors, high CO_2 and high humidity. Fresh food, if you could get it, lasted about two days. The gallows humor was that a Boat might not last as long as the potatoes.

Anti-submarine warfare, or ASW used all of the tools at a crew's disposal that could bear on the enemy submarine or even against our own subs, in practice, although in such practice exercises no weapons were used. In reality, it would become a deadly dance with an unseen partner, each using its instruments and tactics to deceive the other and to destroy the other if possible. The nerve center aboard a destroyer for an ASW attack was the Combat Information Center. There a de'd reckoning tracer was used, an electromechanical device with a glass top and a movable "bug" that moved in space responding to gyro feeds as the ship did its maneuvers. On paper you could see the track of the ship as she circled and thrust across the sub's track or predicted track, with the sub's position coming from sonar and a linking of these estimates of position providing an approximate representation of her track.

Detection devices had their advantages and their limitations. The energy packets used to fix the position of a contact in the air or under the sea were wide in shape, which fuzzied up the bearing of the contact, but the frequency of the transmission of either radar or sonar, with time hacks, provided very precise measurements of distance to the target, albeit not the best directional feedback. In a dance to the death you took whatever advantage you could get. Also the information aged quickly in a dynamic situation that involved a maneuvering ship and contact. What you saw on the trace was where they were at the time the measurement was made. Knowing where they were at the time you released a weapon required sound tactics, some educated guesswork and a bit of luck.

In one on one battles the advantage, at least initially, went to the submarine. But the U.S. didn't go one on one if there were additional assets available. Aircraft patrolled the sub cruising areas and the vicinities of Allied convoys to see if they could catch a sub on the surface or else see its shape at a relatively shallow depth. When aircraft spotted a sub they would immediately communicate with US Hunter Killer, or HUK Groups and steer them in on the location and give them last known course and estimated speed.

On 14 May a British Coastal Command aircraft spotted a German sub, U-616, on the surface. She was an experienced boat on her ninth patrol under command of Skipper Seigfried Koitschka. The call immediately went out to the Ellyson and her Squadron mates, Hambleton, Emmons and Rodman and they got underway from Mers el Kebir making flank speed. Ellyson made the first sonar contact and immediately attacked with a depth charge pattern, after which sonar contact was lost due to the disturbing effect of the explosions and the concomitant bubbles thereby created. A night long box pattern was conducted by all four destroyers including a sweep by Ellyson along the Spanish coast. All they had to show for their efforts on the morning of the 15th was a ten mile oil slick.

In the Ellyson's Combat Information Center, the Captain was discussing their options. "XO, with night having fallen the Krauts will be tempted to operate on the surface, where they can make better speed and charge their batteries." "Yessir, although they will be concerned about being spotted by the Brit's coastal command aircraft." "True, that might force them to snorkel depth so they can reduce their radar cross section, but the seas we're feeling right now will make it tough for them to make any kind of speed, and difficult to control the boat itself." "Sir, did you see the reports of an oil slick?" "Yes, I caught that." "They can't be happy about that as it is yet another possible hampering of their operations." "Agreed, I'll check with the Commodore, going to recommend we set a trap for them, on the basis that they may try for Toulon; They can't make much speed, have to spend more time on the surface than is healthy for them and are likely running low on fuel and out of options."

At that moment in the attack center of U-616 the Captain and his Number two were assessing the state of the crew. The Skipper choked back the nagging cough he had been having, looked with bloodshot eyes at his Exec who reported that the O^2 levels were getting worse, the men were complaining of headaches from the CO^2. "Ya, but how are they holding up, do you think?" "It took us a lot of time to get the jury rig on the fuel line, as close to the tank as the break was, and the fuel level has risen above the deck plates. It's slow but still rising. Losing a bit more of his stoic composure, the Skipper replied, "But Hans, that's the condition of the Boat. I asked for an assessment of the crew." "Sorry, Captain. The senior enlisted are holding up, but the new guys we took on board last time in port are looking very scared. A couple of them were crying and shouting and so I had them sedated. No one is optimistic, Sir, or thinking about anything but survival. I see a lot of wide eyes and scared faces, Sir. It would help if we could just pop up and get some fresh air for awhile. The batteries need charging and the men could take turns on the bridge as lookouts."

It was a close decision, knowing when to risk the boat to improve the lot of the crew and yet knowing that the deteriorating crew, themselves, were an increasing threat to the boat and were fast approaching the point where they might not function well if there was another attack. It was becoming emotional and that was dangerous aboard the Boat; the Skipper knew that. "Very well, periscope depth and then if it's clear we'll run on the surface for a while. Get your best position and we'll set course for Toulon."

The Commodore called in four more destroyers and coordinated a radar search. During the night the sub had deployed decoy balloons to confuse just such a search and yet gunfire was exchanged between U-616 on the surface and USS Nields when the sub dived and suffered additional depth charge attacks. Again contact was lost until just before midnight when another British Coastal Command aircraft spotted U-616 some 40 to 50 miles distant, seemingly headed for Toulon. All ships headed for the last known position of the sub when at 0645 Hambleton made sonar contact, ten miles away from the position of the sub's last dive.

Aboard U-616, the tension was palpable. Driven below again they were listening to their pursuers probing for them and almost like a blind man tapping with his cane in the endless darkness they tried to stay silent while maneuvering at all times to increase the distance between themselves and the destroyers above them. Their situation was complicated by the casualty they had suffered in the first depth charging from Ellyson a day ago by now. The concussion from a depth charge had broken a diesel fuel line, allowing fuel to flood into the sub's bilges. The Pig Boat had gotten even smellier and the fuel fumes were burning their eyes. They had applied patches to the line and isolated the split as best they could with valving in the system but it had split along its length and fuel continued to flow out of the fuel system, albeit at a reduced rate, as the split had occurred between the fuel tank and the first shut off valve. At depth they were, of course, not running on their air breathing engines, and so not using any of their fuel. They could not run their engines at snorkel depth for the boat had not been fitted with the Dutch invented snorkel system. At the depths required to reduce the likelihood of discovery and to increase the distance between themselves and the depth charges, they were forced to run on the electric propulsion system. Their speed was something less than six knots, not much with which to evade the swift Destroyers above, looking for them. Their options were to fight at depth or to take their chances on the surface. In fact they were running out of options, the remaining ones reduced to hoping to avoid detection and limp away until able to surface again and recharge the batteries. Even that option was offering less and less promise as they continued to leak their diesel fuel.

Skipper to XO, "How many contacts does sonar report?" "Sir, they have varied in number but at this time we count four or more, identified as destroyers." "How much usable fuel left in the fuel tanks?" "Sir, enough for two hours at full speed, longer for battery charging and we're down now to two hours left on the batteries." "And the depth of the fuel, sloshing around in our bilges?" "Sir, the men are wading in it, up to their shins in some places." "Recommendations?" "As the Captain knows, we are being tracked very accurately, with two of the destroyers using their sonar to track us while a third is maneuvering to drop depth charges on us. As best we can tell, and we must assume, the tracking ships are guiding the third ship into position to drop weapons on us."

Noting that the XO had not presumed to advise him, the Skipper gave a wry smile, "Hans, we've done all we can for the boat, now we will do what we can for the crew. Prepare to surface, station the gun crew in the tower, ready to man the gun and commence firing immediately upon surfacing." "Aye, aye Captain." He waited until the XO had made his preparations and then the Skipper called out "Surface, surface surface."

Aboard Ellyson, OOD to the Captain, "Sir, sonar reports sounds from the contact, blowing negative. They appear to be surfacing." "Weapons, Bridge, all gun mounts in local control, Chief Dantes to mount 51, fire when ready on the submarine." The Commodore ordered the remaining ships to spread out from the sub's track, giving a clear field for Ellyson to fire. The Chief entered the mount, donned the phones and took the pointer's seat, the one with the firing key. He got a steer of a bearing and estimated range over the phones and exercised the mount briefly to ensure its responsiveness. Then he waited.

It was plain daylight, easy swells less than two feet. A lookout hollered out, "Submarine one point off the starboard bow." Dantes was already on it. As the sub continued to pop to the surface and the deck gun became visible they could see the crew racing to their positions to take them under fire. Before the 4" gun could be trained in their direction, Hod had already cranked off two rounds in eighteen seconds. The first went short, sending up a geyser, the second went long and before the Germans got off their first shot Ellyson had scored with hits from two mounts and had put the German gun out of commission in addition to holing her in the area of the conning tower. "Cease fire, cease fire," the Skipper called out as an explosion wracked the sub.

The German crew was pouring up out of the boat and going over the side as soon as they got topside. Man overboard was called in preparation for rescuing the men in the water as the Skipper maneuvered to place the fantail toward the swimmers. Chief Dantes had run back to the fantail with a Carbine with the sling loosened and the butt to his shoulder, with the weapon still on safe. The Old Man turned over the deck and the conn to his OOD and went aft to supervise recovery operations. Drawing next to Dantes he said under his breath, "Glad you thought of the carbine, I doubt any of them are armed, Guns." "Agreed, Captain. My weapon is on safe." "I don't know whether we sank them or they set charges, themselves," as the boat sank beneath the surface, going on its last dive, "but good shooting, Chief."

Ellyson recovered 30 of the 46 Officers and crew, with Rodman plucking the rest out of the water. Only one German was wounded, all were saved. Elly Mae had blankets and wrapped each sailor as they brought them aboard. When the German Captain came over the side he drew himself up to attention and looked about until he saw the Captain. They faced each other and the German saluted, Ellyson returned it. They were standing on the fantail discussing the battle, when the Skipper asked him how deep the German boat could dive. The German U- boat skipper said, "Deep enough." He then walked over to the depth charge ramp, patted one and said to the Captain, "These, to what depth will they go?" To which the US Skipper responded, "Deep enough." The Germans were treated well and but for another, unsuccessful U-Boat attack against Ellyson, several hours later, were safe until transferred ashore at Mers el Kebir

Aboard USS Ford, Commander J. Lodge in command, in the Atlantic with USS Guadalcanal (CVE-60), part of a Hunter Killer Task Force. The German subs had a limit to how long they could stay submerged, running on batteries. In general it was about three days before they would be forced to the surface to recharge their batteries. Until aircraft with their vast speed advantage and extended search range began to be used in great numbers the U Boats could surface in daytime with relative impunity. Once the aircraft arrived on the scene in effective numbers the Germans were forced to use the cover of night for their surface operations. In the Med which the Romans had called Mare Nostrum, their sea, there was very little protection for Subs from aircraft because the British Coastal Command were able to conduct night flight operations from their airstrips that had effectively turned the Mare Nostrum into their "lake." However in the Atlantic air operations were mostly restricted to daytime flights as night ops were not yet in use aboard the Navy's carriers. The U.S. had in essence shrunk the Atlantic to an effective size similar to the Med. By carrying their own aircraft with them they could operate much as the shore stationed aircraft could. The Germans figured this out and consequently pretty much stayed submerged in the daytime and conducted surface operations and recharged batteries at night.

Captain Dan Gallery of the Guadalcanal, however, was an innovator. He edged toward nighttime operations by taking weapons systems off of some of his Avengers and replacing them with large fuel tanks. Thus equipped, he could launch at sunset and have his Avengers cruise all night in moonlit conditions with a good chance of surprising the U-Boats on the surface, then recovering his aircraft at sunrise. Through trial and error and using a crashed Avenger attached to a winch cable he was able to train his crew to push a crashed aircraft over the side within four minutes. This is turn meant that he didn't risk losing multiple aircraft when one crashed and fouled his flight deck, hence he was able to step up the pressure on the U-Boat fleet considerably. Knowing that most U-Boat Skippers would rather surface when close to destruction from an attack, scuttle the ship, and attempt to save their crews, Gallery also planned an operation to board such a surfaced sub and capture it before it sank.

Ford, as with all of the accompanying Destroyers, was equipped to detect U-Boats and could attack them with torpedoes, surface gunfire and depth charges. The Avengers were also equipped to drop depth charges and could get to the target faster. The DDs also had the mission of screening and protecting the Carrier. Gallery's Hunter Killer group was a potent force and on a mission with a very imaginative Captain. In fact, shortly before D-Day at Normandy, they did manage to drive U-505 to the surface in a German attempt to save their crew. Gallery ordered USS Pillsbury's Boarding Party to attempt to take command of the slowly circling U-Boat and they found her abandoned, got her under control and removed the crypto gear and signal books to the Guadalcanal. LT (JG) Albert David who commanded the party was decorated with the Congressional Medal of Honor for his exploits, while Gallery got a dressing down from Admiral King and was threatened with a court martial for keeping control of the sub. The Admiral was concerned that the Germans would find out and assume the US had the decoding equipment and other documentation and change their system, essentially blinding the US which had already broken their code. The gathering of intelligence and the protection of means and sources had the highest priority for both sides in the war.

Aboard Ford, the Skipper stayed busy as you might expect, with little time to sleep, much less think about his wife, Lydia. But of course think about her he did and worry he also did. He imagined that if she were alive she would be having some of the same worries about him. Their last communications had occurred just before the battles in the Dutch East Indies, which seemed a very long time ago. Just the one message sent by Lydia to Ford, reporting her shift to the Rock, Corregidor. The news they had about the fate of those survivors was skimpy. Lodge didn't know if she was interned or had been killed. He felt responsible for her predicament and very lonely, half a world away. Even if he could just be stationed in the Pacific he would feel better about it, he thought. Chief Wall Locker, almost a good luck charm, had followed him to Ford and he was acutely aware of the pressure under which his Captain labored. The Chief wished that he could do something to resolve the situation, but had not thought of anything to this point. As the Captain's Chief Radioman he knew which traffic interested the C.O. and had noted that he read all traffic having anything to do with operations in the Philippines. He also knew that although Chiefs had great influence aboard individual ships their influence didn't extend beyond the gangway. To effect change in a situation such as the one in which LCDR Lodge found herself took massive pull, or influence. Indeed if one were even thinking about a rescue operation it would require planning and connections well beyond anything currently aboard Ford or on any single ship commander's staff. Still, the Chief let a few notions roll around in his head, conjuring up a picture in his mind of the information they would need about her situation. He, too, was combing the traffic for any hints or ideas that might bear upon the situation.

CHAPTER 51

OPERATION NEPTUNE

The Ellyson was underway and heading for Portsmouth, England. "This is the Captain speaking. I'm allowed to tell you where we're headed and what we're headed for. The Allied Powers are on the brink of invading across the English Channel. Our troops will be going ashore in France and we will be providing shore bombardment, ASW protection for the heavies as well as being on the lookout for enemy aircraft, mines and artillery fire from the Germans. We'll be in fairly shallow water in hotly contested battle space. We have a reputation for our sharpshooting. I know that every one of you will do your duty. I'm proud of you and of our bit of the USA that is our home, the Elly Mae. Here's where we start pushing the Germans back. Well done and Godspeed. That is all."

Down in Chief's Quarters they heard the mike go CLICK as the Skipper finished his talk to the crew. They were at the table and had stopped whatever they were doing to lend a respectful ear. Conversation picked up again. "Whatcha think, Guns?" It was Knucks looking to his shipmate for a comment. "Sounds like a mighty big operation. Those Germans have had a long time to dig in; not going to be easy to get them to leave." Just then the Messenger from the Bridge knocked and came in, walked over to where Hod was sitting and quietly let him know that the Captain wanted to see him on the Bridge, or more accurately in his Sea Cabin. As Hod got up and replaced his chair, Tiny said, "Looks like the *Skipper* wants to know what Guns thinks, too."

"Come," the Hawk replied to Hod's soft knock. He looked up with a smile and offered his Chief a seat and a mug of hot coffee. Hod was not surprised to see the XO there, with them, nor was he particularly taken aback that the Gun Boss wasn't in attendance. Of course he'd circle back and keep his Boss informed. *Guess there's just not enough room for everybody in this small space,* he mused. Commander Dixon nodded at him, "Guns." Dantes replied, "XO, Skipper," and seated himself. The Skipper took a long pull on his coffee and then said, "Chief this is probably the single biggest event of the war to this point. We'll have so many units involved that it will be difficult to keep from running into each other." Hod nodded his understanding. "With all of the roles we have to be ready to play it's going to be difficult to shift from one to the other in a timely fashion, yet it is that instant recognition and quick action that will carry the day. The XO has an idea that I think I like. I'd like your thoughts on it. XO?"

Now it was Dixon's turn to take a moment. Finally he said, "Not running into anybody will be our job, in Combat and on the Bridge. But I think we need a quarterback to be ready to jump in with an instant decision at the right time. It might be a target that you see, or a mine that we need to take under fire or a mount that has a casualty. We think that man is you. And before you ask about the Gun Boss, don't. For all intents and purposes you will be fulfilling many of his functions and I know this will be uncomfortable. I will tell him about our plans at the appropriate time, as I know you would loyally feel obliged to inform him." "But of course we haven't heard from you yet, Chief," the Hawk interjected.

"Sirs, thank you for your confidence. I have one concern, and it is that if we do this, we do it in a manner that makes it seem like I am only supporting my Boss, the Gunnery Officer." Both Officers in the tiny space looked at each other. "If we don't, we will pretty much ruin a man who still has a chance of pulling through. Are you thinking of a special sound powered circuit, connecting me directly to, for instance, the Bridge and Combat?" "Something like that, Chief," said the Skipper. "It'll mean an additional talker," Hod continued, "and I can see the advantage of using a dedicated line, as the regular circuits can get crowded at just the wrong time."

"We're thinking of stationing you amidships and between the stacks where you can get to any other spot quickly in the event of a casualty to a mount, for instance, and where you might also serve as a lookout for enemy artillery on the beach." And the Hawk eased back in his chair. "Sir, I think we might be able to use the Gun Boss on the Bridge as your talker," Hod said. The Hawk looked triumphantly at his XO and they both grinned. Chief Dantes was a problem solver. "And I'd have some small arms available should we spot a floating mine and be able to take a mount into local if the situation seemed to demand it, might even join the crew operating it." All three were nodding at these thoughts. And of course I'll be checking all mounts out over the next few days" Hawk broke out a set of charts that showed the waters in the vicinity of Pointe Du Hoc, on which all of the designated landing beaches were drawn in. They went over the known positions of artillery, troops and armored vehicles. After about thirty minutes of this, they thanked the Chief and excused him while the CO and his XO went over the operations order yet one more time. In the Goat Locker, there were no questions of 'Guns'. None at all, not even Knucks. He had that look, the one that said, *"Don't ask."*

4 June 1944, Ellyson tied up alongside Augusta which was, in turn, made fast to a mooring buoy in Portsmouth Roads. Ellyson, by virtue of being tied up to the seaward side of the big cruiser was providing protection from torpedoes for her. Another Destroyer was on the other side, all three ships rising and falling together as swells made their way through the anchorage. There were rubberneckers as General Omar Bradley made his way across their deck to board Augusta. She was hosting an emergency meeting of Senior Staff to discuss delaying D-Day to 6 Jun. Indeed the swells tossing these ship gently about were part and parcel of the weather disturbance which was forcing the change in schedule. Some several hours later, after one more review of meteorological data the official word of the new date for D-Day was disseminated.

Lt (JG) Rick Hanson ambled up to the gun tub where the Chief was busy as usual. Chief Dantes looked up, stood up squinting in the sun and gave him a salute. Hanson returned it and said, "There's to be a new wrinkle to GQ during the time we're engaged in the invasion. I'm asked to man the Bridge with the CO, to be his talker on a special circuit." Getting no reply he continued, "The XO said he'd inform you of how this change might affect you," "Aye, Sir. The XO did mention that to me. I think it will be okay, maybe with you up there things will smooth out a bit." "That's what the XO thought, too. Have you talked to the men, explained this change to them?" "No Sir, thought I'd wait and see if you wanted to talk to them first." Hansen looked down, thought for a bit and said, "It'll be fine if you instruct them, Chief, you know better what the XO has in mind." "Aye, aye Sir. Any questions, Sir?" "No, Chief, carry on." For anyone watching from a distance it was a display of perfect respect for a commissioned Officer. Chief Locker had beaten that into Hod, they all deserved their salute and his best manners. Hod made sure to honor the obligation. Some were good and some were not, *just like Chiefs*, Hod thought. As he set up the dedicated circuit with the help of the Electricians he went around to each station and told them that they might be getting orders from him, during live fire operations or at any time during GQ and that there should be no hesitation in carrying them out, none at all, and that other than that they were to maintain strict silence on the circuit except to report an unengaged threat. Finally the night before they were to get underway he reported to the XO that all was ready.

At 0630 on D-Day as the Squadron was making its way to assigned patrolling areas, Corry was attacked by a German battery ashore and took a salvo amidships, below the waterline. The keel was broken and a large tear opened up in the main deck as the engineering spaces, a fire room and an engine room were flooded and put out of commission. The ship cross connected the plant and kept steaming but in circles as their rudder was also jammed. A plane that was to have laid down a smoke screen for them had been shot down by the Germans and then the Corry was attacked. By 0700 she was an abandoned hulk with her superstructure poking above the surface, resting on the bottom in thirty feet of water.

Aboard Ellyson it was a sobering start to the invasion, one of their number already sunk. The whole crew topside could see the evidence. What they didn't know for sure was whether it had been artillery or a mine that had sunk the Corry. Hod was looking, though, and he did spot a mine floating on the surface. He said "mine" into his phone and promptly took it under fire with a .50 caliber machinegun on its swivel and the explosion, some one hundred yards away was noted. By noon, with only occasional fire missions called in on spotted targets well inland, Hod was called to the Bridge.

"Chief we've been informed that our Rangers are pinned down on the beach. Their communications are spotty to non-existent. We've been tasked to send a shore party over there and get targeting information from them. I want you to muster our landing party on the quarterdeck immediately and report back when that's done." "Aye, aye Sir." Ten minutes later Chief was back up on the Bridge. "Who you got in charge, Chief?" "Sir that would be me." Hawk swallowed hard. "No one else to do that job?" "Captain it's my job. I have a chart from the XO that shows the positions of the Rangers and I have looked through the big eyes to confirm where they are. I'm taking a party of five plus a signalman who can use semaphore and we've designated one here on the signal bridge to complete the circuit. Ops has given me two walkie talkies that will come in handy in talking to our boat and maybe the Rangers as well.. We've got BARs and rifles and side arms. I think it's best that I be the one to confirm the targets and their positions. I know how the Director uses information and the mounts as well. I have my First Class, Schwartz with me to keep the party together and make his way back to the ship if I am unable to get back. I noted an LCI alongside and assumed they were our transportation, Sir." The Skipper took all of this in and still hesitated. "Skipper, I thought of taking them some ice cream but I didn't want to piss 'em off." That broke the tension and the Hawk laughed and slapped his best Chief on the back, "We don't want any heroes, on this run, just information. If you think it's not possible to get in there to them it'll be your call, Chief." "Aye, aye Sir, we'll see what we can do and we'll bring back the scoop on these German targets."

In the boat, engine full out, headed into the beach at 1230, Hod and his crew were bunched up forward. They felt the judder as the boat ran aground and then the splash as the ramp went down. They piled out into ankle deep water and started running immediately toward the confirmed nearest position of the Rangers held in reserve. They ran a zig zag pattern and soon came up on the spot where they were dug in, rolling into foxholes and settling themselves. An Army Lt Col. pulled him close and looked him over, liked what he saw. "Chief Gunner's Mate Dantes, Sir, from Ellyson, that Tin Can out there. We're here to get the best targeting information you can give us. Then we'll go back to the ship and take those targets under fire." "Cranston, here, Guns. Let's mark up that chart you have and I'll also take you on a bit of a tour so that you can know what you're looking for." "Yessir, and I have a couple walkie talkies that I can leave with you if you need them as well as a signalman who can communicate with the ship by semaphore."

"Chief, you remind me of my first First Sergeant. He knew what to do, too." Hod nodded and grinned and they headed out, running until they had to crawl, stopping where they could see several German tanks. The Colonel handed his binocs to Hod. "Back in there, taking cover among the trees is a tank park. The Nazi tanks periodically come out of there and give us hell. If you could put a bunch of them out of commission it would make this job a whole lot easier, Gunny." Then he rolled over to the west and pointed to the top of the point. Up there just below the skyline the Germans have a concrete bunker with artillery and machine guns. It's covered with camouflage netting. When you get back to your ship, keep an eye out for them. We think they may be the guns that sunk our destroyer out there." They backed away and returned to their foxholes. Speaking to the signalman, "Hayman, We'll check in with you and ask for updates. Get them from the Colonel, here and let us know when he says you can come back. We'll make sure you get back aboard." Colonel Cranston said, "We appreciate anything you can do for us Gunner. When you get ready to run back we'll lay down some covering fire until you get back in your landing craft." "Ready now, Sir."

Under the rattle of small arms fire and a couple of automatic weapons Dantes and the rest of his crew ran back with some zigs and some zags and were glad to be back aboard with the ramp pulling up as mortars were walking their way closer. The Cox'n backed down into deeper water, having already backed loose of the sand bar, spun on a dime and headed for the Elly Mae. Back aboard ship, Hod went straight to the fire control director and trained it exactly on the tank park then he went to the bridge. "Captain, if we could anchor right here, maybe with two hooks down, that would give us the stability and precision we need to take out these Nazi tanks, and he trained the Big Eyes on the park area. Hawk got the Navigator and told him where he wanted the anchors set and the OOD maneuvered in response to the guiding that the "Gator" gave him, setting both hooks within 15 minutes. Hod ran directly to the fire control director and steered him a little closer to the center of the tank park. All they could see was trees. "Commence fire, continuous fire, fire for effect main battery." After the first two salvoes there were explosions in the park and the five inchers kept up the bombardment. With the Big Eyes Hod could see some cripples and he guided the director in on them. The Signalman came running up, "Chief, they say cease fire and well done." Dantes called out cease fire and turned to the Skipper, "We have a likely bead on the big gun and some machine gun nests. We'd better be underway when we take them under fire, Sir."

"Very well, Chief. OOD bring in our anchors as rapidly as possible. As soon as it's safe we'll set course to round Pointe Du Hoc. Well done, Chief." "Sir, I'll head down to my station amidships after I point out the likely spot of the camouflaged artillery to the fire control director. The Colonel ashore said that we had better look out for any tanks we woke up but didn't finish." Sure enough a lone Nazi tank came out and unlimbered his main gun at max range, arcing some rounds over them but they were moving now and gaining speed rapidly. Hod trained the director around to point it at the spot where he thought the heavy artillery was, then went down to his station amidships. On the phone he talked to fire control. "Commence fire on that spot on top of the point and be prepared to adjust fire on the first smoke you see there." After about three minutes they must have been getting close because there was a puff of smoke from the artillery piece. "Adjust fire to that smoke!" As they did so a round came at them and fell short, sending up an enormous geyser. Elly Mae kept firing as fast as they could get the rounds off. Another huge geyser, this one 200 yards long and Hod heard it whistle overhead, thought it could have hit him, standing there, the noise was deafening. He knew for a certainty that their next round would be a direct hit; this was standard field artillery practice. But before the Germans got off their third shot Ellyson fired and the results were spectacular. There was the explosion of the German position with netting, concrete, the gun and people flying through the air visible to the naked eye at their short range. Ellyson kept firing until the Skipper called out "Cease Fire!" Everyone topside was cheering and shaking their fists and you could see the Rangers swarming up and over the cliff. Dantes had the signal bridge raise the beach and they got permission to retrieve their signalman. This was done as the ship shortened the distance. With the pickup completed they moved to their next station, off Cherbourg, cleaning up the debris and preparing for more of whatever the Germans had in store for them.

Ashore back in England General Bradley turned to his Boss, "Ike, reports are we took out that gun emplacement that was holding us up on UTAH. A Navy tin can did the job. Our boys are up and over that cliff and we are no longer bottlenecked." Eisenhower's whole posture shifted as the stress and strain he had been bearing for all these hours was suddenly lifted. "Whew! And his cheeks puffed as he let out his breath in an explosive half shout and half laugh. If you didn't know better you might have imagined a damp eye or two in the room. "Brad, get me the name of that destroyer and we'll set aside a case of cognac whenever we can find it, for that Skipper. Within the hour Hawk read over the1MC, "This is the Captain speaking. Just received from Command, FLASH. WELL DONE, Ellyson. Eisenhower sends."

Resistance at Cherbourg was ferocious but futile. By the time the barrage, both Naval and field artillery lifted, the port was practically useless for Allied use. Hod was still at his station, but they were using the Gun Boss to carry out their Barrage. He had not let down his guard, however and on June 7th, operating between Normandy and Cherbourg Hod spotted in the distance a lone aircraft that had somehow survived and was making a run in their direction, whether to escape or attack he didn't know. "Air Action port," he hollered and the battery responded to his order. "Incoming aircraft, I make it out to be a Messerschmitt. Commence fire." Ellyson started feeding proximity fuses to the mounts and a regular rhythmic pounding commenced with the explosions closing on the fighter until it was hit, a wing coming loose and the aircraft pinwheeling into the sea.

CHAPTER 52

THE NEW COMMODORE

The Ellyson was enroute Gibraltar when Sparks, the Chief Radioman entered the Goat Locker and sidled up to the coffee mess and drew a cup for himself; looked inquiringly at "Guns" to see if he needed a top off and added some 'navy' coffee to his cup too. Aboard most ships there was an unspoken contest to claim the best, or strongest or rankest coffee; the snipes claimed they put boiler compound in theirs, whereas First Division bragged that a spoon would stand up in their coffee. It was almost universal, though, that navy coffee was consumed without any sweeteners and was thrown out if not strong enough. Pulling up a chair to join Dantes, Sparks sat down and buried his face in the fumes coming off his mug. "Trying to wake yourself up?" Dantes asked with a grin. Sparks took a sip, just a small one as it was still too hot. "Got news today that we're getting a new Squad Dog." Hod raised an eyebrow; this was maybe interesting but not that big a deal. Still, he regarded his messmate with interest, "Anybody I know?" "Dunno, but evidently someone coming with him knows you. We also got a radio central to radio central inquiry from a Chief asking if a Chief Dantes was aboard."

Now Hod *was* interested. "Some Chief Locker was asking, says he's coming along with CDR J. Lodge USN." Hod leaned back with a broad smile, "The Chief was my company commander in boot camp; we go way back. He's just the best Chief in this man's Navy." Two days later the word was passed that there would be a change of command when the ship got to Gib. Aboard Ford it had been exciting for Lodge to be highlined over to the Guadalcanal for a sit down with Captain Dan Gallery. "John, I just got word that I'm losing one of my tin can skippers; you're headed to USS Ellyson as the Commander of DES-RON 10. Congratulations, I'll be sorry to lose you. Lodge smiled his thanks as his hand was pumped enthusiastically. "Sir, you've made it interesting, and I'll look forward to having small boys as toys." "That's not all, the word is that you'll take part in the invasion of Southern France and then you'll be taking your squadron back to the States for conversion to high speed minesweepers." Lodge asked, "Any idea which shipyard?" Gallery broke out a big smile, "Word is that you'll be headed to Boston for the modifications, then headed to the Pacific."

Both ships, Ford and Ellyson pulled into Gibraltar, made honors and took up pier space, one behind the other. The ships hooked up to shore power, giving their snipes a break, took on fresh water and fuel as well as fresh food stores and much needed repair parts and eagerly anticipated mail. The prospective C.O. of Ford and Lodge went through a thorough procedure, turning over and signing for all of Ford's material and reviewing the inventory of all Classified material, small arms and an inventory of ship's supplies. They skipped lots of the fine points, didn't inventory tools, for instance, as they were considered consumables. The crew was fallen in and the departing and new Skippers inspected the crew in ranks and read their orders and once Lodge was relieved with a salute and "I relieve you, Sir" he was free to relieve as Squadron Commander. Aboard Ellyson the two Commodores spent a day going over the status of the command and the next day Lodge formally relieved and took command of the Squadron.

Gibraltar, a Spanish rendering of the Arabic phrase, Mountain of Tariq has been of strategic interest ever since ships sailed through its straits connecting the Atlantic with the Mediterranean. Whether Hercules stood astride the opening with one foot in Africa and the other in the Iberian Peninsula is left to one's imagination. Knowing the Greek's thirst for knowledge it is likely he was facing the Atlantic, looking to out sea for as yet undiscovered new worlds. What is undeniable is that various nations arrived on the shores of the Rock and conquered it. Like robber barons of old, collecting tolls for safe passage, modern day nations used their warships and aircraft to detect and take under attack the shipping of enemy nations attempting to make passage through the straits. The Brits occupied the Rock and defended it against the Spanish, Italians and the Germans. They placed an airstrip there and used it to base some of their Coastal Command ASW aircraft. Over the centuries a vast network of tunnels had been dug into the mountain and used for storage as well as headquarters for various commanders. By this time in the war all of the civilian inhabitants of the rock had been evacuated to Jamaica, London and other places. Gibraltar had served as a small staging port for the upcoming invasion of Southern France.

After her successful participation on D Day at Utah Beach and the subsequent assault on Cherbourg Ellyson was ordered, along with her Squadron, to head for the invasion of Southern France. Whereas Stalin thought of the invasion at Normandy as the second front he had been asking for, Churchill and FDR considered the invasion of Southern France as a second front to take some of the pressure off of the troops making their way inland from Normandy and to put increasing pressure on the retreating Germans with a flanking movement out of the Med. Ellyson served as the command center for the Squadron and participated in shore bombardment before troops were deposited on the beaches. There were U.S. troops, Free French troops and an enormous uprising of the French Resistance fighting against a second rate German Army with antiquated weapons. Though more than seven thousand American troops lost their lives in the invasion, the German force was driven to the north and east very rapidly, freeing from German occupation the sea-ports of Toulon and Marseille. The French reoccupied these bases and started operating them as the populace of the region rejoiced and resumed a more normal life albeit in support of the Allied operations in France. The Germans were in headlong retreat.

Of course Chief Locker was welcomed into the Goat Locker and became the source of a lot of inside scoop for the Chiefs. He and Hod spent time catching up on each other's careers and various operations, which means they told a lot of sea stories. Before long the discussion got around to the Commodore. "Hod, you know that you've always been a favorite of the Commodore's, ever since Pearl, when he was a LCDR and you were a Seaman First." With a wry look on his face Dantes acknowledged the fact. "It wasn't always comfortable, that's for sure," Hod replied. "But I thought you both handled it as well as could be done," Locker replied. "Thanks, Wallace, he certainly is a different kind of Officer, not that I've had experience with that many of them. He saw no problem in dropping the bars between us and he afforded me a look at much that I'd have never seen, otherwise." "And the problem with that, Hod?" "Well of course it's all in how the rest of the crew take it and it runs the risk of being called fraternization and therefore deleterious to good order and discipline. I relished our conversations and was super careful not to appear to take advantage." "You knew how to keep your mouth shut." Locker said. "Yes, that too."

Looking around him and dropping his voice, "Hod, I have noticed a decid-ed improvement in the Commodore's outlook since he broke his command pennant aboard Ellyson." Hod just looked at his mentor and waited for him to continue. "I think Lodge has never been quite comfortable with the perqui-sites of his elite status in Boston nor with the automatic respect he gets in the Navy. His leadership is of a more personal nature and it has taken him a long time to get used to the formality. He says his Family expected him to eventu-ally go into business in Boston or New York. Instead he has chosen to go to sea and protect those folks in the steel and glass towers of major cities." "He's certainly been a friend to me, if that's possible in the Navy, between Commis-sioned and Enlisted ranks. In fact, when he and Mrs. Lodge got married up in Makalapa they had me as ring bearer for the ceremony. Mrs. Lodge was the one with the idea and the Commander actually gave thought to me being his best man," Dantes replied. Locker's eyes twinkled at the new knowledge about the relationship between sailor and Officer and a bit of respect that Hod had kept it to himself all this time. "You know, there's a forty millimeter mount in close proximity to the Flag Bridge," Locker said and he got up and put his coffee mug on the peg in the coffee mess and headed back up to Radio Central. On his way out the door he threw over his shoulder, "probably needs to be checked, from time to time."

Flag Bridge, port wing aft, that same afternoon. Chief Gunner's Mate Dantes has freed up the forty millimeter mount and is exercising it fore and aft in train and up and down in elevation. He has a bit of lube oil and a rag and is quietly going about his business, even doing a bit of dry snapping. The racket of cocking and dry snapping made it into Flag Country and the Commodore looked up, saw Dantes and stepped outside. Dantes popped a sharp salute, "Good afternoon, Commodore and may I offer my congratulations." A lazy smile spread across Lodge's face as he returned the salute and reached out to shake hands, only because he couldn't hug him. Thanks, Chief and may I say that your well-deserved status looks good on you." They both turned to the rail and looked out to sea, continuing to talk. Dantes asked after Admiral Fitz, how it was going for him in retirement and also Miz Jane, who insisted on calling him Hod. Lodge gulped and had a hard time getting past his emotions, remembering his wedding and the time they'd spent together.

"Have you heard anything about your own situation in the P.I.," Lodge asked. "I recall that you had quite a nice location up there." "Nothing new, Sir. I am married to a wonderful Yankee, a beauty and we have two kids, a boy and a girl." He held his breath, thinking belatedly about the Commodore's bride, Lydia. "They're all in New Jersey with her Mom, waiting the war out, just like the rest of us." Lodge kept his gaze to sea, "I haven't heard from Lydia since she went out to Corregidor. We keep hoping that she is okay but up until now, no word." Just then chow was called away and as they broke apart, Lodge said, "Good to see you, Chief, I hope your duties will permit more visits like this." "Aye, Sir. You can count on it."

Three days later the messenger from the Bridge knocked and entered Chief's Quarters, found Chief Dantes and quietly told him that the Captain requested he attend him in his sea Cabin. Thanking the messenger, Dantes put on a fresh shirt, changed into his best shoes, lined up his trousers, shirt buttons and belt buckle, ran a comb through his hair and headed up the ladder to the pilothouse. The Quartermaster of the watch sang out, "Chief Master at Arms is on the bridge, Sir!" Dantes smiled at the entirely unnecessary announcement and turned toward the old man's sea cabin, where the Skipper was coming out, uncovered, with a big smile on his face. "Come on in," he said. They went in and the Captain closed the door, pulled two chairs out and invited the Chief to sit.

Turning toward his Chief, the Hawk said, "This is a social visit, Chief." Dantes thanked him, thought about saying something like long time no see and instead just nodded and waited to hear what the old man had to say. He knew or suspected he knew, what this visit was all about. They had met privately from time to time, but most of Hod's contact with the Command was through the XO. "Chief in looking through your Service Record, I'm reminded that you served together with the Commodore on board Detroit. There was also a very interesting commendation in there from CincPac. Is it fair to say that you are shipmates, maybe even more?" "Sir, I appreciate this opportunity to talk about this. The Commodore and I were shipmates when I was just out of Boot Camp. He befriended me and one result was that I was his driver and also a member of the shore party that made contact with President Quezon in Manila. Furthermore his wife requested me to be the ring bearer at their wedding, sometime later in CincPac's quarters in Makalapa. Other than that, there's been no contact between us, as our paths haven't crossed."

The Skipper buzzed for the messenger and requested two coffees, which materialized within thirty seconds. They both eased back in their chairs. "Chief, I imagine he is worried about his wife, who was stationed in the P. I. as I understand." "He hasn't talked about that, Sir, but I imagine the Captain is correct." The Skipper pushed his coffee cup around on his small desk, thinking about how to say this. "Chief, I absolutely approve of your visits to see the Commodore." Dantes nodded, thinking *that's really generous of a subordinate Commander*. "I will want no reports from you on any of your conversations. We all ought to have the comfort of talking to our shipmates, this war is tough enough, as it is." Dantes thanked the Captain, rose and put his chair against the bulkhead and stepped into the pilothouse, then made his way below to Chief's Quarters. It is a measure of the respect that the crew and his fellow Chiefs had for him that he received no questions at all about his visit to see the CO. It was a measure of his integrity that the CO never mentioned it again, though he did manage to drop by the Flag Bridge when Chief Dantes was there and make his manners. They stood and talked a bit, the three of them, nothing particular, nothing operational, just three shipmates being at ease. It was the Hawk's way of saying to his Boss that it was all okay with him.

After the invasion was over and advances consolidated and Toulon and Marseille recommissioned, the Commodore requested permission to take his Squadron into Marseille for a port visit and some badly needed liberty. The word spread like wildfire through the ship and plans were made for one helluva liberty. Those French ladies were grateful and ready to welcome les Americains with open arms. In the Goat Locker the Chiefs reminded Hod that he had yet to buy the drinks he'd promised at the last Kangaroo Court. So Hod made ready to pay up. In an unusual move, the chiefs also invited the CO and XO to join the proceedings; after all they'd been there when court was held. As a last minute gesture, Hawk also invited the Commodore to join them.

With the ship secured and the in-port watch set, including armed sentries on the pier, the liberty party was called away. Knucks knew of a place he'd patronized in years past so it was decided to go there. Of course they were welcomed with open arms, one of the bar girls even recognizing Knucks. They all ordered up and pointed to Dantes as the one who would be paying. It was an enormous table in the middle of a smoky paneled room with the bar off to the side. Up against the mirror were bottle after bottle of wine and also the hard stuff, making its appearance, finally, after the Boche had departed. Knucks hoisted his glass and stood, toasting Hod and retelling the story of his barely getting back aboard the ship that was underway. The Skipper raised his voice and admitted that he had sped up to make him sweat, but that no way was he going to leave his Chief behind. There was general good natured laughter and they all turned toward Dantes, to see what he would say, the three Officers leaning forward with interest, broad grins on their faces.

Dantes downed the rest of his drink, put the glass down carefully and without raising his voice, said, "I bet I can order these exact drinks and get them all correct. And if I do, then each of you has to buy a round. If I can't the rest of the rounds are on me, all night." There had been utter silence while he spoke, a usual thing, for Dantes was soft spoken. When he spoke everybody piped down. The Chiefs turned to each other in some excitement and the buzz increased, "He doesn't know French, does he? Yeah but he has a French name." They were all laughing and someone said, "Hell I'd like to see him try." Knucks, the ring leader for this foray said, "Okay, Chief, you're on." Dantes broke into a grin, the one that said he'd just won another ace-deuce game or had prevailed at darts. He raised his glass and got the waiter's attention and paused for effect. The whole place got quiet and everyone looked at Hod, waiting to hear what this Yank was going to say. Hod stood, saluted them all with his glass and then said, "Garcon, encore." An uproar ensued and they were reminding each other *never* to take a bar bet. The Skipper and the Commodore turned to each other, shaking their heads and then commenced to tell each other their own Dantes sea stories. It was a happy and solidly together bunch that made their way back to the ship, the Commodore and Skipper having bought a round each first and then taking the XO with them and leaving the Chiefs to their merriment.

With orders to return stateside for conversion and upkeep in the Boston Navy Shipyard the Squadron got underway. On one of his trips up to Flag Country, Dantes went into the spaces and knocked on Locker's door. They sat and Locker looked up with curiosity; usually they met and had their chats in Chiefs Quarters, or maybe a stroll back aft to the spud locker on the fantail. "Wallace, I know you've thought a lot about LCDR Lodge and her situation. I know it's wearing on the Commodore." Locker nodded, waited with interest to see what Dantes had to say as Dantes seated himself. "There's been no report of her death nor any confirmation of her being alive, either, right?" Locker nodded. "But there's also been no news either way about Gunny Clancy," and here Dantes leaned forward with an intense look on his face. Locker had a look of slowly dawning comprehension. "Wallace, I'm wondering if maybe Gunny is looking out for Lydia, somewhere in the boonies of the P.I."

Locker looked up, "We can check with the Commodore, but I do believe that the Gunny, once upon a time, made an offer to her to look out for her in the P.I. As I recall it was shortly after she set up her two clinics, one in Subic at the repair facility and one in Manila. Let's say that he has, in fact, been looking after her, what do you have in mind?" "Well, the first step is to make the assumption that what we're saying is true and then we need to determine if she is alive, Gunny, too." Wallace nodded, thinking. "We *did* set up Mamasan, the clandestine intelligence operation on Luzon. And I know for a fact that at one time Lydia went up to your place in the Baguio District and that she met up with Rosario Gabangabang." "And my lawyer, Ricardo Verdad reported an increasing profit out of the place and also reported the purchases of medical supplies." "What this all boils down to is we think there's a possibility that she is alive and performing as a combat nurse of sorts, perhaps operating out of the old Calderone Estancia location," Locker said. "I'll talk to him. Lord knows he needs something to hang onto."

Chief Locker in the Commodore's stateroom, the next afternoon. "Sir I have an interesting possibility brought up by Chief Dantes, thought you'd be interested." "Dantes, huh? By all means, he has the most active and imaginative mind I've ever encountered." "I seem to recall you mentioning once that Gunny Clancy had made an offer, a chivalrous one, to LCDR Lodge." "That's right, it was one evening in our quarters in Subic that Lydia told me about it." And he leaned forward in anticipation. "Sir, as Dantes mentioned, we have not heard any news of either your wife *or the Gunny*. I know I've been looking for any news on your wife for months and in the last 24 hours I've scrubbed all traffic to see what might have been reported on the Gunny or any of the Marines from that Embassy Detail in Manila." Lodge sat back in his chair and mused for a while, staring into the middle distance. Then he said, "I have a few ideas about this and I'm going to write them down. I'd like you and the Chief to see what else you can come up with. It's a full day of training tomorrow. Let's all meet here in Flag Quarters when we're done with maneuvers."

At the end of their meeting the next afternoon Dantes volunteered to Lodge, "Sir, I think that what we've discussed has at least the remote potential to affect the ship's operations. I feel the need to at least mention some of this to my Commanding Officer." Both Locker and Lodge nodded and Lodge told him he agreed, "Good idea. I will chat with him and bring him on board with what we've planned," Lodge said. And at that all three nodded.

And the ship couldn't get to Boston fast enough for the Commodore.

CHAPTER 53

CONVERSION

When they were inport in Marseille the Commodore had gathered his Skippers to Flag Quarters and discussed an idea of his. He wanted a team of veterans, either Petty Officers who had been tasked in training billets or else fairly recently had gone through shakedowns on other ships and passed their training. The concept was simple: write out a complete set of exercises for each department, including imposition of the casualty and then a list of actions to take in the emergency procedure for stopping the emergency and restoring the ship to full function. Each Captain nominated his best guys to the team, which was to be headed by Chief Locker. The Chief informally interviewed all of them and then picked his team of instructors. The instructors wrote down all that they knew about the casualties: how they were imposed, first and subsequent actions to correct and safety procedures to ensure no one was hurt nor any equipment damaged in the "drill". The next step was to send the team to each of the ships in the squadron and hook them up with their opposite number on that ship. He would be the one to impose casualties and score them on his own ship and do the training and repetitions until the procedure was mastered. Chief Locker was to supervise some of the drills in port for all ships and certify that ship's team was ready to conduct training. This quarter they would train on their own ships, next quarter they would all be run through their paces by the overall, varsity team and a competition would be held to determine the ship that was ready for a shakedown cruise. The word was out that they were headed to Guantanamo Bay, Cuba after their modifications and the Commodore thought they'd better have at least their procedures for Engineering, Navigation and Gunnery down before getting there. It was a big enough task to get qualified with the new minesweeping gear. Going to GTMO was a relatively new requirement and nobody really knew what they were in for, so they determined to do all they could in preparation.

The squadron got underway after a week in port in Marseille, formed up and headed for the Straits. Anytime a man of war got underway during a period of conflict she had to be ready for anything. There were the ordinary hazards of running aground or running into extreme weather, suffering a serious casualty to the main plant or in the ammo handling or fuel spaces. On top of 'normal' hazards there were those associated with the enemy. They could be attacked by aircraft, subs or other surface units. Their intelligence told them which ones were the most likely; their experience told them to be ready for any of them or all of them, at the same time. If the Skippers had wondered what kind of Squadron Commander Lodge would be, they had an inkling during the inport training sessions he set up.

A ship at sea is a community in motion. Constant motion, even when trying to remain still. Swells from the beam could impart a pretty large rolling motion, if the period or timing of the swells was just right the rolls could build, even in fairly calm weather. Same for seas off the bow, when swells could make the ship pitch her bow up and down, plowing into seas that washed all the way to the superstructure, bursting against the pilothouse and sending sheets of green water onto the large pilothouse glass surfaces. Then as the ship raised on the next massive wave the bow would send a plume of spray to catch the sun, if it was not overcast, and sparkle like a thousand glittering stars. Everywhere on the ship men were walking or working and their bodies were automatically adjusting to stay upright, though they looked like they were pivoting about their heels, swinging about a point on the deck as the ship danced with the elements. And nobody thought anything about it. If you'd been to sea for a month or more and then went ashore it could be comical watching your shipmates try to walk a straight line. On dry land which was still, it took a seaman a bit of time to not walk funny. Indeed he could look drunk, just trying to walk a straight line, countering forces that were no longer underfoot.

At sea you trained and stood watches and operated your machinery and maintained it and your spaces. There was almost no personal space so you learned a way of being or seeming small, that is you found ways not to be in the way. Since you didn't stop for the night there were constant, round the clock watches just to go to the next rendezvous or else maintain station in the formations. The formations were set up as natural groupings of sensors and interlocking fields of fire so as to detect most surely any enemy threat and then to fire weapons safely at it without hitting one of your ships in company. Every Captain had his Standing Orders and on top of them he wrote his night orders. Officers of the Deck all knew the standing orders and had to review the night orders before relieving the watch. You could be qualified to stand the watch on the bridge for independent steaming or in formation, OOD(I)s or OOD(F)s.

With his formation set for maximum readiness, after they cleared Gibraltar all of the Operations Officers broke out their Op Orders, distributed in port and prepared to participate in the exercises listed there. They would form up on the Flagship which was acting as a carrier and screen it, then the Commodore would rotate the screen to be in position for the next carrier heading, executing the turn of the flagship when all of the screening vessels had arrived at their stations, all ships turning to the new heading at the same time. At the WWI battle of Jutland formations had been in ranks and files, rectangular in shape and to change course had been slow, not responsive enough for a fast moving battle. Once carriers became the capital ship the circular formation first suggested by Nimitz had been a natural one that allowed the carrier to turn into the wind and take her screen with her. In daylight they did these maneuvers with the signal hoists, at night it would likely be flashing light. Or they could do their drills with radio commands. At the same time as they ran their maneuvers they were on the lookout for enemy activity. And navigating. And station keeping. And maintaining their spaces, working and training at the same time. By the second day they had added some of the prepared emergencies. By the fourth day, being Wednesday, they called a hiatus for what the Navy refers to as Rope-yarn Sunday and let the crew have an afternoon for writing letters or repairing uniforms. By then they knew what kind of Commodore they had.

Chief Locker was as busy as the proverbial one legged man in an ass kicking contest and he was happy. His Boss had regained any energy and sharpness he might have lost and was driving his ships hard and himself harder. There was a glint and a confidence about him and it was noticed by all who happened upon the pilothouse or CIC. He never lost patience at missed stations or messed up signals, just happily went about doing it better, again and again. And the ships were all competing to get to their stations fastest and in the most seamanlike manner. Signal Bridges got the hardest workout they'd had in months and were glad of it. Strikers were learning how to recognize the shapes and colors and repeat the hoists and put them at just below the two blocked (uppermost) position. Once the signal bridge and OOD concurred on the meaning of the signal from the signal books, they would two block the hoist indicating they understood the signal, and wait for the command of execution. The Flag Ship was watching for all ships to correctly copy and two block the hoist before executing the movement by quickly dropping their own hoist. Each ship wanted to be the first to answer with their hoist two blocked, and the first to whip it down when the hoist was executed. The same was true of flashing light, you didn't want to be the ship that asked for a repeat. The Skippers sat in their chairs for all of these drills, observing, learning which OODs were the sharpest, the most confident. There was time to run the loading machines and drill the gun crews until they were smoothly operating parts of the overall machine. At chow the talk was about how this had gone or that had failed and how to do it better. The First Class often led these discussions in the messdecks, with their strikers gathered about and listening.

The whole process was not unlike the grinding wheels or chipping hammers and wire brushes used by the deck gang to remove paint and rust down to bare metal. The ship seemed to bang you around, knocking off the rough edges and sharp corners, grinding at your faults and weaknesses until what was left shone like the bare metal of main deck, ready for priming and repainting. The crew had been tested and if any were found wanting and couldn't keep up they were quietly shipped off to a less demanding ship, perhaps an oiler or transport ship. This was true for Officer and Enlisted and Captains as well. You could hack it or you could not. What you were left with was a proud fighting crew that could fight the ship and felt ready for anything.

At the extremes were two types, the short timers and the lifers. The ones in the middle were on their way to becoming either short timers or else lifers. The lifers weren't really comfortable ashore. They saw going to sea as enjoyable, the place where they excelled. Shore was where you went for liberty, spent all your money and your shipmates made sure you got back aboard in one piece and on time. The longer you were aboard the more sea stories you collected. The more sea stories you could tell the more you were likely to be seen as a lifer. Someone in the middle could look at a lifer and see someone who had been institutionalized. If they, themselves thought of the ship as a prison they were soon to be a short timer.

The real salts knew how to tell a funny story. Humor was indispensable aboard ship. And when they went ashore, the stories they told in bars were exotic and filled with foreign expressions from every language, in addition to the Navy lingo that they used without thinking. In their lockers they had an assortment of coins from a dozen foreign lands, all shapes and sizes and colors. They'd had pizza and gelotti in Naples and gambled and gamboled on the French Riviera. Landsmen would go to the beach and sniff the sea air and the sailor would laugh at them because they knew that there was no smell of the sea, at sea, just the smell of the ship. Their wives knew what a ship smelled like as they came home with the smell of NSFO and cosmoline, and as often as not hollered at them while still on the back porch, to not to bring those smelly clothes in here, go throw them in the laundry.

And on the beach, in small cottages in Navy Housing Areas were the families, the ones who lived on base, perhaps, the kids growing up on decks instead of floors, bulkheads instead of walls, dungarees from ship stores instead of civilian fashions and standing still in the yard at evening colors when all stopped until the National Ensign had been slowly taken down. She would be folded just so and in the morning run up smartly. The Navy way. The Military way. The Moms had the child raising to do and the Dad to miss. She made it a honeymoon when he came home and he played Santa Claus after each deployment. There would be linens and small exotic bars of soap and dresses and maybe small carved wooden treasures and always something for the kids. And on duty nights sometimes the family could go aboard and see a movie in Chief's Quarters. And when it was time to go, to go back to the sea, they would all troop down to the pier and stand there waving until the ship was small in the distance. Wipe the tears away and get used to being the one left behind. Again.

Aboard Ellyson the Skipper directed that the Chief Engineer would co-ordinate the upcoming overhaul. He would collect all of the work requests, read them for correctness, sort them by shipyard shop and assign the ship's priorities. A day before making port in Boston, Chief Dantes requested a chat with Lt Sawyer. "Come in Chief, what's up?" Their relationship was one of deep mutual respect; Dantes had on more than one occasion subtly stepped in to solve a personnel problem before it got as far as the XO, and the snipes had at times been the beneficiaries. Taking a seat on the edge of the rack, Hod said, "Sir, I have an idea that might help us in the yard." Sawyer nodded, "Well, we can use all the help we can get, Chief," and he waited to hear what the Chief would say. "Well, everybody uses cumshaw but not everybody does it right. I think we need to requisition beaucoup ten pound tins of coffee and when we get in the yard and put the plant out of commission, perhaps after your guys clean the main condensers, we store the coffee, a couple hundred pounds of it in a condenser and bolt it down and wire it with a lock and a lead seal." A smile started to make its way across Sawyer's face. "Then before our work requests get delivered we send our Chiefs out into all of the shops with tins of coffee. They just drop it off, and mention the ship, howdy with all of the guys in the head shed and, most importantly, don't ask for anything. It's a sure thing that when the Chiefs go back to discuss their work orders and the requests that didn't make it into orders that they will receive a hearty welcome." Sawyer sat back in his chair and gave Dantes an appreciative look. "First we give them our respect, right?" "Yessir and we never put them on the spot. And we get the Pork Chop to open up the mess deck for workers on the swing shift. They'll provide steak sandwiches and hot rations for the welders and shipfitters that come aboard plus the fire watches we provide to go around with them so that they can pull the yard birds' hoses and clean up after the welding or cutting is done. Sir, we'll be the most popular ship in the yard and we'll get lots of extras that aren't even written down in that stack of work requests you have in front of you."

XO's stateroom. Sawyer stepped in and got his usual, "What's up, Chief?" from the XO. The XO was cool that way, called the gunnery Department Officer Guns, called the Chief Engineer, "Chief," or "Cheng," even got away with calling Supply "Pork Chop." For Sawyer, Chief was the highest compliment he could receive, his Dad having been a Chief when Sawyer was growing up. "Sir, I will be putting in a requisition for about 200lbs of coffee, didn't want it to be a surprise or get kicked back by Supply." "What's it for, Scott?" "Planning to store it under lock and seal in a main condenser. We'll make regular deliveries to the main shops in the Yard. For the first delivery we won't ask for anything, just pay our respects." "That ought to be a big hit with them, can't be lots of coffee just floating around, with rationing and such. Great idea!" "Sir it wasn't my idea, your Chief Master at Arms came to me with it." The XO smiled, said "Pergra" and that he'd speak to the Pork Chop. As Sawyer made his way out of the XO's stateroom LCDR Dixon reflected on the value of Chiefs in this man's Navy. And the honor and integrity of every Academy man he'd had the pleasure to run across in his career. Scott Sawyer was a keeper, for sure, and they didn't come any better than the Chief.

In the Yard when the dust settled down and to get away from the constant noise and dust and disruption that a shipyard overhaul or refit always entailed, Locker took Hod on a tour of the Charleston Naval Shipyard. They found the very brick steps that the Brits had used when they landed their troops to quell the rebellion in Boston. Hod felt chills run up his neck, just standing there, and then they strolled over to the USS Constitution. She looked small and solid with low overheads so you had to crouch to move about the gun deck. As a Gunner's Mate Hod took particular interest in the naval artillery on display. He could well imagine and figure out how these guns were operated. It was all manpower. He examined the means to elevate the guns by quoins and wedges, the tackle to absorb the recoil, the crew of several men and one or two boys to clean out the bore and load powder, shot and wads to keep it all in and the brute power and teamwork to operate this whole machine of cast iron and a wooden truck on wheels. Not for the first time he reflected on it being the job of the bluejacket to do the grimy dangerous work, the job of the Officer to order it done. Far from resenting this fact he appreciated the stark division of roles and took pride in his ability to train and refine his gun crews to be able to put out a high rate of fire. Locker had found an old shipmate on board and they got a special tour of the berthing area. "Hmm, not too different from the old Detroit, for living conditions," Hod said. "It's the way we started out, swinging in a hammock and two buckets of water a day if we were in port, maybe one if we were underway." "Wooden ships and iron men," said Locker. "And boys, too," Hod replied. "It took guts for those kids who were powder monkeys to continue serving their gun when arms, legs and splinters the size and sharpness of swords were flying." "Some things never change," Locker replied.

With things settled down in the Squadron and all conversions underway, Lodge started taking his evening meals at home, with Nancy. Sometimes he stayed the night, others he would go to the BOQ, to be closer to the ships. It was a quietly joyful reunion but with the constant reminder that they were not all together and Lodge had no real information about his wife, whether she was even alive. Nancy called Lydia and Sam Crowninshield and after a couple of calls they were invited to join them for dinner one evening. Walking up the walk, John's memories came crashing in on him. He recalled his first and only other time at Lydia's home; that time he had gone there unannounced and been welcomed shortly after his Father's funeral. Lydia opened the door as they got to the top of the stoop and welcomed them with a large smile and hugs all around.

"Would you pass the potatoes?" Sam asked and Lodge passed them across while taking from Lydia a bowl of green beans. There were also Boston baked beans and a roast beef which Sam carved. When everybody had been served, Sam asked for Grace. "Let us bow our heads. Dear Lord we are thankful to be in each other's company and in your presence. Lord we are so mindful of the one who is not with us, today. We pray that she is safe and well and that we may soon hear news of her. God bless us all and bring her home to us soon, safely. Amen." A soft muted chorus of amens followed, along with a few sniffles, with the ladies dabbing a tear or two with their napkins. John picked up his wine glass and proposed a toast. Leaning to the middle of the table, with all glasses raised, "We will find her and we will bring her home, some day."

After dessert the ladies cleared the table and they all went into the study to sit for a bit. There was small talk and then John coughed and claimed the floor. They were all seated and John leaned forward and put his forearms on his thighs, paused and looked at each one of them in turn. "You are not aware, but I have aboard Ellyson, my Flagship, two shipmates from an earlier time, Chief Locker and Chief Dantes." Both ladies remembered Dantes as a Seaman who was in the wedding at Makalapa. They all turned in John's direction, listening intently. "Both of these men were with me on the rooftop of the Manila Hotel when an attack was foiled by Dantes. A third man, a Marine Gunny Clancy was also involved in our actions at that time. While it is true that we have not had any report on Lydia's whereabouts, it is also true that we have had no news of Gunny Clancy. Gunny was stationed at the Embassy in Manila at the time of the attack. He had visited with Lydia when she took over the clinics in Manila and Subic and while there he made a rather chivalrous offer to look after her if and when the trouble started with the Japs.

He paused and took another sip of his coffee. "My hope is that somehow they are together, working together in the resistance, keeping the scouts and guerillas alive in the Philippine jungle. True, it is just a hope but it is also true that there may be a way to communicate and make inquiries, without going ashore. That is my intention, and if we are able to determine their whereabouts I will make all efforts to get approval for a mission to attempt their rescue". As the party took all of this in John added, "It was Dantes who came up with this idea, and he and Chief Locker who have made several suggestions as to how to proceed. It is maybe a small hope but it is a hope. Perhaps you will think on it and pray for our ultimate success." At that the two women broke into tears and the men went to them and comforted them. When everyone had blown their noses and settled back down, Sam broke out the Cognac and poured a healthy shot in snifters for all of them. They sat there for hours in excited talk, happy talk, smiles creasing faces that had not smiled so often in the past months. When at last they rose to go and were walked, arm in arm to the door it was a spirited and determined group that would settle in and pray unceasingly. Pray for Lydia.

CHAPTER 54

A PLAN IS A PLACE TO START

Desron 10 had pulled into Boston Navy Shipyard for conversion to a Mine Squadron, with all ships losing their number four 5 inch guns and replacing them with mine sweeping gear on the fantail. All ships were redesignated as High speed Minesweepers and the Squadron became MinRon 20. Lodge was called to the Navy Annex in DC, made the trip down there by train where he received his fourth stripe in a quiet ceremony in COMINCH offices with Admiral King presiding.

"Commodore Lodge welcome to DC and congratulations on your promotion." "Thank you, Sir." "How's the conversion of your Squadron going, in Boston?" "Going fine, Sir. I expect we will be finished in Boston in a week and then head to GTMO for a quick shakedown." "Tell me, is it true that you put together your own cadre of experts and trained your Squadron on your TransLant, coming back from the Med?" "Sir, that's true, though I don't think we trained enough to skip our shakedown in Cuba." "Very well, but I intend to cut your time there to a week and a half, maybe two at the most." Lodge's head was spinning, wondering how the Admiral kept himself so well informed. "And once you're through at Guantanamo you'll head straight for the Canal and chop to CincPac. We have in mind your performing sweeping operations at Okinawa in preparation for the invasion. You'll shape a course for Pearl and then Ulithi to replenish and get the latest Intel. CinPac has shifted his Flag to Guam, to get closer to the action." Just then the Admiral's Secretary came into the doorway and her expression said what King already knew, there were three more waiting in the outer office to see him. King nodded and before waving them in, turned to Lodge with a look of concern on his face, "Lodge, I understand that your wife is missing, has been since Corregidor, that right?" *This doesn't jibe with his reputation as a hard ass,* and Lodge stammered just a bit, "That's true, Sir. The last we heard from her was that she had gone to the Rock." "I hope that you get some word soon, Lodge, and that it is good news." And with that he was dismissed with a handshake and Captain Lodge went out and got his blues restriped for the fourth stripe, all new gold braid, as the three already on his uniform had tarnished some. He also got new shoulder boards, a new cap while he was at it and a set of eagles for his collar points. Back in Boston there was time for a bit of a wetting down, attended by the Crowninshields and his Mom as well as the Skippers in his Squadron. Also noticed by his Skippers and them not knowing what to think about it, there were two Chief Petty Officers in attendance at the Club for the celebration.

Gitmo went well and in ten days of a crash schedule they were all qualified to run their new gear and deploy it. All other ships there for training were put on hold and the Gitmo cadre concentrated just on MinRon 20. It seemed that what Admiral King wanted, he got. Of course you automatically failed for the first several underway periods, and then were put back together, wounded pride soothed as, miracle of miracles, you passed and received the GTMO seal of approval.

For the trip out to the Pacific Lodge divided his Squadron into its Divisions and gave his Division Commander a bit of time on his own. In the evenings he would often call Locker and Dantes into his stateroom and go over their plan, each of them poking holes in it and the others finding a new approach. Basically it came down to getting permission to use Mamasan to contact Rosario Gabangabang and to determine if the Gunny and LCDR Lodge were alive and their whereabouts known. Given a yes to both of those questions the rest of it, getting approval, was up to Lodge, and he had a pretty good idea of how it would go, if it were to be approved at all. Then, with approval all the way up the line it would be Elly Mae that would likely attempt the rescue, if a rescue there was to be.

They pulled into Pearl and immediately Lodge contacted Uncle Fitz and told him he was in port, would be coming out to spend a night or two and was bringing two shipmates with him. He checked in ashore and went up to visit the remaining CINCPAC staff, asked to speak with the senior Intelligence Staff person. Indeed Admiral Cochrane had gone with Nimitz to Guam, but there was a Commander who swiftly made room for him on his schedule. Over coffee in his office Lodge explained his problem and his need for information and requested the use of the Mamasan network to make a single inquiry. Commander Parsons, who was dating a nurse from the clinic at Pearl, himself, listened closely. "I have in mind that we task a coast watcher to make this signal on whatever previously arranged broadcast schedule you have in place," Lodge said. "We have used the network to make deliveries of medical supplies and perform submarine extractions," Parsons replied. "Then I would like you to get this message out, and it is simple. "Need proof of life of Love Love and Gunny. Chinatown freebie, authenticate." Parsons looked up, "They'll know who LL is?" Yes, that'll be Lydia Lodge, my wife." "And what sort of answer might you accept as a verification?" We expect something, if there is a reply, that will make sense to one of my Chiefs, aboard Ellyson." "Okay, Commodore, I'll have to get permission to do this." "Just out of curiosity, to whom will this request of mine go?" "Why Admiral Cochrane, my Boss." Lodge's dazzling smile set Parsons back in his chair a bit, this four striper was obviously very pleased. "That's perfect, Parsons. Please let me know by SECRET traffic what happens at every step of the way." Aye aye, Sir."

At the Lodge home up Nuuanu Valley, at the table with the Fitzes, the Admiral was in deep conversation with Dantes, whom he found absolutely fascinating. Locker was sitting with them and Lodge was with Auntie Jane. Lodge turned to Locker, "Chief, why don't you tell the Admiral about the little séance we had in Manila, up on the roof of the Manila Hotel? I know that Chief Dantes is too modest to tell it, at least to tell it well." Jane nudged John and they both joined the circle, Jane in Fitz' lap as Locker warmed up to his task. Hod got out of his chair, inviting the Commodore to sit there and went into the kitchen to refresh his Mai Tai. While he was at it he got one for Jane and the Admiral. Hod wasn't listening; instead he was turning over in his mind what he'd learned from Lodge on the way out here. *That message requesting authentication, nice touch. Knowing Gunny he'll say something about our time firing up at Diamond Head or else monkey meat on a stick.* His introspection was broken into as he realized they had turned toward him, were asking that he rejoin them. He gave a chuckle, "As long as y'all have stopped jawing about that night in Manila, okay. I can't stand the thought of violence." That got an appreciative laughing response that died out as he took a seat on the deck with his legs folded.

Auntie Jane spoke up, "As I recall you invited me to address you as Hod, Hod." He immediately blushed down to his toes. "Yes Ma'am but I was just a Seaman First and way out of my depth and had just been asked by the Admiral for an assessment of what was going on in the Pacific. Of course I lost hold of my manners, Auntie Jane," he smiled. Fitz coughed and said, "Well, Sailor, if you like you can call me Admiral." At that they all howled and Locker gave Hod a push that almost tumbled him. There was no getting around it, they were bound and determined to lionize him and it was his job to let them. Fitz asked, "Hod, what's your concept of the way this might all proceed?" Hod immediately turned toward Lodge but he held up his hand, "No, Hod, this is your operation, your idea; we'd all like to hear your concept for going forward."

"I want you all to know how much I appreciate your doing me this honor. You also ought to know that it was Chief "Wall" Locker that got me my start at

Boot Camp and it was a LCDR from Boston who befriended me and gave me opportunities rarely if ever seen by a young Enlisted man. Finally it was Mrs. Lodge who got me invited to the wedding and insisted I have the honor of being ring bearer." Lodge interrupted, "And it was you who got us all together in the Staff car and to the hotel for the show. And did you know that she also was very serious about inviting you to join us at the beach the next day?" And he turned to Fitz, "I've never heard anything from Hod about your conversation that day, nor did anyone else hear about what Makalapa was like. Not from Seaman First Dantes. How about it, Chief?" He was looking at Wall Locker.

"Sir the Chief is the very soul of discretion. He is right now wondering how much he can actually say about the operation we have been discussing." Lodge peered at Dantes, "Yes I can see that. Well then I will say that if we can get proof of life we had better have more than a passing idea of how to proceed." He told them all about his meeting with CDR Parsons and the attempt being made to determine where Lydia and Gunny were, and emphasized that it was only a first step, albeit an important one. Turning to the Admiral he asked, "Admiral, how would you go about this, the getting of permissions, dealing with MacArthur, Cochrane and the rest?" Jane shot a loving look of thanks at John, quickly got up from her husband's lap and Locker offered her his chair, then went into the kitchen for the pitcher of Mai Tais. When all was settled Fitz took a sip of his drink, put it down and leaned into the circle of his admirers.

He was sitting up straighter and he had gotten a glint in his eye. He didn't hesitate or say it was not his place to say, he just laid it all out there. "I knew the Lodge family before you were born, John. Lydia became a regular fixture out at Makalapa, a favorite of ours. Admiral Cochrane and I go way back, too. We spent many an evening going over the tactical and strategic situations confronting us. He got his job as CincAsiaticFlt as a direct result of a recommendation of mine to FDR. Chet Nimitz, before he left, gave me an invitation to come out to the remaining Staff headquarters any time I wanted. John, with your permission I will pay them a follow up visit and drop in on the Intel Section there, Parsons did you say? I hope it will be enough to say that I am very interested in the progress of your communications. As for how to conduct an actual rescue mission, why that depends on so many variables, I wouldn't know where to start without first dealing with the likelihoods, going in." Lodge was looking at Dantes again, the same way he had done on more than one occasion, silently encouraging him to speak. And as he had done before, Hod spoke up, right off the cuff and he had his audience entranced.

Sirs, Ma'am, Chief I have done some thinking about this, for quite a while. My assumption is that the Gunny would have planned to get Mrs. Lodge off of the rock as soon as the scuttlebutt started about a surrender. I know the Gunny and there isn't a tougher, straighter man out there. He was included in the events surrounding the dust up in Manila. I also know that he actually took the Commander up to the old Calderone place a few miles from Baguio. My lawyer has submitted reports to me and I'm generally aware of what has been done with the place." Here Lodge interjected that it was true, Lydia had undertaken providing medical services at Dantes' property. "Ricardo Verdad confirmed Mrs. Lodge's activity and the Gunny's, up there, to me. My feeling, from knowing the Gunny is that he would want to keep on fighting if at all possible. It's just a guess, but I think a good one, that the reason we haven't had confirmation of them as internees is that they found a way to get away from Corregidor and up to the Baguio District.

Taking a sip of the coffee Locker handed him he continued. I think if we can use the network that you set up there, Commodore, we might be able to confirm life and also schedule a rescue mission on the beach closest to Baguio. Those are a lot of ifs. If it all happens and you are able to arrange the rendezvous there's one thing for sure. I am volunteering to go in there and get them out." They all sort of sat back and thought about what Hod had said. Locker spoke up, "Sir I can drive the two of us back to base, pick you up tomorrow, if you like." Lodge thought for a bit, "That would be good, being able to stay here for the evening. The Admiral and I can strategize our approach to the chain of command." With that the party broke up and Hod got his share of tearful hugs from Auntie Jane and vigorous handshakes from the Admiral. Lodge had his memories of time spent with Lydia here and fell asleep with optimism and hope in his heart. At last they were *doing* something.

Admiral Fitz put on his working khakis and got down to Makalapa the next afternoon. He popped into Parson's office amid a flutter of nervous secretaries, was offered a seat and decided instead to stand. "What progress do we have on Commodore Lodge's communications request," he asked Parsons. The Commander excused himself and five minutes later came back with a hard copy reply from Cochrane that he would indeed send the message out. Actually it was addressed to Lodge, Info to him, so there was no question of his need to know. "I'd like to be kept abreast of developments." "Aye aye Sir, we have your address up in Nuuanu and will with your permission brief you by courier when we have any news. "Much appreciated," Fitz said and then he made his way slowly out of the building, stopping to chat with old shipmates. It took him a half hour to leave the building and there were side boys for him when he left, all of them Commanders or above. *"Damn it felt good to be of some use, again!"*

MinRon 20 got underway two days later and two days out were redirected to Guam, just the Commodore and his Flagship, Ellyson. Lodge in turn turned over operational command of the Squadron to his Division Commander before heading for Guam while his Squadron continued steaming to Ulithi. Within the week Lodge had reported ashore to Admiral Cochrane.

He looked about him in some amazement at the size of the Staff. It was huge when you considered the ones still manning the spaces in Makalapa. He and Cochrane sat in Cochrane's office waiting for Nimitz' Secretary to give them the green light. Cochrane had not briefed Lodge on his conversations with Nimitz, only that they had talked and that Nimitz wanted to see him personally, before making a decision and possibly going forward with a request of the Commander in the Area, General Douglas MacArthur.

CHAPTER 55

COMMAND DECISIONS

Cochrane and Lodge were still waiting for the call from Nimitz' Secretary when there was a short knock on the door and Nimitz stepped in. He looked at the two startled occupants of the room who were jumping to their feet and grinned, "I missed our lunches in Pearl, Dick, thought this might go a little easier if we got away from my office." Both of them were standing at a loose attention so he said, "At ease, gentlemen. We can take an hour and I do have lunch coming in." Shortly thereafter a steward came in with a folding table and another brought in sandwiches and drinks. All three got a chair and pulled it up to the table, Nimitz sitting first because the other two wouldn't dream of sitting before he did. Nimitz poured some iced tea in his glass and then hit Cochrane's and with an upraised eyebrow asked if Lodge was having any, then topped his glass off, too. Lodge was taking it all in and felt as though Nimitz somehow looked, well, familiar. Not the looks, necessarily, everybody had seen pictures of this famous Chief in the Pacific. It was just a feeling... *why he reminds me of Dantes!* It was that "Texas" look, eager, curious and taciturn all at the same time. They even sounded alike with a bit of Texas Hill Country in their phrasing. Lodge noticed the others were starting to eat so he started in on his sandwich, waiting for the Admiral to speak.

Wiping with a napkin and then taking a bit of his iced tea, Nimitz turned to Lodge, "Commodore, does your Dad go by the name of Cab?" "Sir, yessir that was short for Cabot." Nimitz looked at him inquiringly, "Sir, my Dad passed away a few years back." "Sorry to hear that. You know he was a first class at the Academy at the time Dick and I were Plebes, and he was a regular hard ass. Good guy, though. I always thought he should've stayed in. As I understand it you and Admiral Cochrane have served together on some three different duty stations." "Yessir." "You went to Harvard, right? Probably not where your Dad thought you'd go." Now Lodge relaxed and sat back in his chair a bit. "Sir as a matter of fact I made mention of that fact at his funeral." Well, if you're anything like him, and I can definitely see the family resemblance, you're a pretty determined guy, one who's used to winning, finishing what you've started." Cochrane piped up, "Absolutely, Sir, I'm proud to claim him."

The stewards came in with another pitcher of tea and some cupcakes. "Well, my wife isn't here so I guess I can eat a couple of these." And he passed them to Lodge first. While he was picking one and putting it on his plate, Nimitz said, "Admiral Cochrane feels some responsibility for the fact that your wife is in the fix we think she's in." "Sir I wouldn't." "Of course you wouldn't and I wouldn't be honest with you if I didn't tell you that I totally understand those feelings, respect them and have a bit of a difficulty getting past them. For of course we have to make our decisions in this theater, these circumstances, mostly on other considerations." Lodge nodded his understanding. "But that does NOT mean we ignore family; when we get a chance to take them into consideration.

"We also have to take into consideration our professional relationships with others whose responsibilities and authority sometimes come into play. In particular if any sort of mission is undertaken in the Philippines, for instance, it must necessarily be with the full knowledge and cooperation of General MacArthur." I sent the Admiral to Brisbane some time back in order to see if he could reduce the amount of distrust I saw between our commands. I'm pleased to say that he somehow managed to do exactly that, serving on his staff for a period of months and proposing and implementing a program of Intel sharing and furthermore cooperation between our submarines and the resistance forces ashore in the P.I. Dick?"

Sir, it is true that the authority you sent with me was key in getting their cooperation. We're all familiar with the General's personality and there are lots of stories about his behavior and habits, some of those stories no doubt overblown. It's not my purpose to carry tales." "Aw c'mon, Dick, you can tell us just a wee bit more than that," said with a bit of a teasing grin. "I've seen him dismiss a three star in a demeaning manner, just because he could. He moves in a regal way and manages to get it all on film and to the press. He is a magnificent speaker and he knows it and he deliberately uses his talent in the belief that he is the savior of the Philippines and it is his job to inspire them. Finally, when we met he brought up a baseball game in which he and I played on the same field, all those years ago. He knows every little thing and prides himself on that. He expects to be kowtowed to, but doesn't respect anybody who does it. You can imagine the task before me, finding a way to serve two commanders so different in every way. The upshot is that by being totally honest I got inside. To give him his due, he was totally honest, too."

"So, where does that leave us...?" Nimitz started when a messenger knocked at the door, stepped inside and proffered his message board to Cochrane. Cochrane signed for a copy and read it, then passed it to Nimitz. Nimitz read it slowly, read it twice. Then handed it to Lodge saying, "Read this out loud for us Commodore and tell us what you make of it." "Aye Sir. From an Australian Command, to Intel, CincPac, subject Coast Watcher communication. The following was received in response to our message, "Request proof of life, Love Love and Gunny. Chinatown freebie, authenticate." Positive both Love Love and Gunny, tight group low and right." Lodge's face crumpled up and he dropped his head to the table, cradled in his arms, silent gut wrenching sobs heaving his back. The two Admirals looked at each other and Cochrane put an arm across John's back while Nimitz nodded, a soft look on both faces. After a short bit Lodge got control of his emotions and sat up, the tears streaming down his face. But by then there were tears on all three faces, Lodge noticed and a laugh bubbled up and he seemed to laugh and cry at the same time. Outside in the passageway passersby heard the ruckus and kept moving. Inside the three man got their napkins and soaked up tears that didn't shame them, passed the cupcakes around again and then got back to business.

"Sir, Chief Dantes is aboard Ellyson, will confirm, but this answer no doubt refers to a pistol practice at the Diamond Head Range. The story was that Dantes, a Seaman First then, fired off a string of shots in rapid fire almost like a machine gun, with a .45. Gunny was the Coach of the Detroit's pistol team and Dantes was trying out for the team. His skill with firearms was and is legendary, Sir. Dantes and I were shipmates aboard Detroit." "Well, I have to say that this is the best news I've had since Midway, gentlemen. Looks like we have a mission to plan and coordination to do. Dick how do you propose we approach this?"

Cochrane got up from the table, swallowing the last of his cupcake, and got a chart he had marked up. "Here is the location of our Mamasan network Command Post on Luzon and it is the place where Gunny and Lydia most likely launch from and return to. The timing for this is exquisite, both fortunate and unlucky at the same time, depends upon how MacArthur looks at it. You see we've been getting observation reports on the Jap POW camp at Cabanatuan, and of course sharing them with MacArthur. That was the biggest accomplishment of our reaching out to him and his staff. We share all of our Intel. MacArthur is increasingly concerned that the Japs will commit atrocities at Cabanatuan, perhaps executing them all, some 500 to 700 still alive there. We know that MacArthur's Staff are planning a rescue operation there which will take place shortly. He might very well look at any attempt to rescue Gunny and Lydia as a distraction and a security risk. Of course his ego will not let him risk an embarrassment."

"I'm sure you've already thought of this, Dick, but maybe we can offer the General a demonstration, some naval shore bombardment in the vicinity, something that might pull some IJA forces away from the main action." "Yessir, I had been thinking of just such a thing and there is a concentration of Japanese regular troops here," and he pointed to a position with symbols for the Unit of troops that were known to be there. "In fact the General's Staff are concerned about those troops and I think that if we sort of made it their idea we might get invited to their party." Looking at the Commodore, "Do you think that Ellyson, your Flagship, has the necessary wherewithal to go in there with a shore party and bring our people out?" "Sir, of course I would need to coordinate with the Skipper, but yessir, absolutely. If necessary our demonstration can also serve as enough force to pin them down." Cochrane interjected, "Can't lose sight of the fact that this will make the extraction more dangerous. It's one thing to come in under the cover of darkness, a new moon night, and sneak two people out of there, quite another to do it after announcing your presence with a five inch barrage."

"Dick, this is your mission to plan and execute. It will also fall to you to coordinate with MacArthur's Staff and get approval on the timing, all of it. Let me know when you have permission or if you run into a stumbling block." They all stood up and before Lodge could offer his thanks, Nimitz held out his hand, shook Lodge's, said, "Good Hunting, Commodore," and was out of the office headed back into a maelstrom of his own.

At Mamasan Headquarters in the Baguio District, Rosario had shared the contents of the incoming inquiry and Clancy had dictated the reply. When they later, within a few days, got the confirming message as well as a rendezvous place and time, they huddled again. No one but them knew that they had received the inquiry, nobody yet knew that there had been a response and now a plan for a rendezvous. Of course there were very important security reasons for keeping this information closely held. But as they whispered together in bed in their hut, Rosario and Gunny talked about another concern. "And I say we do not tell the Commander about any of this." "Why not," Rosario replied. "I just don't know how she would react, that's all," said the Gunny. "Well, it's obviously a rescue mission for the two of you. Either we tell them no thanks, which is unthinkable, or we make preparations." And Rosario rolled over and put her back to him and got silent. She assumed that Lydia would go, but what about the Gunny? Of course she would not ask, her pride would not let her. She would just have to play along and see where this led. With only three days left before the day, they knew they would have to do something and do it soon. Rosario and Clancy met down by the stream. "I am concerned that she has gone native, almost reckless in her forays out into the field," Gunny said. "Yes and that's why we gave her the pill that she keeps hidden on her person," Rosario replied. "I think she keeps it in her bra." And she eyed him jealously to see if that got any kind of reaction. "Here's what I'm going to do, militarily. I will gather together a group similar to what we have used to recover medical supplies. The rendezvous point is down on the beach, the usual place we do this, although we have only done it twice. We'll carry a little bit heavier weaponry and I'll say it is a medical resupply mission. I won't even tell her directly. I expect she will volunteer as she always does. When we get out into the water to receive the supplies and bring them in, that's when I expect we'll hand her over. If she doesn't volunteer to come I'll ask her to come along to verify that we are getting the right supplies. As you know, things are getting increasingly dire at Cabanatuan. Just a guess, but by the requests we've had for more and more recent Intel on that camp and the likelihood of mass executions there increasing, I'd not be surprised if this mission is being undertaken as part of a larger effort."

The word was passed and the group formed from volunteers with experience in bringing medical supplies ashore. Lydia volunteered and was in the party that moved out that night. Rendezvous was to be in daylight in a little more than two days, at noon, actually.

Back in CincPac Headquarters, Guam, Cochrane had sent a flurry of messages to MacArthur, with copies to Lodge. The back and forth continued until an "Eyes Only" exchange between MacArthur and Cochrane. "You must know, Sir that I have a personal interest in pulling off this rescue. The person of interest is the Nurse whom you met in Manila, the one who managed to escape from Corregidor, the one now dangerously known as the White Angel for her medical missions on Luzon and being hunted as we speak. My personal connection to her and her husband is the reason we are suggesting our participation in the rescue effort at Cabanatuan." The answer came back and it was pure MacArthur as only he could have said it, "Dick, we're shipmates and team mates. I have always trusted in the sincerity of your motivations. By all means bring her home safely if at all possible. Please keep me informed. MacArthur sends."

CHAPTER 56

RESCUE OPERATIONS

Lodge met with the Skipper and Hawk was of course totally on board. There would be a small landing party of the motor whaleboat plus two, armed with small arms and with Chief Dantes in charge. Guns had personally met with the gunner's mates and discussed preparations for the shore bombardment mission. After Normandy, Cherbourg and Southern France this ought to be easy, he said. He did one more thing. He went to see the shipfitters and asked if they could make a pair of shields from boiler plate, each to fit at his neck and curved to protect either his front or his back with a soft loop attached so that it would stay around his neck as a collar, keep the plate from falling off. They made them and he tried them on and it was a fit. A bit heavy but a fit and they weren't falling off. Each plate had its own strap to loop around his neck and he had a belt to put around his chest to keep it all in place.

Dantes mustered his boat crew and briefed them on exactly what he expected. He had looked at the charts and showed the Cox'n the depths, coming off of the beach and explained that he wanted them to stay at a distance in case of fire from the shore and yet be close enough so that he could wade and get their evacuee. He directed that they put some blankets in the boat for her as well as some water and had a dowel cut and marked with numbers in feet, from the bottom. "Here, this will be faster than a lead line. Any questions?" "Yes, Chief, is it true, is the person we're picking up the Commodore's wife? "She's a LCDR, Nurse and yes, she is his wife." The crew looked determined and gratified to be on the mission as they cast looks up toward the Flag Bridge. Finally Hod turned to his First Cass Gunner's Mate. "Smitty, you're the back up to me. If you see me go down you're in charge and I expect that you will continue to make the attempt to get the Commander aboard. Using your own judgment, of course." Smitty nodded and Hod was satisfied, dismissed them.

With less than a half hour to go before debarking at the rendezvous point, Dantes noticed that the Commodore hadn't been seen on the Bridge. All outfitted in his protective rig and steel helmet he went into Flag Country and knocked on Lodge's door. "Come." Entering into the space he found exactly what he expected. Lodge looked up from his chair. He had some grease paint on his face and a helmet and some boots to go with his khakis. There was a .45 strapped to his side and a look of determination that would brook no interference.

"I'm a last minute volunteer." Dantes smiled and replied, "Sir, no room in the boat." "I am going ashore with you, Chief." "Sir, all due respect but no, you are not. If you insist on going I will no longer be a volunteer. If you go you will take my spot. It will be your mission and you will lead it. Is there no way you will stand down and let the operation proceed as planned?" Lodge thought for a few seconds, "What kind of man would stay in safety while another man saved his wife?" "A smart one, Sir. Just like a Doctor wouldn't operate on his relative. You pick the next best one in line." Lodge shook his head and Dantes made up his mind. "Sir, as the Officer you give the orders. As an Enlisted man I carry them out." As Lodge stood to make his way to the door Hod said, "Let me check your helmet, looks like it could do with some adjustment." Lodge took it off and Dantes fussed with it for a second or two and then dropped the helmet and cold cocked the Commodore with a vicious right cross. He carefully lowered him onto his bunk, turned off the lights and went down to the boat deck, ready to go, muttering *"First make sure you're right, then go ahead."*

The ship was at General Quarters. When Lodge didn't show up Locker checked the Commodore's Stateroom and saw exactly what had happened. Lodge was out cold and there was a swelling on his jaw, already changing color. The Chief went to the Bridge, told the CO that the Commodore was detained by message traffic and that he was returning to Flag Country. Skipper said, "Thanks, Chief," and went back to his close observation of activities ashore. With his binocs he could see the party they were there to meet. They had just started to break from cover and were making their way toward the waterline. Hawk swung his binocs to the right, further south on the coast line and in the direction from which any opposition would approach. He couldn't see any advancing skirmishers so he said "Fire Control, Bridge, weapons released to deliver fires to targets one and two." The bridge talker repeated the command as well as the reply from Fire Control. A salvo from the three mounts they had left after the modifications went screaming inland to drop precisely on the coordinates given as the location for the enemy encampment. The Army rescue contingent, approaching the Camp several miles away could just barely hear the reports and only because they were listening for them.

The whaleboat had pulled in close enough to shore so that Dantes could get out of the boat and wade ashore as far as necessary to grab Lydia. Gunny and a smaller figure were coming quickly across the sand and entering the water. Gunny had a rifle and a pistol and he had Lydia by the arm. The rest of the "resupply" team had turned their backs on the beach and were advancing back into the jungle to form a defensive perimeter of sorts. Of course they had hoped to melt quietly into the green without being seen. They had been surprised by the Destroyer instead of a Submarine, the use of daylight instead of the cover of darkness.

They were close enough now that Dantes could make out her features. It was Lydia for sure, though not as he remembered her. She had stopped and was looking about her in confusion. Where were the bales of medicine? Why the firing? She was yanking with her arm, trying to get loose just as Dantes made it to their side. "Where are the." And just as she was about to say "med-icines" she saw Dantes. More accurately she saw only the eyes, the same eyes she'd seen in the rearview mirror, the eyes that had watched until the mirror was turned down.

"No medicines, Lydia. John has come for you," Dantes said. Her eyes went totally wide and blank, "NO! I WILL NOT LEAVE MY BOYS." Gunny reached inside her blouse and found the pill and dropped it into the water. "You'd better take her, Hod, she's borderline psycho and a danger to herself. I just got rid of her suicide pill." "You coming, Gunny?" Gunny smiled, "Nah, I've got Rosario to take care of, at least until we win this thing."

Just then a small arms round plinked off of Dantes' breastplate. They both noticed it. "Here, you take my front plate and use it. I'll keep the back one and use it to protect Lydia and myself, going back out to the boat." As he pulled Lydia into his arms and turned back to sea, the hits started coming more frequently into his back plate, each one staggering him a bit as he waded. He had her secured in front of him, protecting her with his body. Gunny headed north along the beach and into cover as soon as he could get there. The ship shifted their fire to cut off any advance by the enemy to the north. Lydia was gazing up into his eyes, unnaturally calm, now. "John, Darling, I knew you'd come. I knew you'd come, I..."

She slipped into unconsciousness, her pale face swaying as Dantes carried her in water getting deeper until he finally got to the boat. The crew yanked her aboard and shielded her as Dantes climbed over the gunwale and threw himself over her and stayed there as the boat peeled away from the shore and headed back to the ship. Only then did he notice that his left forearm was bleeding from what seemed to be a superficial gunshot wound.

Alongside the ship now, he had removed his back plate, grabbed the Jacob's ladder and was getting step by step up the short ladder with Lydia held in one of his heavily muscled arms until several eager hands again grabbed them and pulled them to safety. Locker and Lodge were both there, Lodge with his war paint off, removed by Locker as he was unconscious. He looked none the worse for wear except for the swelling, which was already going down. The medical team had a stretcher standing by and she was put carefully into it and two men carried her up to Flag Country. Locker and the Hawk were standing with Dantes as the boat was brought aboard. "How'd it go, Chief," the Skipper asked. Hawk saw the bloody sleeve and called a Corpsman over, "Better get that cleaned up, Chief." "The home-made armor came in handy, Sir," Dantes answered. "Gunny Clancy, who got her here for rescue took half of it as protection to get back to shore. He felt his place was there and intends to see it through to the end." *As did Mrs. Lodge, bless her poor tortured soul.*

Later that evening, wound dressed and back at the spud locker the two of them, Hod and his Sea Daddy. "You're not gonna' tell me what really happened, are you." "Well, you know. It all went well, that's what counts." "You going to tell Lodge?" "Of course, if he asks." "That was the one helluva most fantastic thing I've ever seen, Hod." "Wallace I will tell you one thing, because I know you've already figured most of it out. Yeah, I did cold cock him when he insisted on going ashore. But before I did I also told him that the way it worked was that he gave the orders and the Enlisted carried them out. It didn't slow him down and I didn't want to see perhaps both of them wounded or dead. So, I did the only thing left that I could think of." Locker stood for a while and thought. "The two of them have got a lot to work out. I don't think you make even the top ten on that list. They just need time to do it, you gave them that time and it's going to be fine." Locker laughed, "Hell by the time they get back in Hawaii and get her pregnant they'll be naming their son Howard, and calling him Hod."

The ship made knots to rendezvous with MinRon20, joined company and took tactical command before reaching their next operation, sweeping the approaches of mines in preparation for the invasion of Okinawa. There was no contact between Dantes and Lodge. The Commander at first was under some sedation and stayed in Lodge's cabin. That lasted for three days. She took her meals there as well. The Commodore bumped the Skipper from his inport cabin and the Hawk shifted to his sea cabin. During the days while in transit Lodge would sit by Lydia's side, caring for her needs. They checked ship's stores and found some khakis, trou that were taken up in the waist and small size shirts. They also found some gold oak leaves and she was able to make a good appearance, though she was very much underweight. The ship's cooks made special meals for her and they were carried up to her by the messenger of the watch. She made do with men's skivvies and had the privacy of Flag Quarters.

The men took to her with great interest and affection, started referring to the ship as the Lyddy Mae, though not in her hearing. Of course Cochrane was given a full report and he passed it along to his Boss who sent thanks and kind words along to MacArthur. A note from Nimitz to the Fitzes was sent and delivered in person by Parsons in Nuuanu. A message was sent to the Commander of the Boston Navy Shipyard who personally took it to the Lodge home and the Crowninshield home. The reactions were explosive happiness and a lot of folks on their knees in gratitude.

For a while nobody made a fuss over the fact that there was a woman aboard. She was getting well, gaining weight by the day, it seemed. They were headed into a live fire Operations Area, actually all areas were pretty much considered hostile. With no ship to which to transfer her, she was going to be aboard in Okinawa. That fact is what probably saved her, or at least brought her back to being a fully functioning human being.

CHAPTER 57

OKINAWA

Captain Hawkins stepped to the mike on the 1MC. "This is the Captain speaking. Well done to all hands and especially to Chief Gunner's Mate Dantes for the successful operation just concluded off the coast of Luzon. Good job delivering covering fire in our shore bombardment. I can now report that at the same time as our shore bombardment demonstration our forces on Luzon completed a daring rescue operation of some 600 or 700 prisoners of war from the Cabanatuan Prison Camp. Our bombardment pinned down some Japanese Army troops, allowing the rescue to proceed with minimal interference. Well done. Now we are headed with the rest of the Squadron to sweep the approaches to Okinawa in preparation for our invasion of that island. We're well trained and that's good because we expect serious opposition from the Japs, including Jap aircraft. We have Radar, and proximity fuzes and we also have a very fine reputation for hitting what we aim at. I expect that we will continue bringing the fight to the enemy. That is all."

Ellyson and her cohorts swept the approaches to the designated landing beaches for six days. Deploying their cutter cables with depressors and floats, the idea was to be able to cut anchored mines loose from the bottom and allow them to float to the surface where they would be destroyed by forty millimeter or small arms fire. Commodore Lodge and his small staff were kept busy coordinating this effort while LCDR Lodge continued to recuperate in her husband's quarters in Flag Country. At the end of this part of the operation all of the high speed minesweepers switched to their roles as radar pickets and ASW escorts and were available for shore bombardment missions.

Hundreds of Kamikaze aircraft launched from Kyushu and Formosa to assault the US and British armada attacking Okinawa. Stationed as they were, some fifty miles from the Island in order to give early warning of approaching Jap aircraft, the Squadron were the first to come under heavy attack. Rodman was hit by three suicide aircraft and a near miss bomb blast. Emmons was nearby providing an air defense of Rodman and was hit by an additional five Kamikazes. She suffered casualties to more than half of her crew and Officers. Ultimately Emmons was scuttled by Ellyson with her five inch gunfire, but before sending her to her watery grave Elly Mae took aboard as many survivors as she could manage, with other ships in the Squadron doing the same.

During a break in the action Lodge popped into Flag Country to check on Lydia and found an empty stateroom. Rushing to the Bridge he was told that the Commander was down in the Wardroom. Dropping down to the main deck he entered the Wardroom. She had on a medical smock over her uniform and was wearing bloody gloves and with the overhead lights rigged to turn the space into a medical center the wardroom table was being used as an operating table. The corpsmen were assisting her as she gave quiet, confident instructions. All of them were wearing masks and from time to time an assistant would wipe the perspiration from her face. Lodge stood for just a short time watching her administer anesthesia and then show an assistant what she wanted done, and then turn immediately back with a saw in hand as she unflinchingly removed a leg above the knee. The deck was slippery and men were doing their best to keep it dry, squeegees being used to pool the blood and blankets thrown to cover it to preserve the footing. Ellyson of course was underway and maneuvering and still the instruments were held in place, the bodies of the living adjusting automatically as required for the rolls and pitching, the unconscious men on the table strapped in. From time to time one of her crew would take the limbs or the occasional dead person into the Skipper's cabin, just forward of the operating room. No sooner did one or two get moved, alive or dead, than another one took his place. There were wild eyed kids getting strapped in and Lydia always took a second to comfort and reassure them before starting her procedure. A corpsman was treating those waiting, for shock, bandaging wounds and ordering them so as to work on the ones with the best chance first. Two with their guts spilling out were given morphine to ease their pain and a towel put over their horrible wounds to hide them as they died. The ship's Protestant lay leader had an open Bible and was reading to his shipmates, another island of peace in the middle of mayhem. But everywhere Lodge looked he saw efficiency and calm. Lodge couldn't imagine the horrors she had undergone in the jungle, just knew she was again intact and had at last come back and he couldn't have been more grateful or proud of her.

Lydia came up the ladder from the Wardroom and entered the space. She had treated all of the men who had come aboard, needing attention. She had been in the Wardroom for sixteen hours and it was now the start of the mid watch. She needed sleep but had left orders to be awakened in two hours or in the event of an emergency. The ship's yeoman had made up folders on each patient and was still typing from her notes, down below. She looked about the cabin and noticed John, seated at his desk. He stood and they came together. At first she was stiff and unyielding. He held her. Then she started to shake and he held her tighter. He felt her back heave as she took deep breaths and let them go, with her tears. Still he just held her. She fell against him and he picked her up in his arms and lay her gently in his rack and put a blanket over her. She fell instantly asleep with a small snuffle, the way she had always snored, up Nuuanu way. John took a seat at his small cubbyhole desk, turned off the small light and repositioned his chair so that he could see where she was, in his bed. *His* bed.

Lodge went below to the wardroom and checked with the corpsmen every couple hours and as long as Lydia wasn't needed for an emergency, he said, please don't wake the Commander. She got a full night's sleep and only awoke with the smell of coffee and toast. She got up and stretched and there was John, still at his desk. As the steward brought in their eggs and grits John told her he'd made the visits during the night and had told them not to disturb her unless it was an emergency. He passed over a written report on her patients, using information from the Corpsmen. She tucked into her breakfast with a relish, and John kept passing it to her.

Finally she looked up, "How long was I gone, John?" "Doesn't matter, you're back, now, Dear." "I wanted to stay there, needed to stay with my boys," and she dropped her head. "Darling, thank you for coming for me. I don't think I would have lasted for much longer." "We got approval to do it as part of a mass rescue of our POWs at Cabanatuan Prison." "We made reports of our surveillance of that prison. The men in there were dying every day. The rescue could not have come too soon for those poor boys. She paused, "I don't think I'll ever forget you in the water, holding out your arms to me. I think maybe it's time you moved back in here, in your own quarters, Commodore."

And very quietly that's just what he did, and they started rebuilding their marriage and were together whenever their duties allowed and slept together on that bed made for one. He realized now that she had suffered some sort of breakdown, had mistaken Dantes for him and it ate at him. It was Dantes who had gone for her, in spite of his wanting to do that very thing. Not only that, but Dantes had slugged him to keep him aboard. It festered and he was not having an easy time of it and it had been several days since he saw Dantes, in fact he hadn't even thanked him for what he'd done, or written him up for assault, for that matter, either.

Locker waited until the Commander was on her rounds, in the sick bay, knocked on Lodge's door, heard "Come" and entered. Lodge told him to take a seat, which the Chief did. Lodge peered at him somewhat querulously, "What's up, Chief?" "Permission to speak frankly, Sir?" Now Lodge colored but swiveled his chair around to face his Chief directly and nodded. "Sir, there are just three people aboard who know that Chief Dantes slugged you." Lodge clenched his fists reflexively, thinking about it. "It was a goddam sucker punch, Chief. You taught him well in Boot Camp." "He always fights to win, Sir. Knows no other way. I'll tell you something else about Hod that he'd rather not you nor anybody else know. He had to fight for his life as a kid, in Texas, together with his brother and sister. They were about to be killed and instead got the gun away from their father. Hod Dantes sees things in black and white and takes action immediately. You were only the latest victim, or in this case, beneficiary. Did you know that he was wounded, getting the Commander off of that beach? He told me that he went ashore thinking there might be only a small chance he could get her out of there alive and he damn sure wasn't going to see the two of you die, just when you had a chance to get back together. Sir, that man idolizes you. He told me that he said some pretty rough stuff to you, right before he hit you. He also said that like Davy Crockett he had made sure he was right and then went ahead. He said it was right to stop you from going ashore with a pistol on your hip when the Squadron needed you here, aboard ship, taking care of *all* of us."

The expression on Lodge's face eased. "*Of course they're right, both of them are. I had no business going ashore and I've been resenting what happened ever since.*" "Chief, no excuse. Of course Hod was right and he most likely stopped me from taking some shots. There wasn't enough home-made armor to go around. Besides, as he so forcefully reminded me, the Officers *give* the orders, the Enlisted men carry them out." Locker stood up, "Sir, I don't have the foggiest notion of what you're talking about. May I be excused?" Lodge stood and extended his hand. "Thanks, Chief."

The Lodges were cleaning up after a light lunch in his cabin. "Dear, I have something to tell you," he said. She turned to him with a smile, "Mmm?" They put their arms around each other. "What, you're gonna' tell me I have to resign my commission, and." He put his finger across her lips and then kissed them. "No, I want to tell you what really happened."

That evening just after chow in the Goat Locker Wallace turned to Hod, "You know, it's been a while since you looked after the forty millimeter. I think right now would be a perfect time to check on it, Chief." Hod looked at his Sea Daddy, didn't say a thing and grabbing his cover he went straightaway to the bridge and made his way to the Flag Bridge. Lydia saw him first, held her hand up to her husband and stepped outside. Hod put down his prop, the oil rag, and saluted her, "Evening, Ma'am." "Hod, from now on we're Lydia and, if I may, Hod." "Why Ma'am." "Lydia," she responded. "Yes Ma'am, uh, Miss Lydia." "No, just Lydia. It's an order and we will observe it when I have the privilege of your company in private or with Family, including my husband." She looked toward the cabin and waited while Lodge came out. By now

Hod was uncovered, holding his cover crushed in both hands. There was no salute. There were no words. They both started talking at once. "Sir I know how much you wanted to go, I *know!*" "I told Lydia exactly what happened. She was out of her mind when she mistook you for me, using my name and all, trying to tell her it was me and not you. She remembers the rescue now, said that all she could think of was that I'd come to save her and she was abandoning her boys. Chief, she said one other thing, she said that you saved my life as well as hers. And we can never thank you enough. And of course you were absolutely correct, my place was here, aboard the Elly Mae." Hod laughed in relief, "Lydia, you should know that the crew now calls the ship the Lyddy Mae." If the bridge watch had looked aft they would have seen a strange sight, but they had their eyes in the boat. Locker and the Hawk were sharing a mug of coffee on the starboard wing. The Lodges and the Chief had one of those instant bits of calm when the crew studiously ignores you. So they stood there in a three person hug. If MacArthur had been there his photographer would have taken a picture.

CHAPTER 58

ZEROS

On the four to eight watch aboard the Ellyson, steaming off of Okinawa, the ship would soon be coming awake to the reality of combat while standing duty as a radar picket ship for the U.S. Invasion force which had been assaulting Okinawa since April. Lt Scott Sawyer USN, the ship's Engineer Officer was the OOD. He had the deck and had turned over conning duties to his JOOD. They were in radar picket station 5, about 50 miles due east of the main island of Okinawa, itself. Their Division of four Destroyers had relieved last night and as part of that taking on of responsibility they had received a good bit of Intel, had an idea of what to expect, if things continued the way they had been going.

But for now, it was a peaceful evening, coming to an end. She was on a course of 000 degrees, heading north so as to take the sunrise on her starboard beam, making turns for fifteen knots. Wind was light, maybe three knots out of the northeast, and combined with the relative wind created by the ship's motion, it put the apparent wind just a point, or so, off the bow to starboard. This in turn kept the stack gas from the two stacks amidships blowing aft, off the port quarter, and giving the watch standers on the bridge clean air to breathe. When apparent wind was from aft it could make the watch miserable, as the ship would keep pace with her exhaust and bathe everyone in the noxious fumes of burned NSFO, Navy Standard Fuel Oil, that the crew called "virgin's breath."

There were no seas of any consequence, just a two foot swell out of that same northeast, taking the bow first, raising it slightly, then rolling under the hull, letting the bow down with a slight yaw to starboard until the fantail also fell off the swell, restoring the ship once again to its intended heading. In heavy weather that motion would turn into a violent corkscrew with heavy rolls, battering the ship as well as her crew. But tonight it was clear, dark and quiet. The OOD knew the position of all of the instruments and gages as well as their knobs for backlighting. He could read wind, course, rudder angle, all by stepping to the readout and finding the knob, a quick flick and back. The idea was to keep the bridge dark and quiet. The surface search radar repeater was covered with a hood, again, to protect night vision.

Sunrise was forecast for 0655, with nautical twilight, light enough to see the horizon, yet still dark enough to see the stars, starting about 45 minutes before that. On this morning the XO, LCDR Bill Dixon was aft, on the signal bridge, getting his star shots before nautical twilight ended. He had his senior Quartermaster getting time hacks as he called the mark, swinging the star's image down to the horizon, rocking his sextant to ensure the star contacted the horizon at the very lowest point, for an accurate elevation angle. Earlier the watch had been treated to the smell of cinnamon rolls, wafting up from the mess decks and the Bos'n's mate of the watch had sent Smiley, the messenger, below to bring a batch up to the bridge. They were sitting behind the pilothouse, next to the Signal Bridge coffee mess as the Bridge team and Combat Information Center maintained a sharp visual and radar watch, on both surface search and air search radars.

Lt Sawyer was glancing at the time, not wanting to miss the call to the CO, for 0530, as requested in the Captain's night orders, when Cdr Dick Hawkins, USN, the Commanding Officer, who had awakened on his own, came out into the pilothouse, around 0520.

"Captain's on the Bridge!' from the Quartermaster of the Watch, Rohde, QM3, as the Skipper returned the OOD's salute and, "Good morning sir."

"Morning, Scott," the Skipper replied, climbing into his chair, on the starboard side of the pilothouse. "Any activity?"

"Sir, radio silence, no surface or air contacts except friendlies, clean screen on the surface search repeater and CIC reports no air nor subsurface contacts." "We have mount captains in the main battery, all mounts slaved to the director, director manned as well."

"And the Chief Gunner, Mr. Sawyer, where's he?"

LT Scott Sawyer let a grin escape his normally serious face, "Captain, Chief has been up and making his rounds since 0200, exercising the mounts in local, checking communications circuits, cycling the loading mechanisms and hoists. He reported a hydraulic leak in Mount 51, fixed it and reported that, too." The Skipper eased back in his chair, asked who the aft lookout was, was told, and asked that he be taken a cup of coffee, and maybe one of those rolls "I smelled, earlier." Everybody on the bridge smiled, that was the old man, checking to see if Jones, on watch aft, was awake and giving him the first cinnamon roll, while they were still warm.

With his sextant in hand, the XO stopped in the pilothouse, reported to the Captain. "Bill, you doing those sights for practice? We have plenty good positioning coming off the surface search."

"Yessir, just keeping my hand in, I'll save these for later, and compare the position to the current one in Combat, once I've worked them out"

"Sounds good, XO, I'm expecting some action, this morning, for sure sometime today"

"Concur, Sir. I'll be in Combat from here on out, make sure we're up on all circuits, and wide awake." He saluted, got an easy salute in return, and "Hey, Bill, take some of those cinnamon rolls to the watch, in there." "And I want your best man on the Surface Search, I think they'll come in low."

"Aye, Sir," and the XO smiled, got a few and left the pilothouse, bearing gifts.

"Rohde, what time's sunrise?"

"Cap'n, I have it at 0655."

"Think the Japs'll be on time, Rohde?"

Sir, I don't trust 'em, wouldn't surprise me if they're early, Sir."

"Yeah, I agree." Turning to the OOD, the Captain said, "I relieve you, Sir." Lt Sawyer saluted and replied, I stand relieved, Sir."

"This is the Captain, I have the Deck and the Conn," "Aye aye sir, the Captain has the Deck and the Conn," came back a chorus of voices from the helmsman, lee helmsman, OOD and JOOD. Rohde went to the log and made his entries of all of this as the Skipper said, "Bos'n, Sound General Quarters."

"General Quarters, General Quarters, all hands man your battle stations, General Quarters," BONG, BONG, BONG, BONG, as the Bos'n made the announcement and moved the switch on the alarm. All the watch standers were relieved by those for whom their battle station was the bridge and the same activity took place all over the ship, in the Engineering spaces Main Control, main and secondary batteries, magazines, sonar, fire control, after steering and Combat Information Center. Everyone ran to their stations, up and forward on the starboard side, down and aft on the port side. It was a smooth and swift transformation of a ship into a bristling, aggressive man of war. The Executive Officer had his stopwatch going, would record how long it took to get reports of manned and ready from all stations. That report would go to the C.O., "One minute, fifty seven seconds, Sir."

"Very well," responded the Skipper, "now where are our Japs?" The crew were still pulling on their helmets and life jackets, folding their trousers into their socks and lookouts adjusting their binoculars as the Captain turned to his talker and said "Fire Control, Bridge, air action starboard." The talker repeated his message into his sound powered phone, got an acknowledgement with an "Aye," tacked on, reported, "Fire Control, Aye, Sir" to the Captain as all three of the ships 5" weapons, under director control, slewed to a bearing of 090 degrees, the hydraulics making a muted, whining humming sound, all weapons loaded. Destroyers were known as the greyhounds of the Fleet, but Ellyson at General Quarters was more like a pointer, nose into the wind, sniffing for her prey. The Skipper noted, with approval, that the JOOD had his head buried in the surface search radar repeater hood; *good, if the zeros are coming in really low, we may pick them up on surface search, be able to steer the director onto target.*

"Captain, I show an intermittent return, at 18,000 yards, 090, could be a maneuvering air target on the deck, sir."

"Very well," "Fire Control, Bridge, probable bogies on the deck, starboard beam, 15,000 to 18,000 yards." "Fire Control, Aye, Sir."

"Starboard Lookout, I have a glint, bearing 080."

"Very Well, Guns free, fire when you have a target." "Aye."

"Combat reports multiple contacts inbound, three bogies at 18,000 yards."

"All ahead flank, make turns for 25 knots, right standard rudder, steady course 045."

"Aye, Captain, right standard rudder, steady course 045," "Engines indicating all ahead flank, turns for twenty five knots, Sir!"

Rohde entered in his log, "0640, Commenced fire, increased speed to 25 knots, maneuvering to avoid incoming bogies."

BOOM, BOOM, clink, clink, the brass shell casings piling up on deck and the burnt powder smell enveloping the ship, all 5 inch mounts firing salvoes, nominally about 15 rounds per minute, but up to 22 rounds per minute, by a smooth, experienced mount. Further, they were using projectiles with "VT" or variable timed fuzes. These were the first smart weapons in the history of warfare, kept secret in order to maintain the advantage over unsuspecting attacking aircraft. The fuze contained a miniaturized radio transmitter and receiver, complete with cushioned vacuum tube, to protect against the shock of initial explosion. Power was from a unique tubular battery, containing the electrolyte in a glass ampule, which shattered upon firing. Then the centrifugal force, caused by the lands in the barrel, cutting into the ring on the projectile, made the round rotate and the acid was flung into the plates of the battery, generating a small bit of electricity. This "juice" was conducted to a capacitor where it accumulated charge and powered the radio and receiver. When the returning radio signal that reflected off the incoming aircraft was sufficiently strong the fuze was fired electrically. All of this was designed to cause an explosion at a distance of 75 feet from the target aircraft, the effective limit of shrapnel from the projectile. The secondary battery of forty millimeter mounts would not commence fire until within shorter range, with their higher pitched contribution to the cacophony of lethal destruction.

Below decks, in the two fire rooms and two engine rooms, another part of the symphony was enacted, an intricate ballet of firemen at boiler fronts, cutting in additional burners delivering NSFO to the fireboxes, and Machinist

Mates, at the throttles, in two engine rooms, maintaining pressure and opening up the valves to admit superheated steam to the turbines, mated to reduction gears which transmitted rotational power to the shafts, which turned the screws. Blowers fed the fires and cooled the Snipes, as they were called, and a full watch kept an eye on all auxiliary equipment, pumps and pressures and electrical generator sets, keeping the ship able to maneuver and giving it the electrical power to operate the mounts, to fight and hopefully to survive.

The engineering spaces were normally very noisy and very hot, and it took a special kind of sailor to spend those hours deep in the bowels of the ship, seemingly protected from an external force, yet isolated in their spaces during general quarters, spaces that could become their coffins, in the event of a serious hit, for all compartments were dogged down with watertight doors and hatches, the principle being to contain flooding or fire to as few compartments as possible.

In Baker 2, Main Control, forward engine room. "Chief, sounds like it's warming up, topside."

Grunting, "Dorso, not the first and won't be the last." Chief George Oakley was rotund, silver haired and mostly content to let his First Class do all the work; the aggressive First Class ruled the roost, and everyone knew it..

MM1 John Dorso,"Five inchers, pounding away, they better hit something."

"Yeah, before something hits us," replied the Chief.

Lt. Sawyer, an Academy man, whose GQ station was Main Control, cast an eye toward Dorso, from Brockton, Mass and the toughest brawler on the ship, "Dorso, I believe you'd rather be topside, kicking the hell out of those Japs, personally."

Dorso, who resembled Popeye, with bulging arms that burst from his dungarees, replied, "not much good with weapons, sir, but I wouldn't mind getting my hands on a few of them." Scott chuckled, remembering the smoker they'd held in Pearl, on the way out here; there were no takers for a bout with Dorso. His arms, reputation and nose, which had been broken multiple times, awed everyone aboard ship. Dorso ruled Baker Two, and nobody gave him a hard time.

The ship heeled to starboard and everyone below decks stiffened slightly, automatically to remain in place, knowing that the ship was making a high speed turn to port. Being closer to the center of mass of the entire ship, motion about the three axes was not felt as strongly, below, as it was topside, especially on the bridge. Sawyer noticed a young fireman, looking spooked and a little the worse for wear, caught the Chief's eye and nodded toward the fireman. Chief Oakley raised a chin at the Fireman, called him over, "Sanders, take a turn on the wheel, Horton, you coach him, no time like the present to get in a little underway training." He looked back at the Chief Snipe as Sanders took the throttle valve wheel to the starboard shaft, and fingered it nervously. The Chief Engineer nodded, just perceptibly, his satisfaction as the Chief made a small smile, headed to the coffee mess for a cup for the two of them.

Meanwhile, topside, Rohde, writing in the Ship's Log, "0650 splashed one bogey," as the Old Man feinted to starboard then shifted the helm, carving the high speed turn to port, felt by the unseeing snipes below. Zero number two had taken the momentary turn, headed to intercept and was late, correcting for the final turn. He flew into a wall of metal, low to the deck, raining parts, cockpit aflame as he sputtered close by, down the starboard side and crashed.

Meanwhile the third Jap Zero had split off from the initial loose formation of three, hauled around to the North and was now approaching, waggling its wings, directly off the bow, and lining up with the ship's centerline. "Right full rudder," "Right full rudder, aye, Sir." The Old man was going to take this one on the port side and cause the Zero to have to maneuver to keep Ellyson in his sights. Now there was less room for pilot error, in glide path; instead of the length of the ship to use for his collision, he had only the width. Conversely, his target was now wider and he could make a greater error in course and still achieve a hit. 'Hawk' knew something about flight and figured he'd just made the Jap pilot's job a little tougher. Sure enough, the pilot had the course figured right, was headed straight for the middle of the ship, but he was losing speed, under the withering fire from the five inchers and the 40mm mounts. Pulling his nose up, to stretch his glide, with power gone, the Zero fluttered as the wings lost laminar flow, stalled and gently eased into the sea and foamed to an oily, fiery stop, less than 100 yards from the ship. The pilot could be clearly seen, moving in the cockpit as his craft continued to float on the surface. "Cease fire, all stations report." Then to the lee helmsman, "all engines stop," a three second pause, "all engines back one third," and as way came off the ship, again, "starboard engine stop," then "all engines stop," as the Skipper had brought the ship smartly to a position from which he could observe this last kill.

Suddenly the port lookout hollered out, "That last bogey, Sir!" Everybody saw it, the Kamikaze pilot had thrown back his canopy and drawn a pistol, was aiming it at the bridge of the ship idling just yards away. Some on the ship that had brought him down were frozen in place: on the bridge, in gun tubs and mounts, between the stacks where a ship's cook had hidden to watch the show, and were waiting for the shot, others were diving for cover. The eerie silence was broken by the chatter of a Browning automatic rifle, BRRRRT, pop, poppop its tracers streaming into the cockpit, and the rounds striking the young pilot, his body jerking spasmodically before falling back into his seat. It broke the tension, like a film jerkily starting again, snapshot images piling atop one another, now the Zero being engulfed in flame, now the craft settling lower, finally at the end of the feature a violent burial at sea for the

Emperor's defender, as the flames reached the explosives he had carried, and parts of the pilot and his aircraft scattered, some even hitting the ship in a weakened last thrust of the Samurai, true to his bushido code even in death.

It was the Chief, he had the BAR and had fired a burst then a few singles, raining fire into the zero until it started to settle beneath the waves. The Old Man looked on in astonishment, as Chief Dantes racked his BAR open and popped the magazine, put his automatic rifle down in the gun tub. The Captain shook his head, waved to the Chief, got a salute in return and the Old Man hollered from the bridge, "Well done, Chief!" Chief just grinned, turned to one of the strikers, told him to clean the BAR, then headed to Chief's Quarters; maybe they had grits, a man could work up an appetite.

The Captain turned to the XO, now on the bridge, from Combat, "XO, set the regular underway watch, port section, and get 'em fed, quickly. That might not be our only raid, today."

"Aye, Sir." And no one noticed the cinnamon rolls, still sitting by the coffee mess, aft of the pilot house.

The ship's Officers started filing into the Wardroom, after going by their living compartments, cleaning up and changing to a fresher set of khakis. The Stewards had already restored the Wardroom table to its dining function, breaking down and storing all of the medical equipment that had been rigged as an operating room, during GQ. The tables had a green felt tablecloth, covered with an ironed white tablecloth, used during meals, with plates and utensils and napkins all in place. In rough weather they would also be fitted with a wooden framework called a fiddleboard, and the tablecloth wetted, to keep crockery and food in place, as the ship rolled and pitched. The Skipper entered the Wardroom from just forward, where his inport cabin was, pushing aside a curtain and going straight to the head of the table. The assembled Officers came to an easy position of attention, sitting after the CO, remaining respectfully silent, until the Old Man spoke.

"Good job, XO, nice early steer to the bogies."

"Sir, they were no doubt inspired by the cinnamon rolls," And the Skipper snapped his fingers, "I *knew* I forgot something!" And those assembled at the senior table chuckled politely, appreciatively; they felt lucky to have 'The Hawk' as Skipper. They all considered the Elly Mae, to be a lucky ship and knew that the Skipper had a lot to do with that.

"That starboard lookout?"

"Yessir, Handy, SN1."

"He had a good, early visual sighting of the bogies, sang right out, too, seems a sharp lad."

"He's had a year of college, sir."

"I'm not surprised, does he want to strike for anything?"

"Not that I'm aware of, Captain, I could find out."

"Very well." And the Captain finished his S.O.S. and coffee, wiped his lips with an ironed napkin and made as if to return to his cabin, which served as an office for him. He waved the table to their seats, then turned, as if just remembering something, said to the Gunnery Officer, Lt JG Hansen, "Rick, a word with you, before you leave?"

"Aye, Sir." And everyone at the table and the next one with the JOs wondered what was up.

CHAPTER 59

LEADERSHIP LESSONS

The Skipper's cabin, or stateroom, was spare, but comfortable. It had a rack, or built in bed, with drawers underneath, a washbasin and separately closeted head, a built in metal desk with drawers and book shelves, with a stacked trio of baskets, titled 'Suction', 'Recirc' and 'Discharge' on top of his desk in the corner nearest the door, giving a hint of the CO's Engineering background. Various cable runs and pipes were solidly attached to the overhead, with their identification and location neatly stenciled on them. There was an industrial beige carpet on the deck, white painted insulation on the bulkheads and a luxury, a door that closed and locked, affording some measure of security and privacy, hard to come by for mere mortals on a man of war. Finally, there was room for a couple, three of the aluminum chairs, found in the Wardroom and Chiefs' Quarters. On this occasion there were no chairs. This was not to be a social meeting.

This was the first time that Lt (JG) Hansen had actually entered the Old Man's inport cabin. He knocked twice, heard, "Come," entered and softly closed the door behind him, trying not to gawk at his surroundings. "Lt (JG) Hansen, reporting as ordered, Sir." He had his garrison cap pulled through his belt, and, as Naval Officers did not salute indoors or uncovered, assumed a position of attention, eyes locked onto the bulkhead, above the Skipper.

"Stand at ease, Rick, be comfortable." And the Junior Officer, yet a Department Head, stood easy and let his gaze drop to the Captain. He didn't know what the Skipper had on his mind, but he was more than a little bit nervous, as he felt the sweat starting to gather under his khaki collar. The Captain put down the papers he had been reading and pushed back from his desk, swiveled to face his Gun Boss.

"Give me your impressions of the action we had, this morning, Rick."

Mind racing, he tried to come up with what he thought the Skipper wanted to hear, instead of just reporting laconically and factually about how his responsibilities had been discharged. "Sir, thought the slight turn to starboard before shifting helm to port was effective, threw the Jap pilot off."

"Ah, Rick, mainly wanted to see what you had observed in our gunnery, this morning."

"Well, Sir, I thought it was effective, we *did* manage to knock down three out of three, no casualties, all mounts ready to go again."

"Did you notice the fall of shot, as the first one got closer, before we got lucky and knocked it down?"

"The shots that missed, Sir? I'm afraid I was watching the incoming aircraft, sir."

The Old Man smiled, "well, Rick, *all* of us were doing that, I take it, then, that you did not notice that one round from every salvo, I think the one from mount 53, all mounts under director control, was off, from the rest. It was hard to tell, since there was a large splash from the rest of the mounts, and the one lone splash, every time. It was to the right, as I recall."

He was crestfallen, now, the starch going out of his posture, as well as gathering at the seams of his shirt and waist. It had suddenly gotten a bit hot in the cabin. "Actually, it makes no difference in local control, as each mount operates independently and has its own accuracy and probabilities of a hit. That's why we train so hard with individual mounts, to sharpen their aim and increase their rate of fire, when in local control." "But in salvo, we need all of the mounts to point at the same target, to deliver the most impact, to be the most lethal."… "Right?" the Skipper prompted him. "Especially true now that we've swapped one five inch mount for our minesweeping gear."

Clearing his throat, feeling the heat in his face, Hansen replied, "Right, I mean yessir."

"So, what do you think could cause that to happen?"

This time the Junior Officer took his time to think, to recall what he knew about the five inch mounts and the gunfire control system, the Mark I Fire Control Computer and director. "Sir, one of the simpler aspects of the fire control solution is for correction of parallax, and,"

"And, how does that parallax manifest itself, Mr. Hansen?"

"Sir, it is a function of range to target as well as horizontal separation of the various mounts from the Director."

"Very good, Gun Boss, and which type of parallax was it that caused the stray rounds, in salvo, do you think?"

"Sir, since you observed this at several ranges, my guess is that mount 53 or else one of the other two is not physically aligned with the director, in train, Sir." The starch was coming back, the blush replaced by a bit of returning confidence, if not bravado.

"Well, Mark, officially we don't ever guess, we find out, but I know what you mean. How, exactly, will you find and correct this misalignment?"

"Sir, I can use the Quarterdeck long glass to sight on Polaris, from the director and from each mount, and ensure they are all reading the same elevation angle."

"In actuality you will be ensuring that the director and the mount are as parallel as possible, since they are both pointed at infinity, right? And then we can rely on the director to alter the train angle of each mount individually to ensure all rounds fall on the same point as the range changes, right?"

"Right, Sir." Hansen was ready to get out of there. "I'll get right on it, Captain."

"Well, you'll have to wait until we're in port to do the bore sighting on Polaris, but there may be some temporary correction we can make, here at sea, until that happens. Get with Chief Dantes and see what the two of you can come up with, then report your plan to the XO. With his approval I'll give you some firing time for training and to demonstrate the effectiveness of your fix."

"Aye Sir."

"And I want action this afternoon. Dismissed."

He got out of there with a final Aye,aye without letting the door hit him in the ass, and felt no small measure of resentment, not yet being mature enough to appreciate that his "training" had taken place in private, instead of before his peers, or, worse, the crew. But that was the Hawk's way, praise in public, chew ass in private, and always give a man his dignity, a way out.

He should've known better, but the Gun Boss called down to Chiefs' Quarters and asked to speak to Chief Dantes. It was near to noon meal and a Filipino mess cook answered the phone, said, "He no here, Sir. Perhaps after chow..." With a gruff thanks, Hansen hung up and went topside, drifted aft, to mount 53, where indeed he found the Chief, bent over an open hydraulic circuit, talking earnestly to two gunner's mate strikers. They were hanging on his every word and nobody looked up when he came and stood next to the mount. He'd noticed that he got a lot of that, the skipping of military courtesies, resented it as he was plenty smart enough to know when he was not recognized, respected. As a result he was often resentful and quick to react, to criticize and show his displeasure. It was going to be an endless cycle, until and unless he woke up. A Destroyer at sea will quickly expose faults, and usually deal with them, mercilessly. They liked to say she was a tough ride, but not a free one. You had to pull your weight.

Wanting his conversation with his Chief to be private, Hansen just caught his eye and asked him to meet him after noon meal, Chief said, "Aye, Sir, maybe back here, at the mount?" Chief had a pretty good idea what this was about, had been expecting something like this, "Either here, or at the director, someplace where we'll have time to ourselves?" "That'll be great, Chief, thanks." And he walked off, trying not to feel dismissed, as he had been at the Captain's cabin.

Chiefs' Quarters, noon meal. Or, perhaps more accurately known as the goat locker, where the Chiefs slept, ate, traded sea stories and simply prevailed as the ship's store of wisdom regarding all things naval, and getting things done.

Hey, pass the spuds, Guns, and what's up with your Boss? "Ahh, he's okay, no problems." "Whaddya suppose the Old Man wanted to see him in his stateroom, about?" It was the Chief Bos'n, who spent nearly all his time on deck and at the scuttlebutt; if anyone on board had the latest skinny, it was Boats. And, if it wasn't a rumor yet, he'd start it. "Where'd you get that, Boats?" They all knew, he just liked to challenge the Boats, every now and then. Boats sneered, said, "Same place you heard, Wardroom steward passed it along, down in the mess cooks compartment and it went wild, from there." Hod had gotten a more detailed briefing than that, however. In his collateral duty assignment as the ship's Chief Master at Arms, he had a lot of contacts, a lot of influence. It paid to be on the right side of the CMOA, you never knew when you might need some slack, and he was known as a power figure, someone who was a straight shooter and who could also deliver results, in tight spots. This overheard conversation was of direct interest to Dantes, the CMOA, and the Filipino wardroom steward described the ass chewing to him, only. The rest of the skinny was unrestricted. Dantes knew that a relatively serious malfunction had been discovered that morning, knew what it was, and had already worked out the temporary solution, was ready to complete putting it in place, this afternoon. His next job was to make it his Boss' idea, and these chuckleheads weren't going to get a word about it out of him.

The naval saying, sarcastic riddle, really, was, "What's long and green and has an asshole at each end?" The answer, fleet-wide was, of course, "The Wardroom table." At one end of the main table was the Captain, at the other end, the XO. They knew the joke, it was an old one, and every now and then one or the other of them seemed to go out of his way to demonstrate the physical reality of it. But for the XO, it was not necessary to try, he proved entertaining in one way or another, without any seeming effort.

LCDR Bill Dixon was a graduate of the University of Illinois, had been a hulking offensive lineman on their football team, was a heavy drinker and had a legendary temper, not a good combination on liberty or anywhere else, for that matter. He had once broken his own arm, pounding on the De'd Reckoning Tracer (DRT) while in Combat, part of the Anti-Submarine Warfare Team. His saving grace was that he was a teddy bear, a really nice guy who was no problem to read and he was dedicated to the ship, the Old Man and his shipmates, in roughly that order. A bachelor, no woman could stay married to him, he often liked to grab a JO or two when in port and say, "Let's go grease the car." Then the two or three of them, dressed in civs, would hit the beach and the XO would drink them all under the table, always making sure to get them back aboard before reveille, always standing tall at Officer's Call, in the morning.

XO turned to the Gun Boss, sitting next to him, at his end of the table, everybody in the Wardroom noticing, figuring he wanted to sit as far away from the Skipper as possible. "So, when are you going to be briefing me on your plan? I want this fixed, and fixed fast." He was talking under his breath, but it was all the more effective for that, coming out as painfully courteous, but presaging perhaps a sudden fit of violence, which the XO was known to have from time to time. Totally lost on Hansen was the XO's use of the first person, singular pronoun. You see, Hansen was not used to using the word "I" when he gave orders. It was usually, "the Captain wants this, or the XO wants that;" never did he muster up the balls to make it a command from himself; it was as though he needed to borrow their authority, a recognition of his own weakness, an apology for his very existence aboard a man of war.

Speaking just as quietly, Hansen replied, "Sir, I'm meeting with Chief Dantes right after chow, have some ideas to go over with him. Should be ready with a plan within an hour, or so. The XO cast a jaundiced eye at him, knew where the ideas would be coming from, and grunted, "Make it so and make it quick! We ain't got the time to be screwing around on radar picket station off no stinkin' Okinawa." With that the Gun Boss sprang from his chair, excused himself to the Skipper and made for the Wardroom door, every eye on him as he went. The Old Man and the XO exchanged glances and conversation resumed, until the Skipper stood and went forward, to clean up before going back to the bridge.

When Hansen arrived at Mount 53, aft the Chief was already waiting for him. "Ahh, Chief, glad you're here. We need to talk about a problem."

"If you mean the stray 5 inch rounds in salvo, I believe we have a fix for that, Sir." Hansen's jaw dropped. What? *Were these Chiefs clairvoyant?* The chief tendered a clipboard with a typed plan for a live firing training exercise. It included a description of the problem, hypotheses rejected and a chosen procedure to isolate the offending mount and put in a temporary fix. Furthermore there was a to/from/subject block, a place for the Gunnery Officer to sign and the Executive Officer to approve. "I chose not to speculate on what caused the mount to come out of alignment, but it should be easy to determine which mount and fix the problem." They went on, to discuss using dye packets on the rounds, and firing three gun salvos, each time not firing a different mount until the one that was the stray was identified by the absence of a stray splash away from the group.

Hansen was suddenly relieved and grateful, and he said, "Then you can go to the XO and brief him."

"No Sir, Mr. Hansen, this is *your* plan, I'll just carry it out for you, if you get the XO's approval. Shouldn't be a problem, just don't make any guesses or guarantees. We're investigating and once we find the offending mount, we'll put in the fix and test again."

"Hmmm, and the fix is just a trigonometry problem, determine the angle off, from the rest of the mounts, and then apply a temporary correction, to the left, of that mount's alignment with the director."

"Couldn't have said it better, myself, Sir, though it may be more trial and error than calculation. Maybe better not to get tangled up in the details of how we accomplish the offset and ensure it doesn't get out of adjustment again. For sure BuOrd would not approve, and it is intended to last only for so long as it takes us to get tied up, somewhere, where we can do a proper bore sighting. If you like I can show you what."

'No thanks, Chief, Well done!" And he headed off, to see the XO, one hugely relieved Department Head. He hadn't shown any curiosity about the fix or how, exactly, after they had put in the correction in train they would jury rig it to ensure it stayed in place. Of course "Guns" noticed and ruefully looked forward to the day when he'd be breaking in a new Gun Boss. *You'd think, even for just self-preservation, he'd have asked, wanted to know.* The Chief shook his head, got a couple strikers to have them make the adjustment for training and for their morale. He picked good strikers and for sure *they'd* be eager to learn. Somehow the mount's response coupling had jumped out of position, probably having to do with worn parts or perhaps a less than tight Allen screw. He'd known of a mount going off in train when this happened. It was the jury rig to make it less likely that the coupling would come out of lock again that wouldn't pass muster with BuOrd.

Bridge, starboard side, Captain's chair.

The rest of the watch had moved quietly away from the Skipper and the XO, giving them some privacy, such as it was. "XO, are you ready to iron out this wrinkle with the stray round?"

"Aye, Captain, and maybe iron out a few wrinkles in our Gun Boss, too."

"Think we're being too rough on him?"

"No sir, just that two black hats might be one too many. Besides, you got his attention and I'm a natural for the black hat, Skipper."

"Okay, then, he's your project, but we don't have a lot of time. I'll give you a few weeks, couple months, at most."

"Aye, Sir."

And, per-gra to conduct your live firing exercise, but keep BuOrd out of our knickers with the fix, and make it temporary."

"Aye, aye Sir."

CHAPTER 60

WAR'S END

Enola Gay, Colonel Tibbetts' B-29 Superfortress taxied to takeoff position at North Field, Tinian at 0200 on 6 August 1945. She carried the world's first atomic bomb, a twenty kiloton device, the result of a race to be the first to obtain the vaunted super weapon. Nazi Germany had tried, as had Japan. The Germans had shipped Uranium to Japan by submarine but in vain for Japan's program was not advanced and the uranium had been intercepted. Russia's weapon program was not yet mature and Germany's had been destroyed before Germany herself had been defeated in Europe.

Not more than four days before, in Cecilianhof, occupied Germany the home of Crown Prince Wilhelm, President Truman had told Communist Party Secretary Stalin, "We have a powerful weapon of unusual destructive force." Since Stalin had his spies in the Manhattan Project he already knew of the United States' success, probably knew more, earlier than the President himself. But a lot had changed. The Principals of the Alliance were fast leaving the world stage. Roosevelt had died, Winston had lost an election and was replaced by Clement Attlee during the Potsdam Conference at which this conversation was taking place. The President was late to the party but was shrewdly aware of Soviet intentions, far better than his predecessor in office had been.

The battle for Okinawa was ended and the Allies had its airfields from which to strike at the heart of Japan, already but six hours away for the immense B-29 heavy bomber fleet operating out of Tinian in the Marianas. General MacArthur was in charge of planning the final invasion of the last islands in the Pacific Campaign, the Japanese homeland. It was feared that the losses in such a bloody attempt would be ten times worse than those at D-Day in Normandy. Truman was loath to use this terrible new weapon, so he issued an ultimatum to the Japanese to surrender or meet prompt and utter destruction.

It was a foregone conclusion that the Japanese had lost the war; now it was time to find out if they were prepared to admit it and lay down their arms.

They were not. The ultimatum was ignored. There had been reconnaissance flights for weeks, practicing the bombing runs against known targets in Japan. They were flown with "Pumpkin Bombs," duplicates in size and shape but holding no nuclear payload. On this morning at Tinian, the bomb known as "Little Boy" had been hoisted from a pit into the specially modified bomb bay in Enola Gay and not yet fully assembled, lest an accident on takeoff cause the bomb to go off and remove maybe a third of the island. A flight of three B-29s made their way separately to the rendezvous point, Iwo Jima. There was the one carrying the bomb, one with instruments to measure the power of the blast and one outfitted to photograph the explosion. At Iwo Jima they formed up to make the run in to their target, Hiroshima. Enroute, a Navy Captain climbed down into the bomb bay and finished assembling the bomb and with thirty minutes to go until over ground zero the safeties were removed. At about eight in the morning from 30,000 feet Little Boy was released and allowed to explode less than 2,000 feet in the air above Hiroshima, instantly killing perhaps 80,000 people, some 20,000 of them soldiers and resulting in the deaths of tens of thousands more in the weeks that followed. Three days later a second device was dropped by Bockscar, piloted by Major Sweeny, on Nagasaki, an alternate target that day, killing 40,000. The primary target, Kokura, had been reported clear by Enola Gay, acting as reconnaissance aircraft, but the city was obscured by smoke from a raid by 224 B-29s the day before, on a nearby city, before Bockscar could get over the target. Of course the Japanese had no way of knowing any of this, indeed had trouble even recognizing what had happened in Hiroshima, with an almost total lack of communications from the region. Emperor Hirohito met with his advisors and they temporized, offering to surrender only if the Emperor could continue in his present position. The answer came back no, only unconditional surrender would be acceptable. The US added that the fate of the Emperor would be left up to the Supreme Commander who would occupy Japan and that there was no intent to enslave the Japanese people.

In his rapid and extensive briefings upon being sworn into office, Truman had come across an intelligence assessment written by an Admiral Cochrane, in which he opined that to defeat the Japanese they would have to become their executioner. Truman learned that he had at his disposal the means to do just that, massively execute the Japanese until they had had enough. He also knew that he would save countless American lives if he did not have to go forward with a protracted conventional invasion. It was not an easy decision but it was the correct one for saving American lives and bringing the war to a swift conclusion. In the event the Japanese announced their surrender on 15 August.

General MacArthur was tasked with conducting the surrender ceremony aboard the Missouri. In fact he'd have been grievously offended had Nimitz been accorded the honor, and Truman must have known this. He satisfied himself with designating Missouri as the location for the ceremony and let it go at that. Ellyson was the first ship into Tokyo Bay, leading MinRon-20 while deploying her minesweeping gear and clearing safe corridors and a vast anchorage for the US Navy vessels that would be on hand to witness the event. MacArthur signed for the United Nations and Nimitz signed for the United States. Though the Japanese showed up in top hats, tails and dress uniforms the victors wore open collar Khakis, a MacArthur decision, perhaps in rebuke to the vanquished Japanese. Having become aware that LCDR Lodge was aboard Ellyson MacArthur extended an invitation for her to be aboard Missouri for the surrender ceremony. Standing on the 01 level in a space of white bleached wooden deck she looked down at the proceedings, was emotionally affected to see Lieutenant General Wainwright there. She found her way into the throng at the end and walked up to him and started to salute, but instead he took her into his skinny embrace as she said, "Sir, I wanted to continue the fight, I wanted..." The General shushed her, "Commander Lodge I understand and furthermore I approve of what you did." Then she did salute him and he returned it gladly. MacArthur had observed the encounter and he walked up to the pair of them. "General I must thank you for the support you gave to us on Luzon and for allowing the rescue operation to go forward, though to be honest, I was not quite ready to leave." MacArthur smiled and said, "If you still feel that way, about not wanting to leave, there's a place on my Staff in Tokyo for you. We have already started the Occupation of Japan." "Sir, thank you. I have orders to a billet on one of the Hospital Ships and will ride it along with our wounded troops back to Pearl Harbor." She again saluted the two General Officers and made her way to the quarterdeck and asked if they would contact Ellyson to send a boat for her. While she waited one of the General's photographers got her contact information and told her she would be receiving photos of her time with the Supreme Commander. She thanked him and watched him return to join the crowd around the General, including three photographers.

"Guns, you shipped over just last year, didn't you?" It was Tiny, making conversation. Everybody was suddenly having to make decisions about where they wanted to go from here. "That's true, Tiny. I figure with thirteen years in I might as well stick around for retirement. I'm looking forward to some leave back on the East Coast, and will most likely look in on my detailer in DC to see about what sort of shore duty billets they have." "Lifer, huh?" "No, I have plans for after I have my twenty in, and a family to raise, probably somewhere in Texas.

In Flag Quarters Lodge and Lydia were sitting and chatting. "It was so good to see General Wainwright. I was surprised he remembered me, my name even." Lodge nodded, "I'll miss you but we'll get back together in Pearl. I've received word that I'll get orders to Admiral Cochrane's Staff there, following a month or so of leave. I'm sure there were raised eyebrows at you being aboard ship with me here," he said. "What about your men, what about Chief Locker and Hod," she asked. "Locker will at last be retired and heading stateside. He would have been out and on the beach a few years ago but of course the war kept him in. Hod has orders to find shipping aboard a troop ship when available and is soon to be detached, perhaps at the same time as I am. He is fairly newly shipped over and after leave he will be looking forward to some well-earned shore duty." She looked at him in concern, "But!" He shushed her, I expect he will funnel through Pearl on his way home. Perhaps we will be able to get everybody together for a farewell up Nuuanu way."

At the Calderone Estancia, Baguio District, Rosario leaned over Gunny's shoulder, watching him sleep. Roosters were crowing and for once there were few concerns. When he had come back after putting Lydia on the boat at the beach she had almost collapsed in joy and relief. They had not talked about the future as it was hard to even picture a future until the Japs were defeated. Now, as things were starting to get back to normal she wanted to know what normal was going to be. She hadn't even known if he would get in the boat with Hod and Lydia or come back to her. She nudged him and a smile started at the corners of his mouth. "What, woman, you want *more*?" She squealed as he spun in her direction, pinning her to her pallet. "I want to know what you are going to do." "I'm going to go down to Manila when the Embassy has been reestablished. I will request to take my retirement right here, in the P.I." "What then?" And she held her breath. "Well, I always said that when I retired I was going to buy a liquor store and set it up with triple concertina, a trip wire and a fifty caliber in a tower and shoot anybody who tried to buy any of my booze." She pulled a face, in order not to cry. "Why, you going back to Manila, going to reopen the Willows?" She nodded, words coming with difficulty past her choked throat. "The thought had crossed my mind, Gunny." "Well then, could you use a bouncer?" And the tears flowed, "No, but I might need a partner." "Let's get married down in Baguio and throw a month long party and then we'll see about going back to Manila," he replied. "Fine, but if I catch you even looking at any of my girls..." "Dearest, you know that I'll look and I know that you'll kill any one of them that makes a move on me and then do the same to me." Rosario smiled in contentment and comfort that her man knew her so well. "Well, I heard you had a favorite in Chinatown in Honolulu. That's off limits too, all of them," and she jabbed him in the ribs, but softly. And then they celebrated the start of their new lives together.

The Emperor of Japan, Hirohito, met with his advisors after the second atomic blast and within five days of the attack on Nagasaki he had signaled Japan's surrender to the Allies. Another five days after that the Japanese sent a party to Manila to meet with MacArthur to learn of his plans and requirements for starting the occupation. That series of meetings lasted for nine days. On the 30th of August MacArthur flew into Atsugi, although warned not to do so, as there were fears of Kamikaze volunteers who might try to kill him. MacArthur brushed aside these warnings, landed in a C-54 and strode across the tarmac to a waiting ancient American Lincoln automobile. Imagine his surprise to find the roadway from the airport to the Hotel New Grand, in Yokohama lined by two divisions of Japanese troops, all standing with their backs to him. It was the same honor they would accord to their Emperor. He would stay for a few nights and the hotel staff noted that he wore a sidearm, worked hard and hardly left his room.

On 6 September President Truman approved and signed the Plan for the occupation of Japan. By that time MacArthur had taken up General Headquarters Offices on the sixth floor of the Dai-Ichi Mutual Life Insurance Building in Tokyo and had moved his family into the U.S. Ambassador's residence behind the Embassy. He kept to a man-killing schedule, having breakfast at seven while he read the overnight traffic, then reporting to his GHQ by 1030 each day, sometimes working until one in the morning.

Upon his arrival in Japan MacArthur decreed three laws. No allied personnel were allowed to assault a Japanese person; no allied personnel were allowed to eat Japanese food and the flying of the Japanese rising sun flag was forbidden. The reason for his second law was that the Japanese were starving. There was practically no food for them to eat and his first problem was to find a way to feed the Japanese. There is no record that MacArthur waited to be named Supreme Commander in the Occupation Plan before acting like he was, in fact, the new Emperor of a defeated nation.

There were calls for the detention of the Emperor and his trial as a war criminal. Also, some of the Imperial Family clamored for his abdication, seeking the honor for themselves. After letting these upsetting facts simmer he arranged a call on the Emperor, visiting him at the Palace. He obtained a photograph of the two of them together, Hirohito dressed formally, MacArthur again in working khakis, no tie, collar open. After letting Hirohito dangle for a bit MacArthur came to his rescue, leaving him in his ceremonial office, although stripping him of his divinity as well as his formal powers. With Hirohito's cooperation in hand things went smoothly. It seemed the Japanese had swapped an Emperor whom they thought of as a God but was no General, for a General who acted as though he thought himself a God.

Truman's Occupation Plan set up an advisory board which was to approve all of the Supreme Commander's actions. MacArthur simply ignored them and did it all by himself. He trashed the Meiji Constitution and replaced it with one that he wrote personally. He gave the vote to women, broke up the huge Industrial Combines and took power away from the labor unions. Truman, himself, engaged in a bit of a power play. Though the Allied Occupation Plan called for the partitioning of Japan among the Allies, similar to what had been done in Germany, it never happened. Truman had had about enough of Stalin, who had come into the war against Japan at the very last minute in order to scoop up some territories. Truman was the man with the bomb, had proved that if pushed he would use it. And though it suited him to let MacArthur run things in Japan he was already anticipating continued hostilities with Russia and becoming more and more discomfited with MacArthur.

MacArthur had stood up the President, begged off on meetings, and caused Truman to come to him instead of putting himself at the convenience of his boss. On the occasion of a meeting in the Pacific, Nimitz had an entire Fleet in Dress Whites, including himself, for a visit by Truman. MacArthur, when he finally showed up did so in working khakis, wearing his Philippines Marshall brass hat and smoking his corn cob pipe. It seemed the General still considered Truman to be Roosevelt's haberdasher who had been a mere Artillery Captain in the Great War. It didn't take much to piss Harry off. He blasted a critic who had panned his daughter Margaret's singing, threatened to punch him in the eye. It didn't help things any that MacArthur had let his name be noised about as a possible candidate for the Republican nomination for President, against Truman.

In the midst of these slights and insults and while transforming a nation and putting it back on its feet, MacArthur found time to arrest, detain, try and execute seven high ranking figures from the former Japanese hierarchy, including Hideki Tojo, the most hated and feared. The Japanese had actually been at war with one enemy or another since 1895, a period of fifty years. It is estimated variously that they killed somewhere upwards of fifteen million human beings during that time. There was lots of evidence and making the case was not very hard. The Japanese warrior code of Bushido, originally an unwritten code of conduct of the Samurai, set forth the ideals by which Japanese men were expected to live. The Japanese had never been invaded, had not been defeated. An invasion of their homeland was unthinkable. In fact defeat of any sort was unthinkable, with many Generals committing ritual suicide, or seppuku rather than live through and suffer defeat. MacArthur of course knew this. When he had the war criminals executed it was a death totally without honor, without the possibility of seppuku. He had them hanged by the neck until dead.

At the Lodge home in Nuuanu Valley, Oahu, Admiral Cochrane and Dame Sandra alighted from their car and walked to the front door. The Fitzes had met Sandy before and wholeheartedly approved of them together. After the initial greetings died down "Great to see you back, Dick." "Sir, it has been too long. Thank you, Jane," and he took a glass of iced tea from her. She rejoiced at her Fitz getting a visit and fussed for a bit, putting some baked goods and the pitcher on the coffee table then invited Sandy outside to give the men some time together. Dame Sandra, more used to the company of men and their routines of course wanted to stay. She was still getting used to the wifely routine but she bestowed one of her brilliant smiles, the nice one, on her hostess and went with her to the garden. "I think we can drop the Sirs, Dick." Cochrane looked at his friend and mentor and relented. "Aye that we can, Fitz. Tell me, what do you hear about the occupation, the politics and what's coming to pass?" "Not as much as I'd guess you know, seeing as how you're still on active duty and over in the Makalapa Head Shed." "Anything from D.C.," Dick asked, "any news on how Truman is settled in, his plans going forward?" "Well, you know he is one feisty SOB, doesn't hesitate to take offense at criticism of his daughter." "Yes, I heard that story. Seems like we all like a little gossip from time to time." They both took some swallows of their tea, Dick topped them off and they munched on a brownie.

Looking up from the table, eyebrows cocked, Fitz said, "So tell me about El Supremo." "Goes no further?" "That bad, huh?" "Good or bad I couldn't say, but it *is* personal and I count the General as something of a friend." As Fitz started to remonstrate and withdraw his request, Dick said, "Fitz, I know you're a student of history." "Not in your class, Dick." "Well, I had the pleasure of serving on Nimitz' Staff and MacArthur's, as well. It was Chet's idea and he sent me to Australia to see if there might be a way to bridge the gap between the two Commands. Australia is where Sandy and I met. She had worked with Mac's Staff and with him personally, in the intelligence business and was able to advise me on how to get along with him and the Palace Guard. He was okay if you stood up to him in private. He seemed to expect people to kow tow to him but didn't respect you if you did. Long story short we had a super relationship and it was key in getting his approval of the rescue attempt of Lydia in the Baguio District. I really think that he was in his element in the Philippines, as their Military Governor of sorts. I know that that experience prepared him for his current role as nation builder and demi-god in Japan, if you will. He has the knowledge and confidence and presence to carry it off, no question." Fitz gave a knowing little grin and said, "But."

"But he has his very own Achilles heel. Back to the history, Fitz. Have you read Caesar's commentaries on the Gallic war." "I doubt to the extent that you have, Dick." Well you know that when a Consul returned in victory from a campaign he was often awarded a Triumph. Part of it was to parade through the streets of Rome in a chariot with all of the slaves and booty in the procession. The honoree was painted red and in the chariot with him was a slave who whispered in his ear, you are only human, you are only human." "Yes, I do recall that." "And after the feasts died down and the games, they might take the defeated General, say Vercingetorix of the Gauls, and hurl him to his death from the Tarpeian Rock, something like an eighty foot drop, unless they strangled him instead. But defeated foes didn't stand much of a chance against the victorious General. MacArthur's arrogance and angry outbursts are legendary. He seems to carry himself as royalty, like a Caesar but with no one to whisper in his ear. With me on his Staff it was almost as though I gave him a good reputation to live up to. Our distant relationship as baseball players in school gave him an excuse to be less overbearing. Nimitz doesn't need anything like that because he knows that all of his power was on loan and only so that he could use it to defeat our enemy. Nimitz was totally loyal to our effort. Unfortunately, not unlike Caesar, MacArthur's highest loyalty is to himself; and we know how that ended up for Caesar."

As they rejoined the ladies Dick said, "Dear, we were talking about something that was more up your alley than mine." "Oh?" And she looked with interest and a bit of a smile hovering. "If you'd like, tell us your assessment of General Douglas MacArthur." "Poor man, he requires everyone to scrape and bow and he hates them for it. He wears a ribbon that is not warranted, the highest one in the land, and he has to try to be regal enough to deserve it. In light of his accomplishments his behavior is understandable and might be okay if his loyalties were to something or someone other than himself." Everyone was mesmerized, in particular Jane. "Does that about cover it, dearest?"

On their way out to the car she said with a leer, "So you were buttering me up for what, Sharrr, just so you could have your way with me tonight?" Dick just smiled and opened the door to the car.

"Come in John, so good to see you." Cochrane stood at the door of his office at CincPac Headquarters, Makalapa, Pearl Harbor and asked his Secretary to hold calls, then returned to his desk and they both sat, as his Secretary brought in a couple coffees and set them on his desk. "How's Lydia doing," with a concerned look wrinkling his brow. "I don't mind saying I held myself totally responsible for getting her into that hell hole in the P.I." "Sir, it was also you who made it possible to get her out of there alive." "Hmm," he grunted, "A certain Chief Gunner's Mate had a lot more to do with that than I did or anyone else for that matter." "Admiral, that's why I requested this time with you." I would like to see him again, Lydia, too. As you probably know the Fitzes are getting ready to return to the states and Boston will be their next stop. We are planning a sendoff, a luau out at the place in Nuuanu. Of course you are invited and we hope you'll come. We'll set the date and time as required to make that happen. Cochrane nodded his pleasure at the invitation. "Sandy and I would be delighted, just let us know when to show up." "Sir if there's any way you might pulse the personnel system and find him, we'd also like your assistance in locating Dantes."

"John, you're in luck. I have been debriefing various members of the Mamasan network and writing up and closing out our files on that operation. As it happens I was just about to involve you in the ongoing debriefs. I have both Chief Dantes and Chief Locker in temporary billeting on the base right here in Pearl. Gunny Clancy has swallowed the anchor and is taking retirement in the P.I. He and the original Mamasan, Rosario Gabangabang, are getting married and settling down in Manila, I believe. Look, here's the number of the duty office at the barracks, you might give the Chiefs a call." As Lodge was rising to retrieve his cover and make his departure Cochrane asked, "Leave going okay? Gonna need any more time or will a month be enough?" Lodge stood easy and seemed to think about it for a second. "Sir we're getting to know each other again and making decisions. I'm pretty sure that Lydia will be putting in her papers. We think she's pregnant." Cochrane came around the desk and slapped him on the back with a huge grin. "Well done, John, well done the two of you." "You're the first to know. We're not even sure of it yet ourselves." "I fully understand, John. My lips are sealed until Lydia makes her own announcement." John was about to go, again, when Cochrane held up a hand. "I have a bit of news, myself. My Boss has asked me if I would consider, as a next assignment, being Superintendent at the Naval Academy. There's been no decision yet." Lodge laughed, "As much as my Dad talked about the Academy, I think I can understand how big this is. He always wanted me to go there instead of Harvard." "Well then think about it some more. After I've been there a year or so I'll be looking for a Commandant of Midshipmen. You'll be at the top of my list. Also I think you should stay on leave until things like morning sickness ease up. Maybe sometime after the party you can come back to work and help me square things away to get ready for my relief." It was a deeply grateful Captain Lodge who drove back to Nuuanu.

The Fitzes had had the good sense and complete understanding to quietly debark from their Nuuanu home on loan, about a week before the Lodges got back. When the couple finally came back out to their honeymoon home and entered it there was the key that they had given to Auntie Jane, resting on a richly embroidered silken Pakemuu. Next to it a note. "Champagne in the fridge. All the love in the world in our hearts for you. Thank you forever for giving us your home, all this time. Uncle Fitz and Auntie Jane." At that Lydia finally broke down, sobbing into John's chest, happy grateful tears flowing freely.

A first Class came into the Senior Enlisted Barracks. A sign on the door said "Chief's Quarters." He spoke up, "A Chief Dantes or Locker in here?" They both looked up from an acey deucey game, 'You want to take it, Wallace?" "Sure, Chief." And Locker went to the wall phone in the passageway. "Chief Locker here." He recognized his former Boss' voice, smoothly going past the need to say his rank, "Chief I'm back on the Island, moved back into our quarters out Nuuanu way. Lydia and I are throwing a send-off party for the Fitzes. Unless I get back to you again, it'll be in two weekends, on Saturday. If you and Chief Dantes can't be there we'll reschedule. Locker broke out a smile and you could hear it in his voice, "Hod is with me now and I'm sure we'll find a way to be there. Could you use any help with setting up, digging a pit for the pig? Anything like that?" Lodge thought for about a millisecond, "Absolutely, Chief, great idea. Why don't the two of you come out on Friday, instead, and we'll get an early start. You can bunk down in the spare bedrooms."

The next weekend Dantes wangled a Staff car and made his way down to the Kekoa's boat yard. Locker had begged off, said he needed a nap. Dantes kidded him about getting old enough to need them. Wall Locker absorbed the jibe; he knew where Dantes was going and he didn't need any help with this one. "It was great getting your call, Bruddah," Kaikane said. The whole family is happy you're back." He went in back to the eating area and poured two rum and cokes, put them on the table and left.

"Dantes, Hod. So good to see you again." It was that voice he had heard in his dreams. There she was, and her face was alight. He turned and beheld a woman, the one who had been his Kuulei, his flower when he wore the green lei and it seemed the whole world could deny him nothing. She saw a man in full flower, all muscle and flat planes, tanned and confident, blue eyes flashing over his smile. All he could think to say was, "It broke my heart to leave." She looked searchingly to determine the truth of those words, "I thought I would die," she replied. Keeping his eyes on hers, "I suppose a hug would be okay?" She answered by embracing him and they stood together that way without speaking for several moments. As they broke Hod said, "I'm married to a wonderful and beautiful woman and we have two children." She laughed, "And my Kane and I have three, two girls and a boy. My husband is a very good man and I love him dearly." They sat and talked for maybe an hour and Hod offered to drop her off. But she said she preferred to say good bye here. And as they did, both mused that this good bye was easier than the last. They didn't bother to deny the attraction that existed between them, nor did they have to do anything about it. It was enough to know that the other one still cared and had moved on and was happy in doing so.

The party up Nuuanu way turned into a weekend long affair that started when the Chiefs arrived on Thursday night, not Friday morning, to watch the fire and put the pig in the ground. The Kamaaina Wahine had been invited, along with J. Akuhead Pupule and there was merriment, lots of Mai Tais and her expert guidance as they made preparations and then put one of the Grandmother's best wild hogs into the ground. On Friday Mama Bishop arrived with a hula class of hers, all Navy wives, and they danced with gourds and bamboo canes as Mama called out the changes and chants. The Fitzes moved back in for the weekend and it turned into a bit of an Island farewell for them, with the Mayor of Honolulu showing up as well as all of the Senior Commanders in the area. Aku knew a band and they played several sets on both Saturday and Sunday.

Chet Nimitz made a surprise appearance but the Chiefs had advance knowledge and as he arrived they broke his Flag on a hastily erected flagpole in the yard. And then they broke another one for Fitz, the one that Nimitz had brought for him as a going away memento. Nimitz could only stay for an hour and as he made to leave, Lodge, Fitz, Cochrane, Lydia and the two

Chiefs formed up as side boys. Nimitz walked slowly through them, saying something to each before going on another step. To Lydia, "God Bless you, Commander, your service in the resistance was magnificent." To Fitz, "You could have done my job better, I hope I lived up to your expectations." To Hod. "I've heard quite a bit about you. Luling and Lockhart, was it?" "Yessir." "My part of the Country, too. Did you work on a farm there as a kid?" "Yessir, my Grandmother's place." "I worked in my Grandfather's hotel, growing up. No place like Texas Hill Country. How do you feel about the Navy, Chief? Are we headed in the right direction?" "Sir I would have been no other place. The Navy gave me far more than I could have possibly given it. She'll be in good hands, Sir, with you on the watch." At that Nimitz turned to Fitz, "You're right about the Chief, Fitz." With that he turned last to Lodge. "You know I like to keep winning teams together. After Dick Cochrane gets settled in Crabtown I'd like for you to go there and join him. The Trade School is the best anchor we have, to integrity, character and professionalism." "Aye, aye Sir."

And then he was gone in the staff car with the five star flags on the front fenders snapping in the breeze, sitting in the stern sheets already reading from a folder given him by his dog robber. He had a tough travel schedule and a bevy of appearances and speeches, starting in San Francisco and San Diego and moving across the Country. The Navy was under attack from the Army and people were demanding that the Marine Corps be eliminated and the Air Corps wanted to own all of the aircraft missions and birds. The man from the Silent Service would be making uncomfortable speech after speech, defending the Service, trying to keep it together in a time of no money and very little interest. One of his most powerful opponents was a certain Douglas MacArthur who had swiftly taken the lion's share of the credit for the victory in the Pacific, with movies and interviews even as he consolidated his position in Japan. It was a close contest but a haberdasher from Independence, Missouri who had responsibility for the whole country dug in his heels. He did not like MacArthur and he wouldn't sign things that crossed his desk until he liked what he read. He was a lot more like Nimitz than he was like the General. Nimitz became Truman's Chief of Naval Operations and wiser heads prevailed.

Finally, Sunday evening came at Nuuanu. Everybody was sitting in the great room, feet up with the windows open and a fragrant breeze lifting the curtains. Fitz motioned to Hod and they went together into what had served as the Admiral's Study when he had been living here. Lodge noticed them go and thought back to that afternoon at Uncle Fitz' Quarters when he'd first met Lydia. "Chief, I'd like you to tell me a bit about that time in Manila, when you pulled duty with Admiral Cochrane." "Yessir, well it was just an assignment as driver, combined with Shore Patrol, sort of like the time earlier in Chinatown, after meeting you in Makalapa. I had gone into the bars in the seedier part of town and drawn the attention of some Tayag insurrectionists. A bar girl there warned me that they were hostile to Americans and put me on guard against them. Back at the Hotel I assumed Shore Duty at the dance they were holding on the roof and when I saw these same Tayags, I knew immediately there would be trouble." His voice trailed off and he stopped talking. "Admiral Cochrane told me that same story and said that you likely saved his life and several others, as well." "Sir it might interest you to know that the commendation you wrote most certainly saved my tail, at the end of my first tour." Fitz looked up with interest. "I had shifted to a tin can, Pruitt, tied up in San Diego so that I could be discharged while my ship, Detroit was at sea. I almost destroyed that ship, Sir, with too much oil in the galley stove. Breakfast was late and everybody on the ship knew who had done it. When it came time to send me off the XO read your comments with great interest and let me know he'd never seen so fine a commendation, and by CincPac, no less. He asked me if I wanted to tell him about it and I said that it had been classified at the time. Your commendation carried a lot of weight, kept me out of some serious trouble." Fitz chuckled. "And please tell me what you think the next fight we might get into as a Country will be." He thought for a bit, not hurried. "Sir, it won't be the Japanese. Those bombs we dropped on them have finished them as a warlike nation for a long time. I see where Russia came in at the last minute, tried to pick up some easy territory but didn't get much. I expect that Russia will be the next one we'll have to watch, Sir, and China after them." "Why China?" "They are fighting among themselves, the Communists and the Nationalists. Depends upon who wins. If it's the Nationalists we'll likely have peace for a while, if not we'll have to handle the communists in China before it's over." As the Admiral nodded his agreement and started to get up, Dantes said, "Sir, if I might?"

Fitz said of course and sat back to see what this extraordinary Chief would tell him. "Sir, this is confidential, just for you to know. Fitz smiled at that. "Of course." "Sir you should know that I'm no hero but Captain Lodge is. Off the beach during the rescue operation he outfitted himself with battle gear and was prepared to leave Flag Quarters and step in the boat and rescue his own wife. Sir, I told him there was no room in the boat, that it was my job. He said that it was his job to go and no man would let another man save his own wife. I admired that but I was worried for his safety. Sir I cold cocked him with a sucker punch and didn't let him come with me. It all worked out and we all got back aboard safely and he did not press charges. Sir I admire the Captain more than I can say. He has given me opportunity after opportunity, beyond anything I could ever deserve. Since you're so close and he's like a son to you I wanted you to know. I am ashamed of what I did, but glad that I did it, at the same time." Fitz was floored. "And I have to keep this to myself?" "Sir, that is entirely up to the Admiral. I feel better that I told you. Thank you, Sir for all your kindnesses to me."

Back in the living area, Lodge and Cochrane were talking and motioned Hod into their group. "Chief, Captain Lodge was just telling me how much he thinks you and Admiral Nimitz are alike." "Well, we *are* both from Texas Hill Country," Hod answered with a smile. "And both of you are at the very top of your professions, Hod," Fitz chimed in. There was thoughtful nodding of heads and then Cochrane spoke again, "Chief I know Admiral Nimitz very well, he's a Classmate of mine and he was quiet, slow to take a compliment and really knew his business and from what I know about the two of you it's absolutely true." At that point Dame Sandy ahemed and hoisted her Mai Tai. Here's to the backbone of this man's Navy. I propose three cheers for Chief Dantes and Chief Locker. Hip hip hooray! Hip, hip hooray! Hip, hip hooray!

The evening had wound down and goodbyes said and Hod was heading toward the door to go to the car when Lydia caught up to him. He held the door for her and she linked arms with him and they strolled slowly into the drive. It was a beautiful moonlit night. Lydia said softly, "Hod, John and I have learned that we're pregnant." He started to congratulate her and she put her finger across his lips. "I'm sure it's a boy. John and I have already picked out a name. He will be Howard Cabot Lodge. And we'll call him Hod. I hope you and your wife will consider being his God Parents." And she reached up and gave him a kiss on the cheek and a hug and went back inside.

Hod stepped down onto the platform in Luling, Texas with his Valpack, golden crow with crossed cannons on his right sleeve and three golden hash marks gleaming. There were campaign ribbons on his chest, a purple heart and a straightness to his posture, an awareness of everything going on about him. A couple young boys idling by stopped and looked at him, slack-jawed, elbowing each other until caught staring and then they remembered their manners. One of them stood as straight as he could and rendered his best salute. Hod returned it without a grin, giving it the seriousness it deserved. *Dang kid doesn't know better; Chiefs don't get salutes.*

Back out at the farm he surprised the two of them. Grandma fluttered as best she could, grabbed hold of him and wouldn't let go. He could feel the soft sobs in her back as they stood there. And he hugged her, feeling the love that made him whole, almost made him a farm boy again. The floor shone dark wood and smelled of wax and the grandfather clock in the hall, a gift of his Dad, ticked in a stately way. He put his things in his old room and went into the kitchen and started cooking. Grandma looked like she hadn't had a lot to eat for a while, looked like she could use the help. Mr. Crowell came in and shook hands, didn't have much to say but handed him the jacket from the smokehouse. It smelled of the place where it had hung for so many years. Hod crushed it to his face and inhaled the memories of the one who had worn it, fighting for his own life. He looked up and Grandma said, "You always were the one just like him, Howard."

Before he left he got a call off to Haze and told her his travel plans, said he'd go by the detailer's office in the Navy Annex first and where did she want to do their shore duty? Haze said surprise me, anyplace you are is where I want to be, Dantes Dantes Darling. He got some time with Grandma alone, asked her how was she doing, really. She said just fine, you go to your own wonderful family; it's been a long and terrible war and thank Almighty God you're back and in one piece. He nodded, "Yes Ma'am. Before she nodded off for another nap he told her she'd forgotten to ask but there still were no tattoos and there would always be a place for her in his home. She fell asleep in her rocker and Mr. Crowell gave him a ride to the station.

In DC it was, miracle of miracles, a different detailer, and it was going to be shore duty of a sort. Hod picked the USS Benewah (APB-35) a barracks ship which was to be homeported in Green Cove Springs, Florida. The joke was that if she were to try to get underway she'd be unable to pull free of her coffee grounds.

101 Mount Vernon Street, Ridgefield Park, New Jersey. A short walk from the bus stop and there was Dance, sitting on the stoop, waiting. He stood up self-consciously with gangly arms and legs, already showing tall for his age, hero worship shining in his eyes. Dad grabbed him, scooped him up in his arms and took the stairs, two at a time. The door burst open and there she was, a vision such as he had never beheld, Loraine hiding behind her skirts and peeking out, shyly. He held them all at the same time and soon the kids were rushing to bring their favorite things for him to see. Dance brought the picture of Hod that had stood on Mother's night table.

And every time someone asked young Dance what he wanted to be, when he grew up, he always said, with a faraway look in his eyes, "I'm going to be a Chief in the Navy, just like my Daddy."

ABOUT THE AUTHORS

Dorse DuBois, a Graduate in the U.S. Naval Academy Class of 1961 served aboard six ships in the Fleet and retired after completing a 20 year career in at-sea operations and high tech field testing of high Energy laser Systems in New Mexico. He was also assigned as a Company Officer at the Naval Academy and a Tactical Officer at the Military Academy at West Point. Married, with six children. He currently resides in Florida where he farms and writes and is working on his "Service Trilogy," a series of books about his family's naval Service over a period of three generations.

Royal Connell, a 1970 graduate of the Naval Academy, retired as a Commander from the U.S. Navy, designated both as a Surface Warfare Officer and as a Naval Flight Officer in the E-2C Hawkeye. He served two tours at the Naval Academy, one as the Piloting Navigation Course Coordinator and then as the Administrative and Personnel Officer.

Upon retirement, Commander Connell became the first Senior Naval Science Instructor for the Navy Junior ROTC (NJROTC) unit in Annapolis where he taught for 18 years, during which time his unit was selected as the Number One Unit in the Nation by the U.S. Navy League. He subsequently moved to Pensacola FL to assume duties as the Curriculum Director and Cadet Education Coordinator for the NJROTC National Staff.

He is the author of *Naval Ceremonies, Customs and Traditions* (Naval Institute Press, 2004)

CHIEF

Chief is the first book in The Service Trilogy, Books titled *Chief*, *Commander*, and *Captain*.

In *Chief* we follow a Texas farm boy, Hod Dantes, in his adventure filled career from Boot Camp in San Diego to the end of WWII in Tokyo Bay. It was a time of great patriotism and idealism. It seems that now is a good time to revisit the Greatest Generation, there to recall their great deeds and our inspiring history of war at sea.

The Service Trilogy illumines the lives and times of one seafaring family and the struggles of our Nation. *Chief* shows us how it used to be and might be again. To that end it contains many Sea Stories, all of which are true.

...or ought to be.